S0-AAE-125

WITHDRAWN

Game of Bones

Center Point
Large Print

Also by Carolyn Haines and available from
Center Point Large Print:

Bone to Be Wild
Sticks and Bones
Charmed Bones
A Gift of Bones

**This Large Print Book carries the
Seal of Approval of N.A.V.H.**

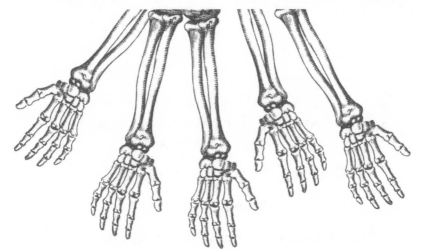

Game of Bones

Bones

A Sarah Booth Delaney Mystery

CAROLYN HAINES

Center Point Large Print
Thorndike, Maine

This Center Point Large Print edition
is published in the year 2019 by arrangement with
St. Martin's Press.

Copyright © 2019 by Carolyn Haines.

All rights reserved.

This is a work of fiction. All of the characters,
organizations, and events portrayed in this novel
are either products of the author's imagination
or are used fictitiously.

The text of this Large Print edition is unabridged.
In other aspects, this book may vary
from the original edition.
Printed in the United States of America
on permanent paper.
Set in 16-point Times New Roman type.

ISBN: 978-1-64358-266-5

Library of Congress Cataloging-in-Publication Data

Names: Haines, Carolyn, author.
Title: Game of bones / Carolyn Haines.
Description: Center Point Large Print edition. | Thorndike, Maine :
    Center Point Large Print, 2019.
Identifiers: LCCN 2019014912 | ISBN 9781643582665 (hardcover :
    alk. paper)
Subjects: LCSH: Large type books.
Classification: LCC PS3558.A329 G36 2019b | DDC 813/.54—dc23
LC record available at https://lccn.loc.gov/2019014912

For Rhee Odom and Beth Marietta Lyons—
we had some fun.

Acknowledgments

Sarah Booth and the Zinnia gang have "lived" for twenty books now—thanks to the dedicated readers who have adopted them as friends and family. I cannot thank you enough. The most precious gift anyone can give is time. These characters are my family, and I am deeply grateful that they are also your family.

Many thanks to my agent, Marian Young. Words are inadequate.

And special thanks to the St. Martin's team: Hannah Braaten, Nettie Finn, Kelley Ragland, Martin Quinn, Lisa Davis, Elizabeth Catalano, Hector DeJean, and Hiro Kimura. They all work hard to make my books as good as they can be. It really does take a village!

Game of
Bones

1

March is the month when hope returns. Even a spirit sorely challenged and worn down finds renewal in a shaft of warm March sunlight or the sight of green pushing through the soil. The new plantings that stretch from horizon to horizon across the vast Mississippi Delta seem to vibrate with a soft green haze that is nothing less than magical.

It's the perfect, crisp morning for a horseback ride, and I've saddled Miss Scrapiron and set off around the western property line with my loyal hound, Sweetie Pie, at my side. The smell of the soil is familiar and calming, as is the motion of my horse. This is a morning of perfect awareness, a feast for the senses. I stop at a brake that bisects a field to take in the tiniest buds on the tupelo gum trees. Miss Scrapiron stamps her foot and snorts, impatient. She is a creature of movement, of elegant maneuvers, of speed and agility. She wants to run, and after I bid the spring buds a welcome, I loosen the reins, lean in to her neck, and let her sweep me across the land in a rhythm of pounding hooves that is as primal as a heartbeat.

I let her run until her neck is flecked with foam where the reins touch her, and when she slows of her own accord, I look back to see Sweetie Pie coursing toward us. She, too, is glad of a rest and flops onto the cool earth for a moment. Horse, dog, and human amble over to a small spring-fed creek swollen with spring rains. Sweetie Pie unceremoniously leaps into the middle of it, despite the chill, and comes out shaking.

In the stillness of the brake, I listen to the trill of tiny songbirds. They flash yellow and brown through the pale and leafless tree trunks. In another two weeks, the green haze will settle over the trees as winter yields to spring.

I awoke this morning after a troubling dream. Only the fragments remain—a bare-chested man wearing a bear-head mask. There are images scrawled across his chest with red, white, and black paints. I wonder if this is a visit from a past dweller on the acreage that comprises my property and home, Dahlia House. Long ago, before the white men came down in wagons to claim the land as their own, the Mississippi Delta was home to numerous indigenous tribes.

At times, most often dusk or dawn, I've seen the spirits of slaves or state prisoners contracted out for labor clearing the land or hoeing the long rows of crops. They are a vision from a long dead past, but I've watched them toil against the purpling sky, hearing the chants of the field hollers that allowed them to work in a steady, unrelenting beat. Those old work songs are the bedrock of the blues.

Today the fields are empty of ghosts. The sun and rain must do the work to bring the tiny plants taller. Humans have no magic for this part of the process. This is Mother Earth's gift to us. The vast acreage of Dahlia House is leased to a local farmer. I have none of the talents—or the love of gambling—that is necessary to put a fortune into a crop of corn, soybeans, or cotton and hope the weather and the market cooperate enough to bring a profit. I've saved out forty acres around Dahlia House for a hayfield where the same man who leases the property cares for the Alicia Bermuda grass pasture to make winter hay for my horses. That's risk enough for me.

I turn Miss Scrapiron toward home. I'm meeting the handsome sheriff of Sunflower County, Coleman Peters, for breakfast. He's cooking and I'm eating, which is a fine arrangement. Last night he worked late, so he didn't spend the night with me, but we'll catch up before we both begin our workday. His inclusion in my life has given me, like the land I love, a sense of balance. I'm still terrified of allowing myself to love him with everything in me, but on mornings like this, as I anticipate seeing him pull into the driveway and get out of his cruiser, I feel the shell around my heart softening. No one can protect us from loss or injury. If you love, you risk. I want to risk. I want to abandon my fear, but right now, caution is the only path I can travel.

"Sweetie Pie." I call my dog from the brake where she's gone sniffing the trail of a raccoon or opossum. She's a hunting dog who now seizes on the scents of evildoers and has more than once saved my skin from bad people. The small furry creatures that roam the land, though a point of curiosity, are safe from her. And from me.

The wind blowing across the wide-open fields has a chill to it, but the sunshine on my back warms me through the light polar riding vest I wear. Miss Scrapiron rocks my hips with her long-legged Thoroughbred stride. I close my eyes and simply enjoy the sensation of sun and movement. My cell phone rings out with "Bad to the Bone."

Tinkie Bellcase Richmond, my partner in the Delaney Detective Agency, is on the horn. Tinkie, aside from being my best friend, is the Queen Bee of all the Delta society ladies. She is a bred-in-the-bone Daddy's Girl, the 180-degree opposite of me. She holds teas, cotillions, garden-club gatherings, and debutante balls for the social elite. She knows the DG handbook of proper behavior backward and forward and manages to cram in her social obligations between caring for her husband, Oscar, and helping me solve crimes. Beneath the coiffed hair and haute couture wardrobe beats the heart of a forensic accountant. Tinkie's daddy owns the local bank and her husband is its president. Tinkie comes from money and she knows how to track it, find it, and sort through the many paper trails every criminal leaves behind.

"What's shaking?" I asked. I like to sit on my horse and talk on the phone. It could only be better if I had a cigarette. Sadly, those days are behind me.

"What do you know about the archeological dig at Mound Salla?" Tinkie asked.

"Let's see. No one knew the mound was actually a real Indian mound until recently, though it's been in plain sight for at least two centuries. Most of it is wooded, and even though it's bigger than several football fields, no one paid much attention to it. I guess we all assumed it was something built way back when to avoid flooding. Then there was that house on top of it that the . . . Bailey family lived in." I shrugged. "It was just always . . . there."

"Until recently. Now it's some kind of archeological hot spot."

"Right. A crew started digging back around Thanksgiving. It's a team of university professors, some students, some archeologists. They believe Mound Salla was a sacred site for the Tunica tribe that once settled all up and down the Mississippi River."

"How did you know all that?" Tinkie asked.

"Mound Salla is not on the Mississippi River but here in Sunflower County. That's why it wasn't really explored or excavated until recently. No one suspected it was a burial mound. It never made sense that Natives built a mound this far from their normal settlements."

"That doesn't explain why you'd know this." She sounded a little testy.

"I thought I might go and volunteer to help with the dig so I read up on it," I said. "I love the idea of studying the original people that lived on this land."

"Old pottery shards, arrowheads, and for your trouble you get dirt under your fingernails that takes a professional manicure to clean out. And for what?"

Tinkie had never enjoyed making mud pies—it wasn't her style. She was more the accessorizing kind of girl. I loved finding treasures, even buried ones. "It's exciting to find things that tell the story of the past. Archeological digs show the day-to-day life of people who lived hundreds of years ago. Their struggles and celebrations. Their beliefs. It's fascinating." Okay, so I was a bit of a history geek sometimes. Most Delta society ladies were all over genealogy, doing their damnedest to prove they were descendants of the original Mayflower refugees. Right. My reading of the Pilgrims made them a club I didn't want to join—they were religious fanatics and a rather unpleasant lot. I kept hoping for more exotic DNA. Maybe gypsy!

"Hey, Sarah Booth. Did you hear me?" Tinkie's voice came over the phone. "We need to run out to the dig today. And Coleman said to cancel breakfast plans."

"Why? Why is Coleman canceling breakfast and why do you want to go to the dig?" Tinkie wasn't about to volunteer as a worker bee. The day was sunny and warming, but the cotton fields were still damp from a recent rain. The gumbo, as the soil was called, was notorious for clinging in thick cakes to the boots of anyone foolish enough to walk through the fields. And Mound Salla was in a large wooded area of low ground between two vast plantings of cotton.

"There's been a death." Tinkie was excited and repelled. I could hear it in her voice. I was aggravated.

"Tinkie! Why didn't you say that right off?"

"It's not like the dead person is impatient, Sarah Booth. Time means nothing to the dead."

I wasn't so sure that was true. My experiences with the ghost of my great-great-great grandmother Alice's nanny, Jitty, had taught me that dead people were keenly attuned to the passage of time, and the ticking biological clock of my eggs. Jitty haunted Dahlia House—and me. She was my family and my bane. "Who died?"

17

"One of the scientists involved with the dig."

"Not Dr. Frank Hafner?" I was shocked at the thought. Hafner had been in and out of Zinnia for the past several weeks and was a poster boy for the dedicated scientist who also worked out at the gym. Handsome, charming, and reputed to be a ladies' man, he'd also headed up three of the most successful archeological digs of the past two decades. He was quickly developing almost a cultlike following among serious archeologists.

"No, not Hafner. It's his coworker Dr. Sandra Wells."

"What happened?" I had visions of walls caving in or perhaps an accident with a pickax. Digs were always dangerous because the method of removing the soil also allowed for cave-ins and mistakes.

"Her body was found hanging above an intrusive burial grave. It's this really deep shaft someone—and not someone associated with the dig—cored out of the mound. They were either going to bury Dr. Wells' body and got interrupted or they were looking for something," Tinkie said. "Oh, yeah. Dr. Wells was tortured."

That was a surprise. "She was murdered?"

"She sure didn't torture herself, so it would seem she's the victim of murder," Tinkie said.

"Thanks for the sarcasm," I said.

"Sorry, it's just that I met Sandra Wells. She

was a guest speaker at the Zinnia Historical Society. Prima donna, and she was a piece of work."

In Tinkie's terminology, a "piece of work" was either a conniving woman who trapped men into marriage or someone who pretended to be someone they were not. "How was she killed?"

"Hung upside down and her throat was cut. She bled out into a bowl just discovered in the dig. A ceremonial bowl that the lead archeologist, Frank Hafner, said could possibly have been used for human sacrifice."

"What?" That was way beyond gruesome for my home county. Things like that didn't happen in Zinnia. We had our share of murders, but not ritualistic killings. "The Tunica tribe wasn't known for human sacrifice. They were peaceful until the whites began claiming all their land."

Tinkie was matter-of-fact. "I'm just reporting what Frank said. By the way, he's our new boss. I took the case. You're always saying how you need money, so he paid the retainer upfront. Now we should hustle over to the dig and see the body before Coleman has it removed. Doc's already there."

I nudged Scrapiron into an easy trot. It was hard to hold the phone, post, and talk, but I managed. "I'll head that way as soon as I get home. Maybe five more minutes."

"I'm going out there. I'll take some photos at

the scene and start the interview process. Hafner hasn't been arrested yet, but Coleman told him not to leave the premises."

"If Hafner is innocent, did he have any idea who the murderer might be?"

Tinkie's laughter was clear and contagious. "He thinks it's a spirit guarding the burial grounds, which means he's not pointing the finger at anyone until he has more information. He has this woo-woo story about the student workers too afraid to stay there after dark because of some spirit plodding around in the woods. But he's smart enough to know he's going to be the first suspect. He and Sandra Wells hated each other."

"Then why was she at his dig?"

"It was sort of *their* dig. She was awarded a grant that totaled over three-quarters of a million dollars and with the grant money, she bought a lot of specialized equipment. That's a lot of money for a dig that isn't likely to yield gold or jewels."

No kidding. Other than pottery shards and a better knowledge of the Native Americans who lived in the region, there wasn't any wealth to be gained. The Tunica tribe that populated the Delta area, adding onto the mounds left by a much earlier people, was not warlike. They'd gotten on well with all the French and Spanish explorers who'd walked through the land, sharing their food and hunting skills. Trouble began when the white settlers claimed the land as their own. In the Tunica world, the earth belonged to all and was meant to be shared. The concept of fences or property titles didn't exist.

Tinkie cleared her throat. "Hafner has made headlines with some of his finds in the mound."

There had been news media, photographers from national magazines, a few international delegates, and some tribal officials at the site. I'd driven by the mound, which had been there for centuries beneath a gracious old plantation house. The Bailey family that owned the house had abandoned it years back, and not so long ago the house had burned to the ground. Until Dr. Frank Hafner showed up with his crew of college kids to excavate, no one had given the property a second thought.

Miss Scrapiron clopped down the driveway with a trot that was easy to post, and I hung up so I could unsaddle and hurry to meet Tinkie. My single desire was to grab a cup of coffee and slap some makeup on my face, more to avoid getting chapped in the windy sunshine than for glamour reasons. When Miss Scrapiron was running free in the pasture with her buddies, I hurried to the back door. Someone stood in my kitchen window.

I stopped dead in my tracks to study the strong profile of the woman in my kitchen. She wore her hair braided and pulled back in a deerskin sheath decorated with beads. Her blouse was of woven fabric. Whoever she was, she was striking and fearsome.

In the back of my mind, I suspected that Jitty was at work, and I had to wonder about my dream of the masked person and the sudden murder at a dig excavating a Native American burial area. Now a bronzed warrior goddess was standing in my kitchen.

When I opened the back door, she turned to face me and I heard the rattle of a snake and the low, throaty tones of a Native American flute.

"There is danger around you." She lifted one hand, palm outward, and made a motion that seemed to encompass the space around me. "The grandfathers are unhappy. The grandmothers weep at the destruction of their rest."

"Who are you?" I asked. I knew it was Jitty, taking on the persona of someone who had come to give me a warning.

"I am Lozen, warrior, medicine woman, and prophet of the Cheyenne Chiricahua Apache. I am the right hand of my brother, Chief Victorio. We shield our people in battle. We protect our right to ride free. Though we are gone now, even our resting places are destroyed for the greed of some."

"Is this about the archeological dig?"

"This is about your need to be strong. You will

be tested. You, too, must stand and fight for what you believe in."

A premonition touched me. Jitty was forever deviling me with half-cocked theories and advice that would land me in prison for twenty years. But this was something different. This was chilling and had the feel of ancient wisdom brought to me from the Great Beyond.

"Don't talk in riddles. Please just tell me."

She lifted a small earthen bowl she held in her right hand. She dipped the fingers of her left hand in the bowl and drew three red marks on each cheek. "Chiricahua for the Red People. For the red clay that is our home. For the right to ride free."

"Jitty." I whispered her name, almost a plea. Lozen was a fierce warrior and she had scared me so badly I found it hard to draw in a full breath.

The face of the warrior began to shift and meld, modeling into the softer features of my beloved haint. "Jitty!" I was so glad to see her I wanted to hug her, but I would clasp only empty air.

When I saw the eye roll that was so typical of my sassy ghost, I exhaled a long sigh. "What in the hell are you trying to do to me? I'm not fond of your impersonations, but sometimes they're at least entertaining. That was downright unpleasant."

"Lozen died of tuberculosis in an Alabama prison camp. Now that's what I would call unpleasant."

She had a point, but I was still glad to see her. "I have to hustle out of here, Tinkie is waiting. If there's a message from Lozen or the Great Beyond, give it to me quick." The whole time I was talking I was walking upstairs to the bathroom to put on some foundation. Jitty followed, still in her Indian garb. "Spit it out, Jitty. Time's a wastin'."

"You want to talk about time wastin', do you? Put a hand on your gut and feel the slow death of those eggs. You want a message from me, get pregnant. You got a good, virile man at last. He knows his business when he wants to bump uglies. Now get out of your own way and let nature take its course."

More than anything Jitty wanted an heir to haunt. I was the last Delaney so it was up to me to provide for her future—or so she thought. I'd fought too hard for the right to be just me to be considered an incubator by society or Jitty. "I don't have time to reproduce." It was a statement of fact.

"Lozen delivered a baby in the middle of a battlefield while she and her people were retreating."

I wanted to know more about this woman, but not now. Tinkie was waiting, as was Coleman and a dead body. I grabbed a cold biscuit from the bread box and some hot coffee in a thermos. I had to get to the site.

"Be safe," Jitty said. She'd returned to the stoic warrior goddess of the Apache tribe. A wind rippled through the kitchen and the rattle shook. Then Jitty/Lozen was gone.

2

Pluto was on the front porch waiting for me when I stepped outside, and I knew there was no hope of leaving him behind. Sweetie Pie magically appeared at the car. I opened the car door for the critters and we were off. I suspected Dr. Hafner would not be happy to see a cat and a dog, but when he paid for Delaney Detective Agency, he got all of our resources.

The dig site was a good forty minutes from Dahlia House down a little-used dirt road that led to the abandoned estate that had once belonged to the Bailey family. They'd fallen on hard times, sold the land to an agribusiness, and shortly after that, the family had left the area. The house had been abandoned for years and had stood sentinel on the high mound until it had mysteriously burned down. No one had lived there, and there were no insurance claims. Rumor was that some kids had accidentally set the fire, but lightning was ruled the official cause.

The blackened timbers of the house had been reclaimed by the woods and volunteer trees had sprouted all over the top of the mound, until the archeological crews showed up. When they'd begun excavating, they'd taken out the trees and plants in their way. Now, after a few rains, parking was a mess at the base of Mound Salla, and the steep sides of the mound, fitted with large timbers to use as steps, showed recent wear. The site had become a big news item, and along with the officials who had a reason to be there, about four dozen gawkers had arrived. I called them the Tragedy Vultures. Whenever disaster struck, the same people came to see the latest accident or drama. Several locals were filming on cell phones. Budgie Burton, one of Coleman's deputies, had them so far back their little phone cameras would be useless.

Tinkie and her dust mop, Chablis, were waiting for me, and Budgie waved us through. He knew we were on official business. I hadn't been to the mound up close and I was awestruck by the fact that something built hundreds of years before had not eroded. It was a steep incline, and the massive cypress timbers used to make steps had weathered the decades and decay. The mound builders had been masters of situating and packing various types of dirt to provide permanence.

It was a vigorous climb up the side of the mound, but Tinkie and I put our glutes into it and made the top where Coleman and Doc Sawyer, the local emergency-room attending and county coroner, knelt beside a sheet-covered body. Before going any closer, I assessed the site.

A large area in front of me had been cleared of vegetation, and this was the primary excavation and where the body was located. Some fifty yards to the east were a number of tents. Several dozen young people huddled around campfires, using the tents as windbreaks. They slowly began meandering down the steep slope. The day was sunny but the wind was bitter. Little was visible of the old Bailey house, and the area where it had once stood was overgrown in vegetation and young trees.

"Sarah Booth, Tinkie," Doc called out, nodding a greeting. "Are you tourists or working?"

"Dr. Hafner hired us," Tinkie said.

"And he's going to need you," Coleman said matter-of-factly. "He's my number-one suspect."

"You know that already?" Tinkie asked.

"I do. When I'm done here I'll tell you why."

Coleman wasn't a man who rushed to judgment. The evidence against Hafner had to be pretty convincing. But it was Tinkie's and my job to look around and find details that would lend themselves to Hafner's innocence, *if* he was innocent, and that remained to be seen.

About twenty yards from the sheet-draped body was a tripod of poles that had been lashed together with stout ropes, which also held a massive hook. I was reminded of the hooks in slaughterhouses, a thought that made me queasy. I stepped over and photographed the rope and knots. It was a primitive hoist, and I knew instantly that Dr. Sandra Wells had been hung from the hook in the center. She'd died on that spot, or if she hadn't died there, this was where she'd been bled.

The earthen bowl that contained her blood remained on scene. I glanced at the symbols drawn into the clay bowl, ignoring the pool of gore inside. The bowl was huge—and I was amazed that it had survived hundreds of years buried in the ground without a crack or chip.

Tinkie seemed to be experiencing the same dismay I felt. "Good lord, Sarah Booth, she was hung up like a cow or pig, her throat was cut, and she just . . . they say exsanguination is painful."

Death was always shocking, but even more so when it was such a brutal murder. I stepped back and looked out over the vista. The flat fields below us, newly planted, stretched for miles to the east, and the dense foliage of a swampy brake extended west. The plantation house had burned, but in the thicket of trees I saw old bricks, rubble, and what had to be a fort made by children. I'd done much the same on the grounds of Dahlia House, taking old boards and scraps of wood, wire, and tin to construct my own secret hideaway. The Bailey family included several children—this had to be their work. For a rural child, a fort was a perfect hideaway.

My father had offered to build a fort for me, but

I'd refused. Then it wouldn't be my secret place. I'd created a hut out of old fencing, boards, weeds, and straw. Those had been good times. I turned away from the past and faced my partner, who was poking at a dead fire some of the dig crew had left behind. At the base of the mound, the student workers were being herded into a group. They milled around like cattle, looking up at the top of the mound with varying degrees of curiosity, horror, annoyance, or sorrow. Sorrow was definitely in the minority.

Dr. Frank Hafner stood with them, consoling some and giving a pep talk to others. He was a very handsome man. Chiseled jaw, dimple in his chin, blue eyes the color of the March sky, light brown hair that ruffled in the breeze. He wore an expensive jacket that fit his broad shoulders and narrow waist to a T. He didn't have the air of any academic I'd ever hung out with. He was more . . . superhero. Any minute he might jump in the air and fly off. He'd leave behind a bunch of broken hearts. Almost all the young women working the dig looked up at him like he was Adonis.

"He's a looker," Tinkie said.

"And he knows it," I added.

"Confidence is very sexy. And so is power. At this dig Frank Hafner has both."

"I wonder if he was willing to kill to retain those things."

"He told me he was innocent." Tinkie kept all inflection from her voice.

I faced my partner. "Then I assume he has an alibi?" Tinkie had spoken with him, but I had not.

"He said he was alone but I think he was with someone."

Oh, I could see this coming a mile down the road. "But he won't say who because it's a student and he doesn't want to be fired or destroy the young woman's reputation."

Tinkie only grinned. "Bwana pretty smart for a country girl."

I only rolled my eyes. Tinkie had developed a fetish for Alexander Skarsgård as Tarzan. She'd watched the movie at least a dozen times and sometimes when we were riding along a country road, she'd burst out in a Tarzan yell that would almost make me wreck. It was a phase she was going through and it would pass, but not quickly enough for my taste. "Stop calling me bwana."

"Yes, bwana." She grinned and stepped out of my reach. "Frank Hafner kind of reminds me of Alexander, don't you think? Tall, sexy. I wonder what he'd look like in a loincloth. I'll bet he works out regularly. I can almost see his six-pack beneath that cotton pullover."

He did look good. "Call him bwana. He'll love it."

"I suspect you're right." She held out a little finger with a crook in it. "Truce?"

"Sure." I hooked her finger with mine and pulled. It was second-grade-secret-pact stuff, but so much a part of our history. "I'm going to see if Doc will give me a view of the body before they move it."

"Someone used an auger to drill deep into the mound. There are some things down in the hole, but Hafner has ordered everyone to stay clear. Coleman believes they were going to put Dr. Wells in the hole. An intrusion burial. Hafner is pissed about the destruction of the mound, though. Digging deep holes with an auger is not how an archeological dig is done."

"Great. Talk to Hafner about who knew how to run an auger. That would take some kind of expertise, I would think."

"Done deal. Hafner can work the auger. A kid named Cooley Marsh and a few locals stopped by to gawk." Tinkie nodded toward the students. "Hey, Hafner is eyeballing you pretty hard. I think he may have the hots for you."

I could feel his gaze drilling into my back. "Poke him in the eyes, then." I wasn't in the mood. "I'll join you when I finish."

"Take photos. I don't want to look at the body, but we might need the photos."

"Sure thing." She was right about that.

Sweetie Pie and Chablis had taken a watchful stance not far from Dr. Wells' remains, but Pluto was nowhere in sight. If he didn't show up in a few moments, I'd begin a search. He was an elusive cat with a nose for trouble—causing it and finding it.

I walked up behind Coleman so that my shadow fell across him as he knelt beside the corpse.

"Death by exsanguination," Doc Sawyer, who was on the other side of the body, said. "Not the method of death I'd pick. The cut was jagged and irregular, like the blade was rough. Maybe even stone."

"Like a caveman's tool?" Coleman asked.

Doc looked at Coleman and his gaze traveled up to connect with mine. "Yes. Like that. I'm tempted to guess that Dr. Wells was killed with a knife found here at the archeological site."

That put a new spin on the death. And it added to the ritualistic element of the murder. "Are you saying Dr. Wells was . . . sacrificed?"

"I'm saying no such thing." Doc was more tired than annoyed. "The use of an artifact as a murder weapon indicates this was a spur-of-the-moment murder. Or it could be the complete opposite—that the killer brought such a tool with him because this method of murder, this particular victim, this location means something to him."

"You're sure it's a him?" Coleman asked.

"Yes. Dr. Wells weighs about a hundred and forty pounds. She was alive when she was hoisted up on the hook, and she was likely fighting for her life. I don't believe a female, unless she was exceptionally tall and strong, could have done that."

"Two females?" I asked.

"It's possible, but not likely." Doc waited for Coleman's response.

"I found footprints by the hoist," Coleman said. "Male, probably size twelve. I'm certain our killer is a male. Dr. Hafner wears a size twelve and the patterns on the soles of his boots match the prints left in the dirt here. The circumstantial evidence is pretty damning."

A few strands of Sandra's hair had escaped the sheet and I could see that they were clotted with blood. I didn't really want to look beneath the sheet, but I asked if I could. Doc held the sheet back and I snapped a few photos to study later. The wound was indeed gruesome. It had not been an easy death for Sandra Wells. She'd once been a beautiful woman. I'd seen her around town with some of the students. She seemed to be held in respect by the young people. Now all of that was moot. Death had left her pale, with an anguished expression on her face.

"Any idea about motive?" I asked.

"That's why Hafner is my number-one suspect," Coleman said as he rose to stand. He was a tall timber, solid and in his prime. He was a magnet for my affections, though I had more class than to put on a public display.

"I heard rumors around town that they were romantically involved," I said.

"I've heard the same," Coleman said. "And they were great competitors. Dr. Wells brought her own funding to this dig. She intended to amplify her standing as an archeologist. Dr. Hafner had separate funding and sought to control the method of excavation. It was a war from the get-go that included yelling matches and threats."

"Why didn't Hafner just kick her out of the dig?" He'd been on the scene first. He was already established here when Wells showed up with fancy equipment and her students and team. The story had flown all over Zinnia—and several magazines and television channels dedicated to history had made the competition into something of a reality TV show. I'd watched a few of the specials—because it involved my hometown area—and thought that both professors had engaged in the lively match to build ratings and gather more donors. Typical reality-show formula and nothing like controversy to bring in the money.

"Frank Hafner's grant only covered some of the cost. Dr. Wells had the equipment grant, the high tech that Hafner needed to complete the dig without destroying critical aspects of the site." Coleman pointed to the hoist. "That hole is twenty or so feet deep into the mound. Yet no graves appear to be disturbed. Someone knew exactly where to dig. Were they looking for something or looking to bury something?" He led me over to the bowl filled with Dr. Wells' blood.

I snapped a few photos and bent closer to examine the markings on the bowl. They were strange hieroglyphics of a sort, the same thing one might find in a pyramid. Or on the painted chest or face of a warrior. I remembered the slashes and symbols from the dream that had so disturbed me. "Is this from the dig here?"

"I don't know," Coleman said. "Hafner isn't talking. But he will."

We both glanced down to the bottom of the mound where Hafner still corralled all the student workers. One was missing, though. The attractive brunette I'd seen earlier wearing overalls with a bright red kerchief tying back her hair was missing. And I could clearly see two distinct groups of students. They were all from a Michigan university. Some were Hafner's and some Wells' students. A handful of them, Wells' students I presumed, looked confused and mournful. Two were crying.

Coming toward the mound was a very official-looking group of men in suits and women in office attire. "Who is that?" I asked Coleman.

"Those are sponsors of the dig. I don't know which ones, but this dig had some serious backing. The National Science Foundation, the Archaeological Institute of America, and one very big private grant from the Americus Cleverdon Foundation run by Elton Cade. That guy with the striped tie is Cade. He's a big philanthropist and scientist."

I knew Elton Cade, but I hadn't recognized him in his business attire. "Why do people invest big money in these digs?" If artifacts were found, they most often went to a museum or public collection. In the narrow, narrow world of archeology there was some smattering of acclaim, but nothing that would bring in the bucks. "I get unraveling the mystery of the past. It's an exciting bit of detective work. But who has half a million to put toward something like this?"

"Rich people." Coleman helped Doc to his feet and signaled the EMTs to come and remove the body. They would take it to the local hospital so Doc could perform the autopsy. "If I had a lot of money, I'd fund cancer research. That's a mystery, too."

"I'd fund vaccinations for children all over the world." It was good to know that we both had a philanthropic bone, though it wasn't likely to get much exercise based on our current earning power.

"History is important, too. If we understand our past, we can better chart our future." Coleman wiped his forehead and gave me a wink. "We can more easily figure out what motivates a person. In crime solving, motivation is ninety percent of the game."

"Well aren't you the philosophic brain today?" I couldn't resist putting my arm around him, just for a moment.

"How about a date tonight? I have body parts that aren't interested in philosophy. I'd like to show them to you."

I laughed, drawing more attention than I wanted. "Perfect. We'll talk later. Those suits are coming up the mound and I need to intercept them and get some answers. If I turn up anything interesting, I'll let you know. As long as it proves my client innocent."

"You do that," Coleman said.

Tinkie approached Elton Cade and as I joined them, I searched through my memory for the tidbits I knew about him. He was an inventor from the disappearing town of Hilo, Mississippi, who'd created a popular action game for children. Instead of selling the toy to a major company, he manufactured and sold it himself. It was the beginning of an empire of toys that included stores all across the nation. His products were safe and healthy and were touted by moms and environmental groups. He had the bucks to invest in digging up bones or buying islands or anything else he wanted. He'd married a local girl, had a kid, and lived a quiet life in a house not ten minutes from the clapboard home he'd grown up in.

I was about to introduce myself to Cade when a tall, handsome man with straight black hair worn in a queue came toward us. "This dig must be stopped," he said, blocking Cade's path and cutting me and Tinkie out of his way.

"What are you talking about?" Cade said. "This will reveal so much about the first settlers of this land. It's a boon for the local economy—hotels are filled and restaurants have catering jobs. Peter, we all benefit from this."

"The first settlers were my people. I'm legal counsel for the Tunica nation. This is sacred ground and all excavation must stop."

I recognized Peter Deerstalker. He'd been in town for a few days, too, and he hadn't bothered to be discreet about his opposition to the dig. The only thing missing from Deerstalker's speech was a court order. He didn't have one and I could tell by the look on Elton Cade's face he had no intention of stopping the dig. Not for a lawyer—not even for a dead woman.

"You know I love and respect you, Peter, but when you have a court order, then we'll talk," Cade said. "This is an important site. This mound is far off the normal geographic location of the other major mounds and it's been hidden here, untampered with, for all these years. Your people stand to benefit with the rest of the area."

"That's your assessment. We believe this was a sacred temple site and was removed from the other sites to keep it safe and hidden. And that's how it should remain." Deerstalker stood his ground.

"I'm sorry. You don't have the say-so in that," Cade said. He shook his head slowly. "Look, I understand where you're coming from. But there is so much to be learned, so much that can benefit the Tunica tribe if their history becomes better known. There's not a downside to this for you or your people."

"Except that if this is a temple site with burials, the bones of my ancestors will be disturbed. In my culture, this is a violation, just as it is in the white culture. Imagine if I wanted to dig up a cemetery."

It was a valid point. I looked at Tinkie, whose gaze was on Frank Hafner. The professor was watching the interaction between Deerstalker and Cade with great interest.

"If there was a cemetery that might lead to a better understanding of the white migration to this land, I would say dig it up," Cade said. "The truth is, we know plenty about the spread of white settlements, the brutal tactics used, the way claim was laid to land that rightly belonged to the Native Americans. The predominant religious belief was Christian. The people who came here were often poor and tempted by the concept of

41

owning their own plot of land. There's no mystery here. The Native settlers are far more intriguing. They could have settled anywhere. Why here? They weren't hunters as much as gatherers. Why here? In the most successful tribes, they had a society based on caring for each other. But they could also exhibit great brutality."

"We love the idea that there is great mystery in studying the *savages*." Deerstalker made his point without raising his voice.

"Can we have this conversation somewhere else?" Cade asked. "We can continue this back at the house. Lolly will make dinner for us, Peter. There's a dead woman here. The sheriff and Doc Sawyer are ready to carry her down the mound and I'd like to speak with the sheriff."

"I'll see you in Hilo," Deerstalker said.

The men nodded and scattered. Tinkie and I looked at each other. "Who knew a dig could be so controversial and fraught with such drama?"

"Let's talk to some of the students here. I want to find out the relationship between Hafner and Wells. And it looks like Hafner has ducked out, or maybe Coleman has taken him."

Tinkie nodded agreement. "I've heard the two competing professors were hostile to each other. Wells made a scene in town a few days ago. She was bad-mouthing Hafner in Millie's when some of Hafner's students challenged her. Millie had to call the sheriff's office. When Budgie and

DeWayne showed up, the students took off."

"Sounds like Wells and Hafner had a very contentious relationship."

As Coleman had pointed out earlier, motivation was one key in finding a villain. Hafner was handsome and had a reputation for charming his students. Perhaps one of them had taken his defense to the point of homicide.

3

Sweetie Pie and Chablis were great icebreakers among the students. The young people—when had I ever looked so wide-eyed and fresh—found comfort in the dogs, stroking their coats and hugging them. Frank Hafner, who'd reappeared in the middle of the kids, watched the dogs with skepticism. He was smart enough not to complain, though. The animals drew attention from him and allowed him to subtly assess Tinkie and me.

When the college kids had settled down, I took their measure. The striking young woman in the red bandana was still missing, and I wondered if she'd left voluntarily or had been sent somewhere by Hafner. The professor's good looks and charm were great manipulation tools for the young and inexperienced. Coleman wouldn't likely miss one student, but I'd suss out where she'd disappeared to. It smelled like a good lead to me. Right now, though, I wanted to hear from Frank Hafner.

Tinkie made the introductions, and I fell under the full power of Hafner's smile and warm hand-shake. "Ms. Delaney," he said. "People in the region sing your praises as a private investigator.

They failed to tell me what an attractive woman you are."

"Probably because the local residents are so full of bull sh— crap," Tinkie said, rolling her eyes at me. "You've already hired us, Frank. Skip the charm session and let's get busy finding you an alibi for the time of the murder. You have to know you're the prime suspect."

"The absurd logic of the undereducated police," Hafner said. "I hated Dr. Wells, that is true, but it isn't in my nature to harm anyone. Especially not a colleague."

"My internal lie detector just hit the red alert," I said. Hafner could deliver a lie with ease, but there were too many instances where he and Sandra Wells had been seen in confrontational conversations. "You hated Wells. Maybe you were hoping to kill her, cut her up, and drop her into that hole you drilled into the mound. No one would ever have found the body. Not even cadaver dogs would have caught the scent."

Hafner looked surprised at the scene I laid out. "I didn't do that, but I have to say, it's a brilliant plan."

I followed with "Where were you last night, Dr. Hafner?"

His brown eyes held a banked fire and his tone was low and seductive. "Wouldn't a better question be: *Where are you going to be tonight?* I definitely see potential with you."

Tinkie winked at me behind his back and gave the famous Daddy's Girl giggle that told a man he was excessively clever. "How you do run on, Dr. Hafner," she said in a perfect Scarlett O'Hara imitation. "I'll bet last night you had six graduate students hanging off your arms and had to beat them away with a stick."

"That's one rule I never break," Hafner said. "I don't date my students. It's an unfair advantage of power."

I concurred with that, but I'd known plenty of professors who didn't mind getting a little action on the side with a student. Some considered it a perk of the job. "So if you weren't robbing the academic cradle, where were you?"

He gave a lopsided grin that was the epitome of sexy with a sense of humor. "I was alone. In my room at the Prince Albert."

"Can anyone verify your alibi?" I pressed.

"Perhaps the hotel staff. I had room service, then worked out. I'm sure someone saw me."

Once Doc pinpointed the time of death, I could match his alibi with that. Assuming someone at the hotel could corroborate he was there.

"Is the crew staying at the Prince Albert?" I asked.

"No, they're at the Budget Inn on the highway. I'm at the Prince Albert because I have meetings with investors." He held my gaze. "And I like luxury. I'm too old to camp out or rough it. I work hard, I deserve the good things in life. I'm the one who brings the grants in to the university."

I had to hand it to him for honesty, at least about his penchant to spoil himself. If the students didn't mind, why should I care? "Do you recall seeing anyone in the hotel? Staff or guests. Maybe you had drinks at the bar? An alibi is only useful if there's proof that it's true."

"I was working last night, so I didn't indulge in alcohol. I'd had an argument with Dr. Wells, a very public argument, and I decided to go over my project's cost analysis to see if there was anywhere I could cut corners enough to dump her. She was a blight on this project. The work wasn't her focus. She had bigger fish to fry, like her own television show. She was willing to wreck this dig to be a star."

"Wreck it how?" Tinkie asked.

"She had no concern for the sacredness of the site or the care needed to find artifacts. She wanted to go in with the laser equipment, for which she was paid to do endorsements, and just blast down into the layers of the mound so that she could time her finds to maximize the presence of camera crews. She just about moved that Memphis television reporter, Cissy Hartley, in with her. Sandra worked every angle. Anything for an audience, and whenever a camera was turned on . . . You should have seen her, all made-up, pretending to be an archeologist. If she got a speck of dust on her boots she made one of her students polish them so they would be perfect for the camera. She wanted to be a TV star. Science was just a stepping-stone to fame for her."

"It's clear you hated her, but did you hate her enough to kill her?" I asked.

Hafner stared directly into my eyes. He had eyes so blue they were almost spooky. Very mesmerizing in the intensity of his stare. "I didn't kill anyone. I'm ambitious and I like pretty women. I enjoy sex without monogamy, but I'm not a killer."

The student with the red bandana had reappeared, and she came up to our little cluster. "Frank wouldn't hurt anyone," she said. "He cares about the integrity of the dig, about teaching the students the right way to do things. He's not a fame hag like Sandra Wells."

The young woman's eyes blazed with the fire of a zealot or a woman in love. She had a tough row to hoe with Frank Hafner. "Who are you?" I asked.

"Delane Goggans."

"You're one of Dr. Hafner's students?" Tinkie asked.

"No, actually one of Sandra's. I'm her graduate assistant."

Oh, that must have made life fun here at the mound if Wells knew Hafner was sleeping with her graduate assistant, and I had no doubt Delane had been caught in the web of sexual excitement spun by Hafner. He was the poster boy for bad behavior.

"Where were you last night, Delane?" Tinkie asked.

"I was with Frank. From about seven—"

"Stop, Delane. It won't help and it'll only compromise your reputation," Frank said, trying to silence her.

"I was with Frank until five in the morning. He didn't want to say because he was protecting my reputation, but I have to tell the truth." Delane's mouth was a grim line.

The young woman was lying. She couldn't look me in the eye when she talked. For all of her bravado, she wasn't a natural-born liar. "The sheriff will have some questions about that," I said.

"I'm not going anywhere," she said.

Shouting came from the other students, and it was clear that two young men were about to tie up. Delane started to go, but Tinkie caught her arm.

"Tell me about this dig," Tinkie said, absorbing Hafner's and Delane's attention so that I was free to talk with the other students.

"I'll handle that," I said and excused myself. The minute I walked toward the two male students, they parted. I went after Pluto, who had headed straight for a thin young man with glasses as thick as bottle bricks. I introduced myself and asked if I could talk with him.

"I don't know anything." He looked around to make sure no one overheard him.

"What's your name?"

"Cooley. Cooley Marsh." He sighed. "I was named for a place in south Louisiana where I grew up, and no, I don't think it's funny."

Okay, so the kid had a chip on his shoulder. He had a right. "What's going on with those two?" I indicated the two students who'd put distance between themselves but continued to glare at each other.

"Testosterone poisoning," Cooley said. "I think they both take steroids. They're on the football team and they came on this dig for extra credit. They need a good grade to stay in the football program next year. They're flunking. Academics and professional football don't mix. As it happens, the dig needs some students with strong backs. They fit the bill."

"Tell me about the dig. Do you know anyone who wanted to hurt Dr. Wells?"

"Even her own students hated her," he said. "Just about anyone here could have killed her. Gladly."

"Including you?"

"Yep. I hated her, too. She made fun of me and only brought me on the trip because my parents made a big donation to the archeology department at the University of Michigan."

"Are you into archeology?"

He shook his lead. "Look at me. I'm a geek. I want to create and develop computer games. My dad convinced me to look at this dig as potential material for a game involving digging up clues and such. He was right. I can call the game Murder at the Mound. It'll be a big hit, especially based on a real story. Wells' murder will get the headlines I need to push this game to the top."

Was everyone here determined to capitalize on tragedy or digging up old bones? "So who's the killer?"

"In my game or in real life?"

I shrugged.

"Dr. Hafner is the obvious choice for real-life murderer. It's hard to believe he and Dr. Wells were ever lovers."

I almost stopped him but checked myself. If Wells and Hafner had been romantically linked at some point, that looked even worse for the good professor. One motive to murder on top of another motive.

"But Hafner is too obvious," the student pointed out. "He wouldn't be stupid enough to hang her from a hoist to bleed into a bowl we just unearthed. Aside from that fact, Hafner would kill anyone who dug twenty feet into the mound with that auger. He would never allow that kind of destruction. No telling what was destroyed along the way."

"Unless he was deliberately trying to throw people off the trail."

His face brightened. "You're pretty good at this. That's a great twist for the plot of the game I'm creating. I might call you for a consultation. You could get a credit on the game and some of the royalties."

"Sounds great. You've got your future all lined out."

"I'm going to be as big in the computer game business as Elton Cade is with the traditional toys. That's why I finally agreed to come to this hellhole. I wanted to meet Cade. He's a genius at creating games and marketing them. I'm hoping to apprentice in his Memphis office. I have a lot of ideas for computer games and someone like Cade could help me jump ahead of the pack. Cade doesn't normally invest in computer games because he wants kids outside and moving, but even he can't hold back the future."

Cooley knew what he wanted. So many millennials seemed lost, but Cooley was on a path. "I'm sure Mr. Cade would love to talk with you as soon as this murder is resolved. So who do you think might have killed Dr. Wells?"

He leaned in closer to me, aware again of any listening ears. "Dr. Wells wasn't a very nice person. She poked at her students and mocked them. Really, they all hated her."

"And Dr. Hafner?"

"Maybe he did kill her. She really got under his skin."

"What about Hafner's students? If he was involved with one of them, maybe Dr. Wells threatened to report him." I left it open-ended to see what Cooley said.

He shrugged. "Rumors are he slept with his students. Food for his ego." Cooley finally grinned and there was something charming in his glee. "The thing is, none of the students are idiots. None of them cared enough to report Hafner. To them, he was just a dirty old man grasping at staying young. Except for Delane. She really seems to care about him."

It was only a little insulting that a man who was suitable date material for me would be considered a dirty old man by college students, but those were the harsh facts. In another few years I'd be forty and over the hill. Cooley and I watched Delane take up for Hafner with Tinkie. The girl was willing to step in front of a train for the professor.

"Delane thinks of herself as superior to us. More sophisticated. She thinks she's a romantic. She reads those old books like *Sense and Sensibility* and thinks she's the heroine. We think she's a sucker."

54

That one statement was a treatise on the danger of perspective, but I didn't have time to really unravel it. "She's a lovely young woman. I hope she doesn't get hurt too badly."

He shrugged. "Some people have to take a lot of knocks before they learn. Me, I watched my parents tear each other limb from limb every day. I've got no illusions about true love or all that hooey. Hafner is using Delane, but she likes it. In the end, everyone gets a little something and loses a whole lot more."

It was one of the most bitter assessments of relationships that I'd ever encountered. If Cooley exemplified the millennial generation, there was nothing soft or magical left in the world of love and romance. I thanked him for his time and stepped back. I immediately glanced over at Coleman, who was helping the EMTs get the body down the steep incline of the mound. My heart thudded with the power of a mule kick. I loved that man, and I didn't want to lose one iota of the power of that love, even though I knew the pain would be equal or greater if we separated for any reason.

"You look gobsmacked," Tinkie said. She'd slipped up beside me without a sound.

"It's been a while since I've been young," I said. Thirty-four wasn't ancient, but it was a long way from nineteen. "I was more . . . romantic and foolish when I was in college."

"Tell me about it. I went to get my Mrs. Degree—a lot of girls did. Now that's slander against our gender to say, but my whole college world was dating and sororities and social events."

"It was a different time."

"I'm glad women are becoming more independent, but I hate that real romance is also taking a hit."

"I know." Budgie was rounding up all the students and moving them toward two buses that someone had sent from Zinnia. They would be questioned and released. "Did Hafner give you any details about what he hopes to find here?"

"He did. It's the historical elements he's after. Dr. Wells had some crazy idea that Hernando de Soto, the Spanish explorer, had a map that outlined three cities of gold off the Gulf Coast. One was in Florida, one in Louisiana, and one up the Mississippi River. Hafner doesn't believe any of the foolishness about gold treasures, but he did believe that the information he could recover from an undisturbed burial mound would cement his reputation as a premier archeologist."

The facts just didn't add up for me. Then again, I thought looking at old pottery was interesting, as was learning about the culture of the people who'd first roamed the Delta. But to kill for such things? I just didn't get it and, trust me, if gold or jewels had been buried in the Delta, some farmer would have long ago plowed them up. While the Mississippi River area was rich in soil and beauty, there had been no gold mines or jewels discovered in the area.

"Let's head to Millie's." I was starving. I'd missed breakfast and Coleman's visit and my stomach was growling.

"Sure thing." Tinkie whistled up the dogs. To our surprise, Chablis ran up to us with something in her mouth. "What is that?" Tinkie wasn't prissy about her dog, but she didn't want her ingesting junk food from a dig site. She reached down and took the loosely woven bag from Chablis' mouth.

The bag was heavy—I could tell by the way she dragged it. And when she upended it, the large pendant that fell into her hand made me inhale sharply. "What is that?" It was lovely in a strange way. A leather thong, which was frayed and dangerously old, held the pendant, which looked to be a ram's head or some animal with horns.

"It looks Egyptian, kind of." That was my contribution to historical culture.

"I think we should take this to Peter Deerstalker," Tinkie said.

It was a brilliant idea, but one that was liable to start a real war with the lawyer. If this pendant was of value to the Tunica tribe, it would give him grist for his mill to stop the dig. We needed to understand what we had before we gave it up.

"Let's turn it over to Coleman first. He can pass it on to Deerstalker or whoever legally owns it."

Tinkie nodded. "After a garden omelet," she said as she put the pendant away.

"If this thing is valuable, it may be why Dr. Wells was killed," I remarked as we made our way down the steep side of the mound. In the quiet of the empty Delta, I felt like ruler of the world. There was something about height that did give a sense of power. The fact that people without any real tools had created such an impressive mound, moving the dirt by hand, made me think of the many changes the Delta had witnessed. The past was gone, though. Our job was to find the person who'd killed Sandra Wells and hope that it didn't put our client in line to be prosecuted for murder.

4

The breakfast rush was over at Millie's Café and we had no trouble finding a quiet table in a corner. Before we'd even ordered, Coleman walked into the café. The sight of him striding through the door gave my stomach a jolt, which was obvious to my partner, who nudged my foot under the table. "Just get it over with and jump his bones," she whispered. "I mean what could be sexier than doing the dirty in the middle of eggs and bacon. Positively *9½ Weeks*. None of that paltry, weak-kneed *Fifty Shades of Grey* for you."

"You only say that because you know I won't." I found her toes under the table and pressed down a little. "If I did, you'd squawk like a chicken laying an eight-ounce egg."

Tinkie shifted her foot away from my pressure and signaled Coleman to join us. "Hello, Coleman," Tinkie said. "Sarah Booth was just remarking how much she enjoyed being fed breakfast."

Coleman gave me a puzzled look, and I had no intention of trying to explain Tinkie's kinky-movie fetish.

Once he had a cup of coffee and had managed to squeeze my hand beneath the table, Tinkie brought forth the pendant. Because Chablis had found it, we couldn't say for certain it was part of the dig or perhaps something left behind by the numerous teenagers who'd used the site for scary stories and petting or even the Bailey family, but the proximity to the dig and the murder made it evidence the sheriff needed to have.

Coleman examined the pendant, then put in a call to Deputy Budgie Burton to join us. Budgie's interest in history and his research abilities would yield answers much quicker than I could. Budgie arrived, setting a land-speed record, photographed the pendant, and tapped away on his tablet—a vast improvement over the research abilities at the Sunflower County sheriff's office prior to his hiring. Budgie knew databases that neither Coleman nor I had ever heard of. And he was on top of science, history, and geographical developments that skimmed over my head.

Budgie held up the pendant. "This isn't from any tribes in this area," he said at last. "And it isn't valuable. Not as a metal. It's a type of pewter, but the design and imagery could have significance to the killer, or perhaps to Dr. Wells. We should show it to her students and see if they know anything about it."

"Good idea," Coleman said. "Sarah Booth, can you handle that? I'd do it but I need Budgie to go with me to talk to Frank Hafner. He was less than cooperative at the dig. He was too busy trying to impress his students with how tough he is."

"Hafner thinks Sarah Booth is beautiful." Tinkie looked so innocent, I wanted to strangle her.

"Sure, Tinkie and I will ask about the pendant," I said before anyone could respond to her ludicrous statement. I looked at Coleman. "We don't mind helping you, just as long as you know we're working to prove Hafner is innocent."

"I know." Coleman looked weary. "I know. And if he is innocent, then that's the outcome I want, too. But if he isn't . . ."

"We didn't have to share the pendant," I pointed out. "We want the truth, just like you."

Coleman finished his coffee and stood. "We'll compare notes later this evening." He bent down to brush a kiss across my cheek. He was not a man for public displays of affection, but he was also a man who felt free to show what was in his heart. I liked that.

As he stepped out the door, Tinkie stepped on my toes under the table. "We should work late tonight, Sarah Booth. Get the jump on this case."

"In your dreams," I replied, smiling. She wasn't going to get my goat now.

At the checkout, I paid and picked up the to-go orders for the pets. I had to have a better routine where I could cook for myself and the pets. Every time I thought this, the secondary thought was—but why? Millie was a much better cook and she only served premium food. And thus the war was lost before the first battle was even fought. Sweetie would have her grilled pork chop with sweet potatoes and green beans. Chablis would have the same—cut into tiny bites for her by the café cook—and Pluto would approve of the fresh rainbow trout with risotto. My own garden omelet had been delicious.

I let Tinkie feed the critters while I drove. We had to pick up her car at the dig, and I hoped some of the students might have returned. I suspected that Frank Hafner had urged them to continue working while he talked with Coleman. Delane Goggans would make certain no protocols were breached.

When we pulled up at the mound, I saw the students at the top. They were gathered around the winch that had once held a dead body. Sandra Wells had died a hard death. The gruesomeness involved could serve two purposes—to punish her or as a warning to others. Or perhaps it was both. If Coleman was done investigating, surely the students would dismantle the winch. I'd be glad when the grisly device was gone. Reminders of the unpleasantness of Wells' death were unnecessary.

"Look, Delane is there." Tinkie pointed her out. She had lost her red bandana and now wore an air of authority as she ordered the other students about. From the looks on the students' faces, a mutiny was about to take place. No one liked to be pushed around by the boss' main squeeze.

We made the hike up the steep side of the mound. I knew I'd pay a big price with sore muscles in the morning. Even Sweetie Pie, who had boundless energy, was huffing and puffing. And she went straight for Delane, who set up a tirade about the dogs destroying the dig site.

"Are you not aware there was a house here? One with children, livestock, dogs, fowl," Tinkie said as she got right in her face. "Stop being a fool. Besides, Chablis found something around here. See." Tinkie showed her a photo of the pendant because Budgie had taken the real deal with him back to the sheriff's office.

Delane's face went pale and her eyes darted to the place where the tripod of death had been erected.

"This means something to you," I said. "Care to tell us about it?"

"I don't have to talk to you. You're private investigators, not cops." She raised her voice. "None of us have to talk to you." Beneath her words was the threat: *None of you had better talk to these two.* "Now, everyone get busy. We don't want to be up here after dark." She looked around as if she expected something dangerous to be lurking about.

"In case you missed the fact, we're working for Hafner," I said with amusement. "Since you two are lovers, I kind of thought you might be interested in helping him."

The pale wash of her skin flushed red. If she stayed out here in the Delta sun for any length of time, the young woman would be risking skin cancer. She didn't have the complexion for a large dose of sunshine. Or humiliation.

"Frank didn't do anything. I told you and those yokel cops that I was with Frank all evening until early this morning. He didn't leave his room."

"Why is it that I don't believe you?" Tinkie asked. "We checked with the hotel and Frank had room service for one. What? You were hiding in the bathroom when the food was delivered?"

I forced myself not to look at Tinkie. She was lying through her teeth. We hadn't talked to the waitstaff of the hotel, but it was a damn good idea.

"I, uh, I—" Delane faltered.

It wasn't like she could claim to have gone to a play or a museum or library. Zinnia shut down at five o'clock. If you were standing on the street the sidewalks might roll you up in them. Millie's Café stayed open until nine or so, and then the only place to hang out was the Sweetheart Ice Cream Bar and Grill. They did the late-night, teenage-dating business.

"We know you weren't with Frank, so where were you?" Tinkie pushed harder.

"I went to Memphis." She looked utterly miserable.

"For what?"

"A doctor's appointment. You can check. I was out of town and didn't get back until about two in the morning. Frank and I were going to alibi each other." She shrugged one shoulder. "I told him it wouldn't work."

"Are you sick?" I asked.

She shook her head. "Amber Johnson had some medical issues. Appendix, I think. I took her to a specialist. Then I took her to the airport to catch a flight back to Ann Arbor. She didn't have the fortitude to be here at the dig."

All of those facts were easily verifiable. It made no sense for her to lie, because she knew I'd check behind her.

"What about the other members of the dig. The students?" I asked.

"They were at the Budget Inn on the highway into Zinnia. We have two vans to haul them and a pickup truck for equipment. Anyone could have gotten a key and taken one of those vehicles out here to the dig. But why would Dr. Wells have agreed to meet up with a student? That doesn't wash. She had only contempt for her students. Dr. Wells had to be meeting someone more important than a student here. To be honest, most of the

65

students wouldn't be out at the dig at night even for a guaranteed A. There's something roaming around in those woods and no one wants to meet it face-to-face."

She had a point. A good one. Sandra Wells wouldn't have climbed up the side of the mound for just anyone.

"So what about that pendant?" Tinkie asked. "What significance does it hold for you, and don't even try to lie." For some reason, Tinkie had this girl pegged. She could intimidate her and Delane knew it.

"You should talk to Kawania. She had the pendant originally."

"And?" Tinkie pressed.

"And she said she was going to put a curse on Dr. Wells." Delane glanced nervously at the group of students who'd stopped working and were sitting in the shade of an oak tree that had to have been growing on top of the mound for over a hundred years. It was a magnificent tree. Delane's gaze swiveled back to us. "I think Kawania killed Dr. Wells. She said she was going to call up an avenging spirit from the past Native American tribes who lived here. They were supposed to do that yesterday."

"Who did they call? I mean what kind of magic were they going to use?" Tinkie asked. I rolled my eyes at her. I was no big believer in magic or curses, though I had kept a small charm Tinkie had gotten for me. One to bring Coleman to my bed. He'd arrived there—and stayed. But I didn't want to believe magic had brought him to me.

"Tinkie, you know they didn't call any spirits. Delane is playing you."

"I'm not playing anyone!" Delane's voice drew the attention of all the students. They watched us. She lowered her voice. "One reason I agreed to take Amber to the doctor and then the airport was because I didn't want to be around voodoo or hoodoo or crazy shit." Delane turned and pointed to an exotic-looking young woman who was staring at us with a Darth Vader glare. "That's Kawania. Ask her. She said she would get rid of Dr. Wells and she did. She said that pendant had great power. And now she's pissed off because she can't find the damn thing. How did you get it?" Delane finally realized she could ask questions, too.

"Stop playing the rube." I was genuinely annoyed. "This isn't going to fly with me. Get Kawania over here."

"She's Frank's student. She doesn't have to do what I say."

That made sense. Frank Hafner's students had no reason to fear or obey Delane. But they had no one else in authority to lead them. "Then please *ask* her to speak with us. And you don't go far. We aren't finished talking."

Delane whipped around and went straight to

the exotic young woman and talked a minute, pointing at us. Kawania nodded, got up slowly, and came toward us. She walked with the grace and confidence of an ancient goddess. I'd never seen such a self-possessed group of kids. I just hoped none of them was possessed with the spirit of a killer. I wondered where that dark thought came from until I realized that Kawania had the lazy, serpentine grace of a snake. She was all fluid power.

Tinkie nudged me. "Check out that guy watching Kawania."

The young man had slowly stood up, his gaze following Kawania as if he were mesmerized. Snake, meet the man you've charmed. He appeared to be in some kind of hypnotic trance, with Kawania the focus of his entire world.

"You wanted to talk to me?" Kawania had the soft, melodic accent of New Orleans.

"We found your pendant."

"Folks who poke around in other people's belongings sometimes lose their nose." She said it like a song or poem, not a threat.

"We weren't in your possessions. My little dog found it on the other side of the mound." Tinkie stood as tall as her four-foot-eleven frame would allow.

Technically, we didn't know where Chablis had found it, but that was good enough. "You've got some people believing you killed Sandra Wells,"

I said. "Not a good move since the professor is actually dead. Murdered."

"People can believe what they want. Where's the evidence?"

She was a cool one. "Why did you want Sandra Wells dead?"

"Did you ever meet the bit—woman? Everyone hated her. I didn't want her dead any more than anyone else here. Especially Dr. Hafner. Delane will lie, but ask anyone else. Frank hated her guts. He used to joke about pushing her off the side of the mound and watching her bounce all the way to the ground."

"What's the story with the pendant, Kawania? The sheriff has it. He's going to be asking you questions."

She sighed. "Look, I need to pass this class. I have to pass it. I have a job waiting for me this summer when I graduate. A good job at a museum in Chicago. I hate this dig but Dr. Hafner said he'd give me the extra credit I need for an A if I came along. So I did. And all I've done is get down in holes and brush dirt away and then move it by the cupful. At this rate it will take a hundred years to find out what's in this old pile of dirt."

"That's what an archeological dig is about," Tinkie said. "The pendant?"

"It was my mother's. She got it at a souvenir shop in New Orleans. She said it had magical powers and I just embellished the story a little to scare the other students. It's good for them to be afraid of me. They do my work, give me extra food . . ." She shrugged a shoulder. "It works out better for me and it entertains me to get them going."

"You didn't put a curse on Dr. Wells?" I asked.

"I would have if I'd known how. That was just . . . a joke. Those morons will believe anything."

"Who hated Dr. Wells enough to kill her?"

"Hafner, for sure. She kept trying to force him to use heavy equipment to get to the real jackpot of the dig. She had TV crews here and she wanted a big find. She was angling for her own TV show."

Tink and I had heard that before, and this validation sounded real. "She sounds very much a—"

"Freaking ego with legs. I've never seen anyone more self-absorbed, narcissistic, and mean."

"Other than Hafner, who wanted her dead?"

"That Peter Deerstalker fellow had a big argument with her. And some of the investors were fighting with her, too."

"Here at the dig?"

She shook her head. "No. I was in that little Laundromat in town. I mean, we have to wash our clothes sometimes. I hate being dirty all the time. Anyway, I had stepped out in the alley to smoke a cigarette and here comes Dr. Wells. She usually made Delane do her wash, but she was carrying a load of laundry when that Tunica Indian guy blocked her path. I peeked around the corner and saw them. He was mad and she was haughty."

"What happened?" Tinkie asked.

Out of the corner of my eye, I saw Sweetie Pie and Chablis circling the students. They had lost interest in watching us talk to Kawania and had opened some beers. Most work for the day had ended with the discovery of the professor's body. Pluto had climbed up to the first branch of the big oak tree. He was watching like a hawk. Many times I envied his ability to get above a crime scene where he could check things out from a completely different angle. When Kawania started talking, I drew my focus back to her.

"That Deerstalker guy, he was really pissed. He told her she had to stop the dig and her TV shows. That desecration of his ancestors wasn't fodder for fat idiots who had nothing better to do than sit in front of a television thinking they were great explorers."

"What did Wells say?" I asked.

"She laughed at him. That nasty laugh of hers, which pretty much said she thought you were a scabbacious worm. When he told her he was serious, she told him to fu . . . to get lost."

"And that was it?"

"Not exactly. He told her she'd regret using his people for her own gain."

"Did he threaten her?"

"Depends on what you consider a threat. He said she'd be sorry for all the harm she'd caused. He said his people were tired of being used by others for personal gain, and that he meant to stop her no matter how he had to do it."

That pretty much was a threat, taken in the context of Sandra Wells' murder most gruesome.

5

While we were at the mound, Tinkie and I decided to poke around. I was curious about the excavation, which was so dang methodical I would have found some dynamite and blown the site wide open. Not really, but the idea of using a small and delicate brush to remove tons and tons and tons of dirt was the road to madness for me. Patience was never a virtue I could claim. Tinkie, on the other hand, pretended fascination and went off with several of the graduate students to get a full-fledged lesson in the technique of archeological digging in this type of soil. Duplicitous was her middle name.

I was merely thankful that Sweetie Pie didn't smell bones and go hog wild. She, too, had thrown in with a couple of students who were taking selfies with her ears. The ears were very long and exceedingly attractive. She looked as if she might be able to fly with them, a la Dumbo. They were so cute I took some photos, too, unbeknownst to the students.

I'd never fully appreciated the size of the mound. It was far off the highway, and through the trees that had grown out of the sides, it had been difficult to see from the road. I'd never known the Bailey family who'd lived atop it.

The old home site was easy to find. Burned timbers and blackened bricks—handmade by slaves, no doubt—were scattered around. Kids and god knew who else had picked through the rubble. When the dig crews showed up, Hafner put an end to local foraging. Before I'd moved home or Coleman was elected, the sheriff had roused high schoolers out of the place on more than one occasion. Not because there was anything there left for the kids to destroy, but when the house was standing it was a danger. The stairs could have fallen or the floor given way. In the humidity of the South, a neglected wooden structure doesn't last long.

The fire had removed the temptation of the old house as a place to gather to drink, smoke, experiment with drugs, and tell ghost stories. Of course the property was said to be haunted by a woman in a gossamer gown who guarded the house from vandals. Or perhaps it was the slender man in a black hoodie, or the little girl with the black eyes, or now whatever was lumbering around in the woods that the students were afraid of.

A grove of oak trees, planted at what would have been the front of the house in an arrangement that yielded a shady and hospitable front yard, were sentinels without a purpose. Other volunteer trees had sprouted up and created a thick veil around where the house had stood. The Baileys hadn't maintained the grounds with the vengeance necessary to keep them in good repair—a reality I knew well with Dahlia House. This climate, with the long, long growing season, the good soil, and plenty of rain, was heaven for weeds and trees as well as cotton. I was one person with a house that needed a crew of workmen and half a dozen gardeners. I did the best I could, but my fence rows were growing up with scrub oaks and maples. Since I wouldn't use chemicals, I'd have to resort to a bulldozer when the fence was replaced. I'd accepted that fact. Nature would reclaim the land—and not long after the humans were gone. In many ways, that was a bit of comfort.

I nudged aside a few of the remaining timbers, upsetting an ant bed that was a reminder of how cruel the land could be to those who muddled about unawares. Fire ants, not a native species, had come into the United States from South America on a ship docked in Mobile Bay. They'd spread like any plague—and their bites were as painful as fire. During a flood the ants would roll together in a ball and continually circulate so that none drowned. They were clever little devils.

Beneath the ant bed was a glimmer of ceramic, and I used a stick to unearth a blue willow china plate in perfect condition. It had survived the kids, the vandals, and the fire. In that split second I understood why digging up old relics was so important. It was that instant connection with the past, with the knowledge that someone else had stood on that exact piece of ground and this had been a part of his daily life. The china pattern told me much about at least one of the people who'd frequented Mound Salla.

"I don't think the 1800s is of particular interest to the professors."

The male voice came from behind me and I whipped around to face Peter Deerstalker. He took the plate from my hand and examined it. "My grandmother admired this pattern. We were too poor for any kind of china, but she loved blue willow. She said it told a powerful story of love and transformation."

I must have looked confused, because he added, "Native Americans can also fall for the legends and tales of china makers who are Chinese."

I had to laugh at that. "Yes, I suppose. It's a sad story, though. My aunt Loulane told it to me. The beautiful Chinese girl fell in love with someone of a lower station. They ran away and married, but the father eventually found them and killed them."

"But you're forgetting the best part. The gods were so moved by their love that they transformed their spirits into two doves where they could be together."

I *had* forgotten that part. "That makes it even sadder." And for me, it did.

"This pattern was a favorite of the Hearst family." Peter handed the plate back to me. "A lot of upper-class women collected the dishes. I suppose you have a set at Dahlia House."

I shook my head. "My mother was unconventional. If there are china patterns at Dahlia House, they're tucked away in the attic. Some future generation will have to dig them out. My mother liked unmatched place settings, handcrafted clay pieces. One-of-a-kind things. Growing up, I had the most unique room décor. My mother would be impressed I saved most of it for my own little girl."

"Are you expecting? I'd heard your detective agency was going great guns. But that urge to have a child is hard to resist, isn't it? I suppose that is the ultimate experience for a woman."

His question and comment startled me, but only for a moment. "No. I remain unwed and unbred. No time now for children. Maybe later." I absolutely would not let the thought of Jitty enter my head.

"I didn't know your parents well, Sarah Booth, but you do remind me of your mom. She had the same . . . saucy tongue."

"Well put." My mother hadn't held back. She didn't conform to expected standards of behavior for Southern women. Not in her actions or her speech.

"Your father helped my father with some land deeds." Peter seemed in no hurry to get to the point of why he'd sought me out. "That was a long time ago. Your dad was a fair man. At that time, a lot of people wouldn't take on an Indian as a client. We couldn't even get haircuts in some of the barbershops."

I'd never heard those things, but Peter was older than I was. And my parents had protected me from some of the worst of the behavior of people around me. "People can be idiotic."

"They can." He looked beyond me to the charred remains of the house. "Three years ago my people wanted to make an issue of this mound, but I talked them out of it. I knew the house was falling down. I figured it would be better to wait until the place caved in and it was obvious there was no interest in the Bailey family claiming it as a homestead. The tribe wanted to stake our claim for what is rightfully a burial ground. I talked them out of it." The muscle in his jaw flexed. "I waited too long. I didn't know about the fire, which was the only thing holding back this dig. Now, trying to assert our claim to this land is going to be even harder."

"The timing of the fire is a bit suspicious." I'd thought that before he said it. "Do you know anything about how the fire started?"

"Nothing. It could have been lightning, as the fire chief indicated. There was no electricity on the property."

"It could have been kids fooling around." Sunflower County was a close-knit area. No one would uphold kids setting an abandoned house on fire, but also it was possible no one looked too closely. The house was gone but the stain of a felony charge could ruin the lives of some teenagers. Another factor was that none of the Bailey family was around to press charges. As far as I knew, if any survived they had scattered to the winds. "Are you claiming that this land belongs to the Tunica tribe?"

"Only the mound, which is where our ancestors have been laid to rest. Although we could make a claim for every acre of land in the region, we haven't. And we don't intend to."

I had to be honest. "I don't think your claim is going to stand up in court."

"I suspect you're right. If our ownership was upheld, then the entire continent would be in question, wouldn't it?" His smile gave his face an entirely different look. Beneath the fierceness of his gaze, I sensed his weariness. He looked like he hadn't slept a lot in recent days, and the first thing I wondered was why. Had he been up all night here at the mound, with Sandra Wells? "Will you be in Zinnia for long?" I asked.

"I'm staying with an old friend near here, Elton Cade. Do you know him?"

"He's an investor in this dig and a phenomenal Mississippi success story." And I'd heard them arguing heatedly not so long ago.

"And an old friend of mine. We shared dreams for Mississippi. Elton has seen his come true."

"He's a big reason this dig is happening."

"I know. We disagree on this, but it doesn't affect our friendship. Elton believes that by learning about the Tunica tribe that lived here, and the people who came before, that understanding will be fostered. He believes people fear what they don't understand."

On the surface, I could agree with that premise. Peter did not. "A tough decision for your people. I'm sure you're eager to learn the secrets of this mound."

"I'm more eager to see that my ancestors rest in peace. I'm a deeply religious man. This is a sacrilege. Elton doesn't understand that, but I can guarantee that if I were in the Sunflower County cemetery digging up graves of prominent white people, there would be an outcry."

He was right. No one dug up European graves to study. "What are you going to do?"

"Nothing. Watch the dig. Make sure all remains are handled properly. There's nothing else I can do."

"What was your relationship with Dr. Wells?"

"When she first came to Zinnia, she was very charming. I met with her, had a few drinks . . ." He shrugged. "Nature took its course. Then I realized she was working me, trying to keep me from getting upset about the dig. She was a shameless woman who didn't understand that limits couldn't be crossed."

"Did you kill her?" My thought was, why not just ask? I would see his reaction, and Peter Deerstalker was a hard man to read.

He laughed. "No, I didn't. My battlefield is the courtroom. Killing people isn't the solution to this. Wells is dead, but if Hafner goes to prison, others will just come to finish. There's been too much publicity. This can't be stopped. You see, killing Dr. Wells wouldn't benefit me in the least."

He wasn't being completely honest. If he could stop this dig—even for a short time—it might give him the legal room to file for control of the mound. "Then you won't mind telling me where you were last night?"

"I was a guest in Elton Cade's home."

"And that's where you were?"

He smiled again. "You should have been a lawyer. I had dinner with Elton and his delightful family." A shadow crossed his features, but only briefly. "Lolly Cade is a lovely woman."

I tried to probe the shadow beneath Peter's words, but without success. It was gone before I could even ask about it. "But you left the Cade house, didn't you?"

"I did. I met a student, Kawania, for a drink."

He was a good twenty years older than Kawania. She was a college student, for heaven's sake. My opinion showed on my face.

"I wasn't robbing the cradle, though that girl could probably teach you and me a few things. She has Tunica blood. I knew her mother, and I wanted to see if she might want to join some tribal gatherings."

"Where did you have drinks?"

"At a local blues club."

And that I could easily check out, seeing as how I knew the owner of the club very well.

6

Peter bade me goodbye and started down the steep side of the mound. I'd failed to ask what he'd come out here for. Maybe to get his story straight with Kawania. She was in a huddle with three other young people who kept glancing at me. I made a call.

Scott Hampton, owner of Playin' the Bones blues club, confirmed that Kawania and Peter were at the club at midnight. Then he lost track of them when the band kicked up a long set. In the middle of the set, a small kitchen fire had commanded Scott's attention. I could not prove or disprove Peter's alibi, at least as far as Scott was concerned. I'd call Cece and see if her beau, Jaytee, the harmonica player, had a memory of Peter and Kawania in the club after midnight. I'd learned the hard way that so many people were simply unaware of the activities around them. Trained observers—not! The bogeyman could be drinking blood at the table beside them and they'd be oblivious. That's why Tinkie and I were so valuable.

Speaking of my partner, I looked around to see that Tinkie had developed a rapport with the students, and I wasn't surprised. She was all high-society glitz, but she never disguised her big heart. People, especially young folks, were drawn to her. I gave her space to work the students and I continued exploring the remains of the old Bailey house.

As I kicked at timbers and poked through rubble, I tried to remember the stories I'd heard. There had been a great scandal in the family. I'd heard different accounts about it. There was a murder in the house—a terrible scene with a hatchet. That had been the beginning of the end of that once prestigious family.

Eventually, the Bailey family had simply disappeared. Rumors were that Martha Bailey had moved back to Oklahoma, where she had a sister. The children moved away. The house had been empty for about a decade. Then it burned.

I came upon a pile of old, charred timbers that had been pushed up with a bulldozer or tractor. Something about the haphazard arrangement of the stack of debris made me stop. It was almost as if someone was hiding something. I pulled a few timbers away. They were mostly ash and lighter than I'd thought. At the bottom of the pile was dirt.

"Damn." I'd gotten all dirty and sooty for no reason. I was about to turn away when Kawania walked up. She stepped onto the area I'd cleared, and stopped when her footsteps echoed.

We looked at each other as the meaning dawned on us both. I signaled her aside and photographed the area. I couldn't be certain because I'd contaminated the scene, but it looked like someone, or something, had shifted the dirt and leaves off the area and then put them back, trying unsuccessfully to disguise the evidence of their meddling. Simultaneously, Kawania and I dropped to the ground and began scooping the soil and debris away. Beneath several inches of dirt was wooden planking with a large thumb bolt. And a round ring.

"It's a cellar," I said.

"Let me call the others over to help."

"No, wait." I waved her down. "Let's take a look before we have a stampede over here." I did manage to get Tinkie's attention, and she headed our way.

"What if Dr. Wells was murdered because of something down in this cellar?" Kawania said. "We should call the sheriff."

"We will." I wanted a look-see before anyone else got down there. Kawania didn't seem impressed with the delay. She nodded toward Tinkie, who was approaching.

"You should step back and call the sheriff," Kawania said. "You two could mess up evidence."

"We work for Frank Hafner," I said. She was bright enough to realize that we were Frank's best bet for freedom. If she cared about that.

"You screw up the evidence and it doesn't matter who you work for. You could destroy something that would save Frank's bacon."

"She's right." Tinkie didn't like siding against me, but she did anyway. "Call Sheriff Peters. Besides, maybe you can have some private time." She said it with a straight face, but Kawania cast me a long, speculative look.

I dialed Coleman. "We've found something at the old Bailey place. A cellar. Tinkie won't let me go down there."

"Thank god Tinkie has some sense," Coleman said. "I'm on the way."

There was nothing to do but wait for Coleman, and that's exactly what we were doing when Elton Cade showed up at the dig. He talked to the college students for a moment, seemingly genuinely interested in their opinions. Then he came over to us. I was struck again by his bearing. He was tall, chestnut-haired, and had a certain elegance. He would have fit perfectly in a Russian or French court. He had that bearing.

Tinkie and I reintroduced ourselves, but Kawania needed no introduction. She gave Cade a big hug.

"I'm so sorry Frank has been . . . cast in a suspicious light," Elton said. "I've made arrangements for his bail if he needs it." He made a visual inventory of the timbers that had been moved and the clearly visible cellar door, but he didn't say anything. "Where is Frank?" he asked.

"He didn't do anything wrong." Kawania was quick to jump to Hafner's defense.

"Of course not." Cade said the right thing, but something in his eyes told me otherwise. "Look, I want to help Frank, and I want to get this dig into high gear." Cade looked down into the open cellar. "Has anyone been down there?"

"No, and no one is going until Coleman gets here." I had to keep the area from being compromised.

"Okay," Cade said. "I agree that's the right approach. Now while we're waiting for the sheriff to arrive, why don't we talk about this dig. Why is this suddenly a site worth murdering for? This mound has been here for centuries. The Bailey family lived here. They could have excavated the scene at any time, but no one even thought that anything valuable was here. Now we have a dead woman, ritualistically killed. Why?"

The whole time Cade was talking, Kawania edged away from us. I reached out and grasped her wrist. "Tell me about the curses you claim to put on people."

"Curses?" Cade was mildly amused. "I didn't realize Dr. Hafner and his students were dabbling in the occult. I thought they were here for serious scientific research."

"It was a joke," Kawania said. She was more

sullen than scared. "Some of the students were slacking off on their work, sneaking away, generally being worthless. I made up a story about my great-grandmother having powers to lay a mojo on people. Worked like a charm. They got to work like motivated little beavers." She grinned.

"Why would they be afraid of your grandmother?" Tinkie asked.

"Helen Laveau. She was a descendant of the great voodoo woman, Marie Laveau."

"Oh excellent. This just gets better and better. A ritual sacrifice of a body, graves unearthed, the Native Americans unhappy, the discovery of a cellar beneath a house that burned mysteriously, ghosts of dead Baileys running around the property, and now a Laveau relative putting curses on people. Can we get any more Gothic?" Tinkie put her hands on her hips. She was outdone.

"My job is to motivate those kids to work however I can. Frank thought it was amusing," she scoffed. "Delane was furious. She said I'd frightened the students so they didn't want to work after dark."

"I guess there's no Equal Employment Opportunity Commission for graduate students." Yeah, I was being a smart aleck.

"Those students are working for a grade. There's no forty-hour week and they knew that when they signed on. We have to excavate and find enough to warrant future grants or the dig will shut down." Kawania had the financial basics of the dig down pat. I was impressed with the students both Hafner and Wells had brought with them. They might not all be completely devoted to archeology, but they were intelligent.

"That's all true," Cade said. "As one of the investors in this dig, I want results. Frank understood that, but he also understood that the integrity of the site was paramount. That's why I hired him and donated so handsomely to this cause."

Now was a chance to understand something I hadn't before. "What results are you after? What is it you hope to discover? Native Americans lived on this land long before Europeans came here. A lot of the burial mounds along the Mississippi River have been examined. What's so special about this one that you'd invest in the excavation?"

"There have always been rumors of gold and treasure brought north by Hernando de Soto and other explorers from South and Central America. Most archeologists believe de Soto followed the Mississippi River very closely. If anything was discovered by him, it would have been left along the river's banks. If it's still here, it would likely be in a protected area. A mound. It makes sense to me that if there was something of great value to the Tunicas, they would have moved it inland to a mound. Like this one. Remember, the Mississippi River flooded hundreds of thousands of acres before the levee system was put in. Moving inland for the most sacred possessions and burials only makes sense."

It made sense, but what a risk of millions on the concept that a tribe of people hundreds of years ago decided to move away from the river. "This sounds more like risk than investment."

"As a young boy, I wanted to be an archeologist. I thought I'd find famous tombs and fabulous wealth." He laughed and there was genuine humor in it. "I wanted to be famous for exploring."

"All young boys dream of that," Tinkie said.

"I studied archeology in college, until my father's death. Then I switched to business and it became apparent that I was very good at it. That and making toys. I focused on my talents, but I never gave up my dreams of participating in a dig. Even if only as an investor. I've had a fortunate life in many ways. You could say I never grew up."

"And this excavation is a chance to reclaim your childhood dream?" I asked.

"Only as an investor. I don't want to physically participate or interfere. I just want to do something to acknowledge a civilization that was here long before my family came. To learn about the native people who worked this land and lived here. To find the lessons always left for us in history."

"Do you know Peter Deerstalker?" Tinkie asked. She knew the answer, but it was a little test.

"Yes, Peter and I have been friends a long time. He's disappointed with me now because I've invested in this dig, which he views as a violation. We've had good conversations about this and, though we disagree, we respect each other. This will pass and we'll renew our friendship."

He sounded very sure of something I didn't see as a solid fact. Peter Deerstalker viewed the dig as a desecration of his tribe. I wasn't so sure he'd get over that.

"Elton, who do you think killed Sandra Wells, and why?" I asked.

"Miss Laveau, would you excuse us?" he said. "I know it's a trudge up and down the mound, but if you could get the food baskets out of the trunk of my car, I brought some refreshments for the students. Take three or four of them with you to help carry the supplies."

He was fluid and accomplished in easing his way through social situations. I had to give him that. When Kawania was gone, he motioned Tinkie and me over to an old oak tree that offered a comfortable place to sit. We plopped on the roots.

"Sandra Wells was a claim jumper, if you want to use old west gold mine terminology. I didn't want her on this dig and I made that clear, but the grant sponsors were determined. Frank hated her interference and her determination to speed the dig up for her theatrical purposes. While Frank focused on the integrity of the dig, she was interested only in results. Her students hated her. The people in Zinnia hated her, just ask around. And her peers back at the University of Michigan loathed her. She made enemies everywhere she went."

"And yet Frank Hafner slept with her." Tinkie just put it out there.

Elton Cade laughed. "So did I."

Now that was unexpected news.

"Sandra had a sexual appetite that was . . . unquenchable. There's not a man alive who can resist that if it's pushed in his face again and again. There was nothing tender or loving or even companionable. Sex with Sandra was more like . . . battle."

"Then why . . ." Tinkie didn't finish. She knew.

"It's not an aspect of my character I'm proud of, but it is very much a part of being male. I'm happily married and I love my wife and son. My fling with Sandra had nothing to do with my daily life."

"Except that's not true." I wasn't a prude or champion of monogamy, but I was a cheerleader for truth. Cheating was, by definition, not telling the truth.

"My wife knows. I told her, which is why I can be so open with you. I know you're working for Frank, and I want you to prove he's innocent. I also knew you'd dig up this affair sooner or later. I thought I'd tell you so you'd realize there are no secrets between Lolly, my wife, and me."

I wondered what Lolly really thought about the affair. Elton Cade didn't realize it, but we now had another suspect. Lolly Cade couldn't have done this particular crime—by herself—unless she was Lumberjack Lolly. To hang Dr. Wells' body in the fashion it was left, she would need help. She had plenty of money—she could have hired muscle *or* she could have asked a friend. "Coleman is going to want to know all about this." Elton was looking more like the prime suspect than our client Frank. Tinkie and I exchanged looks—we were on the same page.

"I'll tell Coleman all of this. I'm the reason Sandra came to Zinnia several weeks early. Let me defend myself by saying her talk about the dig made her seem like an excellent partner. But all that was only talk. She was out only for herself. But I digress. Sandra and I had a thing. The intensity . . ." He looked away and a distant look came into his face, something sad and shadowy.

"It was horrible and wonderful. I've never been so . . . addicted."

"What made you stop?" I asked.

"Common sense. I hadn't been to work for two weeks. I didn't answer my phone. We ordered food sent to the room, and for those days we never left the penthouse of the Prince Albert. I woke up one morning and realized that I'd traded my life, my real life and all I'd worked for and cared about, for a sensation. That was it. I showered, dressed, and went home."

"Mired in the fog of sex," Tinkie said under her breath. "You are one lucky man your wife didn't shoot you."

"Yes, I am. Lolly is an amazing woman. Now that you know my dark secret, I have to return to work. I just came to check on the students and tell you, or the sheriff, or whoever I found here about my affair." His face brightened. "Now that's behind me and I can focus on what I do best. I've invented a new game. Initial testing indicates that the four-to-six age group will go wild for this. The good thing is that it involves puzzle solving and physical activity."

From what I knew about Cade, his toys, and his stores, he did insist that the products he made and sold generated healthy activities for kids. In some stores he'd put in a cross-training track that children—and their parents—had to complete to be able to buy a toy. Everyone said it would doom the stores. Instead, they were one of the few big box chains that gained visitors and sales each month.

"Could we have a number in case we need to reach you?" I asked.

"Sure. And pass this info to the sheriff if you would. Ask him please not to speak with Lolly unless there's no other way. I don't want to rub her nose in this, as it were."

I could see his point. "I'll pass that along."

Cade walked back through the students, who were eating the sandwiches he'd had catered from Millie's and sipping hot coffee or Coca-Cola. Cade was halfway down the side of the mound when Peter Deerstalker joined him. They talked for a moment. Cade held out his hand, but Peter walked away.

"What do you think?" I asked Tinkie.

"Sandra must have had a real action-packed badonkadonk. All she had to do was wag it and the men lost their minds. And I admire Elton. I've never seen a man be so forthcoming about a sexual compulsion. Most of them try to rationalize that they're in love or something."

"Just plain old shagging and the two-backed beast."

Tinkie laughed. "I doubt it was that simple, Sarah Booth. But let's go check with Lolly while we know Elton is out of the house."

"Good idea. And here's Budgie to inspect the

cellar. He's packing about a hundred pounds of lights and batteries."

We helped him carry some of his equipment to the top. When he was ready to open the cellar, he looked at us. "Coleman told me he'd skin me if I let anyone down here."

"But we called Coleman," I protested.

"And I'll call you and tell you everything I find." Budgie pulled his collar away from his neck. He was not comfortable sending us away.

"Oh, Sarah Booth, take pity on the man. We'll find out everything, and we have something else to do." Tinkie motioned me to step away from the cellar. "Probably nothing down there but spiders."

I didn't know what she had up her sleeve, but I had to trust her. "Okay. Call us, Budgie." We made one last trip down the side of the mound and I hoped I didn't have to climb it again in the next decade.

We whistled up the dogs, who were having a second lunch with the students, and Pluto, who'd become besties with Kawania. She was feeding him shrimp from her po'boy. Never let it be said that Pluto missed a meal of seafood for any reason.

As I opened the car door, the wind kicked up with sudden force. A fast-food bag blew across the parking area and into the edge of the woods. Something moved deep in the trees. I caught just a glimpse of white, like a shirt or a dress, and then it was lost in shadows. But thirty yards to the east, Cooley Marsh came out of the woods. He looked around furtively before he broke into a run toward the mound. Perhaps he'd been answering the call of nature, but he sure acted suspicious. It was something to keep in the back of my mind.

7

The Cade house was well known in Sunflower County. When Elton's son, James, or Jimmy, as he was known, was in grade school, the Cades had installed a semipermanent fair on the grounds. There'd been a Ferris wheel, bumper cars, a Tilt-A-Whirl, and a small midway with games of chance. All of the children in the county were invited periodically to come and play with Jimmy. The young boy, who had to be in his teens by now, had been beloved by the local kids. He might have been Richie Rich, but he was a kind boy with a generous nature, like his dad.

There was no sign of any of the thrill rides as Tinkie and I turned down the private road that led through apple and peach orchards to the house. Elton Cade had also had a hand in developing the fruit trees that grew well in the Delta climate— normally too humid and hot for most fruit trees. Along with toys, he was deeply into grafting fruit trees.

The house, which expanded from a central front wing into staggered wings with lookout towers and all kinds of architectural fantasy elements, seemed silent, strangely abandoned. It was a huge house for three people. Once it had been the party center for dozens of kids. It made me sad to think that Jimmy had outgrown that little boy who'd been such an ardent lover of fairies, elves, magic, and adventure. The sadness came because it happened to almost everyone. Puff the Magic Dragon knew these things.

"Do you know Lolly?" Tinkie asked.

"No. Should I?"

"She married Elton, but she was from up around Charlottesville, Virginia. She came down to Ole Miss for school and met Elton. She's a super-sweet person. I can't see her as a killer."

"Probably not, but it won't hurt to talk to her. If she caught on that Elton was sleeping with Sandra Wells, it's a solid motive."

"We aren't going to mention the affair, are we?"

I'd given this some thought while we were driving. "No. Let's not. Elton says she knows and I believe him. There's no advantage in trying to shock something out of her. Let's just talk about the dig and Elton's involvement in it. Peter Deerstalker was supposed to be at their house when the murder occurred so, technically, they alibi each other. Maybe Lolly knows something useful. Maybe she met someone she thinks is suspicious. I'm sure she's eager to clear Frank so the dig can continue."

"Good plan," Tinkie agreed.

"Is Jimmy going to school in Sunflower County? He would have to be, what, sixteen?"

"I don't know. Lolly kind of dropped out of the local society clubs. I think she's writing a book or something. I feel bad I haven't thought to check up on her."

"People with money—folks automatically think they've got everything covered."

"And I'm as guilty as everyone else. I just assumed Lolly could buy whatever she needs. I'm insensitive."

"That's not true, Tinkie. If she's writing a novel, I'm sure she's glad we haven't been aggravating her. Writers need alone time."

"Good point." Tinkie brightened as I stopped near the walk. We got out and strolled to the front door through an alley of beautiful redbuds that were purply-pink—the tiny flowers budding against the gray trunks. The sight was magical. Later, the green leaves would come, but now the flowers were a purple mist against the blue sky.

Lolly answered our knock, and her smile for Tinkie shifted instantly into a hug and kiss. "I'm so glad to see you," she said. Turning to me, she clasped my hand warmly. "And you are Sarah Booth Delaney. I've heard about the detective agency you two run." The smile faltered. "Are you here on business?"

Tinkie laughed, put her arm around Lolly's

waist, and nudged her toward the front parlor.

I gawked at the interior of the house, which was beautiful. The foyer was lovely teakwood and tiled floors, a vaulted ceiling that included a life-size wooden angel. It flew over the room, protecting all who entered.

In the parlor, a full life Pegasus reared in a corner, his wings spread. I was struck by the magnificence of the creation.

"Elton makes those," Lolly said. "They function mechanically. The horse can walk and run and the wings flap. He doesn't fly, though. That was a disappointment to Jimmy when he was young."

It was the perfect opening for Tinkie. "Sarah Booth and I were remembering the days when Jimmy had his fair on the front lawn."

Lolly's smile was tinged with sadness. "Those were great days. How impossible it is when a child grows up." She swallowed. "Let me get some tea." She rang a little bell and when a maid appeared she ordered tea and scones.

"I'm delighted to have company, but what brings you for a visit?"

"It's the dig," Tinkie said. "I'm sure you've heard there's been a murder there."

She looked down at her hands. "I heard. Elton tries to keep such things from me, but there's no way. What a tragic event. Tell me about it."

Tinkie and I exchanged a look. She seemed

genuinely curious about the details. "One of the professors was murdered."

"How?" She waved a hand. "I'm not some delicate flower who'll wilt at the mention of murder. I'm curious. You might as well tell me. It'll be in the *Zinnia Dispatch* in the morning. Elton will hide the paper and I'll send one of the employees to buy me another."

"Dr. Sandra Wells was killed. She was hung upside down over a bowl they recovered from the dig. Her throat was cut and she bled out into the bowl." I didn't hide or embellish.

"Was she dead before she was hung up?"

"Doc is still doing the autopsy." Tinkie looked far more distressed than Lolly.

"And you want to know why Elton invested in the dig and if he had anything to gain from Dr. Wells' death."

I nodded. "Pretty much."

The maid brought in the tea service and conversation waned until she left. Then Lolly picked up the conversation.

"I know Elton invested with Frank Hafner. He felt Frank had the experience and technical expertise to excavate the mound properly." She smiled at my surprised expression as she handed me a cup of tea. "Elton does try to keep the harshness of life away from my door, but we are partners in every sense of the word. We discuss things."

"What did Elton say about Dr. Wells?"

She hesitated. "She was an attention whore. Those are his words, not mine. She desperately wanted to be a TV personality and to quit teaching. She hated her students, the whole academic gig. She was a pretty woman, and she photographed well. She might have been able to parlay this dig into a TV show on Planet Earth or Discovery or GEO." She shrugged. "She didn't have any friends on the dig site, though. No one there has a shred of regret that she's dead. That's kind of sad to me."

All of this was old news. What was interesting was Lolly's opinion of Sandra. It was clear she'd heard negative things about the professor, but it seemed to have no bearing on her feelings for the woman her husband had been sleeping with. It could be an act, but I didn't think so. Scratch her off the suspect list.

Tinkie and Lolly chatted about the garden club and several other civic groups that Tinkie ran with an iron fist. As first lady of the Delta and Queen Bee of the Daddy's Girls, Tinkie had a lot of power and she didn't hesitate to wield it when necessary.

"Where is Jimmy going to school?" I asked when there was a lull.

"He's . . . in a special program." Lolly flushed. "He's so advanced, and he's determined to follow in Elton's footsteps. He's in a computer and mechanical engineering program. He's already developed two toys that have proven very popular with college students."

"Wow. He's only what, sixteen?"

Lolly nodded. "It was a hard decision to take him out of the public schools, but he's working on a graduate-student level now. Time is so precious, as you know."

"I remember how much the other children loved him," Tinkie said. "He was kind to everyone."

"And he still is." Lolly's voice cracked. "I miss him. Elton says I can't be a baby and hold him back. He has to fly." She brushed away a tear. "It's silly to be emotional." She refilled our teacups and shifted the conversation to the good works being done in Sunflower County and finally to the Harrington sisters, who'd opened a Wiccan school. "Elton has donated computers to the boarding school. He's very excited that those witches will get the young people outside and growing their own food."

"Last time I was by there, they'd put in several spring crops. If the weather treats them kindly, those kids will be eating the best organic food around."

"I heard they were going to get a couple of cows to milk and make butter and cheese." Lolly liked the idea. "I wish Jimmy could have participated in that. He would have loved it. He's always had an affinity for cows. All animals. We have quite a collection." She laughed. "His heart is tender."

We'd finished our tea and the delicious cranberry scones. Our visit had netted us nothing, except forty minutes with a nice person I was glad to get to know. But I had one last question. "Lolly, Peter Deerstalker was staying here last night, wasn't he?"

She nodded. "Peter and Elton are going through a rough patch right now. They've always been close, and this dig has put them at odds. But they're big enough to work around it. Peter is always a delight, and I'm equally fond of him."

"So he was here all night."

She looked at me and frowned. "We had a late dinner, then I went up to bed to read for a while. It relaxes me so I can sleep. Elton and Peter talked. As far as I know they stayed up late with cocktails and cigars. But I can check to be sure." She called Annie into the room and asked her about Peter and Elton.

The maid bit her lip before she spoke, "I can't say anything for certain. I cleared away the glasses and dumped the ashtrays. Mr. Elton had gone to bed but Mr. Peter was still up. He could have left, I suppose."

"Thank you, Annie." Lolly gave her a smile. "You always look out for us." She looked from me to Tinkie. "Does that satisfy the requirement for an alibi?"

"Yes, it does." Peter and Elton had alibis. The focus returned to Frank again, whether I liked it or not.

After Tinkie and I said our goodbyes and accepted containers of scones to take home with us, we drove toward town. The critters, full of treats that Lolly sent out to them, were still snoozing in the backseat. They'd tired themselves out running up and down the mound.

As we drove back to Zinnia, Tinkie was contemplative. "Lolly really misses her son."

"She does."

"Eighteen years isn't enough to have your child at home. Jimmy is only sixteen. How do people let their children go?"

"How do we let anyone we love go?" I asked. "I want to have children, but . . ."

Tinkie put her hand on my arm. "I understand. You've lost too much. I'm just glad you have Coleman now. Let your romance take its course. You have another few years to decide about children."

If only Jitty would be so solicitous of my feelings. "Thanks."

"You have to know Coleman is solid before you take it any further."

She was right. Coleman was slowly weaving himself into my life, my world. It was a process

I'd long resisted and now it was inevitable. It was also dangerous. My aunt Loulane, who'd raised me after my parents died in an accident, had been a fount of wisdom, which she often doled out to me and my friends. "You can't miss what you've never had" was one of her favorites. I never doubted the truth of it. As a very young woman I'd wanted only to find someone to love. And then I'd had that and lost it. I'd expected to remain alone for a long time. Now that was in the past and Coleman was becoming a big part of my life. The red-alert button in my brain periodically fired off Danger! Danger! Danger! Talk of children set it off all the time, something I couldn't really explain to Jitty, my tormenter.

"I left my car at the mound," Tinkie said. "Would you drop me and Chablis there? I have plans for this evening. That okay?"

"Sure." I hadn't talked to Coleman so I had no plans, but if I decided to work on the case, I could do that without Tinkie.

"I wonder where Cece is?" Tinkie asked about our journalist friend. Working for the *Zinnia Dispatch* put Cece in a place where she had her finger on the pulse of everything in Sunflower County and the surrounding area. Cece was one of the finest journalists working, and she'd carved out a place for herself in Sunflower County when it might have been easier for her to leave and start fresh somewhere else. It was odd she hadn't shown up at the murder site. She was generally on top of all happenings in Sunflower County. Then again, she knew I'd take photos she could use if necessary.

"I'll give her a call on my way home," I said. Tinkie got out of my car but leaned in the passenger window. Behind her, the sky was taking on the winter tones of an early dusk. The blue hour. In the 1800s, this would be the time when folks gathered on their porches to have a glass of tea—or something stronger—and relax a little before supper was served. The shorter winter days had a rhythm all their own.

I dialed Cece as I drove to Dahlia House. Sweetie Pie jumped onto the front seat to act as copilot as I buzzed through the dying light. Cece had a Spidey sense about her phone—it was seldom far from her hand and she seemed capable of keeping it in a web attached to her body. I wasn't worried about her lack of response, only curious. I left a voice mail for her to call me.

I was pulling into the driveway when thoughts of Cece fled my mind. A beautiful young woman in a long dress with a high collar stood on the front porch of my home. She was clearly from another era. Sweetie Pie and Pluto ran to greet her and I knew it was Jitty, in another disguise. Normally I could figure out who she was pretending to be, but this woman rang no bells. She was beautiful, her curly hair pinned neatly back from her face, her dress beautifully made and presented. She had a satchel under her arm.

"Sometimes having the law on your side isn't enough," she said. "Not for my people, and not for me as a woman." She stared straight into my eyes.

"Who are you?" I asked. Jitty loved to make me guess, but I didn't even have an inkling.

"Lyda Conley."

I shook my head. "I'm sorry. I don't know who you are."

Her smile was soft, but it didn't counter the fire in her eyes. "I'm the first Native American lawyer to be admitted to the Kansas bar, and in 1909, I was the first Native American woman to argue a case before the U.S. Supreme Court."

I suddenly understood her significance on my front porch. "What case?"

"The protection of the Huron Cemetery, where my ancestors are buried, and its designation as federally protected land. My tribe is the Wyandots. I am a descendant of Chief Tarhe."

It didn't take a rocket scientist to connect Lyda Conley to what was happening at Mound Salla. She was here to offer legal advice to Peter Deerstalker. Jitty had always indicated that those in the Great Beyond took interest in what happened on our plane, and sometimes interfered.

Lyda was here to render aid. "Am I to deliver a message to Peter Deerstalker?"

"Your services will be invaluable." Her smile was tentative. "My father believed in educating women. It hasn't been an easy life for me, though. My sisters and I never married, the conflicts of a truly independent and professional woman were too difficult for the men of my time." She stepped toward me. "You're luckier. You can have your career and a family, too."

I realized Lyda was channeling Jitty, who was on her favorite warpath for me to produce an heir. My heirloom ghost was determined that I should get pregnant and today wasn't soon enough. "I'm lucky that I can choose to have neither."

Lyda frowned and I clearly saw Jitty lurking there. "A child is—"

"Jitty, stop it. You can't use dead historical people to try to bully me."

The features of Lyda morphed into another beautiful woman, my haint. "I can use whatever tools are at my disposal. You don't know nothin' about what goes on in the Great Beyond."

She was right about that. "Because you won't tell me." There were days I wanted to wring her neck. "Now quit messing me around. I want to get in the house, pour a nice Jack on the rocks, and see if there's anything in the refrigerator I can pass off for supper to Coleman."

"Cookin' for your man." Jitty smirked. "How

about breakfast for supper? Men love that. Hot grits, eggs, bacon, whip up some biscu—" She clapped a hand over her mouth. "Forget the biscuits. Last time you tried to make 'em you created hockey pucks that could have been used to pave a road."

"The baking powder must have been bad." The biscuits could have been labeled lethal weapons. She was right about that, but I didn't intend to concede a single thing. "I can cook. I'm a good cook when the mood strikes me."

"Like maybe when hell freezes over," Jitty said under her breath. She was still wearing the high-necked dress.

"Change into something else, please," I said. "You're giving me a complex. I don't know how women ever wore all that bull crap. Corsets, high collars, long sleeves and long skirts, pantaloons, stockings, button shoes. Why, if I'd lived back then, I would have set them all on their ears."

"You would have been hanged for a trouble-maker, that's for sure." She was grinning wide.

"What's so funny?"

"You think on Lyda Conley and her work. She was a woman I admired, and she was right. You have a lot more ability to carve yourself out a future you design. Today's women are steppin' on the backs of people like Lyda Conley."

Jitty was right, and she gave me pause. "I am lucky."

"And in other ways, too. Now someone's comin' up on the porch. Jump to it, Sarah Booth. Make your dreams come true."

Before I could answer, she was gone to the beat of a few tom-toms and the cry of an eagle.

8

I'd anticipated Coleman, but it was Delane Goggans who came down my long driveway. I offered her a libation, and we settled in the den where I struck a fire. The days for using the fireplace would soon be gone, and I did love a fire.

"What brings you here?" I asked.

"I know everyone suspects Frank of killing Sandra, but he didn't."

"Okay. Do you have any proof? And just let me add that making up alibis won't help him. It only makes him—and you—look guilty."

Delane tilted her head back and I realized she had a lovely neck and throat. Very Angela Lansbury. "I'm sorry," she said. "I'm not normally a liar and I'm not very good at it. After all these years in school, you'd think I'd have mastered that technique."

I didn't even want to ask. "Why not just tell me why you're here?"

"There are things going on at that dig. They don't make sense. I know Kawania and Peter Deerstalker have something going on. They have a history or family connection. Kawania claims she can curse people, and she really hated Dr. Wells."

I knew that Kawania had Tunica blood but I saw no reason to share that. "Kawania isn't any more capable of putting a curse on anyone than I am."

Delane's gaze drilled into me. "You're kidding yourself if you don't believe that some people can call upon the darkness to help them. There is something going on up there. I'm not saying Kawania is behind it, but something is not right there. There is someone, or something, at that dig. A private investigator has been running around. And that TV reporter, Cissy Hartley, is there whenever a story breaks. It's just too many people who seem to have an agenda."

Her words did evoke a chill, but I wasn't about to let her see it. "Look, if you don't have any-thing better than that, finish your drink and leave. I've had a long day." My butt hurt from walking up and down that mound. I had a sense that Delane was at Dahlia House to pump me or find out something from me, not to give me any clues.

"Look, you don't have to believe in hoodoo. But you do have to believe that Deerstalker has a stake in this game. And Kawania is linked to him. I don't know what they're up to, but you should check into them and also keep an eye on them."

"Good advice. Can you back up your suspicions?"

She thought for a minute. "Maybe." She finished her drink. "Places have a lot of power, Ms. Delaney. That mound is special. There's something there that someone doesn't want us to find. You can scoff all you want, but a lot of the students have seen something in the woods. Something unnatural. Cooley said he saw a woman in the trees, but when we went to look, we couldn't find anything."

I was intrigued and offered her another drink but she shook her head. "I have to go. There are weird things happening at the dig. I've been on digs before, but I've never seen anything like this."

"You're going to have to be specific or else this is just a bunch of suspicions and that doesn't carry much weight with me or the sheriff."

She sighed heavily and stood. "You'll have your proof. I don't know who is behind it, but someone wants that dig stopped. Deerstalker is the obvious person, and Kawania seems to be working with him."

I would believe it when I saw the proof. "I'll be at Millie's Café in the morning at seven. If you have evidence, bring it."

I walked her to the door, where she turned around. "You're lucky to have a home like this. I grew up in a subdivision. Chemical green lawns that no one ever played on and a yard crew maintained, no fields or open spaces to have adventures. I had a safe and happy childhood that was completely bland."

It was funny how people always admired what they didn't have. I'd always wanted straight black hair, like a Native American. It was just human nature. "You have a lot of years in front of you. Maybe you'll have a cabin in the woods. Mountains would be nice."

"Not after climbing that mound day in and day out." She laughed. "But I have buns of steel. I just need to find a reason to use them properly."

Her sharp humor caught me by surprise. We both laughed as she crossed the porch. Darkness had fallen, and I stood in the open doorway until she drove away. Given half a chance, I'd probably really like Delane.

She was gone by the time I realized what she had said. She needed a reason to use her buns of steel. So maybe she wasn't really sleeping with Frank Hafner. It was just one more thing to consider.

The next knock on the door was from the man of my dreams. Coleman came in and accepted the Jack on the rocks I had ready for him. He gave me a long hug and a searing kiss, and then sighed.

"How about some leftover lasagna?" I asked.

"How about we skip eating and head upstairs?"

"How about we race?" I dashed out of the foyer and up the stairs, but Coleman's longer legs gave him the advantage. He caught me at the top of the stairs and gathered me to him.

"You cheated," he said.

"I tried. It wasn't a very successful attempt." I kissed him, and when his arms circled me, I felt the weight of the world lift. I slipped my arms around his waist and rested my face against the starched shirt. "You feel like home."

His hands rubbed my back, a gentle circling that brought great comfort. "That might be the most wonderful thing anyone has ever said to me."

He wasn't teasing me. I could tell by his voice. "We all need such different things from life. What do you need, Coleman?"

"Aside from you?" He kissed the top of my head. "I could go into a long list of emotional and physical and social needs, but how about we leave it at this." He tilted my face up with a gentle finger and his lips pressed against mine. It was a kiss that started tender and quickly grew hungry.

My desire for him burned hot, and I slowly backed toward my bedroom, never breaking the kiss. And Tinkie thought I wasn't coordinated. Hah!

We'd just made the bedroom door when Coleman's cell phone went off.

"Don't answer it." I knew he would, but I had to make the protest.

He hit the button and said, "This is Coleman."

As he held the phone to his ear I started unbuttoning his shirt.

"What?" His hand captured mine and stopped it mid-button. "I'll be right there." He sighed as he stepped back. "That was Budgie."

I'd forgotten about the cellar and Budgie's explorations. "Did he find something?"

"You could say that." Coleman was rebuttoning his shirt. He started for the stairs.

"What did he find? You can't just do that and walk away. I shared my info with you."

"You're going to find out anyway, so you might as well just come with me. Grab a jacket."

I skipped down the stairs after him. "What did Budgie find?"

Coleman paused and faced me. The twist of his grin told me two things. Whatever Budgie had found was substantial. The second was that I wouldn't get a straight answer. Coleman could be the very devil when he chose to be.

"You want to talk or you want to find out what's going on?"

"I want you to tell me and not dangle this in front of me like a carrot for a mule."

"Grab your coat and let's make tracks. Bring Sweetie Pie and Pluto. They might prove useful."

"Flashlights?" I asked.

"Budgie has it covered. I'll need you to take some photos."

"Want me to call Cece?" I still hadn't heard from my journalist friend. Now I was getting worried but I didn't have time to do anything about it since Coleman was hustling me into my coat like he was dressing a toddler. Any minute now he'd wipe my nose and then try to burp me. I liked a take-charge man, but this was making me want to smack him.

"Let's leave Cece out of this for the moment," Coleman said. "I need to evaluate the situation. Then I'll give her free rein."

My radar alert hit priority red. What had Budgie found in that cellar? And why had he waited so long to tell Coleman? I stood my ground on the front porch, glad that Coleman had bundled me so thoroughly against the night chill. The temp had dropped at least twenty degrees and was headed toward freezing. "Tell me or I'm not taking another step. I have to know whether to call Tinkie."

"No Tinkie. Now hurry. The pets are waiting at my truck."

I had to give in. We could drive to Mound Salla by the time I argued Coleman into submission. Which would probably never happen, if I was being honest with myself. I hurried to the passenger side and jumped in. "Let's go. Time's a wastin'."

I wouldn't give Coleman the satisfaction of begging for details on the drive over. I calmed myself by watching the moon over the newly sprouted fields. Some people might see only dirt and tiny plants, but I saw a history of my family, of my connection to the planet. For all of my life, the fertile Delta and the moon would be there.

My roots thrust deep into the land that passed the truck window, yielding an occasional light from a farm or estate far in the distance. There was little light pollution to interfere with the glamour of the moon and stars.

"I'm eager to see the landscape from the top of Mound Salla," Coleman said. "If we look east, toward the open fields, the stars will be magnificent."

"And to the west?" I was curious about his thoughts.

"The river is that way." He shrugged. "I figured there would be more lights. Maybe not. We can check it out. It's a bit comforting and also depressing that life goes on. The stars and moon pay no heed to what happens here, who is missing, who is dead."

There was a hint of sadness in his voice. "Not even the rule of kings can last forever. Even Camelot will pass into the mist of time." I'd been a huge King Arthur fan.

"As I said, comforting and also depressing. No man, no matter how great, can stop the turning of the earth, the passing of the seasons."

Coleman was in a philosophical bent as we drove up to the mound. Far at the top I could see a light. Budgie was waiting for us. "It seems like yesterday that we were teenagers," I said. The younger version of Coleman was woven through my past. I remembered him gawky and awkward. He had the same memory of me. Now we were in the prime of life, and we had many choices to make about our future. But that wasn't a conversation to have as we got out of the truck and started up the side of the mound.

At the first step, just when I asked my thighs and butt to push me upward, my body went into small convulsions. My hips locked, my buttocks started screaming, and I flopped to my side in the dew-covered grass.

"What is it?" Coleman was at my side instantly. "Are you hurt?"

"I-I can't . . . I can't use my legs." I drew into a fetal position, trying to stretch the spasming muscles.

"What's wrong, Sarah Booth?" Coleman was genuinely worried. He tried to help me sit up but the large muscles took a firm grip on me and I thought my ankles would draw up to my butt. I knew what was wrong, but there was nothing I could do to stop the pain or even tell Coleman.

"Are you wounded?"

"Yes," I gasped. "I'm suffering a fatal butt convulsion."

"What?" He reached under me and finally understood. He could feel the contractions. "What the hell?"

"Too much climbing," I managed to get out.

"Oh . . ." That one syllable said it all. He grasped the backs of my thighs with strong fingers and set to work.

I thought I might faint the pain was so intense.

"What's going on down there?" Budgie called from the top.

"Sarah Booth is . . . having a moment," Coleman said. "We'll be up shortly." He leaned down to whisper in my ear, and I realized then he was enjoying himself way too much. "We have to work the kinks out of those muscles. They've seized up."

His fingers were talons of iron, brutalizing my poor legs and butt. I wanted to cry, but I had too much pride. I tried not to whimper as he worked until the spasms slowed and then stopped. He leaned back on his heels. "Maybe you should develop a workout routine. Keep in shape instead of trying to do it all in one day."

"Maybe," I said between gritted teeth. I wallowed around on the ground until I got on my knees. I wasn't certain I could make it to standing.

Coleman stood and lifted me with him. It was sweet relief to stand tall without feeling like my body was going to contort. "Thank you."

"My pleasure," he said, stretching his fingers out. "Anytime you need a glute massage, I'm your man."

"Tread carefully," I said. "I may be hobbled but I can still kick ass."

He only laughed and offered an assist as we made our way to the top of the mound. Budgie was waiting for us some twenty feet away from the edge, giving us our privacy. There was no telling what he thought we'd been doing. I'm sure it looked depraved.

"It's right over here," Budgie said, heading toward the cellar.

"What is right over there?" I'd had enough. I wanted some answers before I took another step.

"A dead body," Coleman said.

"A what?" I couldn't believe it. "You found a dead body this afternoon and waited until now to call Coleman and tell him? Are you kidding?"

"There's a hidden room in the cellar with a very tricky lock," Budgie explained. "It took me a while to research how to open it without destroying the lock. Then there was a bunch of those students around, and I decided to wait until they left of their own accord."

"Who is it?" I couldn't think of anyone who was missing, much less dead. Except Cece. The contracture of my chest was far more painful than my recent butt seizures.

"I think it's one of the archeology students, but it's going to take someone to identify her. There was no billfold or anything with her name on it." Budgie pulled open the cellar door and a foul odor smacked me in the face.

"Did you call Doc?" Coleman asked Budgie.

"He's on the way. He's complaining, but he's coming."

"Good work, Budgie." Coleman started down the steps. Budgie had set up lights. "You coming, Sarah Booth?"

"I'm right behind you."

Coleman disappeared into the cellar and the awful smell of decomp.

9

The body was of a young woman, early to mid-twenties. Even the cool cellar couldn't preserve the body forever. She'd begun to deteriorate, but I could see she'd probably once been quite beautiful. She'd been laid upon a wooden table, and her dark hair hung over the edge, almost sweeping the floor. To my knowledge, she wasn't local. Coleman sighed. "Her throat has been cut. Just like Sandra Wells'."

"Is she one of the dig students?" She had to be, if she wasn't local.

"No one has been reported missing." Coleman was still staring at the corpse, probably because he was processing a lot of information. I turned away. This death hit me far harder than that of Sandra Wells, and I couldn't say why. Maybe it was the way she was laid out, her hair hanging, her hands at her sides, her bare feet pointed to the sky. Bare feet in March in an underground cellar—the sight stirred my sympathy in a way that Wells hadn't. I couldn't explain it and didn't want to try.

"Surely they would report their fellow student missing." But I wasn't sure. The students at the dig were an odd bunch. Most were there strictly for extra credit. Only a few, like Delane, had any real interest in the outcome of the expedition. The rest were unpaid labor praying for a passing grade in the class.

The cellar door opened and Doc came down the steps. "I'm getting too old for this. Climbing that mound is for the young and fit. Where's Tinkie?"

I hadn't called my partner because I hadn't known it was a dead body. Now I didn't have reception. The cellar shut out all cell communication. Again, I was struck by the horror of a young woman held down here and butchered. "When we get up top, I'll give her a call. I don't know that she really needs to see this. I'll make photos and share them with Coleman. How long has this woman been dead, Doc?"

"It's been cool down here in the cellar. Judging from the limited decomp, I'd say three days. No longer than that."

The dig crews had been in town longer than that. She could be one of them.

Doc shifted the body to better examine her. "Wait a minute." He reached beneath her blouse and pulled out a lanyard. We all leaned forward to read it. "Cissy Hartley, WQEX. She's a TV reporter out of Birmingham."

"There hasn't been anything on the news about a missing reporter." Coleman hooked his thumbs in his gun belt. "Wouldn't a news station be a little more proactive about a missing reporter?"

I had a terrible surge of panic for Cece. It wasn't like her to miss a big story with a murdered professor in a ritualistic-style killing. And it had been hours since I'd called her. She hadn't even requested the crime scene photos I always took for her. I started up the steps, where I had cell phone reception.

"What's wrong?" Coleman asked.

"Cece is MIA. I need to track her down and make sure she's okay."

He nodded. "Seeing something like this makes us all realize how fragile life is. While you're up there would you call WQEX and ask them about a Cissy Hartley?"

"Sure thing." It was wonderful to step into the fresh air of a brisk March night. Coleman had been right. The night sky to the east was bright with stars that folks in big cities never saw. Light pollution. I dialed Cece first, and felt a rush of relief when she answered. "Where the hell have you been?"

"I know." She sounded harried. "Look, I've been working on an angle about the dig. I was over in Marksville, Louisiana, on the Tunica-Biloxi reservation talking with some of the tribal elders and leaders."

"And you were there why?"

"Peter told me there's something fishy about this archeological dig. Something . . . hidden.

And now there's a dead woman. I met Sandra Wells and she was awful, but that's not grounds to kill her. There's something else going on. Looks like Peter's instincts were correct."

"Two dead women." I let the silence grow.

"Two?"

"Yeah, a young woman was found in the cellar of the old Bailey house. The house is gone, but the cellar survived. She's been down there a few days. Looks like someone cut her throat."

"Just like Sandra Wells. That's one way to get rid of a problem."

"Wells was a difficult woman, from what I hear, but how was she a problem?"

"That grant she got—the seven hundred and fifty thousand dollars for that high-end equipment?"

"Yeah."

"I'm following a lead that indicates she was blackmailing her benefactor to give her the money for all of that technology. She was determined that this was the dig that would give her a television show. She was obsessed with being a star. If she was blackmailing someone, he might have wanted her dead. Anyway, who's the other dead woman?"

Cece was mighty cool about two dead people being found in the space of twelve hours. "We think she's a news reporter. Cissy Hartley. From WQEX in Birmingham."

"No!" Cece had finally processed that someone was dead and it sounded like someone she knew. "Cissy is a great reporter. What happened?"

I could hear her walking around her house and the TV came on. Sounds of various television shows came through as she channel flipped until I heard a newscaster. "And we have Cissy Hartley live in Zinnia, Mississippi, at the scene of a gruesome murder at Mound Salla."

"She's right there on the television," Cece said. "It's a live feed. She's standing in front of the Prince Albert hotel."

I didn't doubt her, so who was the dead woman in the cellar? One local sheriff was not going to be happy, plus now Coleman and I had another mystery. This latest murder would directly impact my client's appearance of guilt or innocence, depending on the evidence. "Cece, are you coming to the Indian mound or what?"

"I'll be there in twenty."

"Would you call Tinkie? And make it fast. Doc will be moving the body soon. If you want to see the crime scene before it's destroyed, you'd better hie yourself over here."

"Chop, chop, Sarah Booth. I'm walking out the door now."

Tinkie and Cece arrived in tandem. Cece had picked my partner up on the way. It hurt me to admit it, but Tinkie climbed the side of the mound

131

with no adverse effects. Was it possible she was in better shape than I was? It had to be running all over creation in those dang high heels. Tinkie didn't work out. She didn't do housework or farm work. How was it possible she wasn't in *gluteus maximus* distress? She displayed no muscular contractions from our earlier efforts. She strode toward me without a pain in the world. Cece was legging it right beside her.

"You called in the cavalry," Coleman said, but he wasn't upset. He was puzzled. Doc's examination of the body in the cellar had left us with more questions than answers. The unknown woman with a TV reporter's identification had been murdered—that was about the only fact they'd ascertained. Yet again, Doc was waiting on transport of the body back to the morgue so he could run some tests.

"Did you identify her?" Tinkie asked when she stood at my side.

"Not yet." Coleman didn't try to hide his worry. "It's not Cissy Hartley, but the archeology students said the Memphis reporter has been hanging around Mound Salla. The dead woman isn't a student or part of the dig. It doesn't make sense to have a random dead woman in the basement of a destroyed house."

"Is there a serial killer on the loose in Sunflower County?" Cece asked.

That lit Coleman's fire. "Please don't even

say that as a joke. We don't need the county panicking."

"But is it a serial killer?" Tinkie asked in all sincerity. "Maybe it has nothing to do with the dig but is all about the location. I mean there are stories that something is in the woods—"

"Ghosts and spirits, not killers," Coleman was quick to point out.

"Two women, both with their throats slit." Cece put it out there as a fact. "I would never print this with any hint of serial killer, but, Coleman, do you think there's a possibility?"

Coleman focused his attention on Doc and Budgie, who were signaling the EMTs to the top of the mound. "I won't answer that. Be assured, though, that I am taking all possibilities under consideration."

That was the most ominous thing he could have said. "Now Doc and I have work to do. Sarah Booth, I'll need a rain check on our evening plans."

"She can hold off on her romantic impulses," Cece said, winking at my partner. "You two can catch up on that at a later date."

Coleman had the grace to ignore her as he took charge of the body removal.

Millie's was closed for the evening, as was every other eatery in town, so Cece, Tinkie, and I decided to meet up at Playin' the Bones, Scott Hampton's blues club, to catch a set of the fabulous band, and also to talk over the evidence. The club offered only one simple meal—red beans and rice or gumbo or creole. If there was anything left, we'd attack it while we talked. Cece had more to report on her visit with tribal elders, too. Coleman would be tied up for hours, and I needed some friend time, a stiff drink, and to hear the blues.

The band was on break when we walked in and found a table in the corner. The club owner and my ex-lover, Scott Hampton, brought a round of Jack on the rocks to the table. He sat down for a moment.

"What's the scoop?" he asked Cece.

She filled him in after Jaytee, Cece's boyfriend, joined us at the table. We sipped our drinks and listened to the details. Cece had unearthed some valuable information on her trip to Louisiana and the tribal reservation.

"Peter Deerstalker is in great disfavor with the tribal council," Cece said. "He's considered a hothead and a man who crosses too many lines to win a lawsuit or situation. The tribal leader, Joseph Nighthawk, said that Peter is always in trouble. The council feels that he's impetuous and dangerous."

"Dangerous?" Tinkie and I said simultaneously.

"And there's more." Cece almost smirked. Once she had control of the conversation she didn't like to give it up.

"Spill it or I'm going to pinch a knot on your thigh." My muscular anarchy had left me a little cranky.

"Are you sure you can hobble over here to get me?" Cece said archly. "I heard you collapsed on the side of Mound Salla and had to have an emergency butt massage. That's a service I didn't know the Sunflower County sheriff's office provided. I'll have to ask Coleman about it when I see him."

I thought my head would spin around. "How did you know about that?" I demanded.

Cece just grinned. "A little bird told me."

"A little Budgie bird." I knew who the source of gossip had to be. Budgie Burton. He was going to pay. I'd hoped he hadn't seen what Coleman was doing to me but my hopes were in vain.

"What's this?" Scott asked.

"Sarah Booth collapsed on the side of the burial mound. It seems her ham hocks locked up and she went into a muscle spasm. Coleman had to massage the kinks out of her backside." Cece was laughing so hard she could hardly talk. Tinkie was right behind her.

"I'd climbed that dang mound a dozen times. It's steep. I'm not used to acting like a mountain goat." Defending myself was pointless. They were all laughing now.

"You've let your ham hocks atrophy," Jaytee

said. "I could design a workout for you to build those muscles back up."

"I could design a knuckle sandwich for you," I said, but I was working hard not to laugh, too. "Now can we get back to business? My butt is fascinating, I know, but there are higher stakes."

"Let her be," Scott said, rumpling my hair like I was an unruly puppy. I shot a glare at him that made him laugh. Obviously, no one took me as a serious threat.

"Okay, so Deerstalker has a reputation for being a hothead. What else?" Tinkie took pity and pushed the conversation back on track.

Cece motioned us all to lean closer. "No one can say a word about this. Promise?"

We all nodded, and I tried not to get sucked into the moment. Cece was a great storyteller and she knew how to read an audience. She had us in her palm.

"What is it?" Tinkie asked.

"Several women are missing in west Louisiana. It's possible they're connected to the murders here. The thing is, there's no official missing persons report."

That was a bombshell, and I felt suitably shocked. "Did you tell Coleman?"

"I will," Cece said. "I have an interview with Peter first. I want to get that done before I turn Coleman loose on him."

"How did you find out about the missing

women?" If there wasn't an official report, who was Cece's source?

"Cissy Hartley clued me in to the gossip. It seems there was a private investigator poking around Mound Salla. She cautioned the students to be careful, said there might be a serial killer on the loose. The PI's theory was that the serial killer started out in Louisiana but had crossed the Mississippi River. Since we have a murder here, I was thinking they might be connected."

"And you went over to the Tunica reservation to check out Peter Deerstalker," Tinkie said.

"You think Peter killed the two women at Mound Salla and is involved in the missing women in Louisiana?" I asked.

"It's logical. He's here, where there are two murdered women. He's back and forth to Marksville, Louisiana, where the other women are missing. I just want a chance to interview Peter before Coleman locks him up. It could be a big scoop for me. Maybe a book. You know, the whole serial-killer angle is hot."

"No!" Tinkie and I said in unison. "That's too dangerous," Tinkie added. "If you seriously think he might be a psychotic killer, you are not going to interview him."

"I'm not afraid of—" Cece started.

"Well, I am," Jaytee said. "You're not going to meet that man somewhere out of the way to try and pry things out of him. You can't. I won't . . ."

He didn't finish because though Cece loved him more than her own life, she wouldn't be bossed by anyone and Jaytee was smart enough to know it.

"I'm meeting him at Millie's in the morning," Cece said. She looked at Jaytee and her face softened. "Sarah Booth and Tinkie can be at another table. Coleman, too, if he wants. I just need half an hour."

Jaytee's smile was like the sun. "I knew you were too smart to do something dangerous."

"I want this story, but not enough to get hurt. The phrase 'throat slit from ear to ear' is exactly what happened to Sandra Wells and this other woman. I intend to live a long, long time and make an absolutely gorgeous corpse."

"Let's get to work," Scott said to Jaytee. "Hate to leave good company, but the folks came here for a show."

Jaytee brushed a kiss across Cece's cheek and the musicians returned to the stage and kicked up a set that made me want to dance—I just couldn't risk another episode of muscular betrayal. That kind of thing would give a girl a terrible reputation and fast.

Cece, Tinkie, and I huddled close over the table. A new round of drinks magically appeared, and we sipped them slowly. "Do you think Peter is a serial killer?" I asked my friends.

"I don't want to believe that." Tinkie frowned.

"I like Peter. He's done a lot to help his tribe and his community. He does have a temper, but he was a primary force in seeing that the Tunicas' federal recognition gave them the right to build their casino near Marksville. The tribe has prospered since that time."

"Who are the other investors in the property?" I asked. "We know Elton Cade donated a chunk of change to Frank Hafner. Sandra's biggest investor was a private organization that funds archeology adventures, history shows on television, that kind of thing. Delane Goggans believes Sandra was possibly blackmailing one of her benefactors, but who is the person behind the corporation? That's an angle to explore."

"Probably someone she screwed," Tinkie said sarcastically. "Sorry!" She held up both hands. "Sandra was a user. And, really, do we still think the dig is the actual motive behind the murders? This second murder takes the heat off our client, Frank Hafner, don't you think? Looks to me like Sandra flirted with the wrong guy. She met her fate at the hands of a new conquest."

"And the unknown dead woman?" I asked.

"We need to find out who she is and what she was doing on top of that mound. I mean after the fire, no locals hang out up there anymore," Tinkie said. "The young people used to go there, but Budgie said it wasn't a big location anymore. Ghost stories are passé with young people now. They want to sit on the sofa in the air-conditioning and play video games."

I had a great fondness for midnight adventures in the soft Delta nights, but each generation had to find the path to the courtship rituals that defined them. I couldn't imagine anything more romantic than tall tales of a haunted house to induce a cuddle with a crush, but that wasn't appealing to the young people now. "We need to know who she is before we can really begin to look into how she died."

My cell phone rang. It was Coleman. I answered while my girlfriends waited in silence. "Okay, thanks." I hung up.

"The dead woman's name is Bella Devareaux. She's from Marksville, Louisiana. She's a private investigator."

I felt the strangest rush of anger. I'd never heard of Bella Devareaux, but she was one of us—a PI. She'd likely been working a case, checking into the disappearance of young women in Louisiana. The connection to Peter Deerstalker was undeniable. This woman was from the town where his people lived. What had she been investigating that culminated in her death at the same location another woman involved with the Tunica tribe had died?"

"You have to tell Coleman about Peter," I said to Cece.

"Tomorrow, Sarah Booth. *After* my interview."

I didn't like it and neither did Tinkie, but we had no leverage to change it. "We'll be right at Millie's in the morning to look out for you," Tinkie said.

"Fine. You can have Coleman waiting in the wings."

"We will." That was a capital idea.

"I'm meeting Peter at eight o'clock."

I had a tentative appointment with Delane, but I made a decision and sent her a text canceling. If Cece could extract info from Peter, we didn't need Delane there muddying the water.

"We'll be watching you, Cece." It was time to break up the party and head home. Sweetie Pie and Pluto were in Scott's office enjoying a few short ribs, but it had been a long day for all of us. I was sure they were ready to go home. I also wanted to call Coleman back to see when he might be finished with work. I missed our time together, but I wasn't about to say that out loud and give my friends more ammunition for teasing me.

We waved goodbye to the band and headed out. Tinkie had ridden in with Cece, but I volunteered to give her a lift home, which she accepted. We'd barely slammed the car doors before she blurted, "I don't like Cece meeting that man."

"Nor do I. But you know we can't stop her."

Tinkie's mind was speeding far ahead of mine. "Elton and Peter are good friends. Do you think Elton would talk to us about Peter?"

"Maybe tomorrow. Not tonight."

"Let's talk to Elton tomorrow at six, so we have all the scoop we can get before Cece's interview. And we need to find out more about Bella Devareaux. She may hold the key to understanding what's going on with that dig. Or at least with the murderer. And I am going to say serial killer."

"I agree. First thing tomorrow." I drove into the night with my critters in the backseat and my friend in the front seat. The car's headlights cut the darkness and disappeared in the long stretch of straight road. Another beautiful Delta late winter night. I could only hope that there would not be another murder. The reality of a serial killer plying his trade in my little town would definitely disrupt my sleep.

10

As it turned out, it was not dreams of a serial killer that forced me out of bed at two in the morning, but the sound of hoofbeats in the parlor of Dahlia House. My three horses, Reveler, Lucifer, and Miss Scrapiron, were family members, but they'd never been invited inside the house and I knew they preferred it that way. If they were roaming the halls of my ancestral home, that meant someone had opened a gate and the horses were free. It would be dangerous for them and for any drivers if the horses wandered down to the road. How they entered the house was another matter.

Or maybe I was having auditory hallucinations.

The clop clop of hooves on wood told me otherwise. There was definitely a horse in the house. I jumped out of bed and ran downstairs to find a fierce-looking Native woman astride a paint horse. One long braid hung over her shoulder and she carried a spear festooned with eagle feathers and other totems. She stared at me, her dark eyes a challenge.

"Who are you?" I asked. I really sucked at the Native American identification game.

"Buffalo Calf Road Woman. Sister to Chief Comes in Sight. I am a warrior."

I didn't doubt that for a minute. She sat her horse with the grace of a goddess, and her bearing was proud. She wore a deerskin shirt and britches decorated with the images of running horses. A tomahawk hung from one side of her belt and a knife from the other.

"Why are you here? In my home?" I knew it was Jitty, and she'd had her fun by rousing me from a deep sleep. I wasn't going to give her any more satisfaction by freaking out over a horse in the parlor.

"When Three Stars came to kill us, we fought. My brother was wounded, but I saved him. When the yellow hair came to kill us, we fought. I knocked him from his horse and a warrior took his yellow hair." She made a motion of holding up a hank of hair and a slicing movement, a scalping.

I struggled to find the reference she made, and it finally came to me. General George Custer had been called Yellow Hair by the Indians. Another military commander, General Alfred Terry Crook, had been called Three Stars. These men and others had been the fist of betrayal the U.S. government employed to decimate the indigenous population when the government reneged on numerous treaties with the Native Americans. Two major battles that occurred in 1876 were the Battle of the Rosebud, which Crook led, and the Battle of the Little Bighorn, where Custer died. The woman before me had played a role in the death of a man who had slaughtered hundreds of her people. She should have been lauded in history, and yet few Americans knew her name.

"Why are you here to visit me?" I asked a bit more politely.

"The ghosts of the past are restless. They roam the lands they once called home. They are troubled by the disturbance of their bones."

So this manifestation was about the archeological dig, as I had assumed. "Jitty, is this the truth, or are you here to stir the pot?" I asked her directly. "Is something going on in the Great Beyond about that dig?"

The image of Buffalo Calf Road Woman didn't waver, and I wondered if this was truly my haint or some other spirit who'd found a willing conversationalist. "I'm here to warn you," she said. "Disturb not the bones."

That didn't bode well. "Or what?"

"The Crow Moon is waxing. Soon it will be full, and revelations will be told. Your friend is in danger. Grave danger. Blood will spill."

"Cece? Is Cece in danger?" I felt a definite thud in the region of my heart.

"Those you hold dear stand in the light of the Crow Moon, clear for their enemies to see. They are targets for the arrows of the enemy. You must stop them."

"How?" I wanted to stop them. There was only one other person in my life who could scare me with a prophecy, and that was Zinnia's resident psychic, Madame Tomeeka, who was also known as Tammy Odom. We'd gone to school together, and Tammy's dreams were often prophetic. When she told me danger was near, I listened. I felt the same desperation to heed the words of Buffalo Calf Road Woman. "Please, tell me what to do."

"When the moon is full, gather them to you and hold them safe."

She'd said "them," so it was more than just Cece. Tinkie, too, could soon be in danger. "I will. Thank you."

The front door of Dahlia House blew open on a cold wind. Buffalo Calf Road Woman walked through the foyer, the hooves of her horse echoing on the old wooden floors. She crossed the porch at a trot and the horse leaped down the front steps and took off down the driveway. My three horses raced the fence line beside her as she disappeared into the night, leaving only the sound of the running horses behind.

"You certainly do have some strange callers, Sarah Booth."

I whirled to find Jitty sitting on the staircase. She wore a long nightgown and her hair was braided down her back. But she was Jitty, not some long-dead Native woman. "That wasn't you?" I asked, pointing down the driveway.

She shook her head. "She must have felt strongly to come from the Happy Hunting Ground just to pay you a visit."

I didn't believe Jitty was so innocent. She never told me the complete truth. Never. It was part of the gig in the Great Beyond to lie to those of us still alive. "Why would she do that? She doesn't know me. Why should she care if I get hurt?"

Jitty's features softened, and I could see emotion in her eyes. "Perhaps you share the same heart, Sarah Booth. In your own way, you're a warrior like her. She came to warn you, and I do believe I'd pay attention to what she said."

The sound of a vehicle coming down the driveway drew my attention from Jitty and when I turned back, she was gone. A hoot owl sounded, and I remembered the old legends Aunt Loulane would tell me—that when someone heard an owl, it meant a death in the family.

Coleman came across the porch, frowning at the open door. I didn't give him a chance to ask any questions. I ran into his arms, sobbing. He swept me up and held me against him as he stroked my hair and soothed me.

"What in the world?" he asked, trying to get me to look up at him.

"Bad dream." I hadn't told him about Jitty.

I hadn't told anyone. I was afraid Jitty would disappear if I revealed her presence in my life. There were rules about everything in the Great Beyond, and Jitty was my special gift, the link between the long-ago past and my parents. I would never risk losing her.

"Two gruesome murders are enough to make anyone have nightmares."

I nodded. My composure was returning, but I had to check something. "Coleman, would you make us a drink to share?" I didn't really want alcohol, but I had to get to my office. "I'll be right up."

"Sure. Jack?"

I nodded. When he went to the bar in the parlor, I ran to the Delaney Detective Agency office. I settled in front of the computer and typed in the words crow moon.

There it was—the full moon in the month of March was called several names by the Cheyenne, and Crow Moon was one of them. The moon was waxing and it wouldn't be long until it was full. Buffalo Calf Road Woman, whether she was real or Jitty impersonating someone, had come to give me a message. I believed it. Some might say that I was a willing victim of a bad dream and my childish fear of abandonment. Perhaps I was, but I had a terrible foreboding that I was going to lose someone I deeply loved.

It seemed we'd just fallen asleep when I awoke to the sound of my alarm. I'd set it to be sure I was up and at 'em by five when I expected Tinkie to show up. We had a date with destiny. If not destiny, then a very wealthy man.

Coleman was groggy, and I brought him a cup of hot, black coffee in bed, and my reward was a tender kiss. "Why did we wait so long, Sarah Booth? If we'd gotten together in high school, we could have grandchildren by now."

I considered smacking him, but I only laughed. "Yeah, if I'd gotten pregnant at sixteen, and our child had a child at sixteen or seventeen."

"Nothing like a healthy, young breeder," Coleman said, holding the hot coffee up so I wouldn't whop him. "Seriously, I'm glad we're old enough to appreciate what we have here."

"Me, too. Now I need to shower, dress, and head out with Tinkie. Remember, Cece is meeting Peter Deerstalker in Millie's at eight." The worry hit me hard again. "You'll be there, right?"

"I will. If you get there first, order me some of Millie's breakfast scramble, a side of grits, and biscuits."

He could eat like that and never gain an ounce. The male metabolism was a crime against nature.

Fifteen minutes later I was sipping my go cup of coffee, dressed, and waiting on the front porch for Tinkie to arrive. When she pulled up, I motioned her into the roadster with the animals in the backseat and we headed for Elton Cade's home. We'd catch him before he had a chance to leave the house.

We were fortunate to find Elton stepping out the front door. Lolly Cade had been very gracious to us on our last visit, but we were in his front yard at dawn-o-thirty. Even a Daddy's Girl with the rigid upbringing of social awareness before personal comfort could be pushed too hard.

"Elton doesn't look good," Tinkie said.

She was right. He looked harried and upset, but he came over to talk to us. Our news about the second dead body in the cellar of the old Bailey house hit him in the gut. He paled and one hand went instinctively to his abdomen.

"You say the dead woman is a private investigator?" he asked.

"Devareaux is her name."

He shook his head slowly. "Why would she be in Sunflower County? And why would she be near Mound Salla?"

"We were hoping you could help us with that," Tinkie said. "She's from Marksville, Louisiana, which is a bit more than a coincidence, don't you think?"

"How do you mean?" He looked confused.

"The Tunica-Biloxi tribe is there. There are reports of more missing women in that area. And what that has to do with Mound Salla is Peter Deerstalker."

"Peter?" He caught up to my thought train quickly. "There's no way he could be involved in anything like this."

We put the facts out there and Elton sighed heavily. "Look, Peter is passionate about protecting his tribe. You can't blame him if you know the history of how the Native Americans have been treated. But protection is one thing, murder is another. He's just not capable of killing anyone. Especially not two women." He looked out into the cotton fields and thought over what we'd told him. At last he spoke, facing us directly. "Both women had their throats slit. And you say there are more women missing across the Mississippi River in Marksville? Do you think it's some kind of depraved killer at work?"

He went exactly to the same place we'd gone. Serial killer. In Sunflower County.

"There's no evidence of that. And the authorities in Louisiana haven't confirmed the missing women there," I said, "but rest assured Coleman is looking into all angles of the two murders."

"Coleman is a good man, a fine law officer. We're lucky to have him here in Sunflower County," Elton said. "And you ladies, too. Your detective agency has quite a reputation for solving cases. Both of you have brushed against danger, though. It must make your families uncomfortable. I'm so glad you're working on Frank's behalf."

"We're lucky to have your support," Tinkie said. "Elton, is there anything you can tell us about Peter that might help remove him from the suspect list? Lolly said Peter was here the night Dr. Wells was murdered. Was he with you all night?"

"We had dinner late. Then Peter and I smoked a cigar and had some cognac. He said something about a drink, but I went up to bed. Look, we had a good talk, and I'm happy to say we patched up a lot of the damage done by my financial support of the Hafner dig. I believe Peter began to see that good could come of this as well as things he didn't like."

"Peter is very close to all the murders." I had to say it with firmness, and I did.

"He wouldn't do anything like that. He might yell in court or slam books around or file lawsuits against other lawyers, but he isn't a killer. That's what I know."

"Was Sandra involved with him?"

He didn't flinch. "Yes. Sandra has obviously been involved with many of the men linked to the dig. Frank Hafner, too. She had a special talent for making a man feel like he was the best thing she'd ever encountered. As you probably know, the Achilles' heel of most men is their ego. Flattery, especially sexual flattery, is almost impossible for us to resist."

Tinkie understood—and manipulated—the male ego with far more finesse than I had ever managed. She patted Elton's arm. "Women can fall into the same trap when a sweet-talking man comes along. Especially a woman who feels neglected."

That statement wasn't meant to give comfort, and it did make Elton step back. I could almost see him going over Lolly's male friends. It was a good tweak to remind him that cheating was a game both genders could play.

Elton changed the subject deftly. "This Devareaux woman, does anyone know what she was investigating at the dig? I've got a lot of money tied up there and it looks like the whole expedition is cursed." He held up a hand. "I don't mean that literally, it's just that tragedy seems to lurk at Mound Salla. Poor Sandra. She wasn't a nice person but she didn't deserve to have her throat cut."

"Maybe not," I said. "Do you think Frank Hafner is capable of murder? He slept with her, too."

"Frank cut someone's throat? I don't see that." Elton shook his head. "Frank is competitive, but in many ways he's the male version of Sandra. He's handsome and women are drawn to him. I've seen him use that to get something he

153

wanted. But that's still a far cry from murdering two people. There are people at the dig, that graduate assistant, Goggans, or whatever her name is, one or two other young people like that Cooley Marsh fellow. I've heard he's interested in developing computer games, but he's avoided talking with me. I'd look at those people, too. They're smart and a couple of them are at least a hundred grand in debt for their college degrees. If they thought Sandra was going to flunk them, a grade would be good incentive."

He had a point. "And the PI from Louisiana?"

"Maybe she overheard a bargain being made. I don't know. I can't imagine killing someone over anything, not even what would be crushing debt. The guilt of it would eat me alive."

"Because you're a good person, Elton," Tinkie said. "We'll let you get on with your work. We have some meetings. Those kids from the dig are at the Budget Inn on the highway?"

"Yes," he said. "Good luck. Since Frank and Sandra aren't around to ride roughshod over them, they've become very lax about getting out to the dig site, and probably just as well. Someone needs to oversee the excavation. Valuables could be damaged." He nodded slowly. "I am sorry about both women. This will take some time to accept."

We thanked him again and drove away. The sun was lifting over the trees that canopied the

154

driveway. The limbs were bare, but my imagination gave them to me leafed out, full, and beautiful in the first real weeks of spring, which weren't far away. The Cade estate truly was beautiful.

"Want to put some money on who the killer is?" Tinkie asked.

"I don't know. I wish I did, but there's just not enough evidence one way or the other. Let's swing by the hospital and see if Doc has any autopsy reports. Then we can head over to Millie's."

"Good plan."

I checked the backseat to find the animals snoozing. They slept at least eighteen hours a day. I was lucky to get six—less than that since Coleman had jumped into my bed.

Sunflower County Hospital didn't have all the latest technology, but it had something better— Doc Sawyer. He was a much-sought-after coroner and an excellent diagnostician. He had the bodies of both dead women and perhaps he'd found something useful.

My stomach was growling when we parked and hurried into the emergency room. Doc's den of horrors was off to the side, near the ER and operating rooms, and down a little hallway. I could smell the burnt coffee before I pushed his door open. He kept a pot of java on the burner until it was so old and so thick and so strong no one would touch it but him.

"Coffee?" he asked maliciously.

"I'd prefer to have my ptomaine in something delectable," Tinkie said before she kissed his cheek. "What's the word on the dead people?"

"And I thought you were here to visit me," he quipped.

"Doc, we don't have any leads. Do you think Frank Hafner killed either or both of those women?"

"I can't say who did it, but I can say the murders are definitely connected, aside from the method of death."

I stood at attention. "What did you find?"

He brought out his cell phone and shuffled through some photos. The camera phones had changed the world for a lot of professions, even a coroner. "See this design?"

Tinkie and I bent over the small screen. The image was of a horned creature, the forehead broad and the eyes set wide apart. It looked a lot like the amulet Tinkie had found at the dig site. "It's a tattoo," I said. "And it looks like it's a henna dye."

"Right on both counts," Doc said. "It's a mark of belonging, of belief. Some people believe that after death, demons come to punish people for moral failings. Each of the dead women has one of these on her chest."

"Both of them had that symbol?" Tinkie asked.

Doc nodded. "As far as I can tell, they were

applied before death. I don't really have the equipment here to be more specific but I sent some samples off and hope to have firm facts."

So the murders were absolutely connected and the killer was sending a message or working on some twisted pattern or ritual that only he might understand.

"It is a serial killer," Tinkie said breathlessly. "This is really bad for Sunflower County. And Coleman." She looked from Doc to me. "And us!"

All I could think about was my visit from Buffalo Calf Road Woman and her warning to keep my friends close because they were in danger. That visit was even more ominous than I'd thought before.

11

"You're mighty quiet," Tinkie said as we took a table in a corner of Millie's. The farmers, who were in their busiest planting season, had come and gone, but the local businessmen were now filling the tables and counters. The diner would soon be all hustle and loud conversations. There was no sign of Cece and Peter Deerstalker, but we were half an hour early. We ordered coffee and sat back to wait. As hungry as I was, I wanted to delay ordering until Cece arrived. Tinkie said it would give us an excuse to hang around while they talked if we ate slowly.

We looked at the menus, though we knew them by heart. "Are you ordering fried dill pickles again?" Tinkie had been on a binge for those things. I'd never seen her eat a lot of fried food, but those pickles were like crack to her.

"Yes." She waved to one of the waitresses and put in her pickle order. "A little appetizer to get us going."

"Fat and frumpy is where you're going if you keep eating like that." I was amused at my normally disciplined friend.

She shrugged. "I just have to have them. And I've been binging on fresh green peas. I can't get enough."

"Now that is a combo. I have a hankering for some jambalaya. Maybe Scott will have some on the menu at the club. We need to meet up there tonight. It's been too long since we hung out with Scott, Jaytee, and the band. We need to have more fun together, all of us." I intended to drag my friends to the blues club and keep them there all night so I could keep an eye on them. I was forewarned about danger. "Sounds like a good time, doesn't it? Or we could watch a movie at my house or yours. Make some popcorn and Lynchburg Lemonade. That would be good tonight, too."

Tinkie reached across the table and put a hand to my forehead. "Are you sick?"

"Of course not."

"You normally aren't this clingy. What's the deal?"

I couldn't not tell her. If there was danger and I'd been given a warning, I owed it to my friends to tell them. I was just reluctant to reveal the details. "I had a bad dream about a Native woman. It left me on edge. Big massacre. Danger. It was bad." She wasn't my personal ghost and so I wasn't violating any rules of the Great Beyond—I hoped.

"That is terrifying, Sarah Booth." Tinkie looked

a tad confused, but mostly unsettled. "Do you often have such vivid dreams?"

"Sometimes." Maybe Jitty was a dream. Maybe I was narcoleptic and I would fall into a deep sleep and Jitty was just a figment of my imagination.

"Have you told Coleman about this dream?"

I shook my head. "I don't want to unduly worry him, but he is coming to make sure Cece is okay. We'll tell him when he gets here." I sighed. "I just can't believe we're actually talking about Peter Deerstalker being a possible serial killer."

"It is creepy. Oscar told me in no uncertain terms that I was not to go back to that dig at night or alone. Not even with you. He said we had to have some muscle with us. He was pretty firm about it."

"And you liked that, didn't you?" I could see the flush on her face. Tinkie liked her man to be manly and take charge, even though she'd do exactly as she pleased when it came right down to it. Oscar had demonstrated the proper machismo to show that he took her safety seriously. That meant the world to Tinkie—and most of the women I knew. It was the sentiment that counted.

At seven forty-five, we figured Cece would walk in the door any minute so we put in our order. I also got the breakfast scramble for Coleman. He was a timely kind of lawman and I liked that. At seven fifty-five he walked in the café door just as Millie put our plates on the table. The food smelled wonderful. When Millie saw Coleman, she grabbed a pot of freshly brewed coffee, and set a steaming cup before him as he sat down.

"Cece not here?" He'd surveyed the café as he walked through.

"It's only seven fifty-five." I said it with certainty, but for the past ten minutes, my gut was telling me a lot of things I didn't want to hear. Tinkie, too, looked a little green.

"Cece is never late," Tinkie said at last. "She should have been here, setting up at the table she wanted."

I whipped out my phone and called her. It went immediately to voice mail. "Maybe she's late and getting ready." Even I didn't believe my words.

"I'm not happy with this," Coleman said. "On the way over, I checked at the Prince Albert. Deerstalker has a room, but he wasn't there and his bed wasn't slept in. He hasn't been seen since late yesterday evening when he was having dinner in the hotel restaurant."

"Did he go back to Louisiana?" Tinkie asked.

"I don't know. All I know is that he didn't show up here at Millie's like he was supposed to do to meet Cece."

"Where the heck is she?" I asked, tapping my watch. No one wore a watch now except for me.

"Let's start looking." Coleman called the newspaper office and asked to speak with her editor. Ed Oakes came on the line immediately, and Coleman asked about Cece. The furrows on his brow increased as he listened. At last, he thanked Ed and hung up.

"She was in the office at seven. She left about twenty-five minutes ago to come here." Coleman hesitated and then continued. "She got a call from someone just before she left. When Ed asked if it was a lead, she blew him off and wouldn't give any details. He assumed it was one of you two and that she was coming to Millie's."

"We've been here that long," I said. "She never made it here."

"Then she's somewhere between."

None of us would say what we feared—that she'd been taken by someone.

Coleman called Peter Deerstalker, but his phone, too, went to voice mail. Coleman dialed Frank Hafner's cell phone. Hafner had been told not to leave Sunflower County. He was, presumably, in his hotel room at the Prince Albert. His phone went to voice mail, too.

"What is going on?" Tinkie asked. No one had an answer. Or an appetite.

"Let's find her car," I said.

"You look for Cece. I'll tackle it from Peter's end. Surely we can find them."

They had a half hour start on us—if they were together. Peter might not have anything to do with Cece's unexplained disappearance. And he, too, might be in danger. If his lawsuit truly jeopardized the dig, he might have been abducted. We had to find Cece's trail, and fast, before we could even begin to figure out what had happened to the two of them.

Millie picked up our food and whisked it back to the kitchen. She'd box it for my critters. "You come back when you find her and I'll make something fresh for you," she said. She was as worried as we were. We paid the bill and left, Tinkie and I on foot. We walked down the cold brick street to the newspaper. In two hours, the sun would warm the Delta to a lovely spring morning, but old man winter still gripped the landscape. When we got to the paper, we didn't go in, but instead checked the back parking lot. Cece's car was nowhere to be seen.

We went inside to talk to Ed. He was a burly guy with a quick wit and sharp sense of humor. He had the management skill to get the most out of a pack of journalists and photographers who were independent, creative, and cantankerous— but who also had to meet deadlines. When Ed saw us, he knew something was up. Coleman's call had set him up for bad news.

"She left here saying she was walking down to Millie's to meet Deerstalker for an interview. I told her I didn't like the sound of it." Ed ruffled some papers on his desk, but I could see he was worried and angry. "Dammit. Cece thinks she's invincible. She's plenty smart, but that doesn't make me feel any better."

"Coleman is looking for Deerstalker. He's missing, too."

"Because he took her?" Ed asked.

"We don't know." Tinkie put a hand on his arm. She was always the one who knew to offer touch as a means of comfort. "She and Peter could have gone somewhere private to talk, or maybe he had something to show her."

"Or they both could have been taken by the person slitting people's throats." Ed didn't sugar-coat it. "Look, if we have a serial killer on the loose, then Coleman needs to say that. We owe it to the citizens to alert them."

"And he will," I said. "Please don't even say those words. Especially not with Cece missing. If there is a . . . killer"—I couldn't say "serial killer"—"then the worst thing we can do is make him feel cornered, especially if he has Cece as a hostage. Let Coleman collect some facts and make a press announcement when the time is right. I promise he won't hold back if people are in jeopardy."

"Okay." Ed stood and paced his office.

"We'll canvas the neighborhood," I said. "Coleman is talking to other law enforcement, and checking on Deerstalker's record. He grew up in Louisiana, not here."

"Keep me informed," Ed said.

"Will do."

Tinkie and I burst out the front door and started down the street. Few of the businesses had been open at seven-thirty. Zinnia ran on the small-town schedule of eight to five. But we had to take every lead, no matter how slim.

I worked the right side of the street while Tinkie took the left. At the five-and-dime and the lingerie shop, I got the expected answer. No one had been in the store that early. But Junior Wells at the bail bond office had the first bit of good news.

"Yeah, I saw Cece this morning. She was headed toward Millie's about seven thirty-five or so. Walking fast. She didn't stop or come in, just waved as she went by. She looked fine."

"She was alone?" I asked.

"She was." The heavy wrinkles in his face lifted as his eyebrows arched. "But there was someone following right behind her."

"Who was it?"

"I don't know. It was a man, but he had a hoodie up on top of a ball cap. You know like the young men wear now. My thought was it had to be one of those students from the archeology dig. They're all over town and they all dress alike. I didn't think anything about it because it was a brisk morning. Navy blue hoodie, blue jeans, dark bill on the hat. I didn't get a good look at his face because he turned to look across the street when he went by."

It was a good description for a brief glimpse. Junior paid attention to detail because his livelihood rested on his ability to judge whether someone was a bail risk. If they skipped town and left him holding the bag, he took a big hit. "Anything you can add? It's important, Junior. Cece is missing."

"I wish I'd paid more attention, but I was opening up the office, looking at the day's court docket to see what cases I might want to make bond on. I just saw movement and Cece came by, then the man. I'm sorry."

"You've been a big help." I thanked Junior and stepped back out onto the street. I knew Cece had made it almost to the café. The man, if he was the abductor—if there was an abductor—had to have struck right after Junior's. There was an alley beside his building that went back to an unused lot where we'd once found the body of a writer.

Tinkie was working her way down the opposite side of the street, and when she saw me she shook her head to indicate she'd had no luck. I signaled her over. I didn't want to go into the alley by myself. I was afraid of what I'd find.

"Junior saw her walk by. Someone was tailing her."

"Oh, no." Tinkie looked into the alley. "Want me to call Coleman?"

"No, we have to look. He's busy and if this is nothing, we don't want to pull him away from what he's doing."

"Okay." She took my hand, and I wasn't certain if the gesture was to give her courage or to give me strength. I squeezed her fingers and we stepped into the dark alley and walked toward the shaft of sunlight at the back. The one thing I did not want to see was the body of my friend.

We stepped out of the dark shadows into the bright light and stopped. Sprawled against the rickety wooden fence in the back was a body. I recognized Cece's harvest pumpkin coat that I'd envied.

"No!" Tinkie gasped and gripped my arm so tightly I wanted to cry out. But I didn't. Instead I moved forward to the bundle of clothes. I put my mind on autopilot and forced my legs forward. I had to know. It was my job—as a detective—but, more importantly, as Cece's friend.

Tinkie remained at the edge of the lot. She didn't cry, but anguish twisted her face, and her breathing was shallow. Any minute she might faint.

"Cece." I whispered her name as I drew closer. The bundle was misshapen, as if her body had been broken in numerous places. I thought of Buffalo Calf Road Woman and her dire warning. I'd been given a chance to stop this, and I'd failed.

"Cece." My voice broke and a sob tore at my throat. I grabbed a shoulder of the body and turned her over. "Damn!" The word exploded from my mouth as I jumped back. "It isn't her!" I signaled Tinkie over. "It's just her coat. Someone set this up so we'd think it was her."

Tinkie's face was completely white. "Then where is she?"

12

I regretted not photographing the bundle before I moved it, but I took photos once we'd recovered enough from the shock to set to work. Tinkie's question pecked at the back of my head as I waited for DeWayne Dattilo, the head deputy and Coleman's right-hand man, and Budgie to show up. Coleman wouldn't be back for several hours. The only thing we knew for positive was that Cece had been in the alley and was now gone and Peter *could have been* missing for over twelve hours. Or he could have lured Cece into his vehicle and was now . . . holding her.

Tinkie searched the perimeter for clues, moving cautiously to make sure she didn't disturb anything that might have significance to the deputies. DeWayne was good with tracking and Budgie was a whiz on the computer with research. Budgie would come up with something like studying Google Earth to get a bird's-eye view of the terrain. It wasn't a bad idea.

Until then, though, since I'd already moved the coat, I picked it up and shook it out.

"What are you doing?" Tinkie asked.

"Why would Cece leave her coat? Maybe she left a message for us."

Tinkie joined me as we turned out the pockets. A piece of paper fluttered to the ground and I picked it up. *I'm following a lead. Don't worry. Cooley* was scratched on the back of a postal receipt. In an inside pocket, Tinkie found a business card for Cissy Hartley, Memphis television reporter.

"What do you make of that?" Tinkie asked.

"I am going to hurt Cece as soon as I get my hands on her. She says she's okay. She leaves her coat and a cryptic note in an alley. Why not just call?"

"Because whatever she's doing, she knows we would have tried to stop her." Tinkie was as agitated as I was. The other clue was also cryptic. Tinkie didn't have to point out that Cece had never mentioned Cissy Hartley to us as a friend or peer. We knew who Cissy was—she did a good job of covering political events in the Delta. She'd been all over the most recent senate race, but the day-to-day Delta was of little interest. "The students said Cissy has been covering the dig a lot. She isn't exactly Cece's competitor. Maybe they were working together?" I made it a question instead of a statement.

"Maybe. Let's ask Jaytee." Tinkie put in a call to Cece's significant other. Jaytee answered the phone on the fourth ring and Tinkie had her phone on speaker.

"Ladies, you realize it's barely daybreak and I was at work until three a.m." He yawned to emphasize his point.

"It's about Cece," Tinkie said. "Did Cece tell you what her plans were this morning?"

"She was meeting that Deerstalker guy for an interview." Jaytee sounded wide awake now. "Is something wrong?"

"Maybe not," I said. "She just didn't meet him where she said she would. Could you call her? She's not picking up for us." It's possible she really was dodging us.

"Sure. I'll call you right back." The line clicked dead, and Tinkie and I stared at each other, waiting. Not a minute later, Jaytee called back. "She's not picking up. Should I be worried?"

"Not yet." Tinkie decided on kindness and caution. "Sarah Booth and I are looking for her." She pointed to the coat and arched her eyebrows. I shook my head. No point in sending Jaytee over the edge with worry when we'd done everything that could be done. Once the deputies checked things out, we could give Jaytee a full report.

"If you hear from her, ask her to give us a call," I said. "Go back to sleep, Jaytee. Sorry we woke you."

When the connection was broken, I had another

idea. "Call the Memphis TV station and see if they'll put you through to Cissy," I suggested.

The switchboard operator at the TV station refused to put us through to Cissy and refused to even tell us if Cece had called Cissy earlier. Maybe the deputies could worm the information out of her, but where Tinkie and I were concerned, her lips were a steel trap. She took in information but gave none out.

"Would you ask Ms. Hartley to call me?" Tinkie requested in her best Southern belle voice.

"Don't count on it" was the reply.

"We need to speak with Ms. Hartley." I was not as diplomatic as Tinkie.

"If you need to speak with Ms. Hartley, you would have her private number," the operator said in a bored voice. "Leave your name and number, and I'll let her know you called."

Tinkie left her name and number since I'd already been a bit of an ass. Unless we drove to Memphis and waylaid the TV reporter, we weren't going to talk to her.

"Honest to goodness, you'd think she was the president the way they protect her," I said. It was the wrong thing to say. Tinkie blanched.

"Reporting can be a dangerous job," she said.

I had to change the subject fast. I looked at Tinkie and held out the slip of paper with *Cooley* written on it. "You think Cece meant to leave that for us? She had to leave the coat deliberately. I mean no one shucks out of a coat in this cold and just leaves it in a back alley."

"Who else might she have left it for?"

"Only us." I finished searching all the pockets a second time and found nothing else. "The guy in the hoodie following Cece could have been Cooley Marsh. All of those college kids wear hats and hoodies, even the girls."

"What would Cooley want with Cece?" I realized Tinkie posed the question hoping I had an answer that didn't involve blood.

"Maybe to tell her something. Maybe to show her something. He's at the dig but, you know, he doesn't belong there. He's more computer nerd than treasure hunter." I couldn't give voice to the darkest worries that sprang up in my mind. "Let's keep looking until the law gets here."

I searched the area thoroughly, but there was no evidence of any blood, which was hopeful. If the worst-case scenario was true and a serial killer had taken my friend, I had to keep in mind that the killer could have murdered Cece right in the alley with all the privacy he needed. Taking her meant he had another use for her. Or so I hoped. The dark part of my brain told me that if this killer's motive was the ritual of bleeding the victims, he would want to perform the kill in a place where he could indulge his sicko fantasies. I could almost read those same thoughts on Tinkie's face as she tiptoed around the area, photographing everything that might prove the least bit relevant.

"We don't know if Cece is with Deerstalker, or Cooley, or neither. We can't assume she is in danger." I forced my voice to sound firm and authoritative.

Tinkie only looked at me with wide blue eyes and returned to her search.

At last the sheriff's cruisers pulled in front of the bail bond office, which also brought Junior out to see what was happening at the back of his building. I took him aside and told him about Cece's coat and the note.

"I should have paid more attention," he said. The grayness of his skin and the sad, sad wrinkles that his face had fallen into reflected the guilt he felt—even though it was unearned. No one could have known that Cece was in danger—if she was really in danger at all. She was walking down the street in broad daylight, something we'd done a million times as kids and adults. Zinnia was—or should have been—the safest place on earth for Cece.

"Cece could be dealing with anything. Maybe she went with Cooley Marsh because he had something to show her. Maybe she's interviewing Peter Deerstalker somewhere private." I couldn't let Junior buy into all that guilt.

"Keep in mind, she's pissed a lot of people off with her reporting," Tinkie said. "Just last week the square-dancing society got mad at her because they thought she was mocking them." Tinkie, too, was trying to lighten Junior's burden. "Cece loves to stir up controversies on otherwise dull news days."

"She was throwing some shade at those square dancers," Junior said, grinning. "That line where she said she loved the way their flouncy skirts bounced on their fat little thighs. That hit some nerves."

Cece had poked fun at a lot of people, including celebrities. She and Millie, who read all of the trash tabloids about starlets, secret pregnancies, alien matings, and remorse by cheating stars, had teamed up to write one of the juiciest columns in print about the foibles of the rich and famous. What Millie didn't know from her obsessive reading, Cece knew because she was the Queen of Trivia.

"You're right. We shouldn't worry until we have reason to. I'm sure she'll call soon. I'll be in touch. Now I have to go over to the courthouse for a hearing." Junior patted my shoulder. "Cece's okay. She's a tough bird. And when we find who took her—if that's even what happened—we'll make them pay for upsetting us."

I nodded and squeezed his hand. I didn't try to talk because my throat was clogged with a big wad of emotion. Cece had to be okay. She had to be. Had it not been for the warning from a vision of Buffalo Calf Road Woman, I wouldn't have been so concerned. Perhaps I would be better served to worry about my sanity than Cece's safety.

"We'll head over to the dig and talk to Cooley Marsh," Budgie said. "If he knows something, he'll cough it up."

"Any word from Coleman?"

"He hasn't had time to get across the river yet, Sarah Booth." Budgie was the voice of reason. "You know he'll call you the minute he knows anything. He's aware how upset you are about Cece."

Yes, Coleman knew Tinkie and I were emotionally walking on fire, but he was also a professional lawman and if someone had taken Cece, her best chance was in our ability to keep our eye on the prize—finding her and saving her. I couldn't think of slit throats and blood collected in old bowls. I had to believe Cece was okay. She was smart enough to outwit her abductor.

Tinkie came to stand beside me as the two deputies wrapped things up. "What do you think happened to Cece?" she asked, as the deputies pulled away.

"I don't know." It was the truth. "But I don't think she was forced anywhere. I think she left that coat for us to find. The note makes it clear she's okay and Cooley's name was scrawled like she was in a big hurry. She wanted us to talk to him and I think the business card for Cissy Hartley was also left deliberately. Cece is leaving bread crumbs for us to follow. Now, we need to find Peter Deerstalker. He's been missing longer than she has.

"Let's check with the students at the Budget Inn. Maybe they know something. While we're there we can look for Cooley Marsh, too. If anyone knows where he is, it will be Delane Goggans. She seems to be in charge of the students."

"Let's retrieve Sweetie Pie and Chablis from Millie's," Tinkie said. "We might need their abilities to sniff out a villain."

13

Sweetie Pie and Chablis set up a real whine at the Budget Inn when we pulled into the parking lot. Cece's little red Prius was parked beside a big van and I almost didn't see it. Not true for Sweetie Pie. She and Chablis instantly called our attention to it. Pluto, who had insisted on coming along, was too dignified to rub his wet nose on the car windows, but he watched Cece's car intently.

I got out and checked the car, but it was locked and there was no sign of anything out of order. Cece loved the car and kept it immaculate. "At least we know she made it this far," I told Tinkie. "And she was under her own power."

I let the pups and cat out but cautioned them not to wander too far afield. The highway was close, but traffic was minimal, and our critters had more sense than most grown men. Zinnia hadn't been a travel destination until Scott had opened the blues club. Now, more and more tourists were discovering the magic of the Delta—but not in March. The next big event would be an April blues festival, and that was going to be a crowd-buster.

The lobby was empty. It was still relatively early—for some people. The clerk didn't have a room in Delane's name, which was telling, so Tinkie and I started knocking on doors. I wasn't shocked when a large number of the students were still in bed. And I didn't want to know the romantic combos. I just wanted to talk to Delane, who was a bit aggravated that I woke her up in a room registered to Amber Johnson, the girl who'd gone home for appendix surgery. I was honestly surprised she wasn't with Frank at the Prince Albert.

When we finally roused her, I asked, "Where's Frank?"

"He's gone," she said, yawning. "Be back tomorrow."

"He wasn't supposed to leave Sunflower County." Coleman was going to be sore. He didn't detain Frank in jail because of the dig and the need for speed. But the professor had been warned to stay in town.

"Tell it to Frank. He does what he wants."

"Where'd he go?" I asked.

She scoffed. "To give the memorial for Sandra Wells at Ann Arbor. He was asked to do so. He couldn't very well refuse."

"I thought they hated each other," Tinkie said.

Delane shrugged. "University politics make strange bedfellows, you know. She was a colleague."

Maybe he talked to Coleman and got permission. Right now Delane was my focus. I didn't want to jump into the chase for Cece or Cooley, so I started with some basic questions to loosen her up. "Did you ever see a private investigator on the dig site? Female."

She shrugged. "Maybe."

"A simple yes or no will work a lot better." Tinkie was impatient. Behind her, Chablis was wiggling to get into Delane's room. The grad student kept the door at a tight crack, unwilling to step into the hall because she said she wasn't dressed.

"Yes, I saw a private investigator at the dig. About six days back."

"What was she looking into?"

She sighed. "Can we do this later? I can still get another hour of sleep and I'm tired."

"You can do it down at the courthouse. I'll let the sheriff know." Tinkie put her hands on her hips and all but stamped her foot. She'd had enough of Delane. "Now you can talk to us here or a patrol car will be by in about fifteen minutes to get you."

Delane's sigh was jam-packed with exasperation. "The PI was asking about some folklore about the burial mound being protected by a curse. She said she'd been hired by someone to check into a series of misfortunes that happened to people who came to the mound. Accidents,

183

tragedies, that kind of stuff. She was creepy as all get out. I sent her over to talk to the other kook who dealt in charms and spells."

"Kawania."

"That's the one." She yawned. "Now can I go back to sleep?"

I was about to relent, but Pluto slipped through the crack in the door, followed by Chablis. My cat gave an ear-rending screech that was followed by the sound of a male in anguish. "What the hell?" I pushed the door open. Delane fell back and I stepped into a room of empty booze bottles and Frank Hafner wrapped in a sheet and dancing like some animated ghost as Pluto clawed his toes. Chablis merrily barked. Only Sweetie Pie maintained any decorum. She went into the room and flopped down, sighed, and closed her eyes.

Tinkie looked at Frank and then Delane and arched her eyebrows. "I didn't realize Frank could teleport. Must come in handy."

"What do you want?" Frank asked. "You're supposed to be working for me, not against me."

"You're your own worst enemy, Frank," I said. "There are two dead women and you're in a motel with a student."

"She isn't *my* student."

"Like that makes it okay?" Tinkie was disturbed.

Delane was at least twenty. She was plenty old enough to decide what actions she took. But the situation did smack of an older man taking advantage of a young woman, a man who could influence her grade or college career, except she worked for his adversary, Dr. Sandra Wells, the dead woman.

"I've done nothing illegal or immoral." Frank was trying to rear up on his hind legs, but Pluto was still going after those toes, making him dance. He lost a lot of his indignation. "Delane and I are single, free to make our own decisions." He shot her an apologetic look. "You don't understand."

"Uh-huh." Tinkie rolled her eyes. "You should be ashamed." She picked Pluto up. "Enough there, Pluto." She handed the cat to me, but I just let him loose. I liked watching Frank dance around the room. "Why lie about your little rendezvous if you're all so sure it's aboveboard?"

"I'm under suspicion for murder and everything I do reflects back on Delane. I was trying not to sully her reputation."

I choked trying not to laugh. "Good job! Look, we don't care about your sex lives. We want to know about the Devareaux woman and what she was looking into." I sat down in the only chair in the room. "And we're not leaving until we hear the truth."

Frank sat down on the bed. "That woman came poking around on a bull-crap excuse. She said she'd been hired to do an investigation of

185

the dig in relation to some missing women in Louisiana. She never made it clear how that was related to the dig. But she said that Mound Salla was cursed and that tragedy would befall the dig because we were violating the sacred burial site of tribal elders. I've had enough trouble with the students being afraid of the dark, seeing things that aren't there, thinking any minute Leatherface is going to jump out of the woods. I didn't need more drama. I told her to get lost. I threatened to call the sheriff to have her removed if she didn't go voluntarily. So she left. That's what I know."

"Did she talk to anyone but you?"

He shrugged one shoulder in dismissal. "She talked to some of the students. And Sandra, who pissed her off. Sandra was good at that."

"About what?" I asked.

"She asked Sandra if anything unusual had occurred. Sandra fed her a bunch of hokum about the haunted Bailey house and the spirits of the dead Native Americans roaming around. Not what I needed. The students already think there's something in the woods."

"Who was Devareaux working for?" I asked.

Frank frowned. "Not me. I asked but she said it was confidential. I didn't press. I was so intent on getting into the mound and finding something that would shut Sandra up and keep my investors happy."

"What is it you thought you'd find?" I asked.

186

Frank hesitated, and I wondered if he was going to lie. "Pottery, bones, I'm hoping some details on the belief systems of the people buried in this particular mound. If my dating is correct, this mound was developed at a time when the world was changing for the Tunica tribe. They were being pushed farther and farther west. In many ways, this mound was the last holdout of a culture. It could have immense importance."

"Pottery and bones?" I had a sudden realization that something far more valuable had to be at stake for Frank and Sandra to sink so much money into one dig. This wasn't a pyramid or a Pharaoh's grave. There would be no gold or jewels. Those things were of little interest to the Tunica tribe. The Mound Salla site was interesting because it was so far removed from the Mississippi River, where the mound builders had originally lived and died. But there was nothing about the site to warrant such excitement or expense. As far as I knew.

"I'm a professor of archeology," Frank said. Since the cat had quit making him do his Fred Astaire routine, he'd gathered his composure—and his cloak of charm—around him. "While some archeologists are looking for great wealth or treasure or Biblical relics, which are quite valuable, I've focused on the United States sites and the history that has little real wealth but the ultimate value of knowledge. What we learn here tells us many things about the way the planet is developed and our concerns for the future. These mounds show water levels, flooding, so much more, even the more recent ravages of climate pollution."

I almost believed him. Tinkie was looking at him in wide-eyed wonder. Then she glanced at me behind his back and winked. "I can see how much this means to you, Frank," she said. "I've heard there might be a City of Gold somewhere along the Mississippi. De Soto thought so, from what I've read."

"There was always the hope, but I believe the Spanish and French explorers quickly came to understand that the value of the land here was not in metals or jewels, but in furs and colonies."

Perhaps he was telling the truth, but I didn't buy it completely. I realized that I didn't fully trust my client. He could sell sincerity or a snowball in Hell—he had that ability. I turned to Delane.

"What was Devareaux looking for?" I asked.

"Just what we said. She had a tip of some kind that there was an evil spirit attached to the dig. That the ancestors didn't want their bones disturbed. She said it might play into her case of missing women in Louisiana. That's what she was looking into."

"She was tracking down a ghost story?" I found that hard to believe.

"That's right," Delane said. Her face brightened.

"She did talk to Kawania. Maybe that's who was pumping her full of stories about spirits or ghosts or curses. I don't know. I try to stamp that kind of talk out in the other students. It makes for discontent when we have to work late at night. And she was talking with Cooley, and they weren't that happy with each other. It looked personal." Delane stepped closer to Frank.

"Full disclosure," Frank said, "I did take the PI out to the dig late one evening. It was the night before she left to return to Marksville. She was interested in being out there at night to see if there was some kind of ghost."

I perked up at this. Frank had a weakness for women. And he indulged himself whenever he found an attractive woman. "You were out at the dig alone with her?"

Frank had the grace to look a little ashamed when Delane cut him with a glare. "We didn't see anything untoward, no ghostly sightings or signs of spirit activity. She said she was going home to Louisiana."

"Did you leave her at the site?"

"Heavens no! I drove her back to town and left her out here, at the Budget Inn, where she had her room and a car. I went on to the Prince Albert. Delane can vouch for me."

"I was waiting in his room at the Prince Albert. He did come in about midnight, but he didn't tell me what he'd been doing. Now I've got things to do." Delane was miffed and I didn't blame her.

"You haven't seen Cece Falcon this morning, have you?" Tinkie asked. She kept it casual. "She said she was coming to talk to you, Delane." She also lied with perfect ease.

"No, I—" Frank didn't get a chance to finish. Delane cut him short.

"Ms. Falcon was here. Earlier this morning."

My hopes rose. "Where did she go?"

Delane shook her head. "I don't know. She looked upset. She kept looking back at the parking lot as she knocked on the doors of some of the students. It wasn't my business and I was tired so I just came back in the room and went to sleep."

"Why were you outside?" I asked.

"I smoke, if you must know. I was having a cig. Frank doesn't like it when I smoke so I sneak around. He was asleep so I went outside and saw your reporter friend. She didn't look right."

"How not right?" I asked.

"She was nervous. Jittery. Kept looking over her shoulder."

"Was she alone?" Tinkie asked.

"I don't know. She kept looking back at the parking lot, but I was sitting on the janitor's stool by the ice machine and didn't have a view."

"And this was about eight? Did you see what kind of car she was in?"

"Yes, she was here about eight, beating on the

door of Kawania's room, but she didn't get an answer. At least not while I finished my cigarette. I went back inside and crawled back in bed. I never saw the car."

"Does Cooley have a room here with the other students?"

"Not to my knowledge," Frank said. "He was hired by Sandra, not me. He wasn't booked in as one of mine."

Delane shrugged. "I didn't book him a room. He wasn't on Dr. Wells' list, but she didn't always go through the proper channels. Now leave us alone." She edged the door closed.

There didn't seem to be a lot more I could pull out of her at the moment. At least we knew Cece had made it to the Budget Inn in her own car. I suspected Cece had been looking for the same person I wanted to talk to. Cooley Marsh.

14

Tinkie called Coleman the minute we were in the car. While I idled in the parking lot, she put the phone on speaker so I could hear, too. Coleman had an update on his search for Peter. The trail had been hot. Leaving the Prince Albert at seven-thirty, Peter had gotten his car out of parking, and that was the last anyone had seen or heard from him. At least we knew he was okay earlier this morning and he was in his own vehicle. Coleman had called the tribal headquarters but no one there had any knowledge of Peter's whereabouts.

I told him about Cece pounding at the door of Kawania's room. I felt certain Cece was with Peter, but I couldn't explain her weird behavior. She would know we were worried about her, and she was generally considerate of her friends.

"We're far behind Cece or Deerstalker," Coleman said. "At least we know she's alive and she has some freedom of movement. Whatever is going on, she could have screamed for help or tried to run—but she didn't do either. That indicates she's not being held against her will. Have you spoken with Jaytee?"

"He hasn't heard a word, but I didn't tell him

she was missing. There didn't seem to be a point in upsetting him."

"I agree. Sarah Booth, I don't think Cece is a captive, but I also don't think she has the freedom to call you and let you know she's okay. She's not the kind of person to worry you so she must be with someone or somewhere that she can't risk a text or call."

He was right that Cece wouldn't deliberately worry us, but I couldn't concoct a scenario where she wasn't a hostage and also couldn't call. "What about the missing women over there?"

"It's complex. I'll explain when I get home. I'm going to do some more checking on Deerstalker and the dead private eye. There's something wrong with all of this, but I can't put my finger on it. I'll see you this evening for sure."

"You bet." I'd almost said, "I love you," but I'd managed to bite back the words. Our feelings for each other were still new and tender. My reward was a knowing grin from Tinkie as I put my phone away.

We were about to pull out of the lot when I saw Kawania step out of the door of her motel room. She looked left and right and then hurried to a vehicle. I didn't even have to suggest it. Tinkie nodded. We would follow her.

"Somehow, this girl is right in the middle of what's going on," Tinkie said.

"I agree." I didn't have time to say more

because Kawania drove like a bat out of hell and I had my hands full following her without being obvious.

"Where do you think she's going?" Tinkie asked as we crossed the Sunflower River and headed toward the Mississippi River.

"I don't have a clue, but she's making a beeline for somewhere."

Tinkie dialed the sheriff's office again. "DeWayne, Sarah Booth and I are tailing a student from the dig, Kawania Laveau. We're hoping she'll lead us to a clue that leads to Cece." She gave our location and direction.

"We never found Cooley Marsh. He wasn't at the dig site but we have feelers out for him. You keep checking in," DeWayne said. "Coleman just called with an update and he told me to keep you in my sights. If anything happens to you, he said he'd skin me. He wanted you to know he's at Peter's residence, checking to see if there's anything there to indicate what his game is. He's also going to talk with some of Deerstalker's associates in his law firm. Peter has a thriving law practice, and from what Coleman said, he was due in court this morning on a case. He could be in big trouble with the judge for his no-show."

That didn't sound good. No lawyer voluntarily ruined his reputation with such antics. "You keep us informed, and we'll keep you updated on what we're up to," I said.

"Budgie is doing more research on that pendant your dog found," DeWayne said. "All of this talk about ghosts and spirits roaming the dig location and then those tattoos on the two dead women that look like that pendant got him to thinking. He's waiting on a call from someone in Arizona. He'll let me know if he has anything interesting."

"Thank you." I glanced at Tinkie as she clicked off the phone. "We're lucky that local law enforcement works with us."

"And they're lucky to have us," Tinkie said.

Both statements were true.

We trailed Kawania for about ten miles, drawing ever closer to the Mississippi River, when she ditched us. We went through a small forested bit of road and when we came back out of the tunnel of trees and were in the open fields again, there was no sign of Kawania or her vehicle. It was like she'd been swallowed whole by the earth.

"Where is she?" Tinkie asked.

"She pulled off into some side road back in those woods, and by now she's reversed and left us behind." I was annoyed with myself for falling for her tactics. It was basic "how to dump a tail." We'd been bested by a college student. "Damn!" I smacked the steering wheel.

"It's not like you were in a city with a lot of traffic and distractions. She made us because we'd been following her for miles. Heck, we've been the only two cars on the road for fifteen minutes. It was bound to happen. Not your fault."

Tinkie made me feel better. "What now?" I said.

"Looks like she was heading for the Mississippi. I wonder why?"

"She's not going to tell us even if we could run her down and ask."

"Nope, but let's just follow the road and see where we end up."

"That's not very scientific or even practical," I pointed out.

"So sue me. I'm trusting my gut." She poked me in the ribs, but not too hard. "I know what part of your anatomy you've been listening to lately."

I put the car in drive and headed west. Talking to Tinkie was only going to get me teased harder. I was smart enough to know when to just ignore her innuendoes.

The sunshine was warm and the car purred like Pluto with a snack of fresh salmon. The Roadster was an antique, but I took good care of it. I'd have to find something new sooner or later, but not until I'd made some repairs on Dahlia House and settled up some other bills. I had an emotional attachment to the Roadster, too. It was a time machine with a dual purpose. Not only did it haul me down the road, it connected me to my mother in the past and to the future.

When we came to Highway 1, which ran down the western edge of the state beside the big levee on the Mississippi, I looked at Tinkie. "Which direction? North or south? It's your gut leading the way."

"South," she said. "There's a hamlet in that direction. And a marina on a tributary of the river."

"Fancy words for a gut to be using."

"Believe it not, Sarah Booth, while I was at Ole Miss I actually studied. I was proficient in business and geography, though I did major in sorority activities and dating. If I had it to do over again, I would have focused on those two academic fields. I liked studying. My problem was that I wanted to run the bank and I knew Daddy would never let a girl do it. That made it easier for me to blow off any academic pursuit."

"I've never doubted your brains or your ability to apply them." That wasn't totally true. Back in college, I had thought Tinkie was kind of a ditz, but that was because she played the role so successfully. She'd given up all attempts to demonstrate brains and judgment and presented herself as a shallow society girl and man bait. She'd become the perfect upper-crust society girl while I'd focused on theater. Our worlds hadn't crossed that often. When I'd moved home from New York, I'd found there were depths to Tinkie I'd never bothered to see.

"Look!" She pointed through the front windshield to a four-way stop, a blink of civilization at a crossroads. A small country store with gas pumps squatted on one corner, an empty shop was on the next corner, and two houses sat cattycornered to each other. The place was so small it didn't even have a name. But there was a sign in front of one of the houses. SISTER GRACE'S PALM READING. COME IN AND FIND YOUR FUTURE.

"That's the place." Tinkie pointed again. "My gut says go there."

"You're serious?" If we needed help from the spirits, we could go to Madame Tomeeka, the woman I'd grown up with in Zinnia who was truly gifted. I didn't know Sister Grace from Adam's housecat—and I had no reason to believe she might help us.

"Just pull in. And let me do the talking."

"You do remember there's a serial killer on the loose and our friend is missing?" I reminded her.

"That's why I'm talking and you're listening." Tinkie got out of the car and churned toward the front door on her short little legs before I could even climb out. I ordered the critters to wait in the car. Like that ever worked. I hurried and caught up with Tinkie as the front door was opening.

"We'd like a reading." Tinkie was direct. "Do you have time for us?"

I took in the older woman who scrutinized us.

She was in her sixties or else had been a heavy smoker. Impossible to tell. Her dark eyes were sharp, acute. She didn't miss much, and she made no attempt to hide the fact that she was assessing us. Whatever she saw, she kept her reaction hidden. She didn't invite us in, but she stepped out of the doorway and walked into the interior of the house, assuming we would follow. Tinkie was on her like a duck after a june bug. I followed Tinkie. The animals were fine in the car. It was sunny but not hot.

Sister Grace sat down at a small round table and motioned for Tinkie to take the chair opposite her. She gave me a sour look. "You can sit there or pull up to the table, whichever. I know you're skeptical. Just keep your negative energy to yourself, please."

Score one for her. I was skeptical. Reading body language didn't take psychic ability. Instead of sitting at the table, I unobtrusively snapped a few photos of the room. It was interesting and filled with books, some nice pottery, and peacock feathers. There was no evidence of a computer or any electronic equipment, but they could have been in another room.

She motioned Tinkie's hands on the table, then reached across and held them in hers. She turned them over and asked to see the palms. For at least three minutes she studied the lines in Tinkie's hands.

"What do you wish to know?" she asked.

"There's someone killing women in the place where we live. What can you tell us about him?"

Sister Grace looked up quickly at Tinkie, then over at me. "I have no knowledge of that kind of darkness. I don't allow it into my realm. What I can tell you is that danger is close around you both. It's like a fog, a miasma, clinging to your skin. It dims your auras. It comes from a place where old things are buried. You should stay away from that place."

"Are we in danger?" Tinkie asked.

"Yes. From an unexpected source."

"Can you tell us who that is?" I asked.

She shook her head. "I read the energy of the body, the sensations that pulse from you. You know this danger exists." She spoke to me. "You've been told."

Buffalo Calf Road Woman came back to me as clearly as if she sat her horse in front of me. I had been told. My skepticism about Sister Grace was quickly evaporating.

The psychic turned to Tinkie. "Your body is changing. Have you seen a doctor?"

I felt like I'd been kicked in the gut. Why would Tinkie need a doctor? "What's wrong with her?"

Sister Grace held up a hand to silence me. "Let her speak." She dared me to continue and instead gave Tinkie the floor.

"Not yet. I will." Tinkie took my hand. "I'm fine. I promise. I've had cysts on my ovaries before. They treat them and they go away."

I wasn't relieved, but I wasn't going to drag out Tinkie's medical issues in front of a stranger. Sister Grace watched us, but said nothing more.

"Why are you here?" she asked at last.

"We're looking for a young woman, Kawania Laveau."

Sister Grace didn't say anything, but I could see a flicker of recognition, and that she knew the young woman.

"And I wanted to give her this." Tinkie reached into her handbag and brought forth the medallion that Chablis had found at the dig site. Budgie had returned it after photographing it and scanning the photos into his computer to compare against various websites.

Sister Grace took one look at the pewter necklace and stood up from the table. "You must leave."

"What is this thing?" I asked, taking it from Tinkie and sliding it toward Sister Grace.

"Leave." Sister Grace pointed to the door. "You bring evil into my home and I won't allow it." She pushed away from the table.

"What is it?" Tinkie picked up the medallion. "It looks like costume jewelry."

"No!" Sister Grace waved it back from her. "Take it. There is no place here for such. It is a curse on the person who carries it." She leaned in to Tinkie. "Take it back where you found it or you could lose the thing you want most in life."

Tinkie dropped it like it had suddenly become red hot. "We'll throw it out the car window when we're on the road."

Sister Grace grasped Tinkie's hand. "No, you cannot. You must return it where you found it, and bury it. That is a ward against evil. It is enchanted to contain a very bad spirit in one place. The spirit, or *zonbi* as we call it in the Creole culture, will seek to find that talisman. It is bound to it."

"We'll return it where we found it. It came from the archeological dig at Mound Salla," Tinkie said. "They're going to excavate the mound. I don't think I can bury it there, but in the woods nearby . . ."

"You must. This is bad juju. Who does this pendant belong to?"

"We don't know," I said. Tinkie was almost quaking in her stilettos. "Look, I don't believe in cursed things or charmed things or magic. We'll take it back, but lay off scaring my partner."

Grace looked at me. "You don't believe." She laughed. "And you think that makes you immune. You're a fool."

Dang! Sister Grace was a lot more direct than Madame Tomeeka or Jitty. "It's not that I don't believe in things beyond this world, I just don't believe an inanimate object can bring about disaster or tragedy because someone put a curse on it." I reached for the medallion and put it in my pocket. "I will see it's returned to the mound."

Grace sat back down. "The dead are always with us. If they are angry, then they can share that emotion with you. The person who owned that necklace is very angry."

"And who owned it?" Tinkie asked.

"A woman with many needs. Slender, brunette, she thinks highly of herself. She met a bad end."

She described Sandra Wells to a T.

"And this woman, this spirit, is angry?" I hated myself for falling into her mumbo-jumbo but I'd been warned that someone I loved was in danger.

"Much more than angry. She is vengeful. She will have her pound of flesh. And there is something there, at that place, which is of great value. She will protect it."

I couldn't help it that her words gave me a terrible feeling. Cece was missing. I'd been warned to protect my loved ones by Buffalo Calf Road Woman. Now Tinkie had been told she might lose the one thing she loved the most, which had to be Oscar. This was way more woo-woo than I cared to handle, yet I couldn't deny that a tiny part of me believed it. Jitty forced me to.

I clicked on my phone and brought up a photo of Cece. "Have you seen this woman?"

"I know her. She works for the newspaper in Zinnia."

"She does. Have you seen her today?"

"I see everyone who comes and goes through Elmore."

Apparently, this crossroads did have a name. "Has Cece been through Elmore today?" This was like googling. You had to get the question just right to get an answer.

"She was here."

Tinkie started forward. "Who was she with? Where did they go? Was she hurt?"

"She was a passenger in a car. Dark blue SUV. Didn't see the make and they all look alike now. A man was driving. They ran the stop sign—just blew right through it and kept driving. She looked straight ahead."

"The direction they were traveling?"

"South."

I texted the info to DeWayne at the sheriff's office so he could put up road blocks and an APB. "How long ago?"

"Maybe nine this morning."

"Thank you, Grace. And this girl, do you know her?" I had a photo of Kawania from the dig.

"Stay away from her. She is a nasty girl."

"What do you mean 'a nasty girl'?" Tinkie asked.

"She dabbles in the darkness. For personal gain. Beware of her. She brings more bad spirits around you."

I wondered if she knew Kawania's claim to the bloodline of Marie Laveau, and if that was the reason she thought she 'dabbled in darkness.' "Do you know this girl personally?"

"I have met her. She involves herself in the psychic realm, but always for herself. Not to help others. This is dangerous, and though she's been warned, she doesn't heed advice."

"May I ask where you met her?" Tinkie said.

Grace leveled a long gaze at her. "No, you may not. Now you must leave. Get rid of that pendant. Put it back where it came from, and stay away from that area. Light three pink candles each evening at dusk for three nights. Remember the full moon has great power. Ask to be cleansed. Take a bowl of water blessed by the full moon and wash your face. Ask again to be cleansed. Stay away from that burial sight."

"Do you have any pink candles?" I asked. She'd been helpful, and she hadn't asked for pay for her session with Tinkie. The least we could do was buy a few candles.

"In the front."

We returned to the front of the house where sunlight filtered in and gave the room a cheery look. Orange was a happy color on the sofa covers and curtains. Grace went to a cabinet and opened the top. When she reached up for the candles, her sleeve slid down, revealing a tattoo on her upper arm. It was a curious design—and familiar. It was the same horned creature, ram or beast, that had been found on the bodies of two dead women. The only difference was that Grace's tattoo was more colorful.

"That's an interesting tattoo," Tinkie said, pointing to it.

Grace got the candles and moved her sleeve down to cover her arm. "The symbol has great power of protection."

I almost didn't tell her, but then I thought, why not? "Both dead women had a tattoo just like that on their bodies. Why would that be?"

"You would have to ask them," she said. "I suspect if you get that chance, you won't really care about tattoos at all." She handed the candles to Tinkie but refused payment. She opened the front door. The conversation was over—it was time to go.

Once we were outside the house, I felt as if I were waking from a dream. The light inside the house had been dim, and now the sun was almost blinding. I got in the car and put on my sunglasses. Tinkie did the same. The critters woke from a deep sleep as if they, too, had been enchanted.

"Where do you think Cece was going?" Tinkie asked.

"I don't know. If we knew who she was with . . ."

"We have to assume it was Peter Deerstalker, don't we?"

"I don't know." I sounded like the proverbial broken record.

"Where are we going?" Tinkie asked.

"Back to Sunflower County and Mound Salla. I'm getting rid of this pendant as soon as I can."

Tinkie didn't even tease me about it. She was uncomfortable, too. Whatever talents Sister Grace had as a psychic, she sure had a gift for persuasion.

15

We drove back to the burial mound, and to my surprise there were no other cars parked at the base. Midday clouds had rolled across the horizon, and though the fields were greening up, the day had taken on a distinctive gray hue.

"If a wolf howls, I'm outta here," Tinkie said.

"You only have to worry about werewolves on a full moon," I told her.

"Which will be any day now. I was looking at my almanac and it's time to plant. I had some raised beds put in and I'm going to grow some tomatoes, peppers, okra. We need to eat more fresh vegetables. I'll share with everyone."

"You're growing a garden?" This was not the Tinkie I knew and loved. She paid people to do this kind of work for her.

"I am. I'm turning over a new leaf. I'm going to eat healthier, and nothing is healthier than fresh veggies. The almanac says this is the moon to plant under."

The memory of Buffalo Calf Road Woman hit me hard again. The Crow Moon. That was a dangerous night for me and my friends. "When does the full moon occur?"

"I don't remember exactly, but very soon. Tomorrow or the next day. Are you making a garden this year?"

A garden of woe would be my answer. I had the black thumb of death. "Billy Watson has already planted the fields and his crops are coming up. He should be fertilizing the hayfield soon." The full moon was fast approaching and I felt a strong need to reiterate potential dangers—but I knew I'd upset her. Then again, forewarned was forearmed. "Look, Sister Grace isn't the first time I've been warned about danger all around. I told you about my dream. We have to be super careful on the night of the full moon. Things could be very dangerous then."

She looked at me. "I didn't think you were superstitious."

"I'm not. I'm cautious. People get crazy on a full moon. Ask anyone who works in a hospital. Doc will tell you."

"O . . . kay," Tinkie said. "I'll put it on my lunar calendar. Now let's get to the top of that mound and ditch that pendant. I'm hungry, and it's lunchtime. We missed breakfast, as you recall. And we're no closer to finding Cece than we were at eight o'clock."

"We know she's alive, though."

"And headed south in a strange car with an unidentified driver. Whoopee." Tinkie's sarcasm made me smile.

"Do you have a better plan?"

"No." She took off her sunglasses to clean them. "Let's get rid of the pendant and talk to Budgie and DeWayne. Surely they've heard from Coleman by now."

"Good plan." I got out of the car and started the climb up the mound. Halfway to the top, I knew my butt was going to rebel again if I wasn't careful. Tinkie was having a little difficulty herself. "Maybe we can just throw it into the weeds on the side," I said.

Tinkie considered. "Fine by me."

We moved sideways around the mound to the back where the nearby woods had encroached. Saplings and other scrub brush had begun to grow. I pulled the pendant from my pocket and tossed it as far as I could into the thick woods. "That should do it."

"Let's go." Tinkie looked suddenly uncomfortable. "This place is not a good place. I do think the people buried here want to be left alone. I've never given a lot of thought to these archeological explorations, but I wouldn't want my grandmother dug up and exhibited. She was a strong lady and all of that, but looking at her bones or the things she was buried with wouldn't tell much about her. Not the really important stuff. Like how she loved me and Daddy."

Tinkie was right, but we had zero say-so on the

dig. "The body is only a husk, Tinkie. Don't take it personally. I was thinking of donating my body to science."

"You will do no such thing!" Tinkie was emphatic. "You'll be laid to rest right beside Libby and James Franklin in the Sunflower County cemetery."

I hadn't given my burial any real thought, and didn't want to do so at this moment. "Let's head back down."

"I want to take one more look at the site where Sandra Wells was killed." Tinkie started up the side of the mound. I grabbed her ankle.

"Let's just go."

A thicker, darker cloud moved across the sun, and the light grew dimmer. To make it worse, a wind sprang up with the smell of impending rain. "Yeah, let's go."

We'd started down when I heard something. And it wasn't my imagination. Sweetie Pie and Chablis bounded past me toward the top of the mound. Tinkie called for her pooch, to no avail. They blew past us like we didn't exist, and Pluto was right behind them.

"Dammit," I said. I really didn't want to climb to the top. "Just dammit."

"I'll get them." Tinkie started back up and I followed. Somewhere near the area where the dig was going I heard Sweetie Pie baying and howling. Chablis was barking with her rat-a-tat-

tat little bark that could make my eardrums bleed in an enclosed space.

"What have they gotten into?" Tinkie huffed as we neared the top. "Instead of breakfast, I want a drink. Bloody Mary. Spicy. Too bad Millie doesn't have a liquor license."

"I agree." We made it up the last ten feet and turned toward the dogs. "Sweetie Pie!" She was baying like she'd found a batch of meth. "Sweetie Pie!"

We started toward the sound of the dogs. A shot rang out and a bullet bit the dirt not two feet in front of me. I grabbed Tinkie and pulled her to the ground. "What the hell?" she said.

"Either they're a crappy shot or they meant to miss us," I said. "We were open targets."

"What are we going to do?" Tinkie asked.

We didn't have our guns to return fire and there was nothing to hide behind for at least fifty yards, where some dirt mounds would provide cover. It was a long distance to run with someone shooting at us. "We have to go back down."

"If they come to the edge, we'll be sitting ducks going down that steep side."

"We're sitting ducks right here."

She nodded. "You're right. But the dogs!"

"Tinkie, we'll get the dogs. We have to be alive to get them, though."

She scooted back to the edge and disappeared. I was right behind her. When I was almost down,

I called for the dogs and cat again, but I kept moving as fast as I could. If the shooter looked down the side of the mound, we'd be easy targets, Tinkie was right about that.

Sweetie Pie and Chablis rushed past me and I felt sweet relief. Now only Pluto was missing. As Tinkie and I gained the bottom of the mound, I called for him again. He darted out of the trees and ran to jump in the car. We all crammed in and Tinkie and I slammed the doors. I tossed her the key. She had the engine going and I had the phone out reporting the shooter to DeWayne.

"Patrol car is on the way, Sarah Booth. Coleman is still at the Tunica reservation. He should report back soon."

"Thanks."

"Did you get a view of the shooter?" DeWayne asked.

"I didn't see anyone. None of the students are at the dig. Or at least the parking lot is empty. Have they abandoned digging?"

"Peter Deerstalker sent over a cease and desist on the digging. Judge Baxter signed the order based on Deerstalker's pending lawsuit."

"Then Peter *was* in the courtroom this morning?" I was confused.

"Nope. He sent an associate to argue the motion. Nobody in his office has seen Peter Deerstalker. We just assumed he was with Cece since they both disappeared at the same time.

And by disappeared I mean fell off our radar. I wasn't implying anything dire."

Which meant that even DeWayne was worried about Cece. "Any luck with the APB near that crossroads we called in?"

"If they were on Highway 1, they've disappeared into thin air," DeWayne said. "Now you and Tinkie get away from that mound. I mean it. Coleman will do worse than skin me if anything happens to you."

I didn't need to hear that advice twice. I nodded and Tinkie punched the accelerator to the floor. The car roared to life. Once we were clear of Mound Salla and sure no one was after us, I regretted that I hadn't tried to find the shooter. We'd made the right decision to run—I didn't regret that. But whoever was taking potshots at us could probably have yielded a lot of information about what the heck was going on at Mound Salla and possibly even regarding the murders. I comforted myself that we'd find the information another way, and it surely wasn't worth getting shot over.

"Who do you think tried to shoot us?" Tinkie asked. She'd slowed the car to a reasonable speed, and we were in a direct line toward Zinnia.

"Deerstalker? Delane? Marsh? The Ghost of Christmas Past? I don't know. Like I said, I don't think they were really trying to hit us. They had a clear shot."

"Even if we'd had our guns they wouldn't have helped. I never saw anyone or anything to shoot at."

"At least we got rid of that pendant," I said.

Chablis took that as her cue to hop into the front seat with me. She held the leather bag in her mouth. I had a terrible feeling. I opened the bag and dumped the pendant into my hand. "Maybe we didn't get rid of it."

"That's just . . . nuts!" Tinkie was rattled and didn't bother trying to hide it. When she started to shake, she pulled over. We were on the outskirts of Zinnia, and in the distance I could see downtown buildings.

"I don't think the person shooting at us was the killer. That was someone doing something they didn't want us to know about. They just wanted to run us off."

"So they shot at us? Seriously?"

"Trust me. They could have killed us if they wanted." I had to make her see that point.

"And that damn pendant." She picked up the leather sack and was going to toss it out the window when I grabbed it.

"Chill, Tinkie." I took it from her hand. "I'm not superstitious, but between this pendant and the henna tattoos on the two female victims and the same tattoo on Sister Grace, I'm thinking we should hold on to this thing until we solve the case. Then we can drop it down that auger hole if you want to."

"What if it really is cursed?"

A cloud seemed to pass across the sun, and I almost threw the pendant out the window myself. "Let's just hang on to it for another day or so. We'll ask Budgie to get rid of it if we don't need it."

Tinkie nodded and put the car back on the road. "Forget the pendant. Let's find Cece."

That was exactly what I was thinking, too.

16

We put the plans for food on hold—the day was getting away from us and Cece was still missing. We headed instead to Dahlia House and arrived just as Coleman was pulling up. He had news on several fronts, and I put on a pot of coffee so he could tell me and my partner. Tinkie had recovered from the unnerving shooting incident, and Coleman addressed that first.

"There was no sign of the shooter when Budgie and DeWayne got there," Coleman said. "But there was evidence that someone had messed with the expensive equipment. And he found a shell casing. We're trying for fingerprints, but it's unlikely we'll get anything. My theory is that someone was up there, perhaps planning on destroying the expensive equipment, and you two scared them away. They didn't intend to shoot you, but they had to do something to drive you back down the mound."

I'd come to much the same conclusion. "Frank had better post someone to guard that equipment."

Before Coleman could move on to Cece and Peter's whereabouts, his phone rang. "Hello,

Frank." He listened for a moment. "That's a good idea. If I had the manpower to spare, I'd send a deputy, but we're looking for Peter Deerstalker and a local reporter, Cece Falcon. Have you seen them?" He listened again. "Yes, Sarah Booth is here at Dahlia House with Tinkie." He listened another moment. "Thanks." And hung up.

"Hafner's going to post a guard at the dig, and he hasn't seen Peter or Cece."

"What about Peter's involvement in these murders? Did you find out anything?" Tinkie was pacing. Maybe coffee wasn't such a good idea. She seemed wired enough.

"Peter's got a good reputation as a lawyer among the local law enforcement," Coleman said. "He represents his clients with a lot of talent and persistence."

I wondered what he wasn't saying. "And?"

"He's a hothead. The tribal elders are annoyed that he's taken on this fight against the excavation without their approval. When Peter believes in something, he isn't inclined to back down. He'll push to the extreme."

"The tribal elders are in favor of digging up the mound?" I was surprised to hear that.

"They're not *for* it, but maybe not completely against it." Coleman thought a moment before he continued. "They aren't happy with the idea of disturbing their ancestor's bones, but they also understand that a television show could give their tribe a spotlight. Probably ninety percent of the people living around here today couldn't name the Biloxi-Tunica tribe," Coleman said. "I understand this is a chance for them to share their culture, to reveal their role in history, which has been all but ignored."

I could see that, too. It was a dilemma. But not for Peter. He was opposed to it. Enough to wreck expensive equipment? To shoot a deadly weapon at people—even if he didn't intend to hit them? If he was at the top of the mound on a guerilla warfare adventure, where was Cece?

"So what did you find out about Cece?" Tinkie jumped to the heart of the matter.

Coleman shook his head. "No one around Marksville had seen her. Or Peter, for that matter. Not today, at least. But I did find out some things about Miss Devareaux."

The dead private investigator weighed on my mind—especially since I'd been shot at in the location where we'd found her body. "Spill it." I wanted facts that would help me make sense of the mess that was my case. I didn't know that any of the incidents were linked, but I tended to take things personally when bullets were flying around me.

"Devareaux talked with the Avoyelles Parish sheriff's office. They'd had no reports of missing women but agreed to check into it. She told the sheriff she'd been hired anonymously by a man she'd spoken with on the phone. He left a cash payment for her. The sheriff told me she was just starting out as an investigator and she seemed pretty excited about a lead, but she wouldn't share any more information. The sheriff was concerned about the anonymous client business and he said he tried to caution her."

I'd had some pretty sketchy clients before, but none who were completely anonymous. We already knew this had ended badly for the gumshoe. Had she been hired by the killer? And if so, why? "She was investigating the disappearance of several women? Women no one else knows were missing? Were they members of the Tunica tribe?"

"No," Coleman said, and he frowned. "I can't seem to link Devareaux's presence at the mound with anything involving the Tunicas or the archeological dig. Or the missing women—who have not been reported missing. There's no connective tissue except the fact that Devareaux died at Mound Salla. Or at least her body was left there and she'd been there asking questions."

"Do you think she was a . . . sacrifice?" I had to ask it.

"Could be." Coleman looked worried and weary. "This troubles me. Missing women who no one knows are missing. A private investigator with no connection to an archeological dig is murdered and her body found hidden at the dig. The sheriff over at Marksville promised to investigate further but, I have to admit, I'm thinking the whole missing-women thing is a hoax."

"But why? Why would Devareaux show up at the dig talking about missing women, looking for some kind of woo-woo link, according to the students. What am I not seeing? Whatever she wanted must have been worth risking her life."

"I agree," Coleman said. "But I don't know what that might be or why a young woman would pretend to be seeking leads on missing women."

"Delane told us Devareaux was talking heatedly with Cooley Marsh," Tinkie said.

"And it looks like Devareaux was involved with Frank Hafner. Romantically," I added. He was our client, but I couldn't hold back the truth from Coleman while Cece was missing. If her absence was tied to what was going on at Mound Salla, then Coleman needed every scrap of information we unearthed.

"I'll check into that."

I understood what he was saying. "So where is Cece? And Peter?" I was far more worried about my friend than the lawyer, but if Sister Grace was to be believed, it seemed they were in tandem. Find one, find the other.

"I don't have any evidence," Coleman said, "but I believe they were going to the Winterville Mound."

"Why?" Tinkie and I asked in unison. Coleman's statement was a revelation.

"DeWayne got a call."

"From Cece?" Tinkie was hopeful; I was aggravated.

"No, from Cooley Marsh."

"You have got to be kidding me." While Tinkie and I had been chasing all around the Delta searching for Cece, she'd been calling Cooley Marsh. "She called him instead of us?" I was outdone.

"This will answer a few of your questions. Cooley said that he met up with Cece in Zinnia this morning while she was walking down the street. She was asking him about the Devareaux woman, and he didn't want to be seen talking to her so they stepped in the back alley. After they talked, she gave him a ride to the motel. He said she left her car there and got in Peter Deerstalker's vehicle and they took off."

"And she just happened to leave her coat in the alley?" I said.

"Cooley said he didn't know anything about the coat. That she wasn't wearing it when he talked with her."

Which could only mean she'd slipped out of it before Cooley Marsh talked to her in the alley. So she had deliberately left a trail of bread crumbs. "So Cooley was the guy in the hoodie following Cece?" I asked.

"Apparently."

"I don't trust him. There's something off about him, the Devareaux woman, and that psychic—" I stopped but it was too late.

"Psychic?" Coleman asked.

There was no point lying so I told him everything Sister Grace had told us. Coleman took it all in without comment.

"And we still don't know that Cece is unharmed," Tinkie said. "So she's off following a lead with Peter Deerstalker? Why wouldn't she just tell us?"

"That's not like Cece. She knew we were worried. Why would she sneak off with Peter like this?" I was getting a little hot under the collar.

"When you find out, let me know. And her boss, too. Ed's worried about her. And he's upset. I don't envy Cece's return to the newspaper. Anyway, I have no reason to believe foul play is involved in her absence, and I've got two murders to solve, so I'm going to focus on that."

Coleman had a long leash of patience, but he'd finally hit the end of it with Cece, and I didn't blame him. "So Peter has a good reputation as a lawyer, great. But did you find out anything that connects him to the dead women?"

"Only Sandra Wells. It's a fact he slept with her when she first came to town. My assumption is that he was trying to persuade her to abandon the dig. That didn't work, so Peter filed papers asking that Mound Salla be turned over to the Biloxi-Tunica tribe or to the park services. That's likely to go through," Coleman said, "eventually. Which puts more pressure on the archeologists to get busy, and fast, if they intend to find anything before they're shut down."

"Isn't there some way both parties can have a little of what they want? Maybe excavate a small portion of the mound?"

"A compromise is often shunned by both sides," Coleman said. "If Mound Salla is discovered to hold some real significance, then it will become of great value to Sunflower County and the state, as well as to the archeologists. It could very well draw tourists into the area. It's not about what's just or fair."

"I hadn't thought of that." But now I would. "A lot of people have something to gain or lose in this situation. You learned something else at the reservation." I knew it in my gut. And from the fact that Coleman wouldn't look me straight in the eye.

Coleman sighed. "One reason Peter is fighting this so hard is that he believes Mound Salla was built on the spot where a band of Choctaws said the red people had come out of the earth. It's an origin story, and of great value to those who want to protect the tribe and their beliefs. In the story, the first Native Americans came out of tunnels in that mound. They rested on the side of Mound

Salla to dry and prepare to learn to live on top of the earth. Mound Salla is a very, very sacred place to some tribe members."

"Is that what Frank Hafner is really looking for—access to some tunnels?" As crazy as it sounded, it had the ring of truth to it. "To what end?"

Coleman didn't say anything, and this time he didn't break his gaze. "I don't know."

"Why doesn't Frank just say that?" I was puzzled. People were dead, lives were ruined. "What does he believe he'll find there?"

"I suspect it has more to do with Frank's fear of other archeologists trying to horn in on the dig."

Per usual, it all boiled down to ego and greed. The knock at the front door startled all of us. I jumped up and hurried to open the door and found myself face-to-face with Frank Hafner. "Dr. Hafner, can I help you?"

"Coleman invited me over. He said you were in a confab about the case and I want to participate." He leaned closer to me. "I want to spend some time with you, Sarah Booth. I think we have a lot in common."

In the parlor doorway, Coleman cleared his throat. "Frank, you can't be privy to this conversation. You know I didn't invite you here. You're the prime suspect in a murder."

"Which I tell you I didn't commit. And I didn't. What about the other dead woman? That private investigator. Why would I kill her? Clearly you can see that I'm not the villain in this story." He smiled at me. "Sarah Booth knows I'm innocent."

"You're my client. I *believe* you're innocent of this crime." It was a statement of true fact. I didn't think Frank was a multiple killer, though he was pretty ego driven. I did have a question for him. "What are you really hunting for in that mound?"

"Evidence of a fascinating culture. Recognition for a lifetime of research and work."

He wasn't going to come clean. "You're hedging the truth, but I don't believe you're a killer. Did Bella Devareaux ever talk to you about why she was interested in Mound Salla?"

"She was working on a case, she said. I never understood why she thought her missing women were linked to a Native burial mound. She was really interested in the procedures, how we took precautions to carefully remove the dirt. What artifacts we'd already found. She was curious about the family that once lived on top of the mound."

"How curious?" I asked.

He waved a hand, dismissing the question. "She was a layperson, not a scientist. She couldn't appreciate the value of pottery or a glimpse into history. She asked about gold or things of value."

"Did she ask about anything specific?"

Hafner hesitated. "Nothing I put any credence in."

"A specific might help us," I said. "Frank, you could be charged with her murder. If you know something, help yourself."

He thought a moment. "She was fixated on something of value from the past. Maybe it wasn't gold or jewels."

"What else could stand the passage of time?" Tinkie asked.

"Some artifacts can be quite valuable." He hesitated again. "Now that you mention it, her curiosity was out of the ordinary."

And that helped us not at all. "If you think of anything she said that might point us in a direction, please call."

"Oh, I'll call you, Sarah Booth." He grinned at Coleman. "You see, Sheriff Peters, your girl-friend has clearer insight than you do. Sarah Booth is searching for a motive, which is what you should be doing."

I gave Hafner a sidelong glance to see if I could determine what he was up to. Was he messing Coleman around for a purpose, or just for fun?

"Drop it, Frank," Tinkie warned him. "We have a great working relationship with Coleman and you won't impact it. We're not that desperate for a client."

"Ms. Bellcase, your beauty is only exceeded by your brains. I'll heed your warning." He turned to me. "Have dinner with me tonight, Sarah Booth. I don't want to discuss the case or anything to do with the dig. I want to get to know you." He reached and captured my right hand. He looked at it. "You don't wear a ring, so I assume you're free to have dinner with an admirer."

For a split second I considered biting his hand. I hadn't bitten anyone since second grade, when June Caruthers stuck a stick in the spokes of my bicycle and made me wreck. "Actually, I'm not free. Coleman and I have plans."

"Such a pity," Frank said. "Perhaps tomorrow night?"

"I'm trying to prove your innocence, Frank. I believe that should be my priority, not playing at date night."

"Of course." He kissed my wrist in a gesture so smooth I didn't even have time to stop him. "I'll postpone my desire to get to know you until the shadow of suspicion has been removed. Then, Sheriff, may the best man win."

"Where's Delane tonight?" I reminded him that I knew he was sleeping with his student.

"Delane's off with that Memphis reporter. She won't miss me."

"Put a sock in it, Frank," Tinkie said.

Frank turned to Coleman. "Sheriff, Ms. Bell-case, have a good evening. I'll be in touch, Sarah Booth." He walked out the front door and Coleman closed it.

"What the hell was that?" Coleman asked.

"A man with a death wish," Tinkie said. "He's either stupid, smitten, or playing an angle. Either way, he's walking a dangerous line."

17

Tinkie left to meet up with Oscar. They were due at The Club for a social event, so they didn't take me up on my offer of a libation. Coleman and I were left to our own devices. While that tickled my fancy, I also had more questions.

We hadn't watched the news in several days, so we settled in the den on the big, soft sofa. Even with the two of us stretched out together, there was still room for Sweetie Pie. Pluto settled on the top of the back cushion. It was a cozy family setting, and one that touched my heart with a wild joy. Slowly, day by day, Coleman and I were stitching together those rare moments of simple family experience. Sipping a drink as I reclined against him wouldn't be what another person would call earth shattering or spectacular, except that it was. To me. It was that shared intimacy mixed with complete ease in each other's company. It was coming home.

Coleman turned the TV to the local Memphis station—he liked to switch back and forth between Memphis and Jackson to keep up with what was happening in the state and region. Cece was our source of local news—our missing local source. Where in the heck was she?

Just as I was about to speak, the newscast switched over to a live feed of the real Cissy Hartley in front of the Prince Albert. She was a tall brunette who topped the ratings in the regional TV news market. Her light dusting of freckles and dimples were a sure-fire combo with her sharp questions and willingness to back an interviewee into a corner. The camera adored her.

The two Sunflower County murders was the top story. "Sunflower County authorities are working to connect two brutal murders at Mound Salla with an unconfirmed report of three missing women across the Mississippi River in Avoyelles Parish. Authorities believe a killer has been on a spree for the past ten months—the victims all young women." Cissy went into all the gory details of the two real murders and a lot of supposition on the missing women across the river. It was enough to scare the pants off everyone in Sunflower County. She had more details than Coleman had released to anyone, and she played them for all the sensationalism she could.

"How did a Memphis television reporter get hold of that information about the Louisiana missing women, who we don't know are truly missing?" Coleman didn't bother to hide his aggravation.

"Bella Devareaux had Cissy Hartley's press

identification. It would seem that Cissy was helping the private eye gain access to the dig. And Cece had Hartley's business card in her pocket. Tinkie and I called Cissy and got nothing."

"I need to talk to Delane Goggans." Coleman was a coiled spring, ready for action. "Frank said she was talking with Hartley. She's been avoiding my deputies."

"Let me call her." I dialed as I talked. The phone rang several times and then went to voice mail.

"This isn't good," Coleman said. "If she's the one feeding this information to reporters, she needs to stop. She's going to panic folks."

I didn't disagree, but I was snug and comfortable and exhausted. "I'll track her down tomorrow and talk to her. It's late. Let's worry about this tomorrow."

"You got it, Miss Scarlett." He'd just pulled me into his arms when his cell phone pinged. He read the text and grinned. "The Washington County sheriff just confirmed there's a vehicle at the Winterville site. A blue SUV. That's what Peter drives. It would seem Cece and Peter are there."

"Do you know why Cece would be at another burial site in another county?"

"Cece has great instincts as a journalist."

He wasn't going to evade me that easily. "So what lead does Cece have?"

"You'll have to ask her." I felt his rib cage stiffen slightly, and I grinned. Coleman didn't have many tells, but this was one. He was dodging around the truth. When he did that, his torso tightened. I was anxious to know what Cece was up to, but the fact that she was found had lightened a considerable load of worry.

"Oh, I think I'm asking you. You might as well tell. You know I'll figure out a way to get the information. If you didn't know what she was looking for, you'd be out there right now bringing her home."

He had the grace not to deny that. "When I was over in Louisiana, I found out that Bella Devareaux had a lead about the Winterville Mound. The Avoyelles Parish sheriff had her notes when I stopped by. He found them on the foyer table in her home. She'd marked a date to visit Mound Salla, and then she meant to go on to Winterville. There was no indication why."

"And you think Cece knew this?"

"I think Peter did. It's just too convenient that he and Devareaux are basically from the same place."

I nodded slowly. "There's a connection between the killer and the Indian mounds and I mean other than the obvious location for a body dump." My chest felt tight now. If this killer had no connection to the archeological dig but was acting on some deeper, darker impulse involving ritual killing, he would be much harder to catch. Coleman didn't believe there were three additional victims, but he knew for a fact he had two. And no one in custody. The killer was smart.

"How could Dr. Sandra Wells and Bella Devareaux and three women be connected? It just doesn't add up."

"You're tracking my line of thinking exactly," Coleman said. "I believe Dr. Wells and Bella Devareaux were murdered by the same person because of the work at Mound Salla. I just don't have a clue why. If my hypothesis is right, the story about the missing women was a smoke screen to scare the folks at the dig site. Someone—the killer, perhaps—wanted to be at that dig when no one else was there. Scaring people with talk about curses, ghosts, and missing women—that was the aim of our dead private investigator. The Avoyelles Parish sheriff agrees with this."

"But Bella Devareaux is dead. Do you think Bella was just in the wrong place at the wrong time?"

"I don't know. Maybe she saw something. She was definitely looking into the Native American burial mounds. She's connected to that. The sheriff sent a copy of Bella's notebook to Budgie and he's been working on what looks to me like meaningless squiggles. We thought at first it might be written in the Tunica language, but that's been dead for a long time. Budgie couldn't find any written history of the language, so we can't be sure if that's what Devareaux was doing. Keep in mind that she's pretty much a newcomer to the Marksville area and she wasn't part of the Tunica tribe. I think Bella's notes were meant to be found. I'm basing my conclusion on what was in the notebook and how it was left right on a table by her door. It seems like a pretty big coincidence," Coleman said.

"You think someone planted that notebook for the sheriff to find?"

"I do."

"And you think Cece and Peter took off based on that information to find out what Bella Devareaux was investigating at Winterville?"

He finished his drink before he answered. "I do. How would you like to take a ride out to the Winterville Mound tonight? Maybe we can find a hint of what those two are investigating."

"I'm game." My body begged to stay home, on the sofa, in front of the crackling fire, but despite Coleman's logical reassurances, I needed to be sure my friend was safe. There were dangerous people on the loose, whether it was a killer of five or two. "Who do you think was taking a potshot at me and Tinkie today?"

"Not the killer, or you'd be dead. I think it was one of the students or Frank Hafner himself. Someone who was looking for something at that dig site or intending to sabotage the equipment and didn't want to be discovered. They were running you and Tinkie off."

And they'd been successful. Drat it. "Any clue who it might be?"

"I plan on doing some interviews tomorrow. I'm hoping Doc will have some information for me on the autopsies. Dr. Wells' family has asked that her body be shipped back to Michigan. Hafner has been asked to deliver the eulogy. Delane wasn't lying about that." He shook his head. "I don't have enough to keep him here."

"What do you really think is going on?" I asked Coleman.

"I wish I could say for certain. There's something about that dig that's worth a whole lot to someone. And I don't believe it's academic fame or a television show for the killer."

I thought of the people who would gain or lose—Peter, Frank, Delane, Elton Cade, and the other investors. "Coleman, I've talked to Elton and Lolly Cade. Elton seems very open and he has a lot of money tied up in this dig. He had an affair with Sandra. Seems like everyone connected with the dig has at one time or another." I waved that away. "What about Sandra's investors? Have you interviewed them? Or Elton?"

"I've known Elton most of my life, and I did a formal interview with him. As you said, he confessed to an affair with Dr. Wells. He didn't seem to know anything about the dig for a man who put up a lot of money to make it happen. He said it was a childhood interest." Coleman eased to the edge of the sofa, unsettling me from my comfortable perch.

"And Dr. Wells' investors?"

"Henrik Anderson is her primary backer, but he's in Amsterdam. This is business for him— nothing personal. I've spoken with him several times, he seems absolutely legitimate in his financial dealings and in his desire to participate in unearthing important historical facts. Nothing more."

"You sound pretty certain he's not involved in murder," I commented.

"Anytime there's a lot of money on the line, I'm never certain of a person's innocence. But I don't see how killing Sandra could be of any benefit to him, or to Elton Cade. These murders are simply costing them more money and delaying the work." Coleman stood. He checked his phone, though it hadn't dinged or vibrated. "Peter and Elton have been friends a long time. He might lie to protect Peter, but I can't see him involved deeper than that. Elton has more money than he'll ever spend."

"And his son, Jimmy, is in some kind of genius program for computers and engineering. He's only sixteen and developing games that are internationally popular."

"Takes after his dad," Coleman said. "Elton is a genius, too."

I thought of Jitty and her wish for an heir and sighed. "Lolly was really down in the dumps that Jimmy has left home to attend school. If my parents had lived, I probably wouldn't have gone to New York."

"Sure you would have," Coleman said. "And your folks would have gone up all the time to visit and cheer you on. You were never afraid to dream big, and that's something I love about you." He checked his phone again. Coleman was not an impatient man, but he was concerned about something.

"Let's take that ride to Winterville Mound." It would be better to move, and no matter how I tried to roll over it, I was still worried about my friend. If Cece was still at the burial site in Greenville, Coleman could have the pleasure of watching me kick her butt all over the mound.

"I wish this dig had never come to Sunflower County." Coleman was pensive. "I remember the Bailey family who lived out there. Quiet people. The mother was always in church but never said much of anything. They suffered a lot of tragedy."

"One of the sons killed his father?" I had a vague recollection.

"It was a brother who was murdered by a brother, then the father abandoned them. There were five or six children. I don't remember the details, but when Arbin left, the family was in a bad situation. Martha Bailey worked as a teacher's aide for a while, then I remember she was at the Piggly Wiggly checking groceries. She was always so tired looking, and so quiet."

I didn't remember the family, but that wasn't unusual. I'd gone to school in the city limits. There were smaller community schools scattered around the county. Hilo High School, out near where Elton lived, was closer to Mound Salla than Sunflower County High. Had my parents lived, I would have known more community people because of the work they did. But Aunt Loulane was more retiring, more private. My world was limited. My group of friends all attended Sunflower High. In contrast, Coleman knew everyone. He'd worked on local farms all over the county, rotating from one harvest to the next. Good farmhands always found work. Now, as sheriff, it was his job to know his county.

"Why did Mr. Bailey leave?" I asked.

"Folks always thought he had a girlfriend. That's the typical pattern. Guy has half a dozen kids, then decides settling down to family life isn't his cup of tea."

Coleman disapproved. He didn't have to say it. His tone said it, and I valued him because of it. "And why did one child kill the other?"

"I don't remember," Coleman said. "The Bailey kids were a good bit younger than us, so I didn't know them personally and I was away from Sunflower County. That was the summer I went to work in Texas on that ranch. I had to get away from home myself. Things weren't good with my dad. From the stories I heard, things were much worse in the Bailey house. Arbin, before he left, was a mean drunk. The boys were into all kinds of trouble. It seems Martha and the girl put up with a lot. The stories are that Martha haunts the house. She didn't die on the property, but it's said she came back to guard it." He frowned. "As I recall I heard she'd died in Louisiana. I don't remember the details, but there was the sense that her life ended in that house atop a burial mound. No matter how hard she worked, she couldn't change things for her kids. Now her spirit is trapped in a place she was never happy, or so the stories go."

I'd heard whispered stories about Coleman's abusive father. Not a word ever came from Coleman—he had never been one to talk about his personal business. The rumors were vague. When we had high school gatherings, it was always his grandmother who hosted the groups. We were young and no one ever questioned that arrangement but it came back to me now. "You didn't have it easy," I said.

"Neither of us did, but for different reasons."

As soon as I graduated high school, I'd left for college. Coleman had already left two years before to work on a cattle ranch in west Texas. We'd each left Sunflower County as a solution, and yet we'd both come back. The Baileys hadn't been as lucky. They hadn't been able to escape. The kids had eventually scattered, one by one, at least one in a trip to the state prison. I felt a pang for Martha Bailey, who'd worked herself into an early grave. "No wonder folks thought the old Bailey house was haunted."

"It was an old home, built back before the Civil War. As you know from caring for Dahlia House, it takes a lot of money to keep a house up. Arbin Bailey had let things slide for a long time. After he left, things just got worse and worse. Back then folks were too prideful to ask for help, and Martha Bailey worked two and three jobs. That left the kids alone. I think one of the girls went on to become a photographer, and one boy is a dentist." He shook his head. "They came up hard, and everything they got they earned. I don't think any of them have ever returned to Sunflower County."

It was time to change the subject. This talk was depressing both of us. So many people suffered hardship, and at the point in time we were discussing, I lived in a kind of bubble of bliss. I'd suffered loss, but I was never abused or hungry or in any way in danger. It wasn't fair, but so

244

much in life didn't seem to derive from justice or fairness.

"How about I put on a quick pot of coffee and fill a thermos and you warm up the truck?" I was definitely getting the best end of this bargain.

"You got it." Coleman kissed my cheek and headed out the front door.

18

In the kitchen I set up the coffeepot in record time. When it was brewing away, I got the thermos from beneath the sink and rinsed it out.

"History is tricky, fair lady. Facts and truth are distorted."

Although I'd become accustomed, most of the time, to Jitty's theatrical appearances—and vanishings—I still jumped. When I faced her, I saw a handsome Native woman in what looked like Victorian garb. The frilled collar circled her neck like some kind of mini tutu. Her hair was piled high and topped with a clever little black hat. I had no idea who this woman was, though, based on her skin and bone structure, I knew she was of Native heritage.

"Rebecca Rolfe," she said as she dropped a curtsey.

"Sarah Booth Delaney." I could have smacked myself in the forehead. Of course she knew who I was. She was in my home.

"May I consider you an ally?" she asked.

I saw then the loneliness and longing in her face. She was not old, but circumstances had aged her. "Of course."

"You don't know my name, but you know my story. At least you know a part of it."

My memory banks were drawing a big zero. I didn't know this woman. All I knew was that she came from a time when women were forced to wear awful clothing. I could imagine the corset that was squeezing the air from her lungs. "Could you refresh me?"

She smiled. "When the Pilgrims came to my country, I befriended a young Captain John Smith. It's said I prevented Powhatan, a great chief and my father, from killing the captain."

I knew her then—or I knew bits about her past history. Pocahontas, known to be an Indian princess who put herself between John Smith's head and Powhatan's tomahawk.

"Yes, that's the legend." She'd read my thoughts as Jitty could so easily do. She smiled and the years fell away. "It makes a good story, doesn't it?"

"I loved the story of Pocahontas. I wanted to be her when I was a young girl."

"The brave young woman who risked all for an English captive."

I nodded. "For the man she loved."

The smile slipped away. "Perhaps to my people I was a traitor."

Those words stopped me in my tracks. The beautiful fantasy crumbled to dust. I'd been so indoctrinated into the history of the white

248

man—and how all events were told from that perspective—that I hadn't even considered the tragic consequences of the Native American's friendliness to the first white invaders. I swallowed hard. "Why are you dressed like that? Like an Englishwoman?"

"I died in England. After I was taken prisoner and converted to Christianity, my name was changed to Rebecca. I was married to a man, John Rolfe, a pious farmer who meant to save my soul from savagery."

"Did it work?" I had to ask, though I knew it was probably not polite.

"The legends never say, do they?"

I hadn't missed the phrasing of her words "I was married." A far different statement from "I married." The first implied that she was entered into a marriage, perhaps not of her own will. The second, to me, indicated free will. This was a part of history I didn't have an inkling about.

"Did you want to marry?"

"The wants of women were of no consequence in my time. The wants of an Indian woman, even less so."

I wanted to ask if she had any happiness, but I didn't think I could stand to hear the answer. "Why were you in England?"

"I was invited to Whitehall, where I was well received. I could read the Bible and discuss

Scripture; the tamed savage turned into the proper wife."

I wanted to tell her how sorry I was for the course her life had taken, but Pocahontas was not a woman who accepted sympathy. "Did you ever return to America?" I couldn't imagine her choosing to remain in England wearing a getup like the one she had on.

"On the journey home, I became very sick. The ship docked to provide medical care, but I was too weak to recover and died in a foreign land."

Tears stung my eyes but I blinked them back. I would not insult her with my emotions when she was so carefully in charge of her own. "What are you here to teach me?" I asked.

"The only lessons worth learning are those you pick and learn for yourself."

She sounded a lot like Jitty—and Aunt Loulane. In fact, except for the very first things she'd said, she did sound a whole lot like a combination of those two women.

"Jitty!" I needed to see my haint. Pocahontas had left me even more depressed than when I'd been talking to Coleman.

The beautiful woman began to morph. The first thing to go was that wretched collar and stupid hat. In three seconds, Jitty stood before me wearing a sexy Indian maiden Halloween costume. It was scandalous and very inappropriate but a great improvement over Pocahontas'

European garb. "You're going to catch your death of cold running around in that outfit that barely covers possible," I groused.

She set the Native American flutes going in the background. "You'd better heed the words of a Native princess."

"Which words? She said a lot about many things. Betrayal, regret, bad impulse control. What is it I'm supposed to snap on?"

"It's your lesson, Sarah Booth, and you're not a dummy. You'll figure it out."

Outside the house I heard the truck horn toot. Coleman was ready to go. I looked at the coffeepot, which gave a final gasp and hiss. My whole encounter with Pocahontas had taken less time than for my coffee to brew. I poured it into the thermos with the sugar and cream Coleman liked, sealed it up, and took off with Pluto and Sweetie Pie on my heels. It was going to be a cold adventure, that much I knew.

The moon floated high above the treetops as we drove toward the Winterville Mound, and I recalled the words of warning from Buffalo Calf Road Woman and Lozen. The moon wasn't quite full, but it would be the next night or the next. The Crow Moon. Danger to my friends.

I considered telling Coleman, but he had enough worries. He took his duty to protect every single citizen of Sunflower County seriously.

251

Sandra Wells and Bella Devareaux weren't citizens of Sunflower County, not technically. That didn't matter. All who stepped foot in the county became Coleman's wards. Two women had come into his domain thinking to work—and now they were dead. That was unacceptable.

"I'm going to call Cece again," I said.

"Give it your best shot." Coleman kept his focus on the road. It was a cold night, but dry, and the road conditions were excellent. As we cut through the fields—newly planted with only the first sprouting of green—I leaned against his side as he put an arm around me. High school. He'd kept his first pickup truck with a bench seat and it ran great. It also had the advantage of allowing a bit of a snuggle on a cold winter's eve.

I dialed Cece's number and the phone rang six times before it went to voice mail. I didn't bother leaving another message. I'd left half a dozen; some begging and pleading and others threatening.

We rode in silence, enjoying the moonlight, the motion of the vehicle on the road, the sense of being isolated from everyone and everything in the vastness of the Delta. I tried to let go of the puzzle of Cece's behavior and allow my subconscious to come up with some answers, but every time I relaxed, I came back to the problem with a nagging sense of anxiety. My friend was AWOL. The visitations from the Native

American women with their warnings had worked effectively—I was on high alert and there was little I could do to quit worrying.

We arrived at the Winterville Mound, and I was surprised to see two cars parked at the base. One had a Louisiana license plate—obviously Peter Deerstalker's SUV. The other was a tricked-out Lexus with Sunflower County plates.

Coleman was taking no risks. He cut the lights on the truck, pulled about fifty yards closer to the mound, and called in the license plate to the sheriff's office. His answer came quickly.

"Belongs to Elton Cade," Budgie said. "What's up?"

"I'm not certain." Coleman reached across me and got his gun from the glove box of the truck. "Budgie, you might give the Washington County sheriff's office a call and let them know I may need backup."

Coleman's words chilled me but I said nothing and waited for him to make the first move. If I opened the truck door, I might illuminate us. If a shooter was waiting, he'd have an easy target.

Coleman clicked off the dome light in the truck and motioned for me to slip out. I did so and took cover, waiting for him to join me. "You should stay here," he said. "I need to check out what's happening on top of the mound. Make sure Cece and Peter are okay."

Or find out that Peter was doing something

nefarious to my friend. "I'm in as much danger here as with you."

"But if you stay here, you have access to the radio."

He was right about that. "What if this is a trap? You might need my help."

Coleman's focus was on top of the mound. We couldn't see anything, but he finally said, "Okay, just stay behind me. Do whatever I do."

"Okay."

He started toward the mound at a sprint, and I was on him like a second skin. A filmy cloud slipped across the moon and gave us the best cover we could hope for as we started up the incline. My muscles screamed, but I pressed forward, ignoring them. Coleman moved with the grace of a jungle cat, and I did my best to emulate him as I followed close behind. What would we find at the top? I carried a burden of dread. I should have started looking for Cece hours ago instead of going home. I should have kept calling.

My regrets were futile and nothing I could have done would change the situation in front of us. Cece wouldn't have answered her phone no matter how many times I called.

We made it to the top of the incline and I grabbed Coleman's ankle, holding him in place while I crawled up beside him. I was afraid for him to stick his head up—he might get shot. I lifted my hand up, gritting my teeth as I waited for the sound of a gunshot.

Nothing happened. And there was no blast.

"What the hell is going on?" I whispered to Coleman. "If they're here, what are they doing?"

"I don't know." Coleman propelled himself up to the top and froze on his hands and knees. I settled beside him, feeling completely exposed and like someone had eyes on me. I was a sitting duck, as was Coleman.

Like linked shadows, we moved across the mound to what looked like a historical marker. Coleman had a penlight flashlight and turned it on. A small pool of blood had collected around the marker and was coagulating.

"Damn."

"We're going to have to use some light," Coleman said. "If someone is injured up here, we have to find them. That's not a serious amount of blood but it signifies an injury."

"We'll be sitting ducks."

"Go back to the truck. Radio Budgie to call the Washington County sheriff and get an EMT team here."

"What about Doc?"

"It's not my county, Sarah Booth. We have to use whoever they send. Now make that call and wait at the truck. I have to know you're out of harm's way if I need to take a shot."

"But—"

"No buts, Sarah Booth. Promise me."

I touched his arm. "Be careful." I had sworn to myself I would not argue with Coleman when we were in a tight place. He was in charge. I followed his orders. I slipped backward, heading down to do as he bade. We had to get backup and help. I listened carefully as I traversed the side of the mound, but all I could hear was my heart pounding in my ears.

At the truck I put the radio call through to DeWayne, who assured me he'd already called the EMTs and the local sheriff. Help would be there fast. He was also coming, in case Coleman needed him. I felt some relief that the cavalry was on the way, but not knowing what Coleman might be confronting had me so wired I felt like I would explode. My inclination was to rush back to the top, but Coleman had urged me to stay at the truck so he could work without worrying about me. If I ignored his wishes, I could put him in even more danger.

I dialed Cece one more time. The rush of anger I felt was unreasonable, but if only Cece had called us back. If only she'd included us in her plans so we could have been better prepared. If only I knew she was okay so I didn't have that worry piled on top of everything else.

The phone began to ring, and I froze. Somewhere off in the darkness Cece's distinctive cell phone ring broke the night. "Pussycat Moan" was a blues song she loved and she'd had a custom ringtone made. I knew it was her phone, and it rang and rang. I hung up, afraid of drawing attention to my location.

Going by auditory memory, I moved away from the truck, looking for Cece's phone. Coleman and I had driven to the mound site in the darkness. What outbuildings, hideaways, clumps of shrubs that might be near, I couldn't say. I thought of turning on the truck headlights, but we'd rolled up to the location without them because of the risk. I'd have to look for the phone by feel—a task that seemed impossible. Lucky me, I had time on my hands to crawl around searching.

I crept around the truck in the direction I thought the phone ring had come from. Moving on my hands and knees, feeling the ground in front of me, I was determined. If I found the phone, it might yield some clue as to Cece's whereabouts. Because she wasn't sitting around in the dark on top of the mound—not without her phone. Cece's addiction to her phone was legendary. And I could not think that she might be incapacitated, or worse.

When I'd covered the area where I thought her phone might be, I dialed once more.

About twenty feet to my left, I heard it and saw the screen light. I hung up and scuttled over toward it. I had at least accomplished something that would help when the law arrived with searchlights and more artillery. Lots of artillery, I hoped. Maybe a stinger or two.

Patting the ground, I inched along. The location of her phone explained a lot. Cece couldn't return calls without her phone. She may have dropped it accidentally while getting into a vehicle, but I had a sense the location of the phone was a lot more sinister. Moving slowly and methodically, I searched. At last, just as my knee hit a sharp rock that made me flinch, my fingers found the phone. I had it.

Success was indeed sweet. I started to pick it up.

The shot that rang out was like a Taser to the base of my spine. Automatically, I dropped the phone and rolled. Another shot came and clods of dirt exploded in front of the phone. Even as I rolled for my life, I realized someone on top of the mound had a nightscope. And they had zeroed it in on me or that damn phone.

I back crawled as fast as I could until I was twenty feet away. Then I stood and ran back to the truck, hiding behind it.

Another shot rang out and pinged into the side of Coleman's truck. "Damn." I ducked lower.

"Hands up!" Coleman's voice carried to me.

The response was another gunshot—and then silence.

19

It took all of my effort not to call out to Coleman. Instead, I dialed Doc. "You have to come," I told him. I was barely able to control my tears. "I think Coleman's been shot."

"What?" Doc sounded like he'd been asleep. "Can't you tell if he's shot?"

"No, I can't. He's at the top of Winterville Mound and I'm down at his truck. But if he hasn't been shot, someone else has. I don't trust anyone but you." I forced my voice to remain calm, but I was terrified. The image of Buffalo Calf Road Woman came back to me. I'd been warned. It was not quite the full moon, not yet, but it was close enough. "Just come, Doc. Come right now. Please." I opened Coleman's glove box and found the extra gun he always carried. I checked to be sure the magazine was loaded and stuck it in my waistband.

"Stay at the truck," Doc told me. "Stay safe. That's the best thing you can do for Coleman. I'm on my way, Sarah Booth."

I hung up and strained to hear anything from the top of the mound. Where in the hell were Cece, Peter, and Elton Cade? Where was Coleman?

Was he injured at the top of the mound? If he wasn't hurt, he would have found a way to let me know. I couldn't stand it any longer.

"Coleman!" I called as I ran to the base of the mound. "Coleman!"

"Stay back! Don't come any closer."

I could tell by the strain in his voice that he was hurt. "How bad is it?"

"Don't come up here. He's using me for bait."

"I'll stay down here. Help should be here any minute. I called the local sheriff's office and your deputies. They're calling the state troopers, and the state bureau of investigation is sending a team." I was playing to the shooter, hoping to flush him out—or, even better, to make him run away. "This place is going to be crawling with cops in another five minutes." Even as I spoke I was climbing to the top of the mound. Bait be damned. Coleman was hit. There was no way I was going to hide behind a truck.

I scaled the mound, moving steadily to the offside in the hope I could come up behind the shooter. It was a stupid plan. I knew it, but there wasn't a better option. In that strange and eerie calm that comes when a body is flooded with adrenaline, I was up the mound like some kind of supersonic spider. I'd edged to the north side, and I gained the plateau and began moving toward the last place I'd seen Coleman.

At times, the moon slipped free of clouds and

gave good light. That was when I froze and hugged the grass. I could see, but so could the shooter. I waited for those moments of darkness when moving was difficult, but less dangerous.

Creeping forward in one of the dark pauses, my foot struck something solid and I went down hard. Right on top of a human body. One that moaned pitifully. "Help me," a male voice said. It wasn't Coleman, but it was someone hurt.

"Peter?" I asked.

"It's Elton. I've been injured."

"Were you shot?" In the darkness it was impossible to see how badly he was wounded. My hands searched his body, and I found sticky blood at his head and all down his neck and shoulder.

"No, someone hit me with something hard. I lost consciousness."

"Stay still, help is on the way. Just don't move." I didn't want to leave Elton, but I had to find Coleman. "Have you seen the sheriff?" I asked.

"No, I didn't see much of anything."

"What happened?"

"Someone called me and told me Peter was here and in danger. I saw his vehicle. When I called out to him, he didn't answer, so I climbed the mound. I was walking across it to look for Peter when I was struck from behind. I don't even know where my attacker came from." The clouds shifted, revealing a large rock covered in what looked like blood.

"Coleman's been hit." I started to edge away from him but he grabbed my jacket.

"I want to help. What can I do?"

I appreciated his offer, but he could have a concussion or worse. "Just stay put. I'll be back."

Elton clutched my jacket again. "Stay here, Sarah Booth. It's dangerous. Give me a minute and I'll get on my feet."

"The best thing you can do is stay here. I'll be okay." It wasn't lost on me that I was giving the very advice I wouldn't take. I slipped out of his grasp. The moon came on bright and so close to being full, I couldn't be certain that it wasn't. The Crow Moon. An orb of loss and separation. About a hundred yards to my left, I saw a figure on the ground. The silvery light glinted on pale hair. It was Coleman. He'd been hit and he was down. In all of the years I'd known Coleman Peters, I'd never seen him out of control of his physical body. Terror touched me and I ran toward him, heedless of danger or anything except Coleman's prostrate body.

I skidded to a stop and knelt beside him, feeling for a pulse, for reassurance that he was not dead.

"Where are you hit?"

"Shoulder. It's a flesh wound. Get out of here."

I had a reputation for being hardheaded, and now I would employ it. "I'll leave—but only with you. Can you walk? Elton is up here, too. He was struck in the head with something."

Coleman took my offered hand and it took everything I had to get him to his feet. Once upright, though, he seemed able to walk. "Who the hell was shooting?" he asked.

"I don't know. I didn't see anyone, except Elton."

"Get me to the lip of the mound and then get Elton. We'll all go together."

Even injured, Coleman wasn't about to shirk his duties. He wouldn't rest until Elton Cade was safe. "I'll get him. He can walk. Did you find Cece?" I held back that I'd found her phone.

"No. I didn't see anyone. I never saw the shooter, either. I can't figure what he was hiding behind. You'd think he was a ghost or something."

My body shivered as if a cold wind had blown over me. I told him about Cece's phone as I helped him walk back the way I'd come. I wanted him to focus on something other than the effort it took to walk. If he collapsed, I might not be able to get him to his feet again.

Someone approached, and I felt Coleman reach for his pistol. When Elton Cade stumbled out of the darkness, almost ramming into Coleman, I let my breath out. "Help me with Coleman, please."

Cade obliged and put Coleman's uninjured arm around his shoulders. "It's going to be tricky going down, but you can do it. Did either of you see Peter? He asked me to meet him here. I'm concerned."

"We have reason to believe he's with Cece Falcon," I told him. "Did you see her?"

"No one. Like I told you, I'd just arrived when I was struck from behind. I think I've been unconscious for a while."

We were almost to the lip when I realized Coleman was getting weaker and weaker. He had a wound and was likely losing blood. The best thing we could do was get him still and put a pressure bandage on the wound. If we stopped, though, we wouldn't get Coleman back on his feet.

"If we can just start down, you can lay me on the side of the incline. I'll be fine until my deputies get here."

"And Doc. I couldn't help myself. I called him when I heard you get hit. They can use whatever coroner they want to use, but I have to have the best doctor for you."

"Let's get this over with," Elton said. "One, two, three . . ." and we set about inching our way down the steep slope. There were no more shots, though I couldn't stop expecting to hear one. Where had the shooter gone? He had to still be in the area unless he'd parked some distance away, on the other side of the mound. That would have been the smart thing to do.

Coleman was panting and sweating in the cold

night. "Let's put him down." I had to check his wound and see how badly he was bleeding. Elton and I eased him to a sitting position and he leaned back in the grass. "I'll live, Sarah Booth."

"You'd better." I found my phone and turned on the flashlight mode. Coleman's thick dark jacket hid the blood, but the moment I opened it up, I saw his shirt was soaked and blood saturated his pants and jacket. He needed medical attention. I took off my jacket and pressed it against the wound in his shoulder. I ignored his groan as I put my weight into it, forcing the blood to stay in him. Willing it to do so. It wasn't a life-threatening wound and, by damn, he wasn't going to die of blood loss.

Elton touched Coleman's face. "Sarah Booth, he's clammy."

"Listen." I heard the sirens. Help was coming at last. "Go down and see if you can't get the paramedics up here fast. And Doc." I wasn't about to leave Coleman and there was no time to waste for them to stumble around looking for us.

"Will do." Elton was gone, and I was left with the man I loved growing weaker and weaker. I put more of my weight on his shoulder and he moaned.

"It's okay, Coleman. Doc is coming. You'll be fine."

"I'll be flatter than a pancake if you don't quit crushing me."

I gave him a kiss on the cheek. "Love your wit. I'm going to jam a pencil in that bullet hole first chance I get just to show you how much I love hearing you holler."

But I was cheered by his attempt at humor. I couldn't see the patrol cars and EMTs but I heard the ambulances then saw the pulses of red and blue lights when they arrived. At last I heard DeWayne and Budgie.

"Here!" I called them over, waving my phone light to guide them. I was very happy they had arrived.

The moon broke free and I saw the rescue party. DeWayne and Budgie were plowing up the incline and right behind them was Doc and paramedics with a stretcher. Coleman would soon be in good hands.

My legs suddenly gave way and I sat down with a huff right beside Coleman.

"You okay?" he asked.

"I am." But I wasn't. I had no power to stand or walk. "Once Doc is here, I'm going up to look for Cece and Peter."

"Let DeWayne and Budgie do that," Coleman said. "I need you to go with me."

"You're sure?" Coleman's request for me to accompany him was either a ploy to keep me safely with him or he actually needed me. I couldn't risk it. I had to do what he asked.

"I'm with you," I said and grasped his hand. I

managed to hold on to it as the paramedics and Doc maneuvered Coleman down the incline on a stretcher. Doc finally moved me aside so he could pack the wound for transport. I darted away from the ambulance to the area where I'd seen Cece's phone. In a moment I had it in my pocket. When I returned to Coleman, they were loading him into the back of the ambulance and he was grousing and insisting that he would sit up. I used two fingers to press him back onto the gurney. "Behave," I whispered.

"Only because you asked so nicely." He wrapped his fingers around mine and held on until the ambulance was headed to Zinnia.

20

Budgie and DeWayne found no trace of Cece and Peter, but they did find a fine hunting rifle with a nightscope on it. The Washington County deputies took it back for processing, which caused DeWayne great consternation. He wanted to analyze the evidence and draw his own conclusions, but we weren't in his jurisdiction. Washington County was calling the shots and there was nothing he could do to change the situation.

Tinkie and Oscar met us at the hospital, and Tinkie lit into Coleman with all of the things he said to us when we'd found danger and injuries. She was also angry with me.

"How does it feel to have the shoe on the other foot?" Doc asked me. "Normally you're the one who needs medical attention and we all have to hold our breath and pray you pull through."

"It's not much fun to be the one worrying," I admitted. "But Coleman is going to be okay, and that's what matters. Right?" I just needed that one little assurance.

"He is." Doc smiled, and years fell away, giving me a glimpse of the man he'd been when he was in his prime. He patted my shoulder. "Stay in the ER waiting room with Tinkie. Soon as he's stitched up you can be with him."

They rolled Coleman into a treatment room and Tinkie came over and sat facing me so that our knees bumped. "What in the hell were you two up to? They just took Elton back to check his skull. What happened?"

I told her what I knew. "I don't think Cece and Peter were there. I don't know where they are. Peter's car is at the mound. There wasn't a trace of either."

"Jaytee is worried sick. I've talked to him twice." Tinkie sighed. "I feel like we let Cece down. She's so competent, and I just figured she was on a hot lead and that it might be slightly outside the law. We should have been looking harder for her."

"My thoughts, too." I took a deep breath. "We have to figure out who was shooting at us and why. And how do Cece and Peter figure into this? Why in the hell would she take off with Peter Deerstalker?" I put my hand in my pocket and felt the extra telephone. Cece's phone. If I could open it, I'd be able to track who she'd talked to, which might give me a lead to where she was.

"We need to find someone who can hack a telephone." I pulled it from my pocket to show Tinkie. "It's Cece's. I recognized the ringtone."

"Hand it over." Tinkie held out her palm. "Now."

"Why?"

"Because you're going to do the right thing and stay with Coleman, and I'm going to get that phone hacked to the point at least we can find out who Cece was talking to and who's been calling her. Looks like someone hit it with something. That could be why she didn't call us."

She was right. I burned to go with her, but Coleman was where I needed to be. "Call me, please."

"Will do. You let me know if Doc releases Coleman. I did ask Oscar to send someone to pick up Coleman's truck. It's parked in the lot here." She tossed me the key.

"You think of everything." I blew her a kiss and pocketed the key. With any luck, I'd soon be driving Coleman to Dahlia House.

Tinkie hadn't been gone three minutes when the ER door burst open and Lolly Cade rushed in, her face drawn in worry. "Where is Elton?" she asked.

"They're checking his head. He's okay, Lolly. This is just a precaution." I felt the need to reassure her.

"What happened?"

I filled her in on what I knew—just the basic facts without any backstory. That was up to Elton.

"Ever since that horrid Wells woman came to Zinnia, there's been nothing but trouble." She sat down in the seat Tinkie had just vacated. "I wish that dig had never come here. Elton was so determined. He'd done so much research and he said—" She looked up, and I thought she was frightened, but when I looked more closely I saw only exhaustion. "I'm sorry. I know there are more important aspects to this than my personal comfort, but it's just been a difficult time."

Knowing Elton had slept with Sandra Wells, I could see how Lolly wasn't the biggest fan of archeological digs. "I wonder if these murders will shut the dig down." It wasn't unheard-of that a sponsor would pull funding if a dig became too controversial or dangerous.

"Maybe they will." She slumped back into the chair. "I just feel so alone."

Tinkie, not me, was the giver of solace and comfort, and she did it with skill and ease. I leaned forward and awkwardly patted her arm. "I understand. Elton really is fine. He'll be out here any minute."

She sighed, but it seemed her burden had only grown heavier. I didn't know what else to say. I changed the subject. "You haven't heard from Peter Deerstalker, have you?"

"I just spoke with him. He said he was on the way here."

"Peter said that?"

My reaction took her aback. "Yes, what's wrong?"

"He's on his way here?" I had to be certain.

"That's what he said. What's wrong?"

I shook my head. "I've been looking for him." No point going into why. "Did he say if he was with someone?"

"No." She stood up. "What's going on here?"

"Talk with Elton. I have to check on my friend." It was an abrupt leave-taking, but I couldn't help it. I hurried down the hall toward the treatment room where Coleman waited. Doc had to be in there. I didn't bother tapping, just went straight in. Right in time to hear Doc's lecture.

"You need to stay here for the night to be sure you don't start bleeding again. We'll give you some blood for a quick replenish. That'll spur your recovery. Then you can go home tomorrow under the care of Sarah Booth." Doc grinned wickedly. "She's in charge of you. If you don't agree to that, you can stay here in the hospital."

"Doc—" Coleman started to protest.

"Push me on this and I'll call an emergency meeting of the board of supervisors. You're the elected sheriff, but they manage your budget. And the county has a certain liability and concern for your health. You need to heal." Doc winked at me. "And here's Zinnia's own Nurse Nightingale. Sarah Booth, you're going to have your hands full."

"Coleman, Doc is right. You won't be any good to anyone if you bleed to death." I did take a tiny bit of satisfaction in saying the same thing to him that everyone said to me when I was injured.

"We'll move him to a private room in about an hour," Doc said. "Sarah Booth, why don't you run home and grab some personal items. I'm sure you'll want to stay with him tonight."

"You bet!" I walked over and leaned down to kiss Coleman on the cheek. "You are in my power. Doc said so," I whispered before I made a swift exit and headed straight to the parking lot to await the arrival of Peter Deerstalker. If he did show up.

Peter arrived by Uber, and I was standing in the dark night against a pine-tree trunk when he got out of the car. I waited for the Uber to leave and watched Peter square his shoulders before I slipped up on him and tapped his arm. He came around with his fists up. He'd been expecting the worst.

"Where's Cece?" I demanded.

He blew out a breath. "I'd like to know the same thing. What happened? I heard Elton and Coleman were injured."

"At Winterville Mound. Where your vehicle is parked."

Peter motioned me into the shadows of the hospital building. He acted as if someone was after him, and I thought that was a good possibility. He was going to tell me why, because somehow my friends and my lover had been caught up in his mess.

"The last time I saw Cece, we were both at the Winterville Mound. I got a tip that there was information there that would lead to the person who killed Sandra Wells. The caller warned me to come alone and not to tell anyone." He glanced around as if he expected a mugger to jump out at us. "As you know, I was supposed to meet Cece at Millie's Café. I got a call from her that she was giving Cooley Marsh a ride to the Budget Inn and to pick her up in the parking lot, which I did. I didn't want her to come with me to Winterville Mound. I didn't really have a choice. Your friend is pretty persuasive when she threatens a person."

That sounded exactly like something Cece would do. "So where is she?"

"I left her in my car talking on the phone to someone. I darted up the incline, thinking maybe I could find the information about the killer. You know, the clues the caller said I would find to prove I was innocent." He stopped. "You won't believe this, but I was also afraid it might be a trap. Think what you want, but I didn't want Cece to get hurt so I hurried up the mound while she was busy talking."

He sounded sincere, but then again, he hadn't proven to be reliable. "So where is she?" I said it this time a lot louder and with more emphasis.

"I don't know. I searched the top of the mound. I didn't find anyone or anything. No clues. Nothing. When I got back down to the car where I'd left her, Cece was gone. Like vanished. There was no sign of her."

Fear made me more aggressive than normal. "What do you mean? She didn't have a vehicle. Where could she go?"

"She'd vanished into thin air. There wasn't another person around. Elton's SUV was there, but there was no trace of him. I did search every-where. No vehicle, nothing. Cece had been sitting in the passenger seat of my vehicle, talking on the phone, and the next thing I knew, she was just gone."

"If you're jerking me around, Peter, I swear to you—"

"Sarah Booth, Cece believed me when I told her I had nothing to do with Sandra Wells' death and certainly not that other young woman that I didn't even know."

"Bella Devareaux is from Marksville, where the reservation is. You're sure you don't know her?"

"The reservation is tiny. I know all of the native families, but I don't know everyone in the parish by any stretch of the imagination. Bella Devareaux wasn't from Marksville. She'd moved there."

"Bella left a notebook with some strange language in it. It might be the Tunica language."

"It isn't. The Louisiana sheriff showed it to me. I didn't recognize it."

"Did Cece say anything? Anything at all about her plans? If she went to Winterville with you she wouldn't have left without checking out her story. Or I should say she wouldn't voluntarily leave."

"I didn't hurt your friend. I wouldn't. The last time I saw her she was fine."

"Who was she talking to?"

He thought a minute. "On the way over, she did talk to one of the archeology students. Something about a secret organization."

"What secret organization?"

Peter looked even more worried. "She wouldn't say much, only that she believed Bella Devareaux was involved with some other people who had some kind of group desire to disrupt the dig. She said something about tattoos."

"Anything else?"

"Yeah, she was talking to that Memphis TV reporter when I left her. But I didn't hear much of the conversation, certainly not enough to have a clue what they might be up to. That reporter, Hartley, has been hanging out at the dig site and in Zinnia."

"I don't believe in coincidences." I was scared for my friend, and that made me angry.

"Cece believes that I'm innocent. I had no reason to harm Cece and every reason to keep her alive. She was going to help me prove that I hadn't hurt anyone." He leaned closer to me. "I am being framed. I swear to you."

"By whom?" I asked. The prickle of gooseflesh down my spine made me realize that what Peter said could be true. Could. Still, I had to pursue all leads.

"I don't know."

"Where have you been all day?"

"When I realized Cece was gone from the mound and wasn't coming back, I called one of my friends from Marksville. His name is Jonathan Calvarese. He came and picked me up. Check my phone and call him. He'll tell you."

"Why didn't you just drive your car back to town and let us know she was missing? She's been gone hours now and no one knows where she is."

"When Cece left, she took the car keys with her. I thought at first she'd done it to deliberately strand me out there at the mound. I was pretty angry, but now I'm thinking maybe something happened to her. And I didn't rush back to Zinnia to report this because I knew I'd be a suspect and would probably end up in jail where I couldn't help myself at all. Cece told me she had a lead. Because she'd been talking to Cissy Hartley in Memphis, I went there hoping I could find

Cece. Jonathan drove me." He reached into his pocket and pulled out his phone. "See, I called him. Then I called Ms. Hartley, and I called Cece repeatedly. She never picked up."

"She couldn't answer or call you back. I found her phone on the ground."

"I'm sorry," he said. "I really thought she'd pulled a fast one on me. That maybe she had that guy call me about the evidence being hidden at Winterville Mound."

"What guy?"

"I can't be sure who it was. He just said I'd find what I needed at Winterville. So when Cece disappeared, I instantly assumed she'd put someone up to this to get me out of the way. I was pretty upset. It would seem I judged her just the way everyone is judging me."

"Did you talk to Cissy Hartley?"

"I did, briefly. She refused to see me in person and I didn't get much. The only thing interesting she said was that she got an anonymous tip something supernatural was happening at Mound Salla, that the spirits were unhappy because their graves were being disturbed, that something dangerous was walking in the night."

"Cissy Hartley doesn't strike me as someone who would be scared off a story by allusions to unhappy spirits."

"She also said the caller said someone would die."

His words sent a shiver down me. Judging by the staging of the murder scene, it was clear someone had planned Dr. Wells' demise. But hearing that someone knew in advance and had not stopped it made it seem much darker.

21

I warned Peter to check in with Coleman if he knew what was good for him, and he swore he would. He was also surprised that Elton Cade had been injured. I wasn't going to get more out of him grilling him in the hospital parking lot, so I concluded the conversation. He hurried inside the hospital to see about his friend and to sit with Lolly so she wouldn't be alone while she waited for word about her husband.

I stood for a moment in the parking lot, knowing what I had to do but not wanting to leave Sunflower County with Coleman in the hospital. This was the choice I dreaded—duty or the needs of my heart. This was the price of caring I didn't know if I could bear. And yet I had to.

DeWayne had brought Coleman's truck around, and I knew one of the deputies would give Coleman a ride from the hospital, hopefully to my place. I took his truck and headed for Dahlia House to get Sweetie Pie and Pluto. Budgie had picked them up at the mound and brought them home while I rode with Coleman. Now I needed the critters' skill set. In fact, I needed any help I could get.

It was two hours to Memphis, and I'd get there in the wee hours of the morning, a time that could work for me or against me, I didn't know which. Cissy Hartley would never talk to me on the phone—I'd already tried that once—but in person she might not be able to refuse. If she knew where Cece might be, I'd get it out of her. I called Tinkie to tell her what I was doing and check on her work with Cece's phone. I filled her in on Peter and what he said had happened to Cece. "The bottom line is that none of this makes a lick of sense. If Cece is just in Memphis talking to another reporter, why hasn't she called us?" I was agitato by the time I concluded.

"I may have an answer for you," Tinkie said. "Cece did try to contact us. My hacker can't be certain if her phone was damaged before it was thrown out onto the ground, but he discovered a number of text messages to both of us from Cece telling us where she was and urging us to join her at Winterville."

"Damn. I hope she realized the texts weren't going out." I hated the idea that our friend might think we'd been ignoring her requests for help.

"We'll have to ask her when we find her," Tinkie said. "Just promise me you'll stay in touch no matter what. If you go off the radar on me, I'm going to call the FBI, the CIA, the KGB, the NSA—whatever alphabet agency I can think of."

"I'll stay in touch. Just remember, we don't

have the full picture," I conceded. "Something else is going on, and we need to find her." Buffalo Calf Road Woman's warning hung heavily over me. I dreaded the rising of the next moon. While it appeared Cece was the one in danger, it could be Tinkie, too. And/or Coleman. Thank goodness Doc was on my side. He'd figure out a way to keep Coleman in the hospital and out of danger.

"I have a list of calls Cece made," Tinkie said. "The last person she talked to was Cissy Hartley in Memphis."

It was a confirmation of my plan. "All roads lead to Memphis," I told my partner. "I'm headed there now. Could you track down Kawania and find out what she knows about the tattoos on Sandra Wells and Bella Devareaux? That's the connection there. And Sister Grace." Somehow the psychic played into this situation. I just didn't know how.

"Sarah Booth, shouldn't you wait for someone to be with you?"

"It's more important that you run down any additional leads on Cece's phone. I have Sweetie Pie and Pluto. And it's my friends who are in danger, not me."

"What?" Tinkie was rightfully confused.

"I'll explain when I get back from Memphis. If you get something off that phone, call me."

"You do the same," Tinkie said before she hung up.

I pulled out on the highway and headed north. The flat Delta spread out before me, black velvet with pinpricks of starry light that honored the vastness of the sky. High above floated the moon. It wasn't full. And Coleman was okay. But Cece was still missing. I felt like a ticking time bomb was in the sky. I had to find Cece before the Crow Moon rose. And I didn't have a moment to spare.

When I was near Memphis I called Doc to check on Coleman. Yes, I was a coward. Coleman would not approve of me heading off alone. Yes, I had Sweetie Pie and Pluto, but he would have preferred I took DeWayne or Budgie or Tinkie. But both deputies were needed on the job looking for Cece, in case my lead was wrong and she was in the Delta. I could handle one television reporter by myself, even if she did have a reputation for being a land shark—which actually gave me a brilliant idea. Cissy had the reputation for being a ruthless competitor in the mid-market of Memphis television. It was no secret she aspired to a national anchor job on CNN or one of the networks. She came on all sweet and nice, drawing her interview subject into a false sense of safety. Then she struck. She bit a person's head off and crunched it while grinning into the TV camera.

Doc assured me that Coleman was fine. It was a flesh wound and Coleman was sedated and resting. "He'll be awake by seven and fit to be tied, Sarah Booth. I recommend you return before then."

"I promise I'll be careful," I told Doc. "I have to search for Cece."

"I understand, but Coleman isn't going to want to sit this out. If he must participate, which I don't recommend, at least he can do so in your care. You'll bop him on the head if you have to."

It was true. I would not hold back with a smack if I thought it was necessary. "I'll be back before seven. I just need to talk to Cissy Hartley and I need to do it when she can't escape me."

"How are you going to find her? She won't be at the TV station and they certainly won't give out her home address, no matter how nicely you ask."

Doc was right about that, but I had a backup plan. And it involved my lack of talent and Sweetie Pie's solo ability to carry an act.

"Doc, I need a big favor. You can't release Coleman tomorrow until I'm back in town. Whatever it takes, you have to keep him at the hospital."

"Sarah Booth, I don't think that's going to be an option. He'll sign himself out. You know if you two ever have kids, you might produce an advancement in the evolution of mankind. Heads impervious to reason or injury."

"Thanks, Doc. That makes my ovaries do flips." I couldn't help the sarcasm. "I'm serious.

He can't get out in the field tomorrow. He can't."

"Should I ask why?"

"I'd tell you but you'd call it woo-woo and laugh, so no, you shouldn't even ask. Just trust me. Coleman is in danger. Keep him safe, please. It's only one more day."

"I'll do my best, but I make no promises."

When I pulled into the TV station parking lot, I snapped a leash on Sweetie Pie and gave her instructions for her part. I regretted that I hadn't thought of a costume change, but it was too late now. Besides, I was tired. Really tired. My body hurt from the consistent abuse of pushing it up and down the steep inclines of those Indian mounds. I hadn't slept in what felt like a week. When I had caught a nap, it had been plagued with worry. And I was hungry.

"Let's do this, Sweetie Pie." I didn't have a costume, but I could wing it with a country twang.

I warned Pluto to stay in the car, which was about like pissing into the wind. He was catting my footsteps by the time I reached the locked entrance. Gone were the days when anyone could walk into any newsroom with a hot tip. Now the locked door would open only if someone rang me in. I pushed the bell. "Singing telegram for Cissy Hartley," I said.

"She's not here. Do you know what time it is?

No one sends a singing telegram at this time of night."

"Listen, I'm really late. My car broke down, and I had to pick up the singing dog, and—" I burst into tears. "I'm going to be fired and my grandmother is really sick and if I don't make some money, she won't be able to get her medicine." I didn't feel even a wriggle of remorse for lying. And I had to admit, I was selling it.

"Listen, lady, I'm sorry—"

I gave Sweetie Pie her cue. I began to sing the Patsy Cline classic "Crazy." Sweetie Pie howled along as if she'd gone over the edge for love, too.

"Lady! Lady," the guy on the intercom kept trying to interrupt.

I sang with my whole heart—and the voice of a dying toad. Singing was never one of my talents, and butchering the Patsy Cline song in this manner might be considered a musical capital offense. I would pay for my crimes later. I had to get Cissy's address from this man even if I had to torture it out of him.

"Please! Please!" the guy kept saying. "Please, make it stop. Just make it stop! I'll do anything you say."

"Let me in," I said, thinking of some of the more shadowy creatures that might demand entrance. He was lucky it was only one Mississippi gal, her hound, and her cat.

The buzzer sounded and the door unlocked. The critters and I spread into the building like a dark plague. We found the elevator and the production room in short order. Now I had to be my most convincing.

The man who met me at the door to the third floor was older. He had crow's-feet around his eyes and he shook his head and blocked the entrance with his body. "Lady, I don't know who hired you to sing telegrams, but they are either sadists or deaf. I don't mean to be cruel, but you should find another line of work right away." He finally noticed Pluto. "What does the cat do?" He couldn't help his curiosity.

"We'll show you!" It was the opening I craved.

"No, please, no! Don't sing again."

I went into the Shelley West–David Frizzell duet "You're the Reason God Made Oklahoma." I sang the David part and Sweetie filled in for Shelley. When she hit the part about the Santa Monica Freeway, her howl was so piercing I thought my eardrums might rupture.

The man dropped to his knees. "What do you want? Just name it. Make it stop and I'll give you whatever you want."

"I *have* to sing to Cissy Hartley so I don't lose my job. Please, just call her and ask if we can stop by. Or even if I can sing over the phone—I'll leave the sheet here for her to sign. Or she can meet us at the road. I don't have to go inside her house. I know it's really late, but I swear I'll be fired and I can't let that happen. My granny—" I sobbed brokenly again.

"Okay! Okay." He was gasping for air and holding his ears. Sweetie waited until he dropped his hands and then gave it one more shrill howl. He ran into the production booth and I could see him on the phone.

After a quick conversation, he opened the door. "Who sent the singing telegram?" he asked.

"I can't say until I deliver it in person. It's part of my job description. I'm sorry. He did mention something about an opening in the D.C. newsroom for CBS."

He ducked back into the room but before the door closed I heard him saying, "Get your hand camera and record this. We might be able to sell it to the military as a weapon."

Clever man. I petted Sweetie Pie and praised her. She loved to sing, too. It was a shame no one appreciated either of us. When the guy came back to us, a piece of paper in hand, I grasped his hand and shook it hard. "Thank you. Thank you. I'm sorry, I didn't catch your name."

"Completely unnecessary that you ever know my name," he said. He held out the paper with Cissy Hartley's address. "She said she would be expecting you."

"Thanks!" I looked at the address. It was in an older section of Memphis with huge lawns carefully landscaped for privacy. Good. I didn't need any nosy neighbors poking around. "Let's go, Sweetie Pie, Pluto. Our musical career lies ahead of us."

22

It took about thirty minutes to make it to Cissy Hartley's address. When I pulled up behind her cute little Mazda sports car, I heard the soundtrack to *Sexy Beast* going full volume. Sweetie Pie lay down at the door and covered her ears with her paws. I felt her pain. If Cissy didn't turn that off before she answered the door, we'd never be able to sing for her. It wasn't necessary to my goal that I actually sing, but I really wanted to.

I rang the bell and in a moment the door popped open. Cissy Hartley, who was an attractive woman even at the worst of times, beckoned us to follow her, giving me a chance to really examine the leopard-print leggings and sports bra she wore, along with spiked hot-pink high heels.

"I was just doing my Tai Chi routine," she said. "Give me ten minutes to finish. I'm dying to know who sent me a singing telegram. That's so old-school."

I had no words to pause her—hell, with *Sexy Beast* roaring in surround sound, I had no words at all.

Cissy assumed a pose and began to go through the final forms of the ancient Chinese movement.

She did it all in those heels, which was very disturbing for a reason I couldn't put my finger on. It was amazing to watch her move with such fluidity, control, and grace with *Sexy Beast* pounding in the background.

When she finished, she turned off the stereo. "Man, I was thinking about some of my favorite movies. That Ray Winstone gets me hot. I like a lot of American actors, but that guy, he's just so stone-cold amazing."

"Yeah." I had no other verbiage at my disposal.

"So, who sent me a singing telegram?" She held up a hand. "Do *not* sing to me. Do *not* do it. I will hurt you."

I absolutely believed she would, too. "An admirer?" I sounded tentative even to myself. The sad fact was that the sight of Cissy in her leopard skin and stilettos doing the moves of Tai Chi had rattled my game plan right out of my head. It was like the worst melding of East and West, chi and methamphetamines, or herbal medicine and colonic cleanses.

"You don't know, do you?" She was amused. "You look like a seal about to be whacked. Do you know or don't you know?"

"Actually, I don't." The whole farce of a singing telegram had outlived its usefulness. I was in Cissy's house, so I didn't need to pretend to be some kind of singing gift to gain admittance. The next step was the problem. I didn't know how best to wrangle her into helping me. I decided to go for the gold ring. "I'm looking for Cece Dee Falcon. Where is she?"

"And I should know, why?"

"You were the last person to talk to her before she disappeared."

"Oh, really. Can you prove that?"

"Where is she?" I was exhausted, and my patience was even shorter than usual.

"No clue. Now take off before I have you arrested."

"My friend is missing and you're somehow involved. Peter Deerstalker. Did you speak with him?"

"What is this, Twenty Questions? I don't have to answer you. I'm indulging you because you have a set of brass ones, coming here and pretending to deliver a singing telegram. I'm impressed."

"I don't give a hot damn if you're impressed or not. I want to find my friend." I expected she would throw me out. Instead she laughed.

"Calm down. Don't be stupid. Have a drink with me. I just got off work and now I've finished my workout. I need to wind down." She did a big stretch. "I want to talk, so you indulge me and I might answer your questions. Unless you'd like to go another round of Tai Chi with me. That felt really good and now I'm warmed up." She smiled, but her eyes warned me that she was in control. If I wanted to learn anything, I would play her game.

"Isn't Tai Chi supposed to like . . . ground you or center you or something? Connect you with nature?" None of that seemed possible in stilettos with that music blaring.

"There's no one more centered than I am. So what's your point?"

"Doesn't the loud soundtrack kind of get in the way? I mean, I was thinking wind flutes or chimes or something calming."

"That's probably necessary if you have the concentration of a gnat. Look, you want information from me, I want something from you. Now tell me who sent the singing telegram." She motioned me into a club chair while she made drinks at a wet bar. "I need a good martini to unwind. Name your poison."

"Martini is fine." I wasn't going to leave until I had some answers and I was still starving. A drink wasn't food, but one martini to sip wouldn't hurt and it would tide me over. Sweetie Pie moaned softly at my feet. "My hound is quite a talent. Maybe we could sing a few bars—" I was merely delaying the inevitable, when I would have to confess that no one sent a telegram and lose my chance to grill the reporter.

She handed me a martini in a beautiful glass. "I like dogs. What about the cat? What does he do in your act?"

"He does Chilean sea bass, if you happen to have some available."

She actually laughed. "I like you. I think you're probably insane, but you really do have chutzpah. You come in here pretending to have a singing telegram for me and then demand sea bass for the cat." She nodded. "I'll get something for Sweetie Pie and Pluto. You just hang here, Sarah Booth."

The fact I'd been made was a slap in the face. "How did you know it was me?"

"Raily, the production guy, had a camera on you the whole time. I recognized you instantly. I was just in Zinnia, remember? I'm a quick study. Everyone in town knows the local private dick and her clutch of critters."

She was smart. Smarter even than I'd anticipated. "So why did you give me your address?"

"I want to talk to you, silly. I'm a reporter, and I need a good source. I gather the whole singing telegram was a ploy. Poor Raily. He said you made his ears bleed. Anyway, you want information and I do, too. What do you know about those murders in Sunflower County?"

"What do you know about Cece Dee Falcon?" I countered.

"Your reporter friend. She's got a lot between her ears and her facts are accurate. That's what I know."

"Where is she?"

She lifted her head slightly and stared at me

hard. "What are you asking? Is she missing?"

"She came here to talk to you?"

Cissy regarded me. "That's peculiar. I haven't seen her. What makes you think she came to Memphis to talk to me?"

Sweetie Pie had come up beside Cissy and was giving her the hound-dog death stare. "I have a source who said Cece called you and was headed here."

"Oh, that." Cissy waved a hand. She plucked an olive from her martini and ate it with relish. "I love olives. Never get enough of them."

I waited. I'd learned that saying nothing was sometimes the most effective method of questioning. She seemed to be casting about for a reply. What she came up with would be telling. Especially since Pluto was flanking her other side. My critters were partial to Cece, and even if they didn't understand the finer points of this discussion, they could read emotions.

"Cece did call me. She was at the Winterville Mound waiting to find some evidence that an informant left behind which was supposed to clear Peter Deerstalker."

That matched what Peter had said. "Did she make it here?"

"No. She never arrived. When I saw you at the television station, I thought maybe you were delivering a message from her. I know you're friends."

"You didn't see her, but you did talk to her?" I had to be sure. What had happened to Cece after she left Winterville Mound? And how did she leave? She had no vehicle.

"I did. She said she was coming to Memphis, but she never showed up. I was . . . out on assignment until late. But Raily would have let her into the office. She didn't make it."

Cece was still in the wind, and no one had seen her. My worry grew, but I had other questions, too. "How did Bella Devareaux get your press badge?"

"Look, I gave Bella that identification. She wanted to get on the site of the excavation and she figured a press pass would carry a lot more weight than a PI badge. Everyone knew what a glory hog Dr. Sandra Wells was. Bella was pretty green as a private dick, but she had grit. And she was correct in thinking a press badge can open a lot of doors. I shouldn't have done it, but she agreed to share any leads she obtained with me. My success as a reporter is in having good and reliable sources. I saw Bella as just that."

Cissy was an ambitious journalist. She didn't give Bella that identification out of the goodness of her heart. "And what did Bella give you?"

She sighed. "I see my reputation precedes me." She poured herself another martini and offered to top off my glass, but I declined. I really was tired and I had a long drive ahead of me. "Wells and Hafner hated each other's guts." She rolled her eyes. "One of the worst-kept secrets in history was their torrid and tawdry affair. They were hot and heavy for each other about a year ago. Met at a conference, jumped each other and couldn't get enough. One day they woke up, looked at each other, and screamed in terror at what they saw."

I had to fight the smile that wanted to creep up my face. Cissy had an irreverent way of looking at life, but she faced it head-on. She was definitely a shark. When she looked in the mirror, she saw a shark. She didn't delude herself and she wasn't kind to people who failed to face the truth. "Go on."

"I'd hoped that Bella had uncovered evidence that Hafner had killed his partner/competitor. But I didn't get that. As far as I can tell, Hafner is a Lothario but he isn't a killer. And, to be honest, I'm not so certain about his reputation for an aggressive sexual appetite. Men who try that hard generally have something to prove."

I couldn't dispute her theory. "So what did Bella give you?"

Cissy shrugged. "Cece already knows this, so it's not like I'm giving away a story. Bella had that weird tattoo. And so did Sandra Wells."

"Right." I kept my mouth shut about Sister Grace. That was Cece's scoop, if she was still alive when I finally found her.

"That symbol is an original, but it has similarities with some ancient beliefs."

I sipped my martini and fought back true weariness. "Okay. I'm listening."

"Bella said there was something ancient at the site. Something other than old bones and history, pottery shards, and artifacts."

"And do you have proof of this?" I asked.

"That's what Bella believed. And that was what Cece was working on."

"Did Bella say what it was that was so . . . old and valuable?"

Cissy settled on the arm of a big overstuffed chair. "She didn't get a chance. I gave her the press pass, and then she disappeared. I was pretty chapped about it. I thought she'd played me. It never occurred to me that she was dead."

"Who killed her?" I asked.

"I don't know. Not any more than I know who killed Sandra Wells. It all has something to do with that burial site, and it's about a lot more than the history of the Native Americans. I will say Bella had some tight connection with someone on the dig site. One of the students, I think."

"Any clue which one? Delane? Kawania?"

"She knew them both, but I had a sense it was someone else." She shrugged. "I would have gotten it out of her but I didn't get a chance."

Bella had been arguing with Cooley Marsh, but I was under no obligation to tell Cissy that.

"Did Bella say anything about the three missing women in Louisiana?"

Cissy put her drink down and stood up. "That was a ruse, as far as I know. That whole business of missing women was just an excuse for Bella to investigate the dig site," Cissy said.

"So who killed Bella?"

Cissy offered another martini but I declined. "I really don't know. I don't think it was Frank or Peter. The question to ask is what had Bella found before she was killed?"

Her question was right on target. "What had she found, other than the trapdoor to the basement of the Bailey home? Had something significant been in the basement and the killer removed it? Her body was found there, but there was no blood. The blood was either collected and removed or it could indicate she was killed somewhere else."

Cissy kicked off her heels and fell into a chair. "I think there's something else going on at that dig. Something sinister. I'm not sure it has anything to do with digging up ancient bones."

"What lead are you following?"

She examined me with a cool eye. "I need a guarantee. I know you're best friends with Cece, but we have completely different markets. If you find something, you share with me. Deal?"

I nodded. "I will share everything I can, without betraying Cece. That will have to be good enough."

"Don't sandbag me."

I nodded. "Did you ever talk to Sandra Wells?" It felt like a bargain with the devil, but Cissy was good at her job and would gain leads. There was plenty she and Cece could share without stepping on each other's toes. And Cece herself had been talking to Cissy. They'd obviously worked out an arrangement.

"I did, but I didn't get a chance to push her as hard as I wanted. Sandra was so focused on her own needs, she never considered that other people needed things, too. She blabbed all the time about everyone on the dig. She lusted for the fame of her own television show. Everyone knew that. I should have pressed her when I had the chance." Cissy sipped her drink. "I wanted to stay in Zinnia and dig some more, but I had to run back to Memphis for an interview with the head of a tech company who's moving his headquarters here. Big money for Memphis, and while business growth isn't as sexy as a serial killer, we are a local station. What I do know is that whatever Sandra was after, it was something worth a lot more than becoming a footnote in history. As to who killed her, I wouldn't even hazard a guess. Lots of possibilities, but I'm sure you know that. I'd put good money on Delane Goggans. I did my best to break her, but she gave me nothing. She's a tough customer and she hated Wells."

In the role of Dr. Wells' graduate assistant, Delane had the means of going through the professor's notes, of snooping on her private conversations. If there was an ulterior motive or goal, Delane would likely know. The pretty graduate student was also sleeping with Frank Hafner, and while she seemed genuinely fond of him, he didn't seem to consider her feelings. It was hard to keep up with who was sharing whose bed. Maybe it was working all day with the dead that made the archeologists want to suck all the juice out of life while they could. Or maybe they just had poor impulse control. I wasn't going to judge.

"Look." Cissy swung her legs up over the arm of the big stuffed chair. "I don't know where your friend is. I'd tell you if I did."

"But you were talking to her—you were the last person to talk to her."

"Maybe." She stretched, arching her back. She was very limber.

"And Peter Deerstalker said he came up here to talk to you."

"Never talked to him, either. He called. I'm not in the business of giving out information. I'm supposed to be gathering it."

Cissy was all about the story. "Why are you still in the Memphis market?" I'd seen her on the news. She was a great interviewer, she could think on her feet, she asked the hard questions.

302

And she was able to wrap the story up in a neat package and spoon-feed it to the viewer. She had national correspondent or anchor written all over her.

"I like Memphis right now," she said, looking out the window into the night. "It's a sweet town, great music. I'm building a repertoire of stories. And I'm not in a rush. Once you're in that big market, you have a limited time to make your play to be top dog. If you don't succeed, you're gone in two years. It's awful hard to come back to a regional market once you've been national. Maybe it's smarter just to be top of the region." She smiled.

I knew she was lying then. Not because Sweetie Pie watched her with such distrust. Or because Pluto had settled on the pillow above her head and waited for a cue to pounce, if it should become necessary. She was lying because a shark didn't settle for a human finger when it could eat a whole body. Cissy was intelligent and ruthless, and those qualities told me her snow job was false.

"I can see your point," I said. "The competition for those top anchor jobs must be keen."

"Brutal. And it's still weighted toward the male anchor."

That I did believe. I knew then she was waiting for a particular job that was perfect for a female. One where she'd have some job security—a

Barbara Walters situation. "A clever woman can surely turn those odds in her favor." I sipped the last of my drink and leaned back into the sofa. If she put down her guard, maybe she'd give something away.

"Look, Sarah Booth, why don't you stay the night here?" Cissy stood up and stretched. Before I could even blink, she'd done two cartwheels and one back bend. She was like a rubber toy. She reminded me of . . . I thought before I could put my finger on it. The politician's wife in another case. Susan Simpson! She'd been pregnant *and* a contortionist. She almost snapped her cheating husband's head off with the power of her thighs. Cissy had that same crazy flexibility.

"I'd better hit the road. I have a lot of reasons to be home in the morning." I stood up and even in my very flat and stable shoes, I stumbled.

"Sarah Booth!" Cissy shook my arm. "You're too tired to drive. I insist that you stay here until you've caught forty winks. You can't drive home in that condition. At least take a nap. It's not worth killing yourself over to get back to Zinnia in the wee hours of the morning."

"But—"

"How long has it been since you've slept?"

It was a rhetorical question, but I knew the answer—almost thirty-six hours. "I really need to get home."

"It's too dangerous for you to be on the road as

tired as you are. And I have another incentive. I haven't told you the complete truth. I do know where Cece is."

"What?" I thought I'd misheard her. All this time she could have told me where my friend was.

"Cece is here in Memphis. It's a long story and she can tell you in the morning. She'll be here bright and early."

"That's a lowdown stunt, leaving me to worry about my friend, when you knew where she was."

"I was hoping she'd show up and tell you what she was up to herself. She'll definitely be here in the morning. It's only six hours. Grab some shuteye and you can drive her back to Zinnia."

"I can't believe you two are working together."

"Journalism and politics made strange bedfellows. I'll get Neville to show you to a room. The dog and cat can stay with you."

She spoke into her phone and in a moment a tall, muscular man came in and helped me to my feet. I didn't really need assistance, but he maneuvered me like I weighed nothing.

"Put her in the green room, with those animals," Cissy said.

Without a word, Neville took me deeper into the house. Not even my annoyance with Cece and Cissy for their secrecy could keep me awake. The last thing I remember was the click of Sweetie Pie's toenails on the beautiful hardwood floors. The takeaway was that Cece was safe and in Memphis. The relief I felt at knowing that took the last bit of starch out of my spine. I could sort through the rest of it in the morning as I drove home to check on Coleman. I gave myself to the Land of Nod.

23

I awoke with Sweetie Pie licking my face. She had the distinctive scent of steak sauce on her breath and I rolled away, disturbing Pluto, who yawned and stretched. Amazingly, I was clear-headed, refreshed—and very anxious to get the day rolling. Of all times to end up sleeping over in a strange city at a strange person's house, this was the worst. Coleman was waiting for me. Once I collected Cece we'd get on the road home.

My phone was in my pocket and I checked the time. Dawn was just breaking. It was ten minutes after six. I had calls from Tinkie, Doc, and Coleman. I didn't bother listening to the messages but called Tinkie.

"Where the hell are you?" Tinkie was angry, and I knew it was worry more than temper.

"Memphis. Cissy Hartley's house."

"You're still there?" Tinkie was less angry and more annoyed. "You had a sleepover with a reporter friend and couldn't bother to call me. You sure as hell had better have Cece with you."

"I don't. I haven't seen her, but I'm expecting her this morning. How is Coleman?"

"Looking for you. Doc is trying to keep him in the hospital, but he's about to burst out of there and he's wondering where you are."

That wasn't a good thing. "I was exhausted. If I'd tried to drive home I might have wrecked. I did play it safe, and I also have some new thoughts on the case. I'll be bringing Cece home with me. I'm sorry I worried you."

"I'm glad you're sorry, but I'm still annoyed. Things in this case don't add up, especially not you and Cece ending up in Memphis. Care to explain?"

"When I get home. I promise. Cece's been following a lead, or so the television reporter tells me. We'll explain everything when I get to Zinnia."

"Be careful, Sarah Booth. You'd better call Coleman and you'd better have a really good story to tell him. And Doc. Both of them are upset."

"Can you call them, Tinkie? I hear someone coming back. I have to go." I lied with great urgency and hung up before she could protest. Yes it was a lowdown trick, but if anyone could soothe Coleman and Doc, it would be Tinkie. I'd just make a muddle of it.

I found my shoes, picked them up, and opened the bedroom door. I paused with my hand on the knob. From somewhere in the house I could hear voices. It sounded like two women talking, not the big, hulking bodyguard. Sweetie Pie passed me, tail wagging, as she headed toward the voices.

"Sweetie!" I whispered her name, but she kept going. "Sweetie!"

She went down the hall and turned the corner, her toenails clicking. Pluto and I were after her in a flash. When Sweetie entered the kitchen, I heard an exclamation of happiness. I stopped. That sounded a lot like my missing journalist, Cece Dee Falcon.

I burst into the kitchen. Cece sat at a cozy breakfast nook with Cissy and the huge boulder of a man named Neville. They were sipping mimosas and snacking on little toasted triangles of cheese.

"Sarah Booth, glad to see you in the land of the living," Cece said, indicating a chair I should take.

"Where have you been? Half the county is looking for you and I left Coleman injured in the hospital to come search for you. I thought you were in danger!"

"I was," Cece said. "If you'll let me explain, I think you'll see why I had to come up here."

"Oh, I'm ready for an explanation."

"I feared I was in danger. Ms. Hartley saved me. Well, it was actually Neville, but she ordered it to happen."

"What are you talking about? You left Peter

Deerstalker at the Winterville Mound with no way to get home."

"That's not exactly how it happened. Peter left me. He went up the mound ahead of me while I was on the phone. I heard something in the woods. When I went to check on it, I realized I'd dropped my phone. I searched for it but couldn't find it in the dark. I went up the mound to find Peter, he was gone. Not a trace of him. I figured he'd set me up and—" She broke off abruptly. "I thought he was going to try to kill me."

"I was worried you were dead!" The more I talked the angrier I became. "I abandoned Coleman in the hospital after he'd been shot because I was so worried about you. Why didn't you let us know where you were?"

"I did send texts. Didn't you get them? Then I lost the phone."

I remembered what Tinkie had said about the texts that we'd never received. It wasn't Cece's fault. She had tried. Cece looked suitably contrite. Neville continued to eat little toast triangles and ignore me. Cece had the decency to hand a few tidbits down to Sweetie, who was thumping her tail on the floor at her feet. "How did you get here in Memphis?"

It was the television reporter who answered. "Bella Devareaux told me that Peter Deerstalker was into some really weird stuff. She thought Peter had something to hide. I was about to check into the Prince Albert when I called Cece and realized she was at Winterville Mound . . . with Peter. I was talking to her when she heard something in the woods and rushed to check it out. I thought she was potentially in a lot of danger. That's really why Neville and I drove there. Plus I needed some footage."

"Okay, what was the big danger? Did Peter try to harm you?"

"There was someone else at the mound," Cece said. She wouldn't meet my gaze, which was not like my friend.

"Okay, so who was there? Cooley Marsh? Delane? Frank Hafner? Elton Cade?"

"None of the above. It was someone else."

My patience was thin. "I'm done playing sixty questions. Who was there?"

"It's difficult to explain, because it doesn't make sense." Cece hesitated and looked at Cissy again, as if to get their stories straight.

"Stop the footsy with each other and just tell me what happened."

"You aren't going to believe it." Cissy was almost gleeful. "I was about to pop to tell you last night, but I promised I would wait until Cece got here."

"For heaven's sake, spit it out!" I nudged Cece's leg under the table. "Tell me or I promise I'll hurt you."

"When I got to the top of the mound, there

wasn't a sign of Peter, like I said. It was like he'd vanished. I figured he'd lured me out there and set me up to be harmed." Cece held my gaze, almost willing me to believe her. "When the moon wasn't behind a cloud I could see pretty well. There wasn't any evidence Peter had ever been there. When I was on the phone to Cissy, she'd told me about some of the things Peter's name had been hooked to. Supernatural things. Marie Laveau, spells, voodoo. Kawania was also involved."

She glanced over at Cissy. Something like an electric current passed between them. It made me uneasy. I remembered the talk I'd had with Peter at the hospital. "Peter said he was at the top of the mound and didn't see anything. He didn't find any evidence of anything. He said he went back down and you were gone from his vehicle."

"I don't know where he was but he wasn't on top of that mound. I searched for him. I thought he might have gone down the back side so I went to the north edge and looked down. There're some trees there and I guess he could have been camouflaged by the trees and shadows. I guess almost anything could have been waiting in those woods."

I could see her pulse in her throat. She was making me very nervous. "And what?"

"I didn't see Peter, but I saw something else. Someone else."

"Who?" I wanted to shake her. "Quit dinking around and just tell me."

"It looked like someone who shouldn't be there."

"Who?" I was going to have to squeeze it out of her.

"It looked an awful lot like Sandra Wells."

It took a few seconds for what she was saying to really register with me. "You saw a corpse?"

"Not a corpse."

"Then what?"

"I don't know what it was. I didn't get a clear view, but it was walking in the trees. Kind of walking. More like stumbling."

I looked from one to the other, and Cissy confirmed what she'd said with a nod. "Tell me you got a photo," I said. This was too preposterous to be a lie or excuse.

"It was too dark and I was too far away." She held up a hand. "It could have been a trick of the light. It could have been someone else. I couldn't swear to anything. When Cissy and Neville showed up, I'd searched everywhere for Peter and by that time I didn't want to find him. I was more than ready to leave." She sighed. "Peter had abandoned me, and I was creeped out by what I'd seen in the woods." She pushed her hair back from her cheek. "I shouldn't have left Peter but I thought he'd left me. I didn't have a weapon or a camera or even a phone. That . . . thing shifting around in the woods. I couldn't get out of there fast enough. And there was one other thing."

"What?" I still wasn't certain what to make of the scene Cece had witnessed. My friend wasn't prone to flights of fancy or nightmares of corpses walking around.

"This." Cece reached into her purse beside her chair and brought out a beautiful purple cloth. She unwrapped an object. When she pushed the curved stone knife toward me, I eased back from it. It was a beautiful instrument, but wickedly crafted. Deadly. A dark brown crust was near the hilt.

"I found that at the top of the mound," Cece continued. "The cloth was spread out and the knife in the center of it. Look at the handle. It's bone. Probably buffalo bone. The blade is chiseled stone, like the blade used to kill the two women."

I leaned closer. A carving in the bone depicted the very same tattoo that had been found on the bodies of the two dead women. "I think you found the murder weapon."

"I think so, too. And I'm concerned that it was left there to be used on me."

I looked at my friend. I didn't want to imagine her as a ritual sacrifice for some sicko, but it was hard to avoid. The knife told a violent and scary story. "We need to find out what that symbol means and who it's significant to."

"That's what I've been doing here in Memphis," Cece said. "I borrowed a car from Cissy and I've been going to every spiritual healer, card reader, Native American historian—whoever I could find who would talk to me."

"What did you find out?" I asked.

"The symbol isn't historic. It doesn't have a history of use in any organization, religion, or cult that I could find. It seems it's specific to the two dead women."

I had something to add to that—Sister Grace also had the tattoo—but not in front of Cissy and Neville. "I have to get back to Zinnia. Coleman will be awake and waiting for me. Ed Oakes, your boss in case you've forgotten that, is going to be out for blood, Cece. He's been worried and you know that makes him angry. He'd never forgive himself if you were hurt. And taking off with Peter Deerstalker! What was that all about? A man you considered a possible serial killer." I was on a roll and I didn't intend to let her off easy.

"Ed is okay. I called Jaytee and he told me about Coleman getting shot. How bad is it?"

"He's going to be okay. I may not be when he's up and about. I left him so I could find you."

"Thank you, Sarah Booth. I'm sorry. I did try to contact you."

"Did Jaytee say how Elton was doing? He was injured at Winterville Mound also."

"Elton was there?"

I nodded. "He got a call that Peter was in danger."

Cece's brow furrowed. "I know you don't want to hear this, but that makes me question Peter's role in this even more. I really thought he was innocent, but now I'm just not sure. I thought we were all lured to that mound to be either a victim or a scapegoat. How did he miss that knife and cloth? It's possible, in the dark, in the grass." She clenched her fists. "Someone is playing with us. It could be that Peter is behind all of this. He was there. He could have manipulated the whole thing." She frowned. "But he might also be innocent."

"Do you have any evidence, either way? The private investigator whose body was left in the basement of the old Bailey house lived in the same small town as the Biloxi-Tunica reservation. What are the chances of that being a coincidence?"

"I did find out some interesting facts about Bella's background. From Peter," Cece said. "Bella moved to Marksville about nine months ago from New Orleans."

There was another New Orleans connection—Kawania Laveau. And Peter was also connected to Kawania through her Tunica blood. Peter was deep into what was happening at both of the burial mounds.

Cece had accomplished a good bit with her investigation, but I'd wasted hours in Memphis and had little to show. "Get your things. I have to go. Now that you're safe, I'm worried about Coleman."

"Don't be too hard on her. She's been afraid," Cissy added. "And with good cause."

"Ya think?"

"Not afraid of you." Cissy sighed heavily. "She has a reason to be afraid."

She actually sounded sincere. "What are you talking about?"

"Cece should tell you herself."

I focused on Cece. This was worse than pulling teeth. "Can you just tell me the whole damn story and quit piecemealing it out?"

"Let me borrow your phone, please, and give me a moment of privacy. You already know everything." Cece held out her hand and I forked over my phone, but I couldn't resist one last dig. "We need to get back to Zinnia, so make it quick." I went to the back door and let Sweetie Pie and Pluto out into a lovely backyard so they could do their business before we hit the road home. When real spring came, this yard would be a haven for bees and butterflies. Cissy obviously called the shots at her television station, and they paid her plenty to keep her working there. She had to have a gardener along with her chauffeur/bodyguard Neville. Good help didn't come cheap.

I dialed Doc Sawyer to let him know I was delayed but that Cece was safe and sound. Coleman would welcome that news, though he was likely to be prickly over my defection.

"Coleman is fine. Ready to go home. I'll give him the good news on Cece, and let him know you'll be here soon."

"Thanks, Doc." I let out a deep breath.

The back door closed and I heard footsteps. "How about some breakfast, Sarah Booth?" Cissy asked.

"No, thanks. We really have to get back to Zinnia." I was feeling the pressure of deeds undone. "Cece needs to explain to some people. And so do I. I have people upset with me because I came here to help Cece."

"Don't be mad with her. She really thought Peter was going to reveal something that would point to the killer. The problem is, she could have gotten herself killed." She hesitated. "Whatever she saw in those woods scared the hell out of her. I wanted to stay and investigate. I mean, we had Neville. But she wouldn't hear of it. She wanted away from that place."

"Yeah. The knife, Peter disappearing, the thing she saw." I could see how she'd be eager to kick up some heel dust. "How did you get to the Winterville Mound so quickly?"

She blew air out in exasperation. "I was already in the area. I'd arranged to do a live shot on top

318

of the Winterville Mound. You know, the whole full moon, Mississippi River mystique. We chose Winterville because it's a regulated site and has been maintained. Better optics. Then I got a call from Cece and she was really upset. I like her. She's a great reporter. And it was the chance of a lifetime. You have to admit that it's one helluva crime story to run with."

I wasn't certain Cissy was being totally honest, but she was at least 85 percent there. "Did you see anything in the woods?" I didn't believe in the walking dead, but Cece wasn't a person prone to wild imaginings.

She shook her head. "I didn't. I wanted to send Neville to search but Cece was freaked out. I'm telling you, she wanted to go. There was no reasoning with her."

"And so you left a potential killer running around a burial site."

"That was a flaw in our thinking, for sure. I'm sorry, Sarah Booth. It could have been a fatal mistake for you or Sheriff Peters."

The door opened and Cece also came out. "Cissy, there's a phone call for you." She stepped aside as Cissy went into the house.

For a long moment neither of us said anything. Cece put a hand on my shoulder. "I feel like a fool, going off with Peter like that to an isolated place without telling anyone. He told me to keep it under wraps. There was supposed to be evidence there that would reveal the killer." She rolled her eyes. "Right, the evidence was going to be my body. Blood drained for his sicko ritual."

"You did find the knife, which may be the murder weapon. If your scenario is correct, we have to find out, and fast. Peter is either the perpetrator or another intended victim. Remember, if he's telling the truth, he was the one contacted to go to the site, not you."

"Good point."

"We don't know if the killer targets women only, or if he takes whoever is available. Peter could also be in danger."

"He could be." Cece looked perfectly anguished. "And I left him there without his keys."

"He escaped without damage. Now let's head home and put the pieces of this mess together. I feel like we're all being jerked around, and I'm more than a little tired of it."

"I did come to a conclusion," Cece said. Her sassy smile was back in place.

"Yeah? I swear if you don't just tell me everything, I am going to have Coleman arrest you."

"We've been asking the wrong question. What did Bella Devareaux find that cost her her life? The answer to that could unravel the whole case."

24

I navigated the Memphis traffic in silence. It wasn't far to the interstate that would take us straight home. When I was on the four-lane, Cece didn't relax. A tiny muscle jumped in her jaw.

"What gives?" I asked.

· "Some of the students claim that they've seen an apparition at the dig. They swear it's true." She took a deep breath. "I thought they were being hysterical or drama queens, until I saw it, too."

I cast a glance at Cece. She was sitting forward, clearly worried. "Go on."

"I've been giving this a lot of thought. I know Peter is the obvious suspect here, but I think he believed there was evidence at Winterville Mound. He seemed convinced that we'd be able to solve Dr. Wells' and Bella Devareaux's murders and absolve him of any blame." She clenched her fist. "He was positive and eager. I believed him at the time and, now, I'm beginning to swing back to believing him again."

"There was evidence. The knife." I had it safely tucked away with the full intention of getting it right to Budgie and DeWayne. It would have been better if Cece had left it at the mound but, on the other hand, anyone could have stumbled on it and taken it.

"So was the knife left there for Peter to find or left there by Peter?" Cece was piecing it together.

"What do you think?" My gut was telling me one thing, but I wanted to know what Cece felt.

"Go with me a minute. What if he really was following a lead? What if he was tricked, too? What if the killer lured him up there, meant to kill me and disable Peter, and somehow blame him for my death, too? It would be the perfect setup. Also, Peter has strange connections with Bella Devareaux, and he has a link to voodoo practices. He's the perfect scapegoat. Think about it."

"So now you think he was telling you the truth and trying to solve the murders? But you said—"

"I know what I said, but I don't know. That's one problem. But I have an even bigger problem."

"What's that?"

"There is someone lurking around those mounds. Both Winterville and Mound Salla."

She said it with such certainty that it gave me goose bumps. "Someone like a killer?"

She looked straight out the window. "There's an element of this case that . . . is not natural. I know how crazy that sounds, Sarah Booth, but the events that have happened don't make sense in a logical world."

• • •

We drove into Zinnia, and I was amazed to see the normal activities of the town. I felt as if everything had changed, and yet there was Oscar walking into the bank. The shops along Main Street were open and the parking lot at Millie's Café was full. I turned into the residential area where Cece and Jaytee lived in a beautiful old clapboard house with a curved front porch and Victorian turrets.

"Need a lift to your car?" I asked her.

"Could you take me to the newspaper? Jaytee is asleep, I'm sure. I'd like to talk to Ed and get this over with." She looked only a little green. Ed Oakes cared about his employees, and Cece had worried him, too.

"Sure." I drove her the several blocks to the paper on Main Street.

"You good?" I idled in front of the newspaper.

"I am." She leaned over and kissed my cheek. "Thanks for rescuing me, even if I didn't need it."

"Yeah, I just love spend-the-night parties with people I don't know." I patted her hand and gave it a big squeeze. "I'm glad you're okay. What are your plans?"

"I have a few leads to check. And I need to talk to Peter. I owe him an explanation and his car keys."

"Don't go anywhere without telling us."

"Scout's honor."

I had my own fish to fry, so I didn't press her. I drove straight to the hospital and Coleman's room. He was dressed in a clean uniform, sitting on the edge of the bed. He looked like he'd been waiting for a long time.

I breezed into the room like nothing was amiss. "You'll be glad to know Cece is safe. She's at the paper right now. Did Doc say you could go home?"

Coleman lifted both eyebrows. "*I* said I could go home."

"I see." I faced his annoyance and kissed his cheek before I sat beside him. "Flesh wound. Doc says you'll be good as new in a week. We have to be sure the wound doesn't reopen. Do you feel up to something to eat at Millie's?"

"Look, I need a ride to the sheriff's office. Budgie and DeWayne aren't answering their phones."

I eased closer to him. "Where's Doc?"

"Around here somewhere. I sent the nurse to get him a dozen times and he's ignoring me. I'm leaving here, with or without his approval."

I put a hand on his knee. "Coleman, if our places were reversed, what would you do? Would you be glad Doc and my friends made certain I had good medical care? Or would you be mad at people because they forced me to take care of myself for a change?"

324

He put his arm around me. "I hear you, and I'm not mad. I just want to get back to work. We had a shootout at a Native American burial mound in a county where I have no jurisdiction. I was wounded. Elton Cade was bashed in the head. Cece disappeared. And the person behind all of it got away. You go off to Memphis and find Cece, who's been playing coy with us for a whole day. I'm frustrated."

He was indeed. I heard it clearly in his voice. But he hadn't counted that I would be frustrated, too. "I know. I want to wring her neck, but Cece is sorry. She thought she was following a lead with Peter. And she did find a knife at the Winterville Mound. It could be the murder weapon." I held up a hand to stop his complaint. "It's wrapped in some kind of sacred cloth and no one touched it. Cece thinks it may have been left there to kill her and set Peter Deerstalker up as the killer."

"And who would do that?" Coleman asked, watching me carefully.

"The person who would have access to this kind of knife is Frank Hafner who, by the way, hasn't checked in with me in a while. Did you give him permission to leave town?"

"He hasn't been charged yet."

"We'll drop the knife off at the sheriff's office when we leave here." I wanted him to feel progress was being made in the case, even if he was sidelined for a day or two.

"I want to see Cece."

I nodded. "That I can arrange. She can come to Dahlia House to talk to you, as long as you promise to remain calm."

"Don't try to manage me." Coleman's forehead looked like a thundercloud.

I put on the most serious face I could muster. "You would really aggravate me, except for one thing. I look at you and I see me. I act just like you, and now I know why everyone wants to chain me to the bed."

Before he could stop himself, Coleman laughed. "That's a helluva thing to say."

I felt a burden lift. Coleman was going to be reasonable. "Let's go home."

"Did you talk to Doc?"

"He's waiting for us at the back exit."

Coleman gave me a look. "You knew this and were just waiting until—"

"Until you got over your pique." I kissed him before he could say anything else. When we broke the kiss he shook his head.

"Sarah Booth—"

He didn't get a chance to finish. Tinkie sailed into the room. "Will you two get out here? Doc is waiting and I need Sarah Booth to help me."

"Help you with what?" Coleman was all over it.

Tinkie rolled her eyes. "She's going to hate it, but I'm hosting the Young Women of Refinement luncheon today and Sarah Booth volunteered to bartend."

I almost choked. I had done no such thing, and Tinkie knew I wasn't going to spend most of my day serving froufrou drinks to the difficult mothers of bitchy high school girls. I didn't have the temperament for these events.

When Coleman lasered me with a blue gaze, I shrugged. "Cece normally does it. I agreed to fill in. But Cece is back in town. Can't she—?"

"Ed Oakes has her foot nailed to her office floor. I just got off the phone with her. She won't be leaving the newsroom for the rest of the week. Sarah Booth, you promised. I'm in a pinch. Jaytee would do it, but he's already committed to helping Scott with some new wiring at the club. You did promise."

I did not, but I wasn't going to argue in front of Coleman. "Let me get my guy settled at Dahlia House."

"Perfect. I had Marnie send over a ham, potato salad, and fresh rolls. You're set for food. And Harold sent some wine and Jack. You should have everything you need to make sure Coleman heals quickly. But for today, I need you to help me with this luncheon."

There was no easy way out of it. "You can count on me," I said, wondering what in the hell Tinkie was up to. Marnie was the young woman who catered a lot of Tinkie's gatherings and parties. And now she was catering to my injured man. I'd find out what Tinkie was planning when we were alone.

The three of us walked down the hall together. Coleman seemed steady on his feet, though a little ouchy. Doc met us and I waylaid him while Tinkie helped Coleman to the waiting patrol car. DeWayne had shown up to drive him to Dahlia House. That, more than anything, told me how worried everyone had been. Coleman was a huge part of my life, but he was also a big part of the town and community. A lot of people relied on him to be safe and do his job.

"Is he really okay?" I asked Doc. We both stood at the back door, watching Coleman progress gingerly across the parking lot. Tinkie joined our conversation.

"He's good, Sarah Booth, but only because he's lucky," Doc said. "The bullet was a millimeter away from a large artery. He could have easily bled to death. Just a fraction more. It worries me."

"Me, too."

"Who's the shooter?" Doc asked.

"We thought it was Peter, but he was already gone from the site. We don't know. Elton didn't see who hit him, either. Washington County is in charge of the crime scene." I was sure DeWayne was on top of that, but I had to check.

"Sarah Booth, I'm getting too old to go running

out to shootings. You and Coleman need to cut this out. You'll cause me to have a heart episode and then what will Sunflower County do for a coroner?"

He was only half-kidding, and I heard the seriousness. "I'm sorry for the worry we cause, Doc. Just tell me he's going to be okay."

"If he takes care of himself. I'm putting you in charge, Sarah Booth. Sit on him if you have to, but keep him at Dahlia House for the rest of the week. He can talk on the phone, interview people while you're there to make sure he doesn't overdo it. Do whatever you have to do until that wound heals. In a week he can go back to the office. In two weeks he can go on full duty. Remind him that this wound will affect his ability to shoot accurately for some time to come. Those chest muscles come into play and will affect his aim."

The list Doc was running down made me want to cry, but I didn't. Coleman had escaped death. He'd come close, but the shadow had only brushed over him. He and Tinkie and Cece had to play it safe—at least until the Crow Moon was past. Tinkie rejoined us with a happy grin.

"Tinkie, I'm not putting all of this on Sarah Booth. I'm expecting you to help with this. When she needs to be somewhere, you sit on Coleman. You're small but you have great power."

"Coleman isn't as easy to manipulate as some men." Tinkie pursed her lips. "He doesn't fall for flattery or helplessness or the things that generally bring a man to heel. But I have another whole repertoire of talents." She winked at me. "I learned them from Sarah Booth. When she wants a man to do something, she just asks and reasons it out with him. It never works, but if I have to, I'll give it a try."

Doc chuckled. "It'll take the two of you to corral that lawman. See that you do it. I'm counting on you. Now get out of here and I don't want to see any of you until Coleman comes in for a recheck. You hear?"

"Yes, sir!" We almost saluted as we beat it out the door to the patrol car where Coleman waited impatiently.

25

After a quick confab, DeWayne took the knife for processing and agreed to take Coleman and the critters to Dahlia House. I would stop by the sheriff's office and pick up all pertinent information about the case and take it to Coleman. That would give me a moment to find out what Tinkie needed me to do. It wasn't mixing mimosas for her society gathering—that much I was willing to bet on.

Tinkie signaled me into Doc's private office in the emergency room so we could talk. "What gives?" I asked.

"First, don't ever go off by yourself like that again."

She had a point, so I didn't protest or explain. "Okay."

"The Washington County sheriff's department dusted the rifle they found at the mound for prints and it was wiped clean."

"Any registration?"

"None. They're working to trace it but it looks like it was reported stolen from a local gun show. That's one of the many tricks to selling a weapon without leaving a paper trail. What's

331

interesting is the scope. It's a FLIR Systems RS64."

"Cut the gobbledygook and say it plain."

"It's a military-grade weapon scope that images the thermal heat of whatever you're hunting. Costs upward of six grand."

"What? None of those college kids could afford anything like that." Which meant our killer had access to some moolah.

"Right. Unless someone was backing their actions."

Tinkie had just opened the possibility that I'd failed to consider. "What is going on? Is this about the dig, jealousies among the crews, or something we haven't even thought about?" I remembered what Cece had said about apparitions at the dig, of her story of a dead person stumbling about in the woods. I'd seen something too, in the woods at Mound Salla. Not likely a zombie, but it could be someone pretending to be a spirit. Someone with a lot of money for weapons. Someone who wanted to scare away other people.

"Washington County ran a check on the students. There's only one with any connection to a background of that kind of weaponry."

"Cooley Marsh." I knew it. "Where is he?"

"He's gone from the motel. He told Delane he quit and was going back to Michigan. He checked out of the hotel, said he would find his own ride back to the school."

I knew the answer before I asked. "Is he at the university in Michigan?"

"No. He hasn't shown up at his apartment there or at the school. In point of fact, he isn't registered at the school."

Now that was a bombshell. "Anyone else missing from the student workers?"

"No, they're all accounted for." Tinkie put a hand on my arm. "There is someone else with gun expertise."

"And that is?"

"Our client. Frank Hafner is a sharpshooter. Not trained in the military, but he's a celebrated marksman. I did some background research on him and discovered he's a distinguished expert in the National Rifle Association."

That did not look good for Hafner. The person who'd shot at Cece's phone had been a good marksman, because I'd come to believe they never intended to hit me. Only to run me off the case. Same for the shoot 'em up at Mound Salla when Tinkie and I were there. An average marksman could have easily killed us. And Coleman, too. Coleman's wound was serious, but not deadly. And it could have been. "Is Hafner back from his funeral duties? I have some questions for him, and maybe Coleman can get an APB out for Cooley Marsh."

"Hafner checked out of the Prince Albert this morning and took off."

"Are you kidding?" I was fed up with people running hither and yon.

"I'm trying to track him down using credit cards. I don't know, Sarah Booth. There's something definitely not right about our client. He's involved in something, even if it isn't murder."

"Don't tell Coleman that Hafner's out of pocket."

"Of course I'm not going to tell Coleman. Do I look like an idiot?" She held up a hand. "Say it and I will punch a hole in the top of your foot with my stiletto."

I didn't doubt she could do it. "Whatever we do, let's get busy. I can't leave Coleman alone for long."

"Oh, he won't be alone." Tinkie grinned wickedly. "I hired the girls from the hair salon to go over and pretend to be candy stripers. They're offering a haircut and shave, sponge bath, mani-pedi, facial, skin peel, you name it."

I thought of the bevy of good-looking women who cut hair at the Glitz and Glamour. "Cancel that sponge bath," I said.

She only laughed. "They'll trim his hair and wash it, buff his nails, massage his feet. They'll feed him the food I sent over. He'll be occupied."

Coleman was going to kill her. And I had to say, it gave me a bit of wicked pleasure. Oh, yes, this was good. I high-fived her. "You are incredible."

"Tell me something I don't know," Tinkie said, performing a little curtsey. "Now, let's solve this case."

"My car is your chariot."

"Let's go over to Washington County. We'll get DeWayne to call over and say we're picking up the reports for the Sunflower County SO. Unless they have a deputy under thirty they'll never think that they could email them." Few of the rural Mississippi sheriff's offices had the personnel or resources to wade too deeply into the Information Age. Even Coleman was guilty of going old-school, but Budgie was changing all of that.

"You are a genius!" I meant it. "Let's solve this." Cece was back at the newspaper. Coleman was healing. All of the distractions were gone. Now I needed to get to work and clean up this mess of a case.

I stepped out of the hospital into the sunshine. It was a gorgeous March day. A perfect day of bright new green unfurling on the gray trees and a sky deep blue without a cloud. We got in the car and I turned the radio to a blues station out of Arkansas.

"Get ready to howl," the announcer said. "The crops are planted and the full moon comes up at five fifty-two. It's going to be a big moon, a moon for spoonin', so get ready for it."

"What's wrong?" Tinkie asked.

I tried to shift my expression because I knew my face reflected dismay. "Full moon."

"Yes, that happens once a month. On rare occasions, twice. And that turned you into an imitation of the painting *The Scream*, why?"

I was going to level with Tinkie. Not about Jitty, but as close as I could get. "That bad dream I mentioned . . . It was a full moon, and something was after you. All of my friends were in danger. I tried and tried to help you but you kept running away, and the thing was chasing you."

To my surprise, Tinkie looked suitably concerned. "You really dreamt this?"

I was lying, but I couldn't tell her more. That would take me too close to revealing the truth about my resident haint. "I don't remember the exact details. It was upsetting, though, because I knew you were in danger. All of you."

Tinkie considered for a moment. "Let's find this killer before you start going to New Orleans to find a conjure woman to ward off evil."

Her words hit me hard. "There's a part of this case we've really overlooked, Tinkie. Cece said that some of the students believed there was an apparition, a spirit or ghost, who was protecting the dig site. And now Cece has seen something unnatural at the Winterville Mound. Something that looked like a dead woman. We need to dig deeper into Kawania Laveau."

"You think that girl cursed the dig and all of this is part of some hoodoo?" Tinkie scoffed. "And you got after me for wanting to buy into the Harrington sisters as witches."

"What about the henna tattoos on the murder victims? The same design was on the knife handle that Cece found. It means something." I grasped her arm. "I'm serious. There's something occult at work here."

"Posh and shortbread. Budgie looked up those tattoos. They don't really have a sinister meaning—they don't have any historic meaning he could find. And they aren't permanent. I don't think they're occult, but I agree that they mean something to the killer. Even if it's just to psyche the rest of us out."

"Or perhaps the meaning is to the people who wear the tattoo. Maybe the killer didn't put the tattoos on the victims. Maybe they did it themselves."

"Like a secret cult?"

I nodded, my mind racing. "Look, it could be nothing but we need to follow up on this. And we need to check out Cece's suspicions." I told her quickly what Cece had relayed to me. "Some cases we don't have anyone with a motive. This case we have half a dozen people with all kinds of motives. It's frustrating. I guess our first job is to track Kawania down as soon as we get back from Greenville."

"Right. Maybe I should ask DeWayne to pick her up."

I nodded. "Good plan. They can bring her in for questioning and we can just happen into the SO with the information from Greenville. I think Budgie and DeWayne will let us question her as long as we make it clear it's informal."

Tinkie got on the phone and set about putting the plan in action. I pressed the pedal down hard and the little Roadster shot down the highway. Thirty minutes later we were walking into the Greenville sheriff's office.

Twenty minutes after that, once DeWayne had cleared the release of the information to us, we had the paperwork and were headed home. Tinkie read while I drove.

"The deputies or forensic team didn't find any evidence of another person at the Winterville Mound. There were traces of you, Coleman, Elton, Cece, and Peter." Tinkie flipped through the files. "No sign of anyone else in the woods. They weren't aware of the knife at the site. Cece had already removed it."

"Someone else was up there. There had to be another party. Who left the knife? And the rifle?"

"You're right about that, Sarah Booth. Either the shooter is brilliant at covering evidence or the police work was sloppy. I suspect the former—someone knows a lot about how not to leave trace evidence behind."

"Hafner would know forensic procedure as well as anyone." I said it and waited. Tinkie didn't attempt to defend him.

I continued, "I'll bet Cooley Marsh knows a lot about guns. Maybe Delane. Hafner is the most plausible suspect, though." It would take a strong man to hoist Dr. Wells up in the manner her body had been left. And Bella had been carried into the basement of the old house—likely killed somewhere else, based on the lack of blood at the scene. We were talking a physically strong man. There were other possibilities, but we also had to face the fact we might be working for the killer.

"That's pretty much what the Washington County deputies came to determine." Tinkie closed the file. "They want to talk to Hafner. I also found out that Delane Goggans did a stint in the military. She wasn't in combat, but she has basic gun training. The Washington County deputies were thorough."

"Coleman needs to hear all of this. He has to stay in bed, but he can reason through it with us. Yes, we are on Hafner's payroll, but we have no obligation to defend a killer. Especially not one who shot at me and almost killed Coleman."

"I completely agree. In this instance, our goal is the same as Coleman's. If Hafner is innocent, we'll do everything we can to prove that. But we can't protect a killer. A fact is a fact. Coleman needs to know."

"Before we go back to Dahlia House, let's chat with Delane. If Hafner's run off and left her holding the bag, she might be willing to talk."

"And Kawania should be at the courthouse waiting for us." Tinkie was all business now. We were closing in on the bad guys.

"Tinkie, would you feel okay questioning Delane if I take the files out to Coleman first? I can meet you at the courthouse to talk to Kawania." I was having a difficult time with my worry about Coleman and the sense that I needed to be there for him. We were just learning the boundaries of our relationship—the hows and whys of dependence and independence. Coleman would hate it if he thought I shirked my work to be at his side. But I hated the idea that he might feel sick and was alone.

"Good thing we got copies of those files," Tinkie said. "Drop me off at my car and I'll find Delane. Then we'll tackle Kawania together."

"Call me?"

"You bet I will. As soon as I break her."

"Thanks, partner."

I pulled up at the back of the hospital, where she'd parked, and let her out with one copy of the files we'd obtained from Washington County. I'd made another set of files for Delaney Detective Agency use, and those I'd take for Coleman to read. It would keep his finger on the pulse of the case. I knew how hard it was to be forced to sit out an active investigation. This would keep him mentally engaged while I kept him physically restrained.

DeWayne had taken Sweetie Pie and Pluto home when he took Coleman, and I drove straight to Dahlia House with the goal of feeding my horses and checking on my man. I hoped Tinkie's passel of man-tenders had finished and left. I needed some quiet time with Coleman.

The horses were waiting on me when I got home, and I made sure they were all eating with their customary gusto before I went inside. The house was indeed quiet. Not even a sound from the critters. I hoped they were all napping in my bedroom.

I entered through the back door. It was still afternoon, and a steady clack, clack, clack came from somewhere on the first floor of Dahlia House. I paused at the stove, filling the coffeepot and turning it on for an afternoon cup. Fatigue tugged at me. I'd been so exhausted in Memphis I'd fallen asleep in a stranger's home. Now all I wanted to do was crawl in bed with Coleman and snuggle against him.

There was no time for sleep or snuggling. In another few hours, the Crow Moon would climb the sky. Danger would be everywhere. Right now, I had to figure out what the strange noise was in my home. I followed the sound to the offices of the detective agency and stopped in my tracks. A woman with long black hair sat behind my desk, typing on a machine that had to date back to the early 1900s. She typed slowly and carefully, ringing the platen back at the end of each line.

"Who are you?" I asked softly. I didn't want to startle her; she was completely absorbed in what she was writing.

"I have several names," she said. "My professional name is Mourning Dove."

I knew the name—though the connection was tentative and I couldn't quite bring it forward from my memory. She was a Native American woman, one with grace and great poise. That was easy because I could see those things. She wore her long, thick hair in loose braids, and her clothes were made from deerskin decorated with beads and drawings.

"What are you writing?" I asked her.

"It will be published as *Cogewea, the Half-Blood: A Depiction of the Great Montana Cattle Range*."

"You're a writer." I'd never read or studied her work, but I knew of it. "You considered yourself a woman caught between two worlds, the one you knew as a Native American woman and the other world—the one you knew as a student of English schools where you were educated. That's what you wrote about."

She nodded. "I was born speaking Salish, but I easily learned English. Essentially I am a woman without a country because I belong fully to neither. It is said I walk between the worlds."

"And you are respected in both." I couldn't pull up a lot of detail about this woman's history, but I knew enough to pay her a sincere compliment.

"It is flattering to be recognized, but there's a danger there, Sarah Booth. You know this because you also walk in two worlds."

Again, the word *danger*. I pushed past it, hoping to avoid another dire warning. "What do you mean?" I asked. "My world is here in Sunflower County."

She turned away from the typewriter and faced me fully. "You live in the past, too. That is your anchor, the place you always return to. It is a haven, but it can also be a trap."

"The past can be a trap for anyone," I conceded, "but me no more than others." I took a different tack. "You published several books, as I recall. Tell me about your life." It was an invitation to melancholia, because I knew without any certain facts that her life had been hard. The arrival of the white man into the Native world brought mostly suffering and loss to the Native Americans.

"I worked mostly as a migrant worker, picking the fruits and vegetables in the Upper Columbia River Plateau region. Before the whites came, my life was simple and nomadic. For many years, we had no contact with the white world. But then the tide of settling whites washed over us and my world was forever changed."

"Why a laborer and writer? You had skills. You could have had an easier life." I cast about for what job an educated woman might have in those days. The options were nil unless that woman was born into money. For a Native American woman, there were no real options at all.

"I put the stories of my people on the page so they would last forever. My final two books were published many years after I was dead. My voice still speaks for those who take the time to read them. My people will be forever alive in my words. I am remembered as Mourning Dove, but my name is Christine Quintasket."

She'd paid a high price for keeping her people and culture alive in stories. She died at fifty, as I recalled, a young woman by my standards. "Do you regret your choices?"

"I never married and had no children. In the end, we all die alone but perhaps a child would have been a better legacy than a book."

I gave her a hard stare. "Okay, Jitty. Stop it."

The beautiful Native woman morphed into my equally beautiful haint. "Just sayin', Sarah Booth. You can solve all the cases in the state of Mississippi, but who's gonna love you when you're old and wandering around the house here, gibberin' like a happy possum."

"You are incorrigible."

"And you are childless. We're both in a world of hurt."

"I can't believe you'd use a Native American woman to advance your agenda of brood mare and offspring. That's dirty pool."

"And that's why you love me. I'm the one who keeps you focused on the prize. And in case you've forgotten, the prize is that man upstairs in your bed. That man who's been shot and wounded and needs the loving touch of his woman. I can't believe you left him, injured and in the grips of death." Jitty shook off the deerskin dress and long braids and stretched. She was wearing my yoga pants and top. I noted the high arch of her bare foot. She was toned even down to her toes.

"You know damn good and well he wasn't alone. Tinkie sent over the beauty salon posse. Coleman has been pummeled and pampered to a fare-thee-well. I've only been gone a couple of hours. He's asleep." Since I hadn't heard from Coleman—I assumed he was asleep. That was a good thing. He needed rest to heal, and if he was asleep, he was healing.

"I can wake him up."

"Don't you dare." I would wring Jitty's neck. "I have some files for Coleman, and then I need to make some calls."

"Better check on that man."

There was something in Jitty's voice that

warned me. I gripped the files I held and raced through Dahlia House and up the stairs to my bedroom to find the bed empty. There was no trace of Coleman.

26

Once I was able to catch my breath, I looked around my room. Coleman had been there. The bed was mussed and there were medicine vials, massage oil, and water on the bedside table. Evidence of a haircut and a shave proved the beauty salon gals had done their job per Tinkie's orders.

Medicine bottles indicated that DeWayne had taken Coleman by the pharmacy to get his prescriptions filled and then had brought him to Dahlia House, as Doc had ordered. But where had Coleman gone? When did he leave? He didn't have keys to my car or his truck. I had both sets. He couldn't have left on his own.

I checked the bathroom and then the guest rooms along the second floor. No evidence of anyone or anything out of order. I realized then that Sweetie Pie and Pluto were also missing. It was by chance I passed a window and looked out to see a tall silhouette walking past the barn with a dog and a cat in tow. Coleman! He was on the property; he'd gone for a walk. I was going to break his legs.

"Coleman!" I raised the window and called down to him. "You should be in bed."

He motioned me to come down, and I did. No point arguing from upstairs.

When I was right in front of him, he motioned me closer for a hug. "I'm glad you're back."

"You should be in bed."

"I have been. I needed to move."

"Doc said if you got to ripping and snorting you'd reopen that wound."

Coleman nodded. "I'm taking it easy. I'm just strolling. And thinking. Sarah Booth, do you think it was actually Frank Hafner up on top of that mound last night?"

"What makes you ask that?"

"It wasn't Peter. I saw him at the hospital. He came and talked to me. While it isn't evidence, I believe what he said. Unless you know otherwise."

"Cece agrees with the facts as Peter stated them to me. They were lured to the mound with the promise of evidence to clear Peter. They both say Peter went up while Cece took a phone call from Cissy Hartley, who was nearby, by the way. After that, their stories deviate. Cece said she tried to find Peter on top of the mound, but she couldn't. She did find that knife."

"Which isn't the murder weapon."

That was a bombshell. "What about the blood?"

"Chicken blood. I believe Cece is correct. Someone was working hard to set Peter up as the killer. Someone who knew about the tattoos on the dead women—a fact we never disclosed to the public. And someone who knew the type of blade used to kill those women. I think it was the killer who left the knife up there." Coleman was puzzling through the facts. "And who's on the loose with knowledge and time to do all of it? Frank Hafner."

"There's something else." I knew this would send him into orbit. He frowned with impatience. I wasn't helping Cece's case. "Cece thinks she caught a glimpse of Sandra Wells in the woods around Winterville Mound."

"What?" He thought he had misheard me, so I repeated the information.

"Does she really believe that?"

I hesitated. "She saw something. It scared her, and that's one reason she left with Cissy and her driver. I don't know what Cece saw, but it seriously unnerved her."

"You're not thinking it was Sandra Wells? She's dead. You saw her body."

"It couldn't have been Sandra." Not even a serial killer could change the laws of matter and reanimate dead flesh. "Maybe someone costumed to look like her?"

Coleman put an arm around me. "I don't know what's going on. We know Peter didn't shoot at us—he was long gone with his friend Calvarese. DeWayne checked it out and everything Peter said is true. We can safely say Peter wasn't involved."

"Can you tie Hafner into it?" I asked.

"He said he was leaving town. Convenient alibi, that, and he isn't in Michigan. Budgie checked."

I owed Coleman what I'd learned. "Frank's an expert marksman. Holds the highest NRA ranking. Delane also has military training and therefore can handle a rifle. There was no evidence at the crime scene, so whoever was up there knew how to leave without a trace." I couldn't make the facts add up to anything. "Tinkie is talking to Delane right now. DeWayne is holding Kawania at the sheriff's office for questioning. There's some kind of voodoo or cult element in this, whether it's for real or part of the game to confound us. Coleman, I admit it. I'm confused about all of the motives in this case."

"You're right. The case doesn't make any sense." Coleman motioned me toward the front of the house. I walked beside him, aware that attempting to boss him inside was going to have the opposite effect. "We're missing something, Sarah Booth. Something important. We've been distracted by the ritualistic elements of the murder, the location, strangers in town. This has hit a lot of hot buttons that don't appear to have anything to do with the real case. What if Sandra's and the private investigator's murders aren't connected?"

We slowly climbed the steps and Coleman settled into one of the front porch rockers. His thick jacket was around his shoulders because he couldn't move his arm sufficiently to put it on.

"They're connected. I just feel that."

"I agree, but we have no evidence to support it. Only the tattoos and the exsanguination." Coleman snapped his fingers. "Text Tinkie and see if she can find out if Delane Goggans has a tattoo." Coleman handed me his cell phone. "Please. Do it quickly."

I obliged. He had a theory and the only way to tell if it was a good one was to dig at it. Tinkie had a tricky chore, since the tattoos on the two bodies were located on the chest in a place not likely to be seen in the dead of winter. But Sister Grace's tattoo had been on her arm, so maybe . . . "I've thought that maybe the tattoos had more to do with the people who had them than the murderer."

"We have to turn over every possibility." He motioned me onto his lap. "We'll crack this thing, Sarah Booth. I'm not down for the count."

"Of course not." I ran my hands through his hair, feeling a swelling of emotion that was almost painful. "You have to promise me that when I find the person who shot you, that you get DeWayne and Budgie to hold them while I work them over."

Coleman laughed and kissed my cheek. "I love the way you protect your man."

"I'm not kidding." I wasn't.

"Maybe you'll luck out and capture the shooter first. That way if you beat him up, there's nothing I can do about it. At least nothing to prevent it from happening. Of course I'd have to arrest you for assault."

"You're just itching to arrest me for something."

"That's true." Coleman wrapped his arms around me. "And I don't think anyone could blame me. Maybe I'll put you and Cece in the same cell. I'm arresting her for worrying us all to death."

"Now that I agree with. Cece looks great in orange."

Coleman shifted and I popped up out of his lap. He was wounded and didn't need me leaning against him. "Let's go inside. You've been up long enough."

"I know you won't believe it, but I agree. I'm tired."

"You lost a lot of blood and even though you had a transfusion, you still have to rebuild. The more you rest, the quicker you'll heal. Doc said so."

"Could you check the truck and see if I left some files in there? I can do some reading on the case."

"Sure thing. I also brought you the reports from Washington County." Coleman was being far more tractable than I'd ever imagined. "Let me grab the files and we'll get inside. I'll build a fire if you'd like." One of the benefits of Dahlia House was the many fireplaces. There was one in my bedroom, and it made the room cheerful and toasty. I could build up a fire and give Coleman his pain meds and snuggle with him until he fell asleep. I couldn't afford a nap, but a quick snuggle would do us both a world of good.

I went to his truck and got the files he wanted from beneath the seat. Five minutes later I struck the match to light a fire. Coleman couldn't drink with pain meds so I settled for soft drinks for both of us. "Reminds me of high school, drinking Cokes and watching a fire." The flames did crackle brightly. "Except we wouldn't be in bed."

"Being a grown-up has some definite advantages. But I know you have things to do, Sarah Booth. Head out. I'm fine. I can call my deputies if I need anything."

He was being really agreeable. I put a hand on his forehead to check for a fever. "Are you sure?"

"I don't need to be babysat. I'm here, I'm resting. I'll read my files and talk with DeWayne and Budgie and you when I have something to add. I promise not to overdo it. To be honest, I'm exhausted. I think I'll take a nap."

I eyed him warily. This was too, too easy. "Maybe I should call Madame Tomeeka to come over."

"Do not. I'm capable of doing what Doc says. I want to get well quickly."

The debate was interrupted by the ring of my cell phone. Tinkie was calling. She obviously had news. I answered while still giving Coleman a look. "What's shaking?"

"Delane Goggans had plenty to say. Meet me at the courthouse. We have to make Kawania talk. She's the key and DeWayne said he can't hold her much longer. She's demanding a lawyer." I put the phone down.

Coleman shook his head. "I heard. Go. Call me when you find something. I'll see if I can't do my part from this bed."

"A little shoulder wound won't slow you down for long." I leaned over to kiss him. I had the strangest tugging at my heart region—as if a tendon connected us. "Behave. You promise?"

He crossed his heart with an X. "You got it."

My heart was still sore when I drove away. Even though Coleman was doing fine, I had a terrible feeling that he needed me to be there—as if I could throw up a psychic wall of protection. Right. There was truly nothing I could do to make him heal faster. I left Sweetie Pie and Pluto to keep him company.

At the Sunflower County courthouse, I found my partner in an interview room with Kawania Laveau. The tension between them was visceral.

"I know you two aren't real cops and I don't have to answer anything you ask. I've requested my lawyer, Peter Deerstalker, and he'd better be on his way or my rights are being violated." She crossed her arms and leaned back in her chair.

"We can't violate your rights because we aren't police, and you know that."

"Maybe you should just put a curse on us," Tinkie taunted.

I had to force myself not to react. Tinkie was never belittling about supernatural things. She'd been in the room with Kawania for a good half an hour—maybe she had a reason to be so aggressive.

"What kind of curse?" I asked, earning a frown from Tinkie.

"This crazy woman thinks I'm voodooing people to death." Kawania pointed at Tinkie.

"The other students on the dig team say you've gone to a lot of trouble to make them believe in your powers. They say you cursed Dr. Sandra Wells and brought about her death." Tinkie was deadly serious. I desperately needed a private word with her, but now wasn't the time. To interrupt the interview would be to give Kawania the win.

"They are fools and easily led around by the nose." Kawania grinned with pride. "I am good at manipulating them, but I didn't harm anyone."

"What about those henna tattoos? You created

them. You organized a handful of women into a conjure group. You were calling on the darkness." Tinkie got louder with each statement until she was right in Kawania's face, pounding the table. "What did you drag out of the pits of that burial site?"

She had Kawania's attention—and good. A tear slipped out of the young woman's eye and plopped on the ugly metal table. "Dr. Wells put me up to it. She's the one who started all of this. And now she's dead, but I didn't have a thing to do with what happened to her."

"So who did? Spill it," Tinkie demanded. "Fast."

I took a seat several feet back from the table and turned on my phone to record whatever Kawania had to say. Coleman would definitely want to hear this. Budgie and DeWayne were listening, and also possibly recording, but I wasn't taking any chances of missing this interview.

"When Dr. Wells found out I was a distant relative of Marie Laveau, she said I could help her. She had an idea that if we could make people believe the mound was haunted by a ghost or spirit, it would click with the TV producers. Haunted digs, the curse of the pharaohs, you know what I'm saying. There was already a head start with the Bailey family that lived on the property and the rumors of ghosts. All I had to do was get the students worked up and in a receptive mood. That's how the tattoos came to be. We were using them as a . . . ward against evil, I guess you'd say. Sandra got one. So did I. Some others."

"And Bella Devareaux?" I asked.

"Sandra said we could trust her. They knew each other. Sandra said Bella was going to help her get rid of Frank Hafner."

"Did Sandra hire Bella Devareaux?"

Kawania shook her head. "I don't know. They met up in New Orleans, and I know Sandra was cooking up a scheme to push Hafner off the dig. She got me to talk about curses and hauntings and such and keep the students on edge and afraid. I think Bella was digging into Hafner's relationship with Delane. Sandra really wanted Hafner gone and she'd use his sexual peccadillos if necessary. I did overhear Sandra and Bella talking about the missing women. That was just another ploy to keep people upset and in turmoil, afraid to go to the dig at night."

"So they were literally working together."

"Well, it didn't work. Those with the henna tattoos, Sandra and Bella were being killed." Kawania sighed and looked toward the door of the interview room. "Where is Peter? He's my lawyer. I called him an hour ago. He should be here."

"Did he know about this . . . collaboration?"

She shook her head. "It was kind of a girl thing.

Cooley Marsh knew, but he didn't have a tattoo. He was always sneaking around eavesdropping on everyone. Bella really had a burn on for him. She would have pushed him off the top of the mound if she could have."

"Did Dr. Hafner know about any of this?" Tinkie asked.

Kawania looked at the door again, as if she expected help to come sailing in. "Maybe. Ask him. What I know is that all of us, the students, we were just pawns in their game to get grants and become stars. It's what you do for a grade when you have to do it."

"Do you have any idea who killed Devareaux and Wells?" I asked.

Kawania squirmed in her chair. "There is something out there at the dig site. Something evil."

"Don't pull that crap on me," Tinkie said. She had used up her quotient of patience, it seemed.

"It's not crap. When we started with the voodoo stuff and the apparitions, yeah, it was stories we made up to cause unhappiness in the student workers. But I saw something. Something real."

"Oh . . . You saw a ghost, didn't you?" Tinkie was on a tear.

"I don't know if it was a ghost, but it was something. Something . . . wicked."

"Describe it." I didn't believe her but I was curious what she would come up with.

"It was like something dead." She held up a

hand to stop our laughter. "It isn't funny. It was like the reanimated dead. The last time I saw it, I swear it looked just like Dr. Wells. Except it was horrible. Decayed. So ugly and rotten."

She was an effective con woman. Had it been midnight at a dig in the middle of nowhere, she might have scared me. I happened to know that ghosts were real—just not reanimated dead ghosts. Where Cece's description of what she'd seen had gotten under my skin, the same thing coming from Kawania made me skeptical. There had to be a logical explanation, and it wasn't a zombie. "Just so you know, Dr. Wells' body had already been shipped back to Michigan," I told her.

"Why are you even trying this?" Tinkie asked her.

"Because I'm telling the truth. I saw Dr. Wells at Mound Salla after she was dead." She swallowed. "Ask Cooley Marsh. He saw her, too."

How convenient that he was on our suspect list. Not much of a confirmation in my book, but I didn't need to say it out loud. "Anyone else catch sight of this miracle of Dr. Frankenstein?"

Kawania had finally had enough. "Now I'm done talking until Peter gets here. I don't think he's missing at all. I think you didn't call him. But that's all you're getting from me."

27

Tinkie and I adjourned outside and, as I sus-
pected, DeWayne and Budgie were right there.
I sent the download of the taped interview to
Coleman's phone.

"What do you make of her claim about Sandra
Wells?" Tinkie asked the two deputies.

"Reanimated dead?" DeWayne had a slow, easy
smile. "I say call the production company that
does *The Walking Dead*. We may have an episode
for them."

"Very funny," Tinkie said, but she was grinning
wide.

The sheriff's office phone began to ring and
Budgie hurried to answer it while Tinkie and I
talked to DeWayne.

"Any idea where Hafner has gone?" I asked.

"No idea. He isn't in Michigan, though Hafner
indicated he was going to speak at the professor's
funeral. He was giving the frenemy eulogy, I
suppose." DeWayne's grin was out of place. "You
should know where Hafner is. Coleman said he
was hitting on you, Sarah Booth."

"To no avail. I think he was on automatic pilot.
That's his programmed behavior. He'd try it on a

tree stump if he thought he could gain an advantage. In this instance he was just trying to piss Coleman off." A change of topic was in order. "Tinkie, did you find anything from Delane?"

She nodded. "I did. She swears she overheard Cooley Marsh talking on his cell telling someone to meet him at the Winterville Mound. Cooley said that he had evidence that would clear that person." Tinkie pointed to the knife that was on the deputy's desk. "I believe Cooley set up Peter and Cece. I think he left the knife there as part of an attempt to plant evidence against Peter and make him look guilty."

"But it isn't the murder weapon." I pointed out.

"If Coleman or one of us had happened upon Peter holding that knife with Cece potentially as his hostage, it could have ended badly," DeWayne said. "It was definitely a plant, and if Cooley made that call . . ."

"Do you think that nerdy student is actually a killer?" I asked.

"I don't know." Tinkie wasn't rushing to judgment. "He's not around the motel. I can't find him, and Cece did say it was a male who called, so it couldn't have been Delane or Kawania. It could have been Cooley."

Budgie came back to our little group frowning. "I have some strange news. Dr. Wells' body never made it to Michigan. The coffin arrived, but it was empty."

"What the hell?" DeWayne got on his phone immediately and called the hospital. After a brief conversation, he looked at us. "Doc sent the body to the funeral home where she was put in the coffin and sealed. The coffin was driven by hearse to Memphis and put on a plane. They have all the paperwork to document it."

"So where is the body?" Tinkie asked. She shuddered slightly as if someone had walked on her grave.

"Wandering around Mound Salla at night." I couldn't help it. This case had everything, and now there was a missing body. "It would seem Dr. Wells is more dedicated to that dig than we thought."

Tinkie punched my arm. Hard. "Be serious."

I rubbed my arm. "Listen, short stack, do that again and I'll pick you up like a baby and carry you to the car."

DeWayne and Budgie howled with laughter, but Tinkie was not amused.

"What are you going to do about dead professor walking?" I asked them.

"Send you and Tinkie up there to scout it out tonight." DeWayne almost preened with delight at his teasing.

"Sure, I'll check out the burial mound if you find Frank and put him and Delane in lockup, along with Cooley Marsh." The long arm of the law would have a lot more success keeping track of my missing client, his paramour, and one weird student than Tinkie or I would. "Did you guys ever talk to Cooley Marsh?"

"We did," Budgie said. "He swears he's just a student trying to get a grade, but that's not true. He isn't registered at the university as a student."

"Delane said she wasn't responsible for him. She thought Hafner had hired him." Tinkie brought them up to date with what we knew.

"Maybe Hafner brought him in as an outside worker, but he isn't a student." DeWayne was frowning. All trace of teasing was gone. "We'll clear this up when we find Hafner. Also we're going to have to let Kawania Laveau go right now. We can't just keep her in that room."

"We're done with her for the moment. Thanks." I looked at Tinkie. "What's next on the agenda?"

"I've had it with the talk of someone—or some-thing—stumbling around the dig site. We need to set up some cameras on Mound Salla. If there is someone or something up there rambling about, we should capture it on film and then we can do what we must. And, on the reality front, I don't think we'll find any zombies, but we might catch someone snooping around that doesn't belong there."

I checked my watch. It was getting late. The sun would be setting and, to be honest, I didn't want to be on top of the mound in the dark. For any reason. "Let's do it now."

"Let's head to the electronics store. We need motion-activated low-light cameras," Tinkie said.

I was making a list in my head. I wanted to set up the equipment and be gone before full dark and the rise of the moon. I wanted my friends safely tucked into their homes.

Lucky for Delaney Detective Agency, Tinkie had a platinum credit card and no reluctance to use it. We bought cameras and all the necessary gizmos to go with them. If anything moved on the top of that mound or around the bottom, we'd have it on digital files. Whatever was going on at Mound Salla, whether it was supernatural or human, we'd get to the bottom of it. And when we did, someone was going to be charged with two counts of murder.

It was still light when we arrived at Mound Salla and initiated the setup of our equipment. It didn't take long, and we talked as we worked. "We forgot to ask Kawania for a list of everyone who had one of those tattoos," Tinkie said as I pounded a stake into the hard ground.

"You're right. We need to know that."

"I'll call her." Tinkie sat down in the grass and dialed. She frowned and hung up. "It went to voice mail."

"Not everyone answers the phone every time it rings." I couldn't resist a tiny dig at Tinkie for being such a phone addict. "We should call DeWayne to check on her. And mention Sister

Grace, too. Someone should check that connection. How about I call Cece to explore this? She owes you plenty and she can check it out without an official action. Those uniforms sometimes make a girl nervous."

"With your quick thinking, you're leaving me behind in the dust, Tink." Maybe I was tired or had worried myself into dullard mode, but Tinkie was out-thinking me left and right. "Call her, please." Just after I spoke I glanced to the east. The rim of the moon had crept up onto the horizon. The pale slice looked like a portion of a giant disk. I'd never seen the moon come up that big, perhaps because of my vantage point on top of the mound. Or maybe because it was the Crow Moon, an omen of danger.

I took a moment from setting up the cameras and called Coleman, just to let him know I was thinking about him. He answered sounding a little breathless.

"Are you in bed?" I asked.

"No, but I'm fine. I can't lie in that bed. It drives me nuts."

"But you're resting and taking care of yourself?"

"I read the files. I've talked to the Washington County deputies. They're staking out Winterville Mound tonight. The manager of Tibbs Funeral Parlor insists Sandra Wells' body was put on a plane to Ann Arbor. He personally locked the coffin and sent the key. When the coffin was transferred to the funeral home in Ann Arbor, they opened it to prepare the body for viewing. No body."

"What was in the coffin?" There had to be something to give it some weight.

"Sandbags. Budgie tracked them back to a FEMA handout during a flood. Everyone along the river system was given the bags. Sand analysis shows it's local. Anyone could have had those bags."

"But not anyone would want Sandra's body." It was really creepy to think about a body snatcher. Very Victorian, with shades of Frankenstein. I didn't need that as the moon inched up the horizon. It looked so close, with all the topographic shadings clearly visible. "That's just gross." I told him about what Kawania had said about the students sighting something shambling around the mound late at night.

Coleman's laughter at least made me feel better. He didn't believe them any more than he believed Cece's "faulty vision," as he put it. "Okay," I continued. "Cece is on the trail of Kawania, who isn't answering her phone. Cooley is MIA. Those students are jumping ship like rats. That's all we know."

"What are you doing now?"

"Setting night-vision cameras on top of Mound Salla. If Sandra Wells is shuffling around here looking for brains, we'll catch her on video."

"I don't think you'll catch anything on film, but it's a great idea to use cameras."

"Tinkie and I are finishing here. I'm going to do some more digging on Bella Devareaux. There's something not right there."

"Be careful."

"Will do. You stay in the house. It's cold now. You need to let your body rebuild and recover."

"Yes, Nurse Ratched."

He could call me all the names he wanted, but I would be relentless. That was my job, according to Doc. "See you soon. I'll bring something from Millie's for dinner." I realized I'd missed a lot of good meals in the past two days because I'd been on the run from zip to zap.

"No worries. I'm a long way from starving, but your hound and cat are pretty pissed at you."

"I'll make it up to them." Tinkie was signaling me. "Gotta go. Talk soon." I slid my phone into my jacket pocket. "What's up?"

"Delane hasn't checked out of the motel, but no one has seen her for a while."

"Maybe she's with Dr. Hafner. Do you think Hafner has his competitor's dead body?" That idea was just too creepy.

"No, I don't, and that is sick, even for you," Tinkie said. "When she finishes up her story, Cece is going to join us here at the mound."

The moon was rising and the sun was slipping

away. The long shadows of ten minutes earlier were fading into dusk. It was still winter in the Mississippi Delta and the days were short. The sound of the wind soughing through the trees at the base of the mound was mournful and nerve jangling. It sounded like the trees were singing a warning. "Let's just get away from here. We'll meet Cece somewhere else."

"Let's put a camera at the trapdoor to the basement. We have one more. Let's use it. Maybe the killer will return to the scene."

Tinkie was all perky about meeting a killer. Me, not so much. I snatched the camera and ran toward the barren area where the Bailey house had once stood. The volunteer trees that had jumped up around the old homesite were so thick not even the silvery moonlight could penetrate.

While I was seeking a place to put the camera to best advantage, the huge moon rose completely above the horizon. It was big and pale gold, so close it seemed if I walked to the end of the mound's plateau I could touch it. I'd seen beautiful moons in my past thirty-four years, but never one like the Crow Moon. It was mesmerizing. I was frozen with the camera in my hand as I stared into the golden orb.

A sound deep within the woods stopped my thoughts and nearly my heart. It was probably a raccoon or possum rambling through the undergrowth, but I was on edge. I found a sturdy branch in an oak and planted the camera. It was time to go—past time. I made sure the camera lens was pointed at the area of the trapdoor that led to the basement where Bella Devareaux's body had been found. The wide angle of the lens would cover a good bit of turf, and once I had the equipment set up, the need to leave pushed hard at me. I was about to call out to Tinkie when again I heard something in the woods. It was a strange slump, shuffle, shuffle. Slump, shuffle, shuffle. Like someone with a pronounced limp was moving about in the brambles, undergrowth, and leaves.

Had Tinkie slipped past me and into the woods? She was stealthier than I realized and maybe she was trying to put one over on me. I turned around and saw her standing at the edge of the mound, looking down into the parking lot. She was nowhere near the creature moving in the woods. Behind me, the noise continued, making the hair on my neck stand on end.

Facing the woods again, I waited, watching the dancing shadows created by the moon and wind skitter about in the deadfall and rattling branches. In the bright light, I saw something through the trees and underbrush. Someone. The person moved awkwardly, stumbling from tree to tree almost as if he were blind. Something was definitely wrong.

"Tinkie." I said my partner's name, hoping

she'd hear me. I certainly didn't want whatever was in the woods to hear me.

"Tinkie!" I called a little louder, my gaze never leaving whatever was stumbling around. The person stepped into a shaft of moonlight and I saw long dark hair and a blue blouse stained with what looked like blood. It was a woman. She lifted a hand in front of herself as she shambled forward.

"Tinkie!" I yelled her name. The woman turned to look at me, pausing mid-step just as my partner joined me.

"What's up?" she asked.

I pointed to the woman on the edge of the woods.

"What the heck?" Tinkie took two steps forward for a better view. "Who is that? What's wrong with them?"

"I don't know." I could feel my heartbeat thumping in my chest. As much as I loved a good ghost story on a stormy night, this was too real.

"What's going on with that person?" Tinkie asked, her voice rising. "They look—Holy crap, that's Sandra Wells!"

"No." I wouldn't believe it. She was dead. I'd seen her body. I would not believe this—and I would not look.

"Let's get out of here." Tinkie grabbed my arm. "Sarah Booth, I don't care what it is—that thing looks like Sandra Wells. Her body is missing.

Maybe this is why. She's running around the woods up here at this dig. Maybe this place is cursed. Maybe those archeologists should never have started digging up the bones of dead people. I don't know. I don't care. We're leaving!" She grabbed my arm and tugged me with her across the moonlit plateau of the mound.

Behind us, limbs crackled and snapped and the wind sang a dirge in the trees. I glanced back. Dead Sandra had begun to follow us. She stayed at the edge of the woods, but she could move pretty fast for a corpse. I froze. I couldn't look away.

"Damn! She's coming! Run!" Tinkie pushed me hard to get me going and then she tore toward the edge of the mound. She cast one last look at me as I hesitated. "You'd better run, Sarah Booth, or she'll eat your brains!" And then she started down the incline.

I looked back at the pitiful creature that came toward me. If that was Sandra Wells, whatever had made her unique and human was gone. The creature loped and faltered toward us, a sad imitation of what once had been.

I didn't know which rule in the Daddy's Girl rulebook would cover the etiquette of what to do when approached by a zombie, and I sure wasn't going to wait around to ask Tinkie for the finer points of good manners. She wasn't waiting either. The top of her head disappeared down the side of the incline, her golden, glitzy hair more of a halo than real. I was hot on her heels. No way did I want to confront whatever was haunting the dig site. While I didn't believe in zombies, I couldn't deny what was right in front of my eyes. And hopefully the cameras we'd set up would capture it—whatever it was. It sure looked a lot like Dr. Wells, but I refused to wait for it to get close enough to make a positive ID.

Tinkie was talking on her phone as she slid down the grassy side of the mound. When we got to the bottom, we made a run for the car. It wasn't until we'd pulled out and were at least a mile away from the mound that Tinkie blew out her breath. "What the hell was that?"

"Clearly, it was a zombie." My remark earned another hard slug to my arm, but I was too traumatized to even react. We drove as fast as we dared, focusing on the road, the moon, and each trying to sort what we'd witnessed.

There was nothing else to say until we arrived back in Zinnia. "We should check those cameras," I said to Tinkie. "We have evidence of what we saw. You realize no one is ever going to believe us without proof."

Tinkie was quiet for a long moment. "What did we see, Sarah Booth?"

I wasn't all that quick with an answer, either. "It seems we saw the reanimated corpse of Dr. Sandra Wells stumbling around the dig site."

"It did look like Sandra." She fiddled with the buttons on her coat. "But did we think it was Sandra only because we know her body is missing? Because others had suggested they'd seen her?"

"No, I'm pretty sure we thought it was Sandra because it looked exactly like her. Right down to the blue broadcloth shirt she often wore."

"No kidding. I'm just thinking maybe we were played."

"In what way?" Tinkie was smart and it would behoove me to listen to her. I drove down the Main Street of Zinnia and pulled into the parking lot of the Prince Albert hotel.

"Think about all of this. The dig, the ritual killings, the tattoos. The very first day we find a talisman, a ward against evil, that amulet."

"Which may really be something intended to prevent the dead from returning to life."

Tinkie didn't contradict me. She just kept talking. "I have a sense that all of this is being orchestrated by someone. We've been chasing our tails since the very beginning."

I couldn't argue with what she was saying. "But a reanimated corpse. Who would do such a crazy thing? Why? And even more importantly, how? And how did it get from Memphis, or even from Tibb's Funeral Parlor in Zinnia, to Mound Salla? Can you imagine carrying a body up that incline?"

"I don't have any answers, but we saw what we saw and, by the laws of science and all that is holy, there is no way to reanimate the dead. Not Dr. Frankenstein. Not Mary Shelley. And not anyone in Zinnia." The creature we'd seen had frightened her badly and made her fractious. I knew exactly how she felt.

"You think the whole thing is a charade? Why would anyone do that?"

"Maybe to destroy the dig? Maybe to get rid of Hafner and Wells so a competitor could come in and take over? Maybe a publicity stunt for some reason I'm not seeing."

Tinkie had good ideas. And it was far easier to believe what we'd seen was some kind of prank or setup than a true zombie. "We have to find Hafner, which is why we're here at the Prince Albert. Someone is going to know something, and I put my money on him. We just have to make him talk."

"Call Coleman." Tinkie wasn't kidding.

"I can't do that. He needs to heal."

"You know damn good and well he isn't in bed. He's up doing something. We're just asking him to talk to the hotel staff. They'll tell him a lot more than they'll tell us."

She wasn't lying, but I couldn't, in good conscience, involve Coleman in the case. He had been shot, for pity's sake. Doc had warned me to make him stay at home and heal.

Tinkie pulled out her phone. "DeWayne, run by Dahlia House and pick up Coleman. We need him at the Prince Albert. We're onto a lead he needs to follow and then we want to have dinner at Millie's. You and Budgie are invited. My treat." She hung up and looked at me. "A man has to eat. He can sit at a table and ask a few questions while he's filling his pie hole."

"He needs to rest."

"If you honestly think he's lying around, you're deluding yourself."

Coleman wasn't the kind of person to lay about. Tinkie was dead right about that. At least if he was with us, I could make him stay calm and see that he had a good meal in him. "You win."

"But of course, my dear. Now get Cece here. I hope she hasn't already left for the mound. We need a powwow of the best and brightest. Then we can make Budgie and DeWayne retrieve the zombie footage." She grinned. "Because I'm not going back up there. I can tell you that wasn't a zombie and, intellectually, I know I'm right. But my body tells me to run in the opposite direction. Let DeWayne and Budgie take this one."

"I agree." I did as she bade me, and then motioned her out of the car. The one thing we could get at the Prince Albert that we couldn't get at Millie's was a drink. I was badly in need of some liquid fortification, but I would have to settle for caffeine since I was on the job.

28

"Tell me one more time what you saw," Coleman said as he sipped a cup of coffee. The five of us—me, Tinkie, Coleman, DeWayne, and Budgie—were parked at a small table in the bar of the Prince Albert hotel. "I want to be sure I've got a clear picture."

I looked at Tinkie and rolled my eyes. We'd told him and the deputies twice. Cece had confirmed, over the phone, what she'd seen on that fateful night with Peter Deerstalker. At first the lawmen had guffawed. The second go-round they'd laughed and frowned. Now they looked serious, but it was clear they didn't believe us. We went through the story one more time, taking care to give each detail. "We're not making this up," I told him. My tone should have been enough for them to knock off the teasing.

"If you'd had Sweetie Pie, Chablis, and Pluto with you, they would have rounded up that zombie and kept her at bay until you could get help." Coleman was straight-faced when he talked but he wasn't taking us seriously.

"Hey," DeWayne said, "what about we catch that zombie and use it for a tourist attraction. I know Sarah Booth and Tinkie hate zoos because the animals are in prison. But the thing with a zombie—it's already dead! Perfect."

"You are cruising for a bruising," Tinkie said to DeWayne. "I mean it."

"Just think of the crowds we could draw." Budgie picked up the thread of torment. "Maybe we could get Zombie Watch added to the blues trail that runs through the Delta. What if there are more zombies out there just waiting to be captured? Or capitalized on?"

"Do they really eat brains?" DeWayne asked.

"Maybe Millie could add something to the menu like roasted brains or maybe Zombie Pot Pie—a light crust filled with vegetables and fresh brains. It would be a big hit with the zombie population."

"There. Is. No. Zombie. Population." I said each word clearly.

"There is only one zombie and she's haunting both burial mounds. Let Budgie and DeWayne retrieve those cameras," Tinkie said. "You'll see, and then you'll be sorry you doubted us."

"Budgie, why don't you fetch those cameras," Coleman suggested. He was working hard to hide a grin.

Budgie sat up taller. "DeWayne and I will go get 'em."

Coleman arched one eyebrow. Now he was truly amused. "You don't need DeWayne. You're not scared to go alone, are you? DeWayne's going to find Cooley Marsh for me. He knows something and it's time for him to talk."

"I want to look for Cooley Marsh, too," Budgie said. "DeWayne and I can pick up the cameras and then jump on Cooley's trail. We'll be more efficient as a team." Budgie looked at the table-top as he spoke. Two little red spots of embarrassment touched his cheeks. He was creeped out by the zombies and didn't want to go alone. And I didn't blame him.

I grinned. "They would work faster as a team," I said to Coleman. I gave Budgie a long look so he would know I knew I was saving his butt. "While they're gone, we can talk to the hotel staff. Rain check on dinner at Millie's?"

Coleman relented. "You two take off," he said to the deputies. "Report back when you have Cooley. I did a little background check on him and found some interesting history. He's a bit old to be a college student, though he doesn't look it. Turns out he's in his late twenties."

"He couldn't be." He looked like he was in his early twenties, at most.

"Since Cooley didn't check out as a student, I did some digging." Coleman was no longer teasing. "Cooley Marsh doesn't exist. It's an alias, and we need to discover why he's using an alias."

"Why indeed." I pulled up my conversations

with him. "He said he wants to make computer games. He wanted to connect with Elton Cade, maybe have a shot at creating games for Elton's empire."

"Elton's pretty accessible," Tinkie said.

"I need to speak with Elton, Frank Hafner, and Peter Deerstalker," Coleman said.

"Is Hafner back from giving the eulogy?" Tinkie asked.

"No body, no eulogy," DeWayne noted. "He's arriving back here this evening. He knows to come by the sheriff's office."

"We still have a lot to do." Coleman stood and we all rose to our feet. It was time to get about our work. It was six o'clock, and everything in Zinnia except the hotel, Millie's Café, and the Sweetheart café, which was more of a teen hangout, had closed.

"Where's Cece?" Tinkie asked. "She was supposed to be here by now."

"I'm here, dah-link!" She came out of a hallway, pushing Kawania Laveau ahead of her. "Or should I say we're here. You should know all of the students are leaving town as quickly as they can make travel arrangements. Kawania was walking out the door when I apprehended her. And she has something to tell y'all."

I looked at the young woman who seemed to be perfectly miserable. "I didn't tell the truth about Bella Devareaux."

• • •

An interrogation in the lobby of the Prince Albert was out of the question. I whispered to Coleman that I thought he'd get more out of Kawania if he kept the questioning informal. With some reluctance he agreed to walk down to Millie's Café. He'd been nibbling on ham and potato salad, but I was starving. Tinkie, too. We'd gone all day without sustenance and, besides, I could not go home without something for the critters. They were already miffed by my neglect. Sweetie Pie, for all of her good nature, and Pluto, who was a black cat after all, could be quite vengeful.

We took a seat in a quiet corner of the café and Millie came to wait on us herself. She put a hand on Coleman's shoulder and kissed his cheek, a rare moment of open affection for him and concern for the fact he'd been shot. "Worry me like that again and I'll pour a pot of hot grits on your head," she said.

"I've surrounded myself with bloodthirsty women," he replied. He turned to Kawania. "So tell me the truth before you get yourself into more serious trouble."

I couldn't tell it if was Coleman's laser-blue gaze, his blunt honesty, her tiredness, or pent-up emotion—whatever, she began to cry. Not ugly sobbing, but tears slipping down the curves of her cheeks. "I never wanted to be involved. I didn't.

But my mom owed a lot of money for my degree. Dr. Wells said if I went along, I'd get an A. I hate archeology. I just wanted to get my degree and go home to New Orleans."

"Are you really a descendant of Marie Laveau?" I asked.

She nodded. "That's true. Probably the only thing that's true."

Millie brought our food and, while Tinkie and I ate, Kawania talked, prodded on by Coleman or Cece.

"I knew Bella from before I went to college. When I first met her in the Quarter, she lived on Barracks Street with her mom. She read tarot cards and bartended and wrote for some of the free shopper magazines. You know, she made ends meet. She's about six years older than me, and after she graduated high school, she just sort of disappeared. We lost touch until she called me and said she wanted to meet, that she was interested in the archeology dig at Mound Salla and could use my help."

"When was this?" I asked.

"Sometime last fall. In fact, Bella is the reason I signed up for the archeology class and the dig. She said if I came to Sunflower County we could renew our friendship and I could also get a good grade. My GPA isn't the greatest, and I don't have the time or money to repeat courses. An A would keep me off academic probation, plus I would be close to home so I could visit with my mother. I miss New Orleans."

For the first time I felt Kawania was being sincere. Cece must have scared the socks off her.

"What's the real story of your relationship with Peter? And what was Bella Devareaux after?"

Kawania frowned. She pressed her lips together and Coleman, not so subtly, took his handcuffs from his belt and put them on the table. It was incentive enough to get her talking.

"I told you the truth about Peter. I'm part Tunica, and he knew my mother from some tribal gatherings. As to Bella, I'm not completely sure. She was interested in the dig, but not because of missing people in Louisiana. I don't think that was ever real. She mentioned that was a good excuse to poke around here, but she was after something else. That was the whole point of her being at the dig. There was something there she wanted."

"How did Bella and Sandra become friends?" Cece asked.

"I never heard either say. But they knew each other, at least since last summer. I was on the fringes of whatever they had going on. I'm on the fringes of all of this. I only did what I was asked so I'd get an A. But I can tell you that Bella and Sandra were thick. And that creep, Cooley Marsh, was spying on them all the time."

"And what were you asked to do?" Coleman

said, but he spoke gently. "Tell the truth, Kawania. We've had enough half-truths and lies."

"Bella knew that I was a pretty good scary storyteller. She asked me to get the students goosed up about the place being haunted or cursed or whatever it took to keep them on edge and away from the site during the night. That was basically it."

"What went on at night that was so important?" Coleman followed up.

"I don't know. Something unnatural was going on, but I didn't care. I wanted a good grade. Every chance I got I headed to New Orleans to visit my mama."

"And Peter Deerstalker? What was his role?"

She looked around at each of us. "Peter wanted to stop the dig completely."

"How was he hooked in with Bella and Dr. Wells?" I pressed.

She shook her head. "He wasn't, that I know of."

"Was he involved with Hafner's schemes?" Tinkie asked.

Kawania continued with the head shake. "No. I mean, I don't know. Not to my knowledge." She blew out a long breath. "There was a lot going on under the surface, so I can't say anything for absolute certain. It seemed to me that Hafner was sincere in wanting to excavate the site and document his finds as a scientist. But who knows. There were so many rumors about who was sleeping with whom, about jealousies." She shook her head. "I stayed clear as much as I could."

Millie refilled our coffee cups and put a platter of pastries on the table. We'd consumed a huge meal, but the flaky crust and drizzled sugar wrapped around cream cheese centers was my undoing. We all grabbed one, even Kawania, who seemed to have loosened up. She acted like telling the truth was a huge relief.

"We need to know about those tattoos," I said.

"I knew that was a mistake. I should never have let Bella talk me into doing them. I just thought with the henna, they'd wear off, no one the worse for wear."

"Both dead women had tattoos. Who else?"

Kawania pulled the edge of her blouse down to reveal a tattoo on her upper chest. "I was going to give one to Delane, but she balked. She was smarter than the rest of us."

"What's the significance of the tattoo?" I asked.

"Bella had an amulet. I used that for the pattern. She told me to tell everyone it was mine, part of a voodoo inheritance, but it was hers. Everyone thinks I'm the creepy one, with my links to a dead voodoo queen, but Bella was really into the occult. Seriously. She claimed she could raise the dead."

Tinkie and I exchanged glances.

"Could she work . . . magic?" Tinkie asked.

Kawania shook her head. "I don't know. She creeped me out so I didn't hang with her. Anyway, Bella said that particular design was a family inheritance and it would seal evil in the earth. She had an idea that digging into the burial mound would release some kind of cosmic evil."

"And you believed that?" Coleman continued with his questioning.

"Doesn't matter what I believe. The students believed, and those were the people Bella and Sandra wanted to manipulate. At any rate, Bella supplied me with plenty of stories about the Bailey family and the old tales of hauntings." She gave a rueful smile. "The stories were really scary, and really sad. Poor Martha Bailey had a hard life. One son in prison, one dead, the rest scattered to the wind. I don't think Martha Bailey does very well as a fortune teller out on Highway 1."

"Wait!" I held up a hand to stop all conversation. The diner was almost empty, but even the people across the room paused. "Are you referring to Sister Grace?"

Kawania rolled her eyes. "She's about as much a palm reader as I am an astronaut. She and Bella Devareaux have known each other for a while. Bella said they met in the French Quarter when she lived there."

I looked at Tinkie. I could see the facts adding

up—her expression went from calculating to angry. "She played us like a cheap harmonica," she said.

"What are you talking about?" Cece asked.

Instead of answering her, I turned to Kawania. "How are Bella Devareaux and Sister Grace related?"

She shook her head. "I don't know."

But I did. "They're mother and daughter. They were working this dig for some reason."

"That can't be true," Kawania said. "Bella told me her mother had died several years back. That would mean that—"

"Bella Devareaux is a Bailey. That's how she knew about the basement. After all this time, she came back to find something at their old family homesite. What in the hell was she hoping to find at this dig?"

29

Coleman started toward the door. I dodged around three tables and got there before him. "No. You're not going to help DeWayne and Budgie." The look in his eye made me step back. "Please, Coleman. They can find Cooley Marsh. You need to heal. I'm asking you to do what Doc said." I put a hand on his cheek. "I swear that if I'm hurt again I will obey Doc to the letter."

His grin was slow, and I knew it cost him. "I'll hold you to that."

"I expect you to."

"Remember, we don't know how Marsh—or whatever his real name is—figures into things, but his background is suspect, and if he made that call to Peter Deerstalker to lure him to the mound where I was shot . . ."

I could tell Coleman was itching to go. "I'll take Coleman back to Dahlia House with the food for the critters. I can also drop Kawania off where she needs to be."

"I want to go home to New Orleans and see my mama." Her eyes filled with tears, but she didn't cry. "Can I?"

Coleman nodded. "We may need to talk to you

again, but for now you can go. Don't make us come looking for you if we call."

"I won't. I'll help any way I can. I just want this all to go away. I'm sorry I ever took the class. I'm not going to get a good grade and I've wasted a whole semester."

For the first time since I'd met her, Kawania sounded like an average college student. Priorities were grades, grades, grades.

We broke into our respective chores. Cece was on deadline at the paper and only a moron would brook the ill favor of Ed Oakes after the disappearing stunt Cece had pulled earlier. Tinkie and I took Coleman home and the deputies headed out to Mound Salla to check the footage on the cameras we'd set up.

Sweetie Pie and Pluto greeted us on the front porch. Though they were clearly miffed at me for abandoning them, they were glad to see the food boxes from Millie's.

Tinkie took care of feeding the critters while I led the way to my bedroom. Coleman willingly went upstairs and stretched out on my bed. The moonlight pouring through the window limned the entire room in silvery gold. I gave him his antibiotics and pain medicine. "Sleep if you can. If we need you, I promise I'll come and get you."

"I am bone weary, and my shoulder is really starting to throb. I may have overdone it."

That worried me—Coleman had a tough time

admitting any vulnerability, just like me. But it was good he could be honest with me. It showed a trust between us that I valued and intended to study. This was what it meant to be in a real relationship. To be able to share even your fears with the person you loved. I needed a lot of work in that area. When my parents were killed, my survival response had been to show no weakness. Ever. Not to others and not even to myself. I thought of a song my mother had loved by Simon and Garfunkel. The lyrics had gone on about a rock never feeling pain and an island never crying. But rocks and islands also never shared intimacy. Double-sided blade.

I turned off the lights in the bedroom and kissed Coleman tenderly on the lips. "I'll be back." Tinkie and I had plenty to do. Delane and Frank Hafner were out of pocket, but I was most eager to visit Sister Grace.

"Be careful, Sarah Booth. This has gone on long enough."

It did seem like I'd been on this case for a month of Sundays but it really had been just a few days. Time had collapsed in on itself. "If we find anything interesting, I'll call." I didn't want Coleman to feel left out. I knew that misery.

"Please. I'll be eager to help. Right after I take a nap."

Since the room was already dark, I kissed his forehead and tiptoed out. "Sweet dreams," I said at the doorway, something my parents had always said to me. He didn't respond but I listened for a moment to the steady whisper of his breath as he slept.

My bedroom was toasty warm and the fire was still banked—things would hold there until I finished what I needed to do. I found Tinkie in the kitchen, and I whistled up Sweetie Pie knowing Pluto would be right with her. We all loaded into my car.

"Going to pay a visit to Sister Grace?" Tinkie asked.

"You're a regular mind reader," I told her. "She could have mentioned to us that she had a long and unhappy history with the dig site and a relationship with Bella Devareaux."

"It's strange that she wasn't visibly upset about Bella's murder." Tinkie hit the nail on the head.

"Very strange."

"Who owns the property now?" Tinkie asked.

"I don't know, but that's definitely something we should find out." It was a point we shouldn't have overlooked. "Call Cece and see if she can access the land ownership records on-line."

Tinkie placed the call. She chatted with Cece for a moment before she hung up. "Cece's on it. She's also got a lead on Delane."

"Is she up at the school in Michigan?"

"No," Tinkie said. "She's at Elton Cade's house with Peter Deerstalker. As Coleman requested,

Peter checked in with the deputies. He took it seriously when Coleman told him not to leave the county. He's staying there until all of this is cleared up. Elton invited him."

"Elton's a good guy. I know he has a lot of money riding on this excavation. These murders have messed it all up. I guess when you have as much money as he has you don't let the small stuff get under your skin. What about Frank Hafner? Anyone run him to ground?"

"Not yet," Tinkie said. "Or if they have, no one has told Cece. She's still after him."

I got the Roadster on the road and headed west for Highway 1 and a fortune teller going by the name of Sister Grace. It should have been Sister Liar Liar Pants on Fire.

"You should call Coleman," Tinkie said when we were about five minutes away from the palm reader's house. "Just to let him know where we are."

"Let's wait until we have some news," I told her. "I hope Coleman is asleep. He was snoozing pretty good when I left, and those painkillers should help him stay conked out."

"You really do love that man, don't you?"

Tinkie's question held a certain longing. "I do. And you love Oscar."

Her momentary melancholy disappeared. "We're both lucky in love."

"And a lot more." I pulled into the front of

the modest house with the palm reading sign. It looked as empty as it had the last time we were there. I almost told Tinkie to put my gun in her purse, but Sister Grace was an older woman. We could easily handle her, if it came to that. It had been a long time since I'd thought about another older woman who I'd sorely underestimated— Gertrude Strom. Gertrude, an unassuming B and B owner outside Zinnia, had tried to kill me more than once—and she'd shot my fiancé Graf Milieu in the leg and could have crippled him. My nemesis was still on the loose, but she hadn't been seen or heard from in months. And I was a person who believed in letting sleeping dogs lie.

"You ready?" Tinkie asked. "I vote for direct confrontation."

"I'm backing your play."

We walked up to the front door and knocked with authority. The door opened instantly and Sister Grace, aka Martha Bailey, grinned at us. "I guess the jig is up," she said.

"Martha Bailey?" Tinkie asked.

"She is my past. I've reincarnated. I've trans-formed." She laughed out loud. "I have left that poor pathetic woman behind and become a whole new person."

I couldn't help it. I stepped back. There was something wrong with Martha Bailey—a hint of madness in her eyes. "We need to talk to you." I kept it low-key.

"Come in." She pushed the screen door open so we could enter. "Excuse the mess."

The place was wrecked. It looked like someone had gone through everything in the house looking for something. "Did they find what they were looking for?" I asked her.

She looked around and shrugged. "Who can tell? First I'd have to know what they sought."

She might be on the verge of madness, but she was cunning. I'd completely missed the glint of obsession in her eyes when we'd first stopped by looking for Cece. "Who tore up your house?" I asked. A direct question might prove easier for her.

"Oh, you know how it is with children. No matter how old they are, they're still Mama's babies." She waved a hand around. "Ingrates. That's what Arbin called them. They came out of the womb sucking at everything around them." She chuckled. "Maybe he was right all along."

Whatever bit of sanity Sister Grace had held on to two days ago, it was gone. She'd slipped into Oz, and I couldn't make head nor tail of what she was saying.

"Sit down, Martha," Tinkie said gently, assisting her to a chair. "Who came into your house and did this?" she asked.

"What difference does it make?" The madness receded and there was simply hopelessness in her face. "They come and go. Always the big dream.

Frank hasn't helped them. Not at all. Not like he promised. Now I'm getting the blame."

"You know Frank Hafner?" I asked, trying to emulate Tinkie's soothing tone.

"Yeah, sure. He went to school with Arbin over in Georgia. He always thought he was better than us. He got his doctorate. He had a tenured position. He went to cocktail parties and hobnobbed with the intellectuals while Arbin worked at the locks on the river, drank beer with the boys, and I raised a brood of thankless young'uns."

"You sacrificed everything for your children." I remembered what Coleman had said.

"And all it did was make them think I owed them more."

It was a harsh indictment. "Did your children come here and tear up your house?" Glass and knickknacks were scattered on the floor. Drawers had been pulled out, the contents thrown about the room. Smaller pieces of furniture had been overturned and the backs and sides sliced as if someone had been searching for something stuffed inside.

"I suspect it was one of them. I didn't see who it was."

"What were they looking for?" Tinkie asked. She'd sat down beside Martha and patted her shoulder.

"They believed all that foolishness about something of great value in that Indian burial mound. Arbin filled their heads full of nonsense to make up for the things he didn't provide for them. Stupid brats. They hung on his every word. Me, I worked three jobs, stopped buying clothes or doing anything for myself. They had no use for me. It was always Arbin and his foolishness."

"What stories?" I asked gently. "What was the valuable thing at the burial mound?"

"Dirt." She laughed. "Nothing there but dirt, some pottery shards, and bones. That and the spirits of the dead. That's the other thing. What none of the kids counted on." Her grin was filled with malice.

"What didn't they count on?" I asked.

"Something evil walked that mound late at night and protected all the secrets hidden there. Arbin ran across it a time or two when he thought he'd get wise and dig around to find that secret treasure he was always going on about. I told him not to mess with dead Indians, that they deserved to rest in peace. He couldn't help himself, though. He'd drink with 'the boys' and ended up out there with a flashlight and shovel. It was bad enough when he was doing it by himself, and then he got the boys going. And Bonita. They were all caught up in it. They'd sleep all day to go hunting for treasure at night, leaving me to run the house and earn a living. Worthless."

Time had not been kind to Martha Bailey. The

bitterness had festered and changed her into someone who had lost her joy.

"What was this big treasure?" Tinkie asked.

"Who knows? It was some kind of fountain of youth or some such foolishness. To hear Arbin spin a yarn, the people buried in that mound lived to be much older than normal humans. They'd found the secret to heal illnesses and such." She waved a hand through the air in a gesture of dismissal. "Arbin was a fool and my kids fell right in with him. He's the one planted that seed of hatred between Bradley and Jason. He's to blame for setting them against each other to the point that Brad killed his brother. Arbin was gone by then, only coming back to dig and stir up trouble with the boys. I shoulda killed him years ago, putting that ignorant bullshit in their heads and then taunting them into hurting each other."

I couldn't imagine a father pitting his kids against each other, but lots of tragic things happened in "average" households every day. "Did they ever find any signs of this miracle . . . solution?"

"Are you kidding? Arbin lived in the realm of *The X-Files* and *Ancient Aliens*. He was certain some space creatures had come down, lived with the Indians, and given them the cure for old age and illness. Even after he abandoned us, he'd sneak back up to the mound and dig. I called the cops on him more than once, but he always got away sliding down the backside of the mound and cutting through the woods."

"Was Bella Devareaux your daughter named Bonita?" Tinkie asked gently.

For a moment Martha's face changed to sorrow. "She was. She changed her name when she moved to New Orleans. I didn't blame her. I was sorry to see her come back here. I tried to make her leave, tried to make her step away. She couldn't, though. She was as caught up in this as Carl."

While Tinkie was consoling Martha as best she could, I stepped to the place where someone had swept everything from the top of a dresser. Amidst the fragments of glass from a broken frame I picked up a picture of a family gathered in front of an old Southern house in disrepair. The Bailey house. A much younger Martha Bailey stood with a brood of kids. I recognized the slender girl who would grow up to be Bella Devareaux. And there was a boy, standing beside Bella. The years had changed him, too, and I couldn't be positive, but I thought I knew him.

"Mrs. Bailey, is this your son Carl?" I held the photo out to her.

"That's him. Changed his name, too. No one wanted to carry the Bailey name."

"Is his name Cooley Marsh?" I asked.

"That's him. He's the one came in and tore up my house."

My cell phone rang, and I heaved a sigh of relief. "We'd better be on our way."

"Yeah, we have a lot to do," Tinkie said. She was as eager as I to get out of there.

"If you see my worthless kids, tell them not to bother to come by unless they bring money to pay me back."

We didn't respond as we got in the car and drove away. When we were several miles down the road, I pulled over. There was a weight on my heart. When I looked at Tinkie, she, too, was upset.

"Her daughter is dead and her son is likely in some trouble," Tinkie said.

"It just seems like a terrible waste. Do you think Cooley killed his own sister *and* Dr. Wells?"

"There's a family history of sibling-on-sibling violence. What do you make of this elixir for health and immortality?"

"There's no such thing as this fountain of youth. You know that. Arbin Bailey must have been half a bubble off, and his kids didn't fall far from the tree. But why go to all the trouble of this subterfuge? Why didn't Bella or Bonita or whoever just show up and volunteer at the dig? They would have accepted her."

"I don't know," Tinkie said. "But we're going to find out. But first we need to stop by Hilltop to get Chablis."

"Absolutely." I pulled the car back on the road,

did a U-turn, and headed to Zinnia. "We have to find Frank and make him tell us what he knows about this elixir. He's lied to us the whole time. If he knew about this . . ."

I didn't have to finish the threat. Tinkie already had blood in her eye.

30

By the time we'd picked up Tinkie's pup at her home and driven to Dahlia House—I had to check on Coleman—we'd figured out some of the major connections of the case. While the waters were still muddied with lies and false motivations, we'd linked some dots in the pattern. I couldn't wait to tell Coleman that Bella Devareaux was none other than Bonita Bailey and that Cooley Marsh was her brother, Carl.

The day was ending and I had a terrible, nagging feeling that I was neglecting something important. I fed the horses while Tinkie went inside to put on some coffee. In the quiet of the barn, I listened to the horses snuffling as they ate their grain. Bonita and Carl Bailey had returned to Mound Salla to follow the obsession their father had instilled in them—the idea that some magical elixir was hidden in the mound. It was cockamamie bull, but people sometimes needed a Camelot to believe in. I understood that perfectly. But the question of their relationship was whether they had been so competitive with each other that Carl had murdered his sister. The Baileys had a history of fratricide, so perhaps sororicide wasn't out of the question.

Once the horses had finished I put out three flakes of hay for each one and made sure their turnout blankets were snug. The weather prediction was for a warm-up beginning tomorrow, but the night would still be cold and bitter—and bright from the full moon.

I went inside to find Coleman at the kitchen table, sharing a cup of coffee with my partner in solving crime. "That's some good detective work, Sarah Booth," Coleman said when I walked in.

"We stumbled into it."

"You found the Sister Grace connection and you worked it. That's the legwork that always pays off."

I didn't want to preen and flutter at his praise, but it did make me smile. "Thanks."

"I was thinking about the Baileys," Coleman said. "Martha, I remember. I had no idea she'd turned herself into a palm reader, but I guess it beats standing at a conveyor belt checking groceries."

"I guess." I shook off the sadness that came from realizing people had wrecked their own lives. "Peter and Kawania are linked into this. Either innocently or because they knew the legends. This may be why Peter was so dead set against the dig. If he thought something of value was in the mound, it should go to his people, but it wouldn't."

"You're likely correct. Depends on the contract. But as you well know, it was also highly likely that if someone found something of that value, it might just disappear."

"We need to talk to Peter."

"He's at Elton Cade's house."

"I'll give him a call." When Peter didn't answer, I dialed Elton Cade. I watched Coleman make ham sandwiches as I talked to Elton. My man looked like he was preparing to feed a battalion of men. I counted at least seven sandwiches.

"Do you know where Peter is?" I asked Elton.

"He said he had to look at something out at Mound Salla. He was insistent. I offered to go with him, but he said he had to do it alone," Elton said. "Can I help?"

"No. But thanks." I hung up with a sick feeling in the pit of my stomach. "Peter went to Mound Salla."

"I'm making sandwiches for DeWayne and Budgie. They were supposed to come by here with the camera images so we could watch together. I'm eager to see what scared you so." He checked his watch. "They should have been back by now."

"Yeah. They should have." I looked at Tinkie. We both knew what had to happen. No matter how much we didn't want to do it. "Tinkie, call Delane Goggans. See if she answers."

"I think she's flown the coop," Tinkie said, but

she dialed. Her eyebrows jumped up her forehead when someone answered the phone. "Delane?"

The person on the other end of the phone answered, but I couldn't understand what they said.

"What?" Tinkie put the phone on speaker so Coleman and I could hear.

"Leave me alone." The young woman's voice sounded muffled or maybe she'd been crying. "I'm safe, but leave me be or I'll be in danger. Don't call me again."

"Where are you?"

"I'm at the bus station. Frank told me to beat it. I'm going home." She sounded breathless.

I kissed Coleman on the cheek and motioned Tinkie toward the door. If Delane was at the bus station, we'd have her in our custody in under fifteen minutes. We just had to hustle. Tinkie was still talking soothingly to her when we hit the door. Sweetie Pie, Chablis, and Pluto were not going to be left behind this time, and I let them into the backseat.

"Delane, just give us a chance to talk," Tinkie said as I drove. "Where is Frank?"

"I have to go." Delane sobbed. "I have to go. Frank told me to run. I should have listened to him but I love him." Her voice faded, and in the background I thought I heard a male say something.

"Delane!" I had to keep her talking. "We're

coming to the bus station. Just stay there. We can help you."

"No one. No one can help. Save Frank. I know you think he's a horndog, but he truly loves me. The whole thing between him and Sandra was fabricated to gain attention for the dig. I told him it was stupid. He doesn't sleep around. I want you to know he loves me enough to send me away to keep me safe. Something terrible is going to happen tonight and no one can stop it." She broke the connection.

Tinkie put her phone away and looked at me. "She isn't right. Something is wrong with her."

"I agree." As I pulled out of the driveway on the county road, a bank of clouds parted. I looked to the pasture where my horses grazed and felt a stab of fear in my heart. Standing alone was another horse. Astride the horse was Buffalo Calf Road Woman. She held a war staff in her hand, the feathers ruffling in a gentle breeze. Her gaze found mine and held. She nodded briefly, as if to say that I'd been warned. A whisper of a wind flute came to me, and then the clouds shifted and the image was gone.

"What's wrong?" Tinkie asked me.

"Get my gun out of the glove box. You keep it. Put some bullets in your pocket."

"You're kind of creeping me out," Tinkie said. "What do you know?"

"You heard Delane. Someone very dangerous is

out and about tonight. I'm afraid we're going to run into them."

"I'll call Budgie and DeWayne."

Coleman was waiting for them, but I'd feel a lot better if they met us at the bus station. "Okay."

Tinkie dialed both cell phones but neither of the deputies answered. "I wonder what they found on those cameras," she said as she put her phone down and checked the pistol to make sure it was loaded. Meanwhile, I called Coleman. When he didn't answer, I felt again the brush of disaster that swept over me like the shadow of a raven's wing.

"Where is everyone?" I asked as I turned into the parking lot by the bus station. The lot was devoid of cars, and the bus station was empty except for an older man behind the counter.

"Can I help you?" he asked.

"Is there a young woman here?"

He shook his head. "There was a brunette here. The bus to Memphis just pulled out. That's the last bus for the evening. Nothing until morning."

"Thanks." I made a quick check of the ladies' room just in case Delane was hiding. It was empty, and I had no reason to believe the elderly clerk would not tell me the truth. Delane Goggans had made a bid for freedom and we'd just missed her. Now I had to round up Budgie, DeWayne, and Peter Deerstalker. "I guess we're going to

Mound Salla," I said to Tinkie as we left the bus station. "Something is going on there."

"I'd rather go to hell in a handbasket," Tinkie admitted. "I don't know what we saw there the other night, and I don't want to find out."

"If something's happened to the deputies, we have to find them. Else Coleman will drive out there and you know it. Peter's supposed to be there, too. We'll honk the car horn until they all come to us. To be on the safe side I'll text Coleman our plan."

"Let's go." Tinkie was resigned. "The sooner we get there, the sooner we can leave."

I parked beside the Sunflower County sheriff's cruiser and Peter Deerstalker's SUV. There was no sign of the people who should have been *in* the cars. Tinkie put a hand on the door handle but didn't open it.

"I don't believe in zombies," she said. "Just so you know."

"Are you telling me something new or trying to convince yourself?" I nudged her in the rib cage. "Personally, I'd prefer to load up our friends, snatch those videos, and get out of here."

"Yeah." She reached over and laid on the horn for a full minute. As the sound blared, the clouds parted and the full moon lit the scene. The night was peaceful and serene once the noise stopped. We waited, but there was no sign of anyone.

I had the sense that we were truly alone at the old burial site.

"This is not good," Tinkie said. She opened the car door and stood. Sweetie Pie, Chablis, and Pluto cascaded out of the car. The hound sniffed the air, testing. Pluto stretched and yawned, then began licking a paw as if he had all the time in the world.

I laid on the horn again, for a full minute. As we scanned the area for signs of life, we found nothing. Near the tree line, a breeze whispered through the bare limbs and set a few pine needles to rattling. The dread that I'd felt leaving Dahlia House hit me hard again.

"Do we have to go to the top of the mound?" Tinkie asked.

"I don't want to."

"Do you think Budgie and DeWayne are here?" she asked.

"I don't know, which is why we're going to have to look. Their vehicle is here. We can't just leave without seeing if they're in trouble. If they could answer, they would have come when we blew the horn."

"Look at Sweetie Pie." Tinkie pointed to my hound, who was sniffing the ground, moving quickly, stopping to lift her muzzle to test the air. She moaned softly in her throat and looked at me.

"What is it, girl?" I hated to ask because I was afraid she'd tell me.

She moaned and shook her head until her ears flapped, then she started up the side of the mound. She looked back to see if we followed.

"Let's go," I said. "Be sure you have the gun."

"Check." Tinkie sighed. "I don't want to do this."

"Nope, but we're doing it anyway."

Sweetie Pie was halfway up the mound under a moon so bright that we all cast shadows. The pale gold orb floated just beyond the edge of the mound. "Where in the heck are DeWayne and Budgie?" My voice held a slight whine. I was scared, and that made me angry and irritated.

"They would have come if they could have."

Tinkie said what I knew—and didn't want to acknowledge. The two deputies were in trouble. "Peter is here, too."

"Maybe." Tinkie was huffing slightly. "Damn, I hate this mound of dirt."

We made it to the top and peeped over. The grassy plateau stretched out in front of us, empty in the moonlight. The area where the most extensive digging had been ongoing was empty. The tent camp was abandoned. I motioned toward the area where trees had grown up around the old Bailey plantation. "They have to be over there."

"Let's check for fresh signs of digging. If someone is looking for treasure, it won't be where the Bailey home stood."

She was right. We moved across the top of the

mound in a crouched position because we were completely exposed—a perfect target. When we got to the area where sifting tables and machinery to carefully excavate the site had been left in place, Tinkie put a hand on my arm. Beside the hole that had been dug, presumably for Dr. Wells' body, were fresh marks of excavation. This had been done with a backhoe and without care. Someone had been in a great hurry.

"Dr. Hafner is going to be PO'ed," I said. Whatever else Hafner might have done, I didn't believe he would destroy the integrity of his site.

Tinkie knelt at the edge of the pit. "How can we tell if they found what they were looking for?"

To the right of us, near the tents, I sensed more than saw movement. I checked around for the dogs and cat, but they were on the other side of the mound where the old Bailey house had stood. I put a hand on Tinkie's wrist. "Someone is over there."

She followed my gaze. "You sure?"

"I am."

"Let's check for the deputies and get out of here. Sarah Booth, they have to be up here. The car is here."

I nodded and we went toward the tents. Neither of us spoke what was heavy on our minds—if the deputies had been able to answer us, they would have. Either they were gone from the dig or they were detained in a way that prevented them from answering. First, they wouldn't have abandoned the patrol car. Second, it would take a lot to contain DeWayne and Budgie. They wouldn't go down quietly, a fact that resulted in the pounding of my heart.

Tinkie and I moved toward the first of the six tents. Sweetie Pie took a flanking movement on the left, and Pluto on the right. Chablis clung to us as Tinkie and I advanced down the center.

The scene, silvered as it was by moonlight, was unnaturally still. A breeze kicked up and the fabric of the tents began to move softly. It wasn't hard to imagine someone, or something, hiding behind a flap, waiting for the right moment to strike. Every ion of my survival instinct screamed at me to run—to step on anyone who got in the way of me getting off that mound and into my car and driving away.

I watched the dogs and cat creep forward, and I stilled the impulse to run. Two women were dead. Coleman had been shot, and two deputies were missing. Tinkie, Cece, and I had been terrorized. If the answer to what was happening at Mound Salla would put an end to the violence, I was going to find the solution. I would not run. There was no such thing as a zombie.

"The dead can't return to life," Tinkie said out loud, as if she sensed where my thoughts had gone.

"Let's do this." I stepped into the first tent and shined my flashlight over the bedrolls, duffle bags, and general mess that people camping out acquired. The tent was empty of all living creatures.

We moved on to the second tent. Pluto stood at the entrance and when I started inside, he caught my jeans with a sharp claw and held me in place. Tinkie ran into the back of me, but neither of us uttered a peep. Aware that Pluto was warning me of danger, I pushed the flap of the tent back and stepped inside. Tinkie peered around my shoulder.

"Oh, no!" She whispered her dismay.

Delane Goggans lay in the dirt in the middle of the tent. Her still body made me think she was dead, but I knelt beside her and felt for a pulse. There was a faint throb beneath my fingers. "She's alive."

"What's wrong with her?" Tinkie whispered.

I rolled her slightly so I could see her face, which was bloodless, but there were no signs of injury. "Delane." I patted her cheek, hoping to wake her. "Delane."

She moaned softly but didn't wake.

"She's been drugged." Her skin was chill beneath my hand.

Tinkie knelt down beside her, too, and put a palm on her face. "She's too cold, Sarah Booth. I wonder how long she's been laying here on the ground. It's freezing. She was never at the bus station. When she called, she must have been here."

I grabbed a sleeping bag and put it over Delane. She looked like such a child. "We need to get her to the hospital."

"Yeah." Tinkie snugged the covers up to Delane's chin and tucked it around her. "What about DeWayne and Budgie?"

"We have to call for help. If they're up here and injured . . ."

"Right." She reached for her cell phone, but a noise from outside stopped us. It was Sweetie Pie growling deep in her throat. Beside me, Pluto arched his back, every hair on end. Chablis, who weighed five pounds, took a stance to guard the entrance.

"Who's out there?" Tinkie asked in a barely audible voice.

I didn't answer. I was too busy looking at the shadow the moon cast on the side of the tent. Someone was outside the tent. They stepped forward, dragging one leg behind, lurching and then stumbling. Primal fear blocked the scream in my throat.

Tinkie and I clung together, hovering over the prone Delane. Sweetie Pie, Chablis, and Pluto took point, prepared to defend us to the death.

The shadow moved along the tent, struggling. It looked an awful lot like a zombie shuffling about. I hated that my mind went there, but I couldn't stop it. Tinkie gripped my hand so hard I thought she might break the bones in it. "What is that?" she asked.

The thing stopped and turned to face the tent, as if it had heard Tinkie's whisper. Or maybe it could smell us. I shook my head at Tinkie and put my finger to my lips. After a moment, it began to limp forward.

We could see only the shadow, but the moon was bright enough that the creature's actions were clear. I pulled out my cell phone and began filming. If something had happened to the cameras that we'd set up, at least we'd have proof. The creature lifted its face to the moon and I swear it was sniffing, like a dog on a scent.

When it was at the back of the tent, I motioned Tinkie to move the flap aside. We had to make a run for it. Tinkie pointed at Delane. She was still unconscious and completely defenseless.

"We'll call reinforcements. We also need to find the deputies." I was genuinely worried about DeWayne and Budgie. If anything happened to them—or anyone—Coleman would blame himself. We had to get out of there before we were trapped inside the tent. We'd be no help to anyone. And we needed backup. The entire Sunflower County sheriff's office was out of commission. "We can call Junior at the bail bond office. He'll get help here."

"And Doc." Tinkie looked at Delane. "There's something really wrong with her."

"She's probably been drugged, but I don't know what to do until we find out with what substance. So let's go." I put a hand on the tent flap and pulled it back. The limping, shuffling creature thing was at the back of the tent. Now was our chance to make a break for it. I grabbed Tinkie's hand. "Let's go!"

We bolted out of the tent at full speed, only to meet with an unmoving obstacle. I hit someone hard and fell back into Tinkie. When I regained my footing, I saw Cooley Marsh standing as cool as could be.

"What's the rush?" he asked, and I knew we were in big trouble. In the strong moonlight, I finally saw the resemblance. His forehead and eyes, his nose, the line of his jaw—Cooley Marsh was indeed Carl Bailey, sister to the dead Bella and son to Sister Grace.

"Hello, Carl," I said. "What brings you out on such a fine night?"

"So, you finally figured it out."

"I haven't figured out how you could kill your own sister. But Bella wasn't the first of your siblings to die because of something here at Mound Salla, was she?"

"I didn't have anything to do with Bella. You can't pin that on me, either. I warned her to stay away. I did. She wouldn't listen. She thought she

417

was working with Dr. Wells, but I knew Wells would betray her at the first chance."

"So you killed Dr. Wells," Tinkie said.

Cooley shook his head. "You're still in the dark."

"What are you doing up here?" I asked. "You're digging for something." I pointed toward the trench someone had dug with a backhoe. "Did you find anything?"

"It's not a good idea to be poking around here, ladies." He held a gun loosely at his side. Tinkie had one tucked in the back of her belt and I put a hand on her to stop her from reaching for it.

"Who do you work for, Carl?"

"Now that's the big question, isn't it?" He was perfectly at ease, and the look in his eyes said he was no stranger to doing whatever was necessary. "Maybe I work for myself."

"Then you did kill Bella and Dr. Wells." I could see he was following my logic.

"I told you, I didn't kill anyone."

"What did you give Delane? She's been in the cold for too long. She needs medical attention."

"She'll be fine. Those two yokel deputies, too."

"Where are they?"

"They took a little tumble into the basement. Nosy parkers get their just deserts. Now you're going down there, too. We'll be finished here in another hour and gone."

"'We'? Finished with what?" I asked.

He chuckled softly. "If I told you I'd have to kill you. And you don't want that, now, do you?" He motioned for us to move toward the area where the old Bailey house had stood.

"Let us get Delane. We'll take her with us. She'll die of hypothermia if we don't." Tinkie stood her ground.

"Well hurry up, then," Carl said. "She won't be the only one dead around here if you don't get moving."

31

Tinkie and I bundled Delane in the sleeping bag, where we also hid the gun. Between us we got her to her feet and dragged her out of the tent. Carl/Cooley made no effort to help us. Delane wasn't big, but she was dead weight and we struggled. As we made our way across the grounds, I looked for my cat and the dogs. They were AWOL, and I was glad they'd had sense enough to cut out. They might be the only help we could expect if Cooley locked us in the old basement.

"Are DeWayne and Budgie hurt?" I asked Cooley.

"They aren't dead. They got some bumps and bruises, but nothing life-threatening. I told you before, I don't have an interest in killing anyone."

I tamped down the impulse to try a roundhouse kick. "Why are you doing this?" I asked. "Do you really believe there's something here so valuable it's worth all of this?"

"My whole life everyone's taken what I should have gotten. I spent my childhood hunting for this treasure, but we never had the tools to really look. My dad couldn't get the right equipment. We dug with our hands and shovels." His bitterness was clear. "We just never had the money to do it right." In the pale light of the moon, he grinned. "Jason was gonna dynamite the mound. He was gonna get that treasure. That's when he and Brad got into it. End result was one dead brother and one still in prison."

Tinkie and I finally made it to the trapdoor. Cooley opened it.

"Hey! Get us out of here." DeWayne sounded okay. "Budgie is hurt. We need a doctor."

"It's me and Tinkie," I said. "We're coming down with an unconscious woman." I'd explain later. "Help me with her." Tinkie and I managed to position her so we could lower her into DeWayne's arms.

"Get down there!" Cooley pushed at Tinkie and almost made her fall in. "Move!"

"You're going to pay for being such a—"

I didn't get to finish. He shoved me right on top of Tinkie. We both made it into the dark basement without breaking our necks—but just barely. The trapdoor slammed hard and I heard the bolt shoot home. We were prisoners.

"Budgie is hurt pretty badly," DeWayne said. "He broke his leg. The bone is sticking out."

Tinkie knelt beside Budgie, who now had the unconscious Delane beside him. "Try to keep her warm, Budgie. We'll get out of this. Doc is only a phone call away." She whipped out her phone.

"No reception down here," Budgie said, gasping a little from the pain as he talked.

"Who knows you're here?" DeWayne asked.

"Coleman," Tinkie and I said in unison. I added, "Don't worry. When he can't raise any of us, he'll get help. He'll call the Mississippi Bureau of Investigation, the state troopers, some of the other counties."

DeWayne eased me to the side. "Budgie has lost a lot of blood. He needs help now."

"As quickly as we can," I promised.

"Did you see anything . . . out there?" DeWayne asked.

The way he phrased the question told me instantly what he was talking about. "I saw a shadow of something limping around the tents. Did you?"

"Something." He hesitated. "I swear, Sarah Booth. It didn't move like it was human, but I didn't get a good look. What did you see?"

"I didn't get a good look either. But I did clearly see Cooley Marsh, aka Carl Bailey, and he's a lot more dangerous than something limping around in the moonlight."

"So Cooley is a Bailey. As was Bella Devareaux. And their mom is still in the area going by the name Sister Grace. What are they up to?"

"Some kind of buried treasure," I said.

"An elixir," Tinkie clarified. "If it even exists."

"Was the whole dig centered around this? Was Hafner in on it?"

"I don't know, but maybe Delane can answer that when she comes to."

"Right." DeWayne took a deep breath. "I'm going to rig a lift so I can haul Budgie out of here the first chance we get. That winch and hook are still over by the dig site. We can use that and I'll have him out of here in a blink. The girl, too, if she isn't awake by then."

"I'd like to know what Cooley gave her to knock her out." Budgie was using his own body to warm her up, but she wasn't responding. Tinkie chaffed her hands and feet. My concerns for Delane were growing. "Do you know what he used?"

"He didn't say. I swear, it would be karma if there was some dead thing out there waiting to extract revenge on Cooley and everyone involved with him." DeWayne was busy making a rope harness from some supplies he'd found in a corner.

Delane moaned softly and began to thrash. Tinkie tried to soothe her but she seemed to be in pain—whether it was physical or some mental torment, I couldn't say. "At least she's moving," I said, trying to be positive.

"I don't want her to convulse," Tinkie said. "We've got to get her and Budgie out of here."

"I know." I went up the stairs to the trapdoor

and pushed hard. It was bolted. I'd seen the thumb bolt that held both sides of the exit closed. I banged on the wood. "Cooley, we have two injured people down here. You're going to be responsible for their deaths if you don't let us out."

There was no answer.

I paced the enclosure for what seemed like an hour. Finally I found an old desk to sit on and stopped. "Did you see Peter Deerstalker or Frank Hafner up here?" I asked DeWayne.

"Budgie and I were busy gathering the cameras, which that criminal Cooley Marsh took from us. We didn't get a chance to check them out, either. And we didn't see anyone else. I have no idea where Cooley came from. He was suddenly just there, a gun barrel poked in Budgie's rib cage." DeWayne shook his head. "That Bailey family just disappeared. I never thought to look for them or ask what had happened to them. Bad luck, bad decisions. I thought they'd packed up and moved on," he said.

Budgie was doing his best not to show pain. "Did Cooley, or Carl, say anything that might make you believe Deerstalker or Hafner is in on this scheme to find this elixir? Surely Cooley hasn't been pursuing a fantasy elixir all these years."

"The archeological dig brought all of this back up," I said. "There was a lot of publicity. My guess is that it didn't take long for word to get back to the Bailey family members. I'm sure they felt if there was anything on that burial site worth anything, it belonged to them."

"Believing it doesn't make it true," Budgie said. "The treasure belongs to whoever leased the rights to excavate the property."

"And who would that be? Hafner?" I asked.

"I didn't get a chance to look," Budgie said. "That's what makes sense, unless it was one of his backers. They might have done the paperwork. We'll check when we get out."

I climbed the stairs and pushed hard against the doors again. They were shut solid.

"If we get out," DeWayne said direly.

I wanted to curse and ram the wooden blockade, but standing precariously on the top of the stairs I had no leverage. I was about to give up when I heard the soft sound of scratching.

"Sweetie Pie?" I knew it was my dog. She had a keen ability to untie knots and I'd seen her and Pluto open doors and windows with skill. Could she slide the thumb bolt? "Sweetie Pie, help us."

More scratching ensued. I listened carefully and finally heard the screech of rusty metal against metal. Uttering a prayer, I pushed at the door. It opened an inch. Sweetie Pie had cleared the latch. "DeWayne!" I looked at Tinkie. "Give him the gun."

She didn't argue but pulled it out of a deep fold in the sleeping bag. "I wish I had more bullets but the clip is fully loaded."

"That little bastard took our guns," DeWayne said. He would be sore about that for a long time to come. "Let me get out and make sure it's clear. Then you come out and we'll haul out the sick ones."

"Our phones will work once we're back on top."

"I don't care if you call the paratroopers at Fort Benning. Just get everyone here," DeWayne said.

I wasn't about to argue. It really was time to call in reinforcements. Anyone who could possibly help.

The minute I was out of that dank basement, I put in a call to Coleman. When he didn't answer, worry crashed over me like a tidal wave. Where could he be? I called Doc while Tinkie called the Washington County sheriff's department at DeWayne's instruction. Budgie and Delane remained in the basement. We had to move the winch and rig before we could get them out.

"Doc, we need you at Mound Salla. It's Budgie. He's got a broken leg with the bone through the skin and Delane Goggans is out cold. Been that way for what looks like hours. I have no idea what drug she's taken."

"Tell me Coleman isn't there." Doc sounded truly stressed.

"He's not here. He doesn't know about any of this."

"He's not at Dahlia House. Harold stopped by to visit and no one was there."

"When did Harold drop by?" Harold worked at the bank with Tinkie's husband and he was a friend of both Coleman and me.

"It's been awhile. Harold said Coleman wasn't on the property. He searched the barn, too."

All of this time, he'd been up and running around, doing everything he could to reopen his wound, which was why he wasn't answering his phone. He was a devious piece of work. "Call the EMTs and come out here, please."

"You find Coleman. Sarah Booth, this could be serious."

"I know. I'll find him."

Tinkie was watching my face as I put the phone away. "Coleman's on the loose."

She nodded. "Then let's get out of here."

"Doc and the EMTs are on the way."

We went to help DeWayne move the winch and tripod. It felt like it was made of cast iron and was much heavier than it looked. We were almost back to the basement with it when a bullet zinged into the ground at DeWayne's feet.

"I told you to stay in that hole. You were safe there. Now you've aggravated me." It was

Cooley's voice, but I didn't see him anywhere. How the hell could he hide on a flat surface with a bright moon blazing down?

"Where is he?" Tinkie whispered. She pointed to the weapons, all piled in a stack, that Cooley had taken from the deputies. She picked up both guns and handed one to me. "I still wish we had more ammo."

DeWayne signaled us to be quiet as he broke away and darted behind some of the tents. Tinkie and I looked at each other before we headed in the opposite direction toward the woods. With any luck we could circle behind Cooley and catch him in the crossfire.

"I'd be careful in those woods, Sarah Booth," Cooley called out. "There's something in there would really like to meet you."

"Shoot him," I said to Tinkie. "You're a good shot. Wing him."

"I would if I could see him. He must have a bunker or something dug where he's down in the ground."

"Dammit." I didn't have time to play dodge bullets with Cooley. I had to find Coleman before he hurt himself. "I'll flank—" I stopped talking. I'd heard something in the woods. Someone was moving around, and they weren't being delicate about it. Limbs crackled and it sounded like a body crashing through the underbrush without care.

I grabbed Tinkie's shoulder and held her steady as something lurched out of the trees about twenty yards from us.

Fifty yards to the east, there was the sound of a gunshot and then several more. Pop, pop-pop, pop-pop. It seemed to be coming from several directions.

Behind us, the thing in the woods kept coming toward us.

"Sarah Booth!" Coleman called out to me from the far side of the mound, the place where the gunshots had come from. The dig site and the tents were between us. The moon had gone behind a cloud, leaving us all in darkness. "Are you okay?"

My heart registered the danger before my brain could. Coleman was on top of the mound. Bullets were flying. I had to stay calm. "We're good, Coleman. Stay where you are." He had to be near the side of the mound that led to the parking lot. That was the direction Tinkie and I wanted to go anyway. "We're headed toward you, Coleman. Just stay there."

"Sheriff! Get down!" DeWayne's voice came out of the night, just before the sound of a gunshot. And then silence.

32

"Coleman is hit!" DeWayne yelled the words. They seemed to be coming from a hollow drum. I heard them but I couldn't react to them. "Help, the sheriff's hit. It's bad." DeWayne, who was normally so taciturn, was yelling.

I started to run toward Coleman across the open ground but Tinkie grabbed my arm. "No! Getting shot won't help Coleman." She held on to me in a death grip.

Behind us, whatever was in the woods crashed forward. At last it stepped into the moonlight. It was indeed Dr. Sandra Wells, or what was left of her ravaged body. She still wore the bloody blue shirt I'd seen on her body. Her hair was ripped and torn out in hunks, and the gaping wound beneath her chin told me she was dead. Yet she was upright and walking toward us.

"Run!" Tinkie grabbed at me to get me moving, but I couldn't. My body refused to respond to mental commands.

The pathetic thing that Sandra had become came ever closer. She seemed to sense us more than see us. She made guttural sounds, as if she'd forgotten human speech but had some great need

431

to communicate. Adjusting her course, she came straight at me.

"Sarah Booth! Get over here! I'll give you cover," DeWayne called out. "Coleman is dying!"

"Sarah Booth!" Tinkie dragged at my shirt. "Come on!"

Sandra lurched toward me, now only fifty feet away. Without any real thought, I lifted the pistol and pulled the trigger. Her head exploded. There was a sizzle, lights in the skull fragments blinked and went out. She crumpled to the ground.

"She's a robot." Tinkie still had her hand on my shirt. "She's a damn robot."

"Sarah Booth, come now!" DeWayne sounded panicked.

I ran then. I crossed the open ground, dodging past the dig site and the tents and finally dropped to my knees beside DeWayne, who cradled Coleman in his arms. The moon came out, the very full Crow Moon, shining light on the dark blood that seeped from Coleman's torso. This time the shot was truer. It had gone into his stomach and the blood was coming out too fast, a red-black pool in the silvery moonlight.

"Sarah Booth, I love you." Coleman gasped the words. His gaze sought and held mine.

"Doc's on the way. You're going to be fine." I spoke with a calm I never knew I possessed. I grasped his hand and squeezed. I willed the life into him. "Put pressure on the wound," I said to Tinkie. She and DeWayne disrobed, using jackets and shirts to staunch the flow of blood. We worked in the quietness of a night suddenly completely still. Whoever had been shooting at us had stopped.

"Sarah . . ." Coleman's eyes rolled.

"Come back." I touched his face. "Come back!"

He focused on me once again. "I love you." Then his eyelids fluttered.

"Don't you dare leave me!" I would not lose him. Not when we had just begun to understand our roles in life's journey. I had lost those I loved most, and Coleman would not be one of them.

Hands pushed me aside, and I looked into Doc's sorrowful eyes. "Let me work."

Tinkie pulled me to my feet and pushed me away. In a moment we were joined by Cece and several paramedic teams. Tinkie sent them to recover Budgie and Delane from the basement. There was nothing they could do for Coleman. Doc was doing all that could be done.

"He can't die." I said it to Tinkie. Someone had to understand this and make it true. "Don't let him die."

Tinkie didn't make a sound, but the tears slid down her face.

"How bad is the wound?" I asked. I wanted her to lie to me.

"Very bad." She wouldn't lie. Not even when I needed it so desperately, because the truth would have to be faced eventually. "Doc will save him if he can be saved."

"He's going to die, isn't he?"

She didn't answer, and Cece pulled me against her, as if she could protect me from what was happening only thirty feet away.

"Who shot him?" I asked.

"I don't know." Tinkie wiped her tears away. "We have to find Cooley, too. I'll go look for him. If he's running around here with a gun he has to be stopped. I'm the best shot, though Sarah Booth took that robotic zombie out like she was Rambo."

"No! No one leaves my side!" Not another single one of my loved ones would be hurt or taken from me.

"Sarah Booth—" Cece started but never finished.

"Stay here." I stalked away, heading for the tents. If Cooley Marsh was in one of those tents, I meant to kill him. I was helpless to do anything for Coleman, but I could do something for me. In all the times that I'd lost the ones I loved, I'd been helpless, a victim who could only endure the loss. Learn to live with the pain. Not this time. This time I would inflict the pain.

"Sarah Booth!" Tinkie called after me.

"Let her go," Cece said. "We can't help her."

They were both crying now.

"There's a man with a gun out there," Tinkie said.

"I know," Cece answered. "God help him."

I stepped behind a tent before I allowed myself to crumple over. A pain as sharp as a knife tore at my heart. In the distance there were sirens, but they were too late. Coleman was mortally wounded. I'd never seen so much blood, and what could Doc or anyone else do to stop it? I was a coward because I could not watch the life leave the man I loved. The only path left to me was revenge.

The moon slipped behind a cloud and left me in darkness. Near the edge of the mound where Coleman lay surrounded by Doc and paramedics, there was a circle of light and movement. All else was still.

The gun in my hand was heavy. This was a deputy's gun, bigger than my own. I'd used it to kill the robotic Sandra Wells that someone had set out here at Mound Salla to scare people. I didn't have to ask myself who had done this. With Coleman's life hanging by a thread, a lot of things had become clear to me. Who had the talent and skill to create an animated contraption that could move about Mound Salla like a former human? There was only one person—toymaker Elton Cade. Elton's life's work was toys, many of them engineering marvels. But why? Why would

Elton want to create a zombie to scare away the very people he'd given money to conduct the dig?

In all of the whirling motives I'd plumbed, I'd never considered Elton Cade might be sabotaging his self-funded dig. But I would learn the truth. Once I'd taken care of Cooley Marsh, I intended to get that answer.

The moon darted out of the clouds again and I saw the blood on the ground. The flow was enough to track, and it went straight into one of the tents. Someone wounded was hiding out there. Wounded animals were always more dangerous. I didn't care. I pulled the flap back and stopped. Sweetie Pie, Chablis, and Pluto stood guard over a body. When I stepped inside I heard the rasp of breath. Whoever it was remained alive. For now.

I stepped past my dog and delivered a kick to the back of the man's thigh. "Roll over."

With a groan, Elton Cade shifted so I could see his face. He held a blood-soaked pillow to his shoulder. In his other hand he clutched some kind of vial. His fingers tightened around it as he realized I'd spotted it.

"You shot Coleman."

He tried to sit up but I kicked him hard in the wounded shoulder. He cried out and stayed down.

"Tell me or I will hurt you in ways you've never imagined."

"I winged him the first time. I never wanted to hurt him."

The details of that night came back to me. Elton had been hit on the head—or so he'd claimed. "You stumbled into that historic marker on Winterville Mound and hurt your head. Then when you needed me to believe you were a victim, you hit yourself on the head."

"I never meant to harm Coleman. Not then or tonight. He was intent on stopping me, and I had to get . . . I had what I needed and I only wanted to leave. He should have let me."

The idea that he wanted to pretend he was the victim made me want to kick him in the shoulder again. Repeatedly. He sensed my pending action and turned slightly away, revealing the vial in his hand.

"What's that?"

"The thing I need to save my son. Jimmy is dying. He's not away at a special school. He's in a hospital in Switzerland. Just let me go. I'll turn myself in as soon as I—"

I stepped closer and squatted down. Elton was no danger to me. He was too weak to fight. "Give it to me."

"No." He tried to push away from me but I reached across and grabbed the vial. It was more of a clay tube with strange markings on it. It was sealed with a substance that might have been bee's wax.

"What is this?"

He refused to answer, and I picked up a heavy lantern. I put the vial on the ground and raised the lantern. "You're going to answer my questions or I'm going to smash this."

"Stop! I'll tell you. That vial is why I funded the dig. There have always been rumors of the Natives possessing an elixir that could heal the most grave illnesses. I grew up on those stories, and when I began to explore them, I realized they might be true. I knew Frank's reputation. He would use the utmost care while excavating this burial mound. If the elixir was here, Frank would find it without damaging it."

"Only it didn't work that way, did it?" My desire to hurt him was hard to control. If I thought about hurting him, I couldn't think about Coleman dying. "You didn't count on Sarah Wells showing up or the Bailey family returning here to claim what they viewed as their right."

"I would have paid them. I would have given Sandra a television show and the Baileys more money than they could have spent. I only wanted the elixir. Money means nothing when your son is dying."

"Or the man you love." I wanted to choke him with my bare hands.

"I'm sorry. I didn't mean for anyone to get hurt. I only wanted to save my son."

"Why did you kill Sandra Wells?"

"Dr. Wells overheard me . . . That private investigator woman showed up. I had no clue she was a member of the family who'd once lived on Mound Salla. They started working together and were coming to the dig at night to search. I couldn't let them find it. They would never have given it to me. Never. I had to kill them both. Once Sandra was dead I realized I could modify my robot and really scare people, so I stole her body."

"And Delane? What have you done to her and why?"

"She's only drugged. It will wear off. She found the vial today. She called Frank and when he didn't answer, she called me. I couldn't risk that she'd take the elixir. I had Cooley drug her."

"So you had one of the Baileys working for you."

"I didn't know who he was. He approached me about computer games and then feigned an interest in archeological digs. I needed an inside source to keep an eye on this so I made sure he got put on the dig crew. He played me."

I held up the vial. "Was it worth it?" My voice broke and the reality of losing Coleman hit me hard.

"If it cures my son, it's worth everything I had to do." He grabbed at it but he wasn't quick enough.

"You really believe something you found in a

vial buried for hundreds of years can cure your son?"

"I know it can." He reached for it again and I let him take it.

My head was like an echo chamber. One word repeated over and over again. Cures. Cures. Cures. I had come into the tent intending to kill whoever was responsible for hurting Coleman. The gun slipped from my fingers and thudded into the dirt. Elton lurched for it, and when he did, I kicked him in the side of the head with my boot. When his hand flung backward to try to gain balance, I grabbed the vial and wrested it from his grip.

I left Elton in the tent, out cold and guarded by the critters. The bright moon gave me a clear view of the cluster of EMTs, Doc, and my friends hovering at Coleman's side as I began to run.

"Use this! Doc, use this!" I pushed my way to Coleman's side and dropped to my knees, holding out the vial to Doc.

"What is that?"

"Use it." When Doc didn't take it, I picked up a rock and broke the sealed top. I didn't know what was inside. I couldn't wait to see if it would work or not. Coleman was ashen, and he was no longer conscious. He was slipping away despite the bags of blood and fluids the EMTs and Doc were pumping into him. His blood had soaked through the bandages. I opened his mouth and poured the contents of the vial into him. Then I moved the bandages away and poured the remaining drops directly into his wound.

"What is that, Sarah Booth?" Doc grasped my wrist. He looked up at Tinkie and Cece. They moved behind me and grabbed my arms, lifting me away. "Get her away from here," Doc said. There was no censure in his voice, only sadness. Doc motioned to the paramedics. "Let's move him now. He's as stable as we can make him here. Our only hope is to get him to the hospital before he dies."

"Coleman!" I broke free of my friends and grabbed his hand. "You're going to be okay. I promise!"

"Sarah Booth, we have to go." Doc spoke with urgency. "Move him."

Tinkie sobbed, but she gripped me with a strength born of desperation. "Come on. We'll follow the ambulance." She turned to DeWayne, who was about to cry himself. "There's another paramedic team coming. The other guys need help to get Budgie and Delane out of the basement."

"Can do. And we have to find that Cooley Marsh guy."

"Elton Cade is in one of the tents. He's been shot. And kicked unconscious." My gaze watched the medics hustling Coleman down the side of the mound.

"Shot? Elton? How?" Cece was shocked.

"He's behind all of this. All of it."

"Did you shoot him?" Tinkie asked. "Is he alive?"

"I think Coleman shot him. He's alive. Maybe."

DeWayne took off for the tents as he was yelling orders to the paramedics who'd just arrived.

"Let's go." Tinkie nudged me toward the precipice. "Hopefully this will be the last time we have to go up and down this stupid incline." Tinkie put a hand on my cheek. "Remember the time I was poisoned and you were the only one who believed I'd live? They brought Oscar in to tell me goodbye, but you believed I was going to make it. And I did."

I remembered that nightmare in Greenwood. I'd found an antidote. At first it had looked as if it wouldn't work but, finally, just as Oscar kissed her, she'd awakened. "Yes, I remember."

"Coleman is going to be okay." Tinkie turned my face so I had to look into her blue gaze. "What did you give him?"

"I don't know. Elton had it. He killed all those people to get that elixir. To save his son. But I gave it to Coleman."

"It came from the burial site?" Cece tried hard not to sound disgusted, but she wasn't successful. "It had been buried for hundreds of years?"

"Elton said it was the elixir of eternal youth," I

said. "He believes it can heal." I looked at them, suddenly aware of a new possibility. "I believe it, too. It's a gift for us. To save Coleman."

"That's perfect," Tinkie said. "Come on now, Sarah Booth. We have to get to the hospital."

Cece took my other arm and together the three of us descended. By the time we were in Cece's car, the critters had joined us and hopped into the backseat with me.

As the time passed, more and more people began to show up at the emergency room as Coleman's surgery continued on into the wee hours of the morning. Peter Deerstalker paced the hallway. Junior came over from the bail bond office. Millie closed the café and came to sit with me. Madame Tomeeka leaned against the wall. She made no predictions. She didn't need to. Coleman had little chance of surviving the gunshot wound that had struck his liver.

A surgical specialist had arrived from Memphis and two other surgeons had come up from Jackson to set Budgie's leg and patch the wound in Elton Cade's shoulder. Not a single person questioned me about the goose-egg knot on the side of his head where I'd kicked him.

Budgie was in surgery getting his leg set, and Delane was still unconscious but was showing signs of waking. Doc's examination showed she would not be harmed by the drug.

Cooley Marsh was still missing. At last Frank Hafner arrived and was sitting with Delane. Watching the way he stroked her face, I believed what Delane had said. He truly loved her.

Kawania Laveau was in the waiting room with Peter Deerstalker and Lolly Cade. I didn't know where their allegiances might lie now, but they were staying the course until the case could be closed. The other students had gone— back to school or simply away from danger and unhappiness.

DeWayne entered the waiting room and signaled for me to meet him in the hall. Cece and Tinkie were reluctant to let me go, but I stepped free of them.

"I took Sweetie Pie, Chablis, and Pluto home. Fed the horses and gave the dogs and cat some kibble."

"Thank you, DeWayne." I spoke automatically.

"Yeah, well, they weren't too happy with the menu but I told them you'd be home with Coleman to make it up to them."

I'd held rigid control for so long, and his tender words were nearly my undoing. "Thank you."

"I found that thing you shot. You know, the Sandra Wells look-alike. By the way, it was a perfect shot, Sarah Booth." He tried for a grin but failed. "That robotic zombie. It's all plastic. Nothing to do with a human body. Elton made it to scare people away from the dig. Late at night, when all the students were gone, Elton was going up to the dig to search for the vial. He needed privacy to do that."

"And Hafner is innocent of all wrongdoing?"

"So it would seem. Elton has confessed to everything."

"Frank and Peter are completely innocent."

"They are." DeWayne put a hand on my shoulder. "And there's another bit of good news. The Washington County sheriff's department picked up Cooley Marsh on the highway headed south. He'll be going away for a long time. He was the one who called to lure Peter and Cece up on Winterville Mound. He meant to kill Cece and set Peter up for it. Get rid of both of them. That was his idea, not Elton Cade's."

I nodded. "Thanks for telling me."

DeWayne sensed my burden of worry. He put an arm around my shoulders. "I've never seen the sheriff as happy as he's been the last few weeks. Don't give up on Coleman. He's a fighter."

"He shouldn't have been at Mound Salla. I should have been home with him."

"If you'd been at Dahlia House, you couldn't have stopped him. Coleman would have been at Mound Salla no matter what. You know that, Sarah Booth. Everyone else knows it, too."

"Why did Elton shoot Coleman? Couldn't he have just slipped down the back side of the mound and run for it? He'd recovered the vial.

All he had to do was run." I was having difficulty grasping Elton's actions once it was clear he was going to be caught.

"He had that elixir, and he believed it would cure his son. He was only intent on getting home to give it to his son."

"Damn." I didn't want to ask, but I had to. "What's wrong with Elton's son?"

"It's some autoimmune issue. His body is attacking itself. It's progressive and incurable. The boy won't be able to walk or talk in another six months."

I didn't want to feel sorry for Elton Cade, but I did. I still blamed him for his actions, but I also understood his desperation.

I looked down the hallway to see Doc coming straight for me. His stride was long and purposeful, and he zeroed in on me. I held my breath when he drew abreast of me. "What?" I whispered.

"I don't know what to say," Doc said. "It's not possible, what I saw. It's not possible but it's happened nonetheless."

"What?" I grasped his arm. "Is he alive?"

"Oh, he's alive," Doc said. "Amazingly alive. We got into his abdomen and I was sure his liver had been blown to smithereens. The hole, the bleeding, there's no way he should be alive. But he is."

"He isn't going to die?"

"No, he's not. Unless he disobeys me again and then I might have to kill him myself."

"Can I see him?"

"You can sit with him in recovery, as long as you don't mess with him." Doc rumpled my hair like he used to do when I was six. "Go on. The nurse will show you where he is. He should be awake in a bit."

I didn't need a second invitation. I was down the hall like a shot. When I turned the corner into the surgical ward, a nurse flagged me to the recovery room. I stepped inside and felt my heart pumping hard. Coleman looked dead. He was pale, his lips blue. But his chest moved up and down. I took a seat beside his bed and captured his hand. As long as I could hold on to him, could feel him alive and getting better with each passing second, I would not ask for any more miracles.

33

Coleman sat propped in the bed, the sun coming in through my gauzy bedroom curtains. He'd been home for two days, healing with amazing speed. I put a tray of country fried eggs, bacon, and biscuits on his lap. "Millie brought the biscuits. She was afraid if you ate mine they would kill you."

"Gotta love a woman who knows true danger when she sees it."

I didn't care that he teased me about my biscuits. I was just glad he was alive and able to tease. "How are you feeling?"

"Good. Actually great. Doc said I'm healing ten times faster than anyone should." Coleman reached for my hand and held it firmly. "He said I should be dead, Sarah Booth. He said you gave me some kind of ancient elixir."

"It could have killed you."

"I was dying." He pressed the palm of my hand to his lips. "I could only think of one thing— that I didn't want to leave you. That I wouldn't do that to you, or to myself. When I felt myself slipping away into that warm place filled with light, I came back to you."

I didn't want to cry. I hated crying, especially in front of people. But the tears slipped down my cheeks. "If you'd left me, I would have killed you."

Coleman laughed. "No doubt. You would have revived me just to have the pleasure of sending me to the Great Beyond. Doc said he didn't know what you gave me but that he wants more of it."

"The truth is, no one can say that it did a thing to heal you." I'd been over this with Doc and everyone else. I might have given him rainwater, for all I knew. Doc was running tests on the empty vial, but so far he'd had no luck identifying what was in it, only that it was organic.

"Doc believes it was a miracle." Coleman held me with his gaze. "Elton killed two people and was willing to kill more to get that elixir for his son. You gave it to me."

"And I would do the same again. He shot you. His actions resulted in my behavior. I'm sorry for his son, for the horror of what's happening to a really good kid. Too bad we don't have any more elixir."

"You gave it all to me."

"I did."

"I owe you my life. Doc said my liver should never have recovered, but it did. I should have died on top of Mound Salla, Sarah Booth. He has no explanation for it."

"Okay, I saved your life." I forced a teasing

note into my voice to hide the fact that my heart pounded painfully in my chest. "Oh, you are going to owe me big-time. Don't ever doubt it."

"And that's one debt I'll gladly pay." Coleman tugged my hand gently until I leaned down and kissed him. Really kissed him, all too aware of how close I'd come to losing him forever.

While Coleman napped, I went out on the front porch with a cup of coffee, Sweetie Pie, and Pluto. The black cat stretched in a sunny spot, and Sweetie Pie sat at my feet on the steps. The coffee was black and strong, and I sipped it slowly, thinking about how close I'd come to tragedy yet again.

My friends had come and gone, making sure Coleman was on the mend and I was giving him the care he needed. Budgie was still in the hospital, but his leg would mend, good as new. Delane Goggans had awakened with Frank Hafner by her side. He'd proposed to her while she was still in the hospital.

Peter Deerstalker was holding a press conference at one o'clock to announce that the dig had been stopped and Mound Salla transferred over to the Biloxi-Tunica tribe's care. Perhaps it would one day be explored. Maybe not. It was up to the descendants of the people buried there.

My cell phone rang and it was Tinkie. "Hello."

"They found Sandra Wells' body."

I'd forgotten all about the missing corpse. Since I'd "killed" Elton's robotic Dr. Wells, I'd put aside all thought of her and her missing body. "Where?"

"In the barn at Elton Cade's. He'd been working on robots for a while. Another game or adventure experience he was re-creating in his toy empire. Elton confessed that he took Sandra's body so folks would be afraid."

"Why wouldn't Elton just say what he was looking for? Things could have gone so differently. The elixir would have been found and perhaps it could have been duplicated."

"I know." Tinkie sounded pensive. "I understand how desperate he was. I mean . . . his son."

Something in Tinkie's voice stopped me cold. "Are you okay?"

"Never better." She sighed. "I've been waiting for the right time to tell you, but I need to get this done."

"What?" Fear hit me hard.

"I'm late. I haven't checked yet and I'm not going to be crazy and go buy a bunch of pregnancy kits. It's only been a few weeks. I feel different, though. I think I'm pregnant."

I wished she were sitting on the porch with me, but I figured it would be easier for her over the phone. This was such a big dream. "What does Doc—"

"I haven't told him or anyone. Just you. I know

you're skeptical of magic, but what happened with Coleman is . . . a miracle. He should be dead. Everyone knows that. But he isn't, and I think it wasn't because of some elixir that no one can identify. I think your love healed him. Maybe my love for a child will be my elixir."

Life or fate or help from the Great Beyond—I didn't know where it came from—had given me another chance at a life with Coleman, and I was not going to step on Tinkie's dream. "I hope you're pregnant with twins." I meant every word of it.

"Thank you. Now tend to that man. Millie and I are bringing some supper over tonight so we can all catch up. See ya soon."

And she was gone. Tinkie wouldn't tell Oscar or anyone else what she'd shared with me. Too much was at stake for her. And I would honor her by keeping my silence.

Sweetie Pie rose slowly from her reclining position and pointed her nose down the driveway. She gave a soft "woof" of welcome at an approaching figure that instantly captivated me. The woman was slender, and she wore a cloche on her head, a big coat with wide shoulders and a fur collar—fake, I hoped. She was very young, maybe in her early twenties. She came down the driveway straight toward Dahlia House. Definitely an aficionado of the 1920s, based on her attire.

She came right up the steps and took a seat beside me without invitation. Pluto sat down beside her and Sweetie Pie yawned and settled back to continue her nap. I knew it was Jitty. It could be no one else. "Tinkie is pregnant." I said it as a fact.

The woman arched one eyebrow. "Science makes great strides, particularly in medicine."

"It wasn't science. It was a miracle."

She nodded. "Once upon a time, man dreamed of conquering space, of transporting humans to other planets. Now it's a reality. I played a part in that."

She was definitely Native American, and a lovely woman. But she was also something else. "Who are you?" I asked.

"Mary Golda Ross." She held out a hand that I shook. "First Native American space engineer."

"First but not last."

"You can't have a second or two-hundredth until there's a first. I broke ground for my people, for all people."

"And you were a flapper." I found both facts to be amazing.

"Only part time, in my youth. But I was a full-time rocket scientist. The only Native American and the only woman among forty engineers."

Mary Ross was truly a groundbreaker, and she'd done it with her own individual flair and style.

"Are you glad the dig at Mound Salla has been discontinued?" I was curious. Mary Ross had stepped into modern times. She'd achieved in a world that her ancestors had never imagined. She'd achieved in a world where both Native American people and all women were still held back.

"We can learn from the past," she said, "but so often we don't. That's a crime. We are impervious to history and keep repeating the same mistakes. If we could truly learn, the world would benefit in many ways. The future could be so . . . incredible."

"Don't give up on us. We can't give up. Not you. Not me. And not Tinkie. We have to hold on to our dreams."

Mary Ross stood, and I could see the cotton fields green with new growth through her. She was fading from this world. "Always believe in miracles, Sarah Booth. For Tinkie and for yourself." In her words I heard the whisper of my mother's voice.

"I will. You have my word on it."

| Books are produced in the United States using U.S.-based materials | Books are printed using a revolutionary new process called THINKtech™ that lowers energy usage by 70% and increases overall quality | Books are durable and flexible because of Smyth-sewing | Paper is sourced using environmentally responsible foresting methods and the paper is acid-free |

Center Point Large Print
600 Brooks Road / PO Box 1
Thorndike, ME 04986-0001 USA

(207) 568-3717

US & Canada:
1 800 929-9108
www.centerpointlargeprint.com